A HEART FULL OF MALICE

TONY DEBAJO

ISBN 978-1-8383586-4-8

Published by De-Bajo

A HEART FULL OF MALICE

For Remi and Arianna

GLOSSARY

Agbada
Traditional West African loose-fitting, robe-like garment worn by men.

Agogô Bells
A musical instrument consisting of a single or multiple sets of connected bells originating from West Africa, mainly amongst the Yoruba people.

Baba
A term used to describe an elderly male. The female equivalent is 'mama'.

Babalawo
Many names have been used to describe this group – witch doctors, medicine-men or women, and herbalists, to name a few. Their areas of expertise are often varied. Some are healers and purport to have the ability to cure any form of ailments, while others claim to possess the power to cast spells that can ward off evil spirits, create wealth or guarantee a positive outcome to any endeavour. However, their services tend to come at a cost, that is not always forthcoming or apparent at the onset.

Babariga
Similar to agbada, this is a traditional West African garment worn by men.

Burukutu
An alcoholic beverage popular amongst the northern tribes. It is brewed from the grains of Guinea corn and millet.

Calabash
A fruit indigenous to many parts of Africa, that was also used traditionally for medicinal purposes or harvested mature and dried to be fashioned into utensils like cups, water bottles, plates and spoons.

Danshiki

Traditional west African attire. It tends to have varying designs and patterns around the neckline and sleeves and are usually colourful. The more elaborate the patterns, the wealthier the wearer is assumed to be. However, the northern tribes prefer more subtle designs and plain colours.

Harmattan

This is a season in West Africa that occurs during the winter months between late November and mid-March. It is characterised by a drop in temperature and a large amount of dust carried in the wind that hangs in the air and obscures visibility.

Hoe

An agricultural hand tool used to cultivate root crops or break up the soil.

Iro and buba

Traditional attire worn by west Africa women, translated in the Yoruba tongue to mean wrapper (see description below) and blouse or upper clothing. These items are designed with a variety of materials ranging in colour and texture and are accessorised with matching headgear.

Iroko tree

A large tree of hardwood commonly found in west Africa and some species can live up to 500 years. The wood from this tree is favoured for crafting expensive furniture, spear shafts and sword handles.

Juju

Synonymous with black magic or dark arts, practiced by small groups in several African countries and other parts of the world. Juju can relate to minor incantations for protection, wealth and prowess, while other times it can be associated with much darker spells to inflict harm or summon evil spiritual beings.

Kabiyesi

A title given to Yoruba kings and said to be translated to mean, "He who cannot be questioned".

Kaftan

Similar to the danshiki, a kaftan is a long flowing garment that is often accessorised by a belt at the waist. Commonly worn by men, however, they can be fashioned into women's clothing, having more elaborate designs and colours.

Kakaki

A musical instrument like a trumpet commonly found in eastern Africa. The four-meter-long wind instrument is famous amongst the Hausa tribe and is associated with royalty, often played at ceremonial events and functions in the palace.

Kola nut

The kola nut is a fruit of the kola tree and grows in tropical African countries. It has a bitter taste and contains caffeine and is used as a flavouring in different types of beverages. The nuts also hold a traditional significance in west African countries, often used traditionally for celebratory purposes and a sign of friendship and respect, like the sharing of mead.

Marabu

Marabus are the Hausa equivalent to the Yoruba Babalawo.

Masquerade

These are long-standing traditions of Nigeria and span across the various tribes. It is essentially an elaborately designed mask and outfit worn by a tribesman that represents the essence of their tribe. Some are perceived as a manifestation of spirits, good or malevolent, while others are simply entertainers. They are usually accompanied by large processions, mostly musicians, who serve as their heralds. The ones who entertain tend to be acrobats, performing energetic dances, while others carry bamboo canes to lash those that would stand in their path.

Modakeke

These people are a sub-tribe of the Yoruba, who also claim to be descendants of Oduduwa, the Yoruba deity. They are a warrior-elite group whose loyalty lies solely with the Kingdom of Ife. They are the kingdoms deadliest military force and have no rivals to that claim.

Ncho

Also known as *ayo*, ncho is said to be one of the oldest board games known, dating back thousands of years. It is a pastime of the elders in Yorubaland and is fashioned from wood with pits carved in rows into the board. Stones or seeds are placed within the pits, and the aim is to move them around.

Oba

This is a title given to a Yoruba ruler, which is used as a form of address.

Ogogoro

An alcoholic beverage, which is indigenous to Nigerian. It is a spirit distilled from the fermented juice of a palm tree. It holds traditional value and is a typical drink of choice at ceremonies and gatherings, such as weddings.

Orisa

This is the collective name for the deities of the Yoruba people.

Palm wine

Similar to ogogoro, palm wine is another alcoholic beverage that is extracted, or tapped from the tallest section of a palm tree and is left to ferment with the yeast present in the air. This drink is a favourite of many of the Nigerian tribes and is also used traditionally like ogogoro.

Shahbanu
This is a title given to a queen of north African or middle eastern heritage.

Wrapper
This is a typical garment for west African women and in simple terms, is a length of cloth wrapped around the waist and tightened by several folds at the hip. Men also wear this attire, but have it tied in a knot over one shoulder and draped around their body, which is common in the Igbo tribes. The designs and texture often vary, some being heavy and coarse, while others could be light and fine.

TRIBES & CHARACTER LIST

YORUBA

Often referred to as the westerners, are homogeneous people made up of numerous sub-tribes that all speak the same language of Yoruba but with varying dialects. Some claim to trace their lineage directly to the gods that once roamed the earth. They consider themselves to be the most intellectual and progressive amongst the tribes, and they pride themselves for their great warriors and hunters.

Adeosi Adelani

(ah-day-o-see / ah-day-la-nee)

Father of Jide and Olise, former king of Ile-Ife (e-lay-e-fe), also referred to as Ife, and all the provinces and tribes south of the rivers Niger and Benue.

Bunmi Adelani

(boo-me)

Mother of Jide and Queen of Ile-Ife.

Enitan Adelani

(eh-nee-ton)

Third child of Jide and prince of Ile-Ife.

Jide Adelani

(je-day)

King of Ile-Ife and all the provinces and tribes south of the rivers Niger and Benue.

Kayode Adelani

(ka-yor-day)

Father of Adeosi and grandfather of Jide. Fabled king of all the lands south and north of the rivers Niger and Benue (although he never completely conquered the north, but he claimed it as part of his dominion).

Lara Adelani
Queen of Ile-Ife, wife of Jide and mother to the three princes; Toju, Niran and Enitan.

Niran Adelani
(ne-ron)
Second child of Jide and prince of Ile-Ife.

Olise Adelani
(oh-lee-se)
Half-brother of Jide and son of Ekaete. He also has Igbo and Calabar heritage from his mother.

Toju Adelani
(toe-ju)
First child of Jide and heir to the throne and southern kingdom.

Adebola
(ah-day-bo-la)
Commander of the guard in the Ondo province under Olusegun.

Adedeji
(ah-day-day-je)
Head of the Modakeke warriors (the royal family's personal army and warrior class of the tribes), and the council of ten (elders/ leaders of the Modakeke).

Ayo
(ah-yor)
Blood-guard to Enitan and Modakeke warrior.

Dami
(da-me)
Wrestler from the Ogun province.

Dare
(da-ray)
Chief of the island provinces (the islands that make up Lagos).

Dimeji
(de-may-je)
Blood-guard to Olise.

Dotun
(dor-toon)
Head of a prominent family in the Ogun province.

Femi
(fe-me)
Modakeke warrior and eldest son of Adedeji, head of the Modakeke.

Goke
(go-kay)
Elder from the village province of Inisa. / Minor Chief from the Ogun province

Idowu
(e-doe-wu)
Chief of the Lagos province and nephew of Dare.

Kola
(kor-la)
Chief of the Ogun province, father of Lara and grandfather to the Adelani princes.

Lanre
(lan-ray)
Former royal guard of Ile-Ife and one of Niran's trusted warriors.

Leke
(lay-kay)
Blood-guard to Toju and Modakeke warrior.

Ogie
(o-ge)
Commander of Olise's army.

Ogogo
(o-go-go)
Commander of the Adelani royal guard.

Olusegun *(Segun)* **Lawal**
(oh-loo-sheer-goon / la-wal)
Chief of the Ondo province.

Seun
(shay-un)
Blood-guard to Niran and Modakeke warrior.

Taiwo
(tie-wow)
Captain in the Adelani royal guard.

Tunji
(toon-gee)
Head of a prominent family in the Ogun province.

Wale
(wa-lay)
Commander of the guard in the Ogun province.

CALABAR & RIVER TRIBES

One of the tribes of the rivers and considered to be the most powerful across the River-lands. Located in the south east, their provinces are based around the many veins of water that feed into the two great rivers Niger and Benue that flow through the country. Fishing is their trade of choice, but they are also known to breed exceptional warriors.

Atai
(ah-tie)
High ranking Calabar warrior.

Edem the ugly
(eh-dem)
Chief of the Akwa-Ibom province.

Efetobo
(eh-feh-toe-bow)
Chief councillor in Ile-Ife and relative of Ekaete.

Ekaete
(eh-ky-e-tay)
Second wife of Adeosi and mother of Olise. Claims Igbo heritage from her father.

Essien
(eh-see-yen)
Chief of the Calabar tribe and provinces.

Etido
(eh-ti-doe)
Commander in Olise's army.

Etim
(eh-tim)
First son of Edem the ugly and heir to
the Akwa-Ibom province.

Odafe
(O-da-fay)
Commander in Olise's army.

IGBO

The Igbo also claim to be decedents of the gods and are perhaps the proudest
people amongst the tribes. They dominate the eastern region of the country,
with borders deep into the south that overlap the River-lands. They are a tribe of
warriors and farmers and are known to be an amiable people.

Achike
(ah-chi-kay)
Chief of one of the Igbo provinces.

Boniface
(bunny-face)
Councillor in Ile-Ife.

Ikenna
(e-cain-ah)
Chief of one of the Igbo provinces.

Ngozi
(n-gor-zi)
Daughter of Zogo the black.

Nnamdi
(n-nam-de)
Cousin to Zogo, chief of the Anambra
province.

Obinna
(oh-bin-a)
First son of Zogo the black and heir to
the Igbo provinces.

Uzoma
(u-zoor-ma)
Warrior and distant relative to the
Chidozie family well known for his
humour and good nature.

Zogo the black
(zo-go)
Renowned warrior and head of the
Chidozie families, lord of all the Igbo
provinces. Also, a relative of Ekaete
through marriage.

HAUSA

The horse tribes dominate the northern lands beyond the great rivers. Little is known about this elusive tribe other than the fact that their provinces, which are mostly deserts, make up for half of the landmass of the country, which could easily make them the most populous amongst the tribes. They are expert horsemen, adapting this to their style of warfare, making them a formidable foe. They are mostly herdsmen by profession.

Mustafa Abubaka
(mus-ta-fa)
Emir to all the lands north of the rivers Niger and Benue.

Habibah Abubaka
(ha-bee-bah)
Second daughter of Mustafa and princess of the north.

Danjuma Abubaka
(dan-ju-ma)
First son of Mustafa and prince of the north, heir to the northern kingdom.

Usman Abubaka
(us-man)
Third son of Mustafa and prince of the north.

OTHER

Amina Rabiu
(ah-me-na / ra-bee-you)
Shahbanu and ruler of the middle eastern hordes.

Hassan
(ha-san)
Emissary and advisor to Amina

THE GODS (ORISA)

Aganju
(ah-gan-ju)
The god of the earth and often associated with volcanos. Also known to be close to the deity Shango, some claiming that they are brother gods.

Chineke
(chi-nay-kay)
Is the king of the gods to the Igbo as Olorun (Olodumare) is to the Yoruba.

Esu

(a-shoe)

The trickster god synonymous with misfortune, chaos and death. Once the messenger of all the orisa able to speak the language of every creation but later becoming forgetful and misconstruing the messages that led to chaos.

Obatala

(o-ba-ta-la)

The god of the sky and rumoured to have been instrumental in the creation of the human form before life was blown into them by Olorun (Olodumare).

Oduduwa

(o-do-do-wa)

A lesser god sent by Olorun to help with the creation of the Yoruba lands. He was also known to have created Ile-Ife and settled there as its first divine king. The Adelani family claim to trace their bloodline directly to him.

Ogun

(o-goon)

The god of war. Depicted with a machete and a hammer. He was also known as the god of blacksmiths who forged all the metals used to create instruments of war.

Oko

(o-ko)

The god of farming and agriculture. He is celebrated especially during the seasons of crop harvesting.

Olorun

(o-lo-roon)

Also referred to as Olodumare (o-low-do-ma-ray) is the king of all the gods in the Yoruba tribe and the creator of everything.

Oshosi

(o-show-she)

The god of hunting and all things associated with the forest. He is known for his cunning and astuteness and is said to favour the bow and arrow over the spear.

Shango

(shon-go)

The god of thunder, often depicted as a bolt of lightning in human form. Considered to be the most feared of all the gods for his fiery temper and known to shoot flaming arrows from his hands when angered.

Yemoja

(yay-moe-ja)

The goddess of the rivers. Known as a protector of women and healer in matters regarding fertility and childbirth.

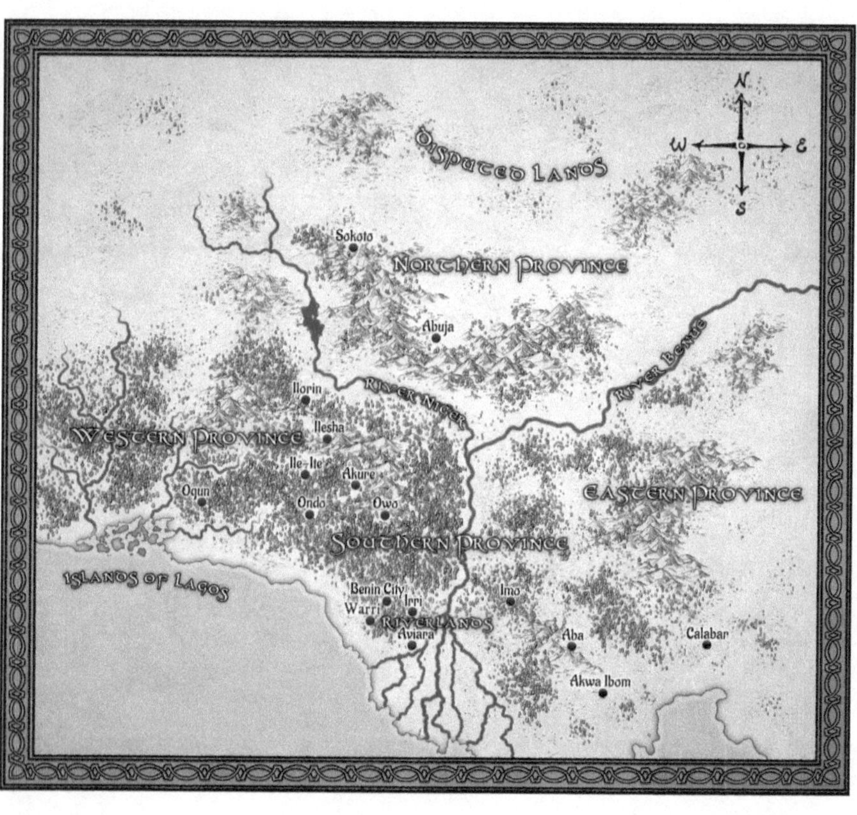

N
W
E
S
DISPUTED LANDS
Sokoto
NORTHERN PROVINCE
Abuja
Ilorin
RIVER NIGER
RIVER BENUE
Ilesha
WESTERN PROVINCE
Ile-Ife
Akure
EASTERN PROVINCE
Ogun
Ondo
Owo
SOUTHERN PROVINCE
ISLANDS OF LAGOS
Benin City
Irri
Imo
Warri
RIVERLANDS
Aviara
Aba
Calabar
Akwa Ibom

AN UNKINDNESS
OF RAVENS

Black wings, black tidings. This was the old saying. An omen, that much was true. Most would prefer to avert their eyes as soon as the caws of the large bird carried on the wind, not willing to be burdened with whatever sorrow it brought along with it. But in this case, the message could not be avoided.

King Jide was dead, there was no hiding from it. This sorrowful news would be far reaching, festering in the hearts and minds of many. There was no denying the misery that would befall the realm. All would mourn with the knowledge that the realm had never before seen, and never would again see a man of such stature walk upon the soil of this accursed earth. All that was left was the memory of his greatness. And his sons.

Sons that would be left with the bitter taste of vengeance on their lips. Sons that would be prepared to bring this fragile kingdom to ruin and put it to the torch to appease their unquenchable desire to see those responsible pay in blood. And blood is exactly what the realm would see; spilt from the guilty and the innocent alike.

King Jide had been the only obstacle stemming the kingdom from teetering on the edge of anarchy, and now, nothing could prevent the tide that would burst and flow forth, consuming all in its wake. His life's work had been to unify the tribes and provinces under one crown. Those hopes had been dashed the moment his blood had mixed with the soil of Ife. And now, all that could be expected was many more years of unrest in the realm.

Upon Jide's death, ravens had taken to the sky, perhaps prompted by the gods, to bear word of what had been witnessed in the ancient city of kings. The birds had scattered to the furthest regions of the realm. And dark tidings travel fast. Many had perceived the birds as a sign of dread, and those gifted with the sight had interpreted the display of dark wings as the passing of something, or someone, significant. Before long, word of the events in Ife had surfaced, and the realm held its breath in anticipation of the worst.

Each of Jide's sons had reacted to the news differently; Toju had been enraged at the folly of his father, who he blamed for being the architect of his own demise by placing his trust in lesser men and not holding a tighter rein on his subjects. He was still indignant at the fact that Jide had welcomed the displaced and destitute into their capital city with open arms, throwing caution to the wind, allowing the tainted amongst them to infiltrate their very foundation and feed on it from the inside. But his anger had slowly been tempered by his new wife, princess of the royal courts of the Hausa, and the distractions of his recently won title – the prince of two kingdoms. A title never claimed by any of his forebears or anointed princes before him, and one that came with great responsibility.

This placated him somewhat, but he was plagued by moments of deep sadness that could only be sated in battle, causing him to push himself further than any warrior prince should ever be allowed to, sometimes to the point of recklessness. With the strength of his spear, he continued to capture new lands for his adopted people and further establish a name for himself as the fearless prince from the south. *Ogun's* hand, however, had always been upon him as he also expanded his own empire in the far northern territories.

Niran had been devastated by the loss of the greatest monarch of a generation, and an even better father. The kingdom had lost a bastion of society, one who inspired countless individuals and gave them hope and the means to write their own destiny. He swore anew to bear his father's torch with dignity and honour in the best way he could by following in his footsteps and fighting to try and mend the fracture that had befallen the kingdom. He would stop at nothing to fulfil his father's ambition of uniting all the tribes under one throne and the house of the Adelanis.

He had continued his campaigns deeper into the eastern provinces, and had been rewarded with a firm grip in the region. In so doing, many more spears had sworn their allegiance to him, swelling his ever-growing army, and proclaiming him as the true heir to the throne. His name spread across the lands as if carried by swarming locusts. But his conquests had not been without difficulty as the river tribes of the southeastern provinces had not taken kindly to the prospect of another Yoruba monarch, and vicious battles had continued to rage over these lands, with both sides bitterly fighting to secure and expand into the imaginary borders set by their forebears. However, Niran's influence was strong and with the combined might of the Igbo tribesmen, it remained but a question of time until total dominance of the region would be assured.

Enitan, on the other hand, burned inside. He cared not about inheritance nor titles and the riches and power that accompanied them. He burned with a desire to cleanse this so-called kingdom and visit his vengeance on everyone, to a man, that bore the same blood of those that betrayed his house and stole everything that he had ever known and held dear. His heart was consumed by loss and a slow flame that was at the edge of exploding into a raging inferno at the thought or mere mention of the fate of his father.

His disposition had not always been so. He was once a carefree child, only concerned with adventure and mischief. Playful, affectionate, and inquisitive. But all that had changed; his innocence had been stolen, replaced by the image of the horrors he had witnessed during the sack and destruction of his home, and from the hardship he had endured when he was forced to flee Ife and seek solace with the last remnants of his family in the western city of Ogun.

Now, his eyes did not only burn with the image of his city, Ile-Ife, aflame, but also with the fire of retribution. His sorrow, anger and fears now served as a conduit for the will of the gods, and one god in particular. *Shango*.

Without truly understanding his actions, he had sworn himself to *Shango*, his protector, the deity that had taken a keen interest in the young prince and set him on the path to realising his destiny in the world of men.

He gave himself over to the god, and with his so doing, his childhood innocence slowly ebbed away into the recesses of his subconscious. Slowly fading was the playful boy, bright-eyed and eager to explore the world. In his place was a shell, hard and cold, with a brittle temperament to match.

But the gods are fickle. Their desires and motives are only known to them and change more frequently than the passing seasons. *Shango*, however, truly loved this child, and there was a saying – If the gods so love a man, no feat desired by that man was unachievable.

In the centre of it all was Olise. He sat on a throne he had built on the ruin of the old city. A throne that was soaked in blood and erected on the bones of the people. He had silenced all his opposition in the surrounding provinces and struck fear in the hearts of all his new subjects. He created a far-reaching network of spies and cutthroats that worked from the shadows, weeding out would-be perpetrators of treasonous acts that threatened his rule. He vanquished whole cities and everywhere his warriors marched, they brought fire and death along with them. No one dared to voice their contempt for his reign.

The west, by and large, was under his control, with only a handful of cities and towns that remained defiant, including the province of Ogun, where Enitan had sought refuge. But this didn't matter to him. He knew that it was only a matter of time before the region yielded. They didn't possess the military might or resources to match his vast and ever-growing empire, which continued to build in strength with every passing moon. Not only that, but his mother, Ekaete, ever the master that pulled the threads from the shadows, continued to exert her influence, and support for the traitor king never waned.

However, deep down, Olise was embroiled in an internal battle, one that weighed heavily on his conscience. His dreams were haunted by the memory of his brother, King Jide, and the fate he had written for him. Everywhere he turned he saw Jide's face, with the same accusing eyes and the expression of sorrow mixed with pity he had worn the night Olise had passed judgement on him and put him to the axe. The sound of Jide's voice uttering those final words – *"He who laughs last laughs the hardest"*, still lingered in the halls of his memory. He had never truly wanted him dead, only for him to suffer and live with the knowledge that the throne had been taken by the better man, one more deserving to be called the king of the tribes.

Now, the crown he had coveted for decades left him with a sense of emptiness, a black gaping hole that slowly diminished his will to rule, tainting all his accomplishments. He drank more and spent his days wallowing in self-pity, seeking comfort in the company of bed warmers. To further compound his growing apathy, he had lost the closest people to him; Dimeji, his ever-loyal blood-guard and Ogie, the former commander of his army, both falling to the spears of Jide's allies. He was now surrounded by fools, who only stood by his side out of fear or their self-interest to raise their station in the realm. He would sooner see them all stripped of their newly found titles and lands, and hanged for good measure, but Ekaete had vehemently persuaded him of the importance of maintaining old, and forging new, alliances, which he reluctantly entertained. For now.

All was not lost, however, as he still possessed a handful of warriors that he could trust. These were high-ranking commanders in his army that had survived the battle of the tribes, and they carried out his bidding; they were his blades in the dark, as he referred to them. They spoke with his authority, not that of Ekaete, and their loyalty was to him alone. These warriors were his inner circle, men that had earned his respect through the passage of battle, a baptism in blood of sorts, and were ever eager to appease his every whim.

But now there was a new threat from the east. One that threatened to challenge the very essence of his stolen crown with the potential to have a rippling effect in the kingdom and embolden the hearts of those that would sooner see him dethroned. This was the only thing that drove him forward, his only motivation, which he embraced wholeheartedly. He thrived on challenges, anything that ignited a fire under his feet. After all, he was a warrior. One that believed that all he needed was a blade in his hand, and he could take whatsoever he desired, not least something that he believed belonged to him by right of birth.

He would seek out this so-called prince of royal blood and put an end to the rumours for good. Besides, it was time he brought the River-lands to heel. The decades-long enmity they had towards him for spilling the blood of one of their greatest sons; the warrior Abasi, had not been forgotten, and the chiefs of this region had openly expressed their intentions not to rest until Olise's blood was spilt in return. Olise would oblige them, but it would not be his blood that would spill. He would personally see to it that all the rebellious River chiefs and their allies were scratched from the history of the tribes, banished to antiquity like the ancient names of those that roamed the lands before them. By the time he was done with them, they would be but a memory, a mere smudge under the great heel of time.

He planned to use this opportunity to kill two birds with one stone. Maybe that would restore his passion to rule and forever cement his name as one of the greatest rulers to have ever sat upon the throne.

Yes. The stones would be cast, and the future of the tribes would be written by his hand and his alone, not that of his mother, Ekaete, or by some pretender claiming to possess the blood of kings. No. The scrolls of history would tell the tale of the great deeds and the conquests of one man, Olise Adelani. The one and true king of the realm. And he would carve out his own destiny in blood.

BLESSED ARE THE CHILDREN

ONE YEAR EARLIER

The stench of rotten eggs was almost suffocating, tinged with the scent of decaying vegetation and other sulphide gases emitted from the swamp-infested jungle that stretched for miles around. The smells were a constant companion, seeping into the fabric of their clothing, and almost under their skin. This was no place for the delicate.

How anyone, hardened or otherwise, would even contemplate inhabiting an environment such as this was beyond imagining. As if the smell was not deterrent enough, there was a plethora of ungodly creatures lurking under every bush and hiding in every tree, just waiting to pounce and take a man to a murky grave.

The group had already lost several men to gods-know-what, unfortunate souls who were dragged off in the night screaming and splashing about through the undergrowth, with only traces *of them found in the morning when there was sufficient light to carry out a hesitant search.*

To say they had to tread lightly was an understatement by all accounts, and yet, every day, they trudged through the harsh terrain, grim-faced, and anxious to reach their destination and fulfil the task their prince had set them. The only consolation was that some of their numbers were somewhat familiar with the topography here, being locals of the surrounding villages, and adept at surviving in these very conditions. These men were the local militia, and they served a double function; guides and the vanguard of the group, ranging deep into the jungle to map out the safest routes for the large party of men and warn against the potential threat of being discovered by scouts. Not that they expected to see anyone insane enough to be patrolling these jungles, but it harmed not to take precautions.

It was almost impossible to imagine that the locals braved this perilous wilderness every other moon for the sake of earning a meagre wage. Traders would labour with wagonloads of supplies and other necessities, risking life and limb to reach the stronghold nestled in the heart of a land that could only be described as a place suitable for no man. New routes literally had to be carved out every time the treacherous journey was made, as they were overgrown by various species of invasive plants or saturated from the constant torrential rainfall that fed the swamps, creating new habitats that bred the cyclical ecosystem that was the jungle.

And suddenly, standing prominently just above the bushes and tree line on what appeared to be a man-made rise, was the welcoming sight of the bronze-studded gates of the town of Ada, promising civilisation, and a haven away from the mosquitoes, pests, and creatures of the worst kind.

This had been Olise's little kingdom. A kingdom granted to him in banishment more than 20 years ago. This is where he plotted to wrest the power he believed was denied him by right of birth. Now, it was home to a garrison with a small complement of soldiers, and the hostages his mother, Ekaete, had advised him to take to ensure the continued fealty of several significant chiefs across the eastern and southern provinces of the realm.

'Thank the gods! I thought I'd never be in the midst of humanity again. I had already resigned myself to my destiny being to die in this gods-forsaken natural splendour!' said a stocky warrior wrapped from head to toe in rags.

'You call this "natural splendour"? Those are not the words I'd use to describe this place at all. More like a wilderness of flesh-eating monsters,' said another man, called Uzoma, who was obviously the jester amongst the bunch.

'Do not presume to think that our focus can be eased now that we have reached our destination. Only death and the princes' vengeance await beyond those gates. Gods willing, we'll be the ones doing all the killing. Nevertheless, make your peace with the gods and prepare yourselves,' said a third man. He was clearly in command. His accent, which differed from the eastern accents of the other two, marked him out as a native of the western regions, Ile-Ife more specifically. He was once a royal guard that had witnessed the fall of the great city and had to flee with the princes. But here, he served as prince Niran's spear, entrusted with the deliverance of all the captured children of the tribes, a

task that bore a considerable significance in the determination of the balance of power. A task which he could not fail under any circumstances, and one that he had accepted gladly.

'If I'm honest, I most certainly prefer my prospects behind those gates. At least if I'm to die, it'll be with a blade in my hand, not in the jaws of some wild animal. Imagine that. When they write songs about me, they'll say — there he lies, that steaming pile of crocodile faeces. But he was brave, and he died for his kingdom,' said Uzoma, which immediately caused a bout of nervous laughter amongst the men.

'And what makes you think that anyone would write a song about you? Besides, if you die, within the confines of the gates or out in this jungle, you'll certainly end up as food for the wild. Nobody will have the time to dig you a grave. I would imagine that the town's dead receive this very treatment,' said the stocky warrior.

'Why be so cruel? I would dig a grave for you if you fell in battle, and you wouldn't do the same for me? How disappointing,' said Uzoma as he feigned sadness.

'Enough! No one is dying, or digging any graves, for that matter. Provided we follow our plans, it should all work out exactly as expected,' their leader said with finality. The respect he commanded was evident, as no further comments were made; rather, the group of men started to check their weapons and move into position.

Several of the soldiers placed themselves strategically around the wagons that snaked further back into the jungle, obscured by the thick vegetation, while others tentatively moved away and out of sight to conceal themselves amongst the foliage, ready to reveal themselves when they were called upon.

The men that remained with the wagons began to pull hoods over their heads or wrapped lengths of cloth about their faces to disguise themselves. Others, despite being clothed in rags, smeared mud on their attire to complete the pretence of being poor merchants and field hands.

'Right. Remember the words, and do not try to get smart with the guards. Keep it simple and to the point,' whispered the royal guard to Uzoma as he locked eyes with him to further emphasise how serious he was. Uzoma only smiled back in return and tilted his head in acknowledgement.

'You there on the wall!' he called out when the party of men were within a spear's throw of the gates. 'We come bearing gifts. Your monthly supplies have arrived. Please open the gates before the crocodiles get what's left of the food. I've already lost good men on my journey here and I would sooner raise a horn to their memory and have a warm meal in my stomach,' he finished, drawing a sharp look from the royal guard and a look of exasperation from the stocky warrior.

Soon enough, a begrimed face with shifty eyes popped up from the wall adjacent to the gate, followed by another face just as filthy as the first. 'I don't recognise you. Where is Ike? He always leads the supply baggage,' said the man with shifty eyes. He had a slight slur in his speech, and red-rimmed eyes — the tell-tale signs of a drunk. Who could blame him? Anyone who had been posted here would do well to dull their senses in such a desolate and depressing environment.

'I fear Ike is currently making his way through the digestive systems of several animals. He should have known better than to

urinate in a snake's pit. The resident of the pit didn't take too kindly to that and bit him. He died two nights ago, so we left him in the wild. But do not despair, it was his dying request to be laid to rest in the jungle he knew all too well. Honestly,' replied Uzoma.

The royal guard standing behind Uzoma slowly moved closer to him and discreetly poked him in the small of his back with a dagger, signalling that he wasn't amused in the slightest. So, Uzoma quickly added, 'But he entrusted me to fulfil his duty; I am his cousin and, besides Ike, no one knows this jungle better than I. Please let us in so we can unburden ourselves with this load, it's been a long and sad journey and I would like to pray for Ike's soul. Besides, I've brought some perishables, delicacies from my village, and fresh palm wine. I'm sure the commander of the garrison would not be best pleased if the food were to spoil before it reached him, eh?'

The man with the shifty eyes licked his lips, clearly visualising a welcome change to whatever vintage of jungle brew he'd been forced to endure for gods-know how long.

'Okay. Wait there,' he said after a hushed deliberation with his dirty-faced companion, who was nodding his head approvingly, no doubt having the same thoughts as shifty eyes.

'You fool! Are you trying to get us killed before we even pass the gates?' hissed the royal guard, once the men on the wall disappeared. He still had his dagger pressed in Uzoma's back as if daring him to make another smart remark before driving the blade through his spine.

Uzoma only shook his head, just before the loud rattling of metal signified that the locking mechanism of the gate was being engaged, and the bronze-studded mass of wood slowly began to swing outwards.

'You see? I told you I'd get us in,' Uzoma said triumphantly with a slight nervous smirk.

'Lucky for you. You would have had one less kidney otherwise. No more games, you hear me?' The royal guard hissed as they stood before the gates groaning from the unoiled hinges and snapping off the unruly ivy that had sprouted from the cracks in the wooden frame of the gates.

It took several minutes for the gates to fully open, revealing what seemed to be a considerably well-maintained series of stone and wooden buildings erected haphazardly within the compound, a huge contrast to the green hues of the jungle they had travelled through for days.

Several soldiers idled about but looked on expectantly as the wagons were pulled into the open courtyard. The arrival of provisions was obviously the highlight of their time here, and judging from their seemingly relaxed disposition and lack of attentiveness, they probably had not seen any action for some time. Only a few of them were visibly armed with daggers hanging from their waists, and other than the men on the wall, there was barely a spear in sight.

Townspeople were dotted around the courtyard and, at a glance, they seemed to be the workers, carrying out menial tasks, while the soldiers clearly ruled this little part of the world.

This would be an easy town to take, *thought the royal guard satisfactorily as he scrutinised his surroundings from under his ragged hood. With a keen soldier's eye, he took in the layout of the town, the buildings likely to house more men, the armoury, potential escape routes, and so on.*

Then, his attention was drawn to the sound of the gates being closed behind them. They had planned for every eventuality, including this one. The men that had made it into the town would wait for nightfall, take the guards on the wall, and drop ropes down for the rest of the men lying in wait in the bushes. Now, they just had to exercise a little patience and avoid being discovered; the night promised to be fuelled by drunken revelry as the soldiers indulged themselves on the casks of palm wine, which was a benefit rather than a hindrance.

Uzoma was already ingratiating himself with the guards, talking animatedly, whilst making them laugh uncontrollably. The royal guard signalled to the stocky warrior to keep his tribesman in check, a hard task as Uzoma was clearly in his element, but one that needed to be done.

Similar orders were discreetly issued to all the men that had accompanied the supply wagons, forbidding them from indulging in drinking, and to keep their weapons close, but they were disciplined men that knew the gravity of their mission and suspicion was miraculously never aroused.

Nightfall. Darkness was accompanied by the familiar sounds of a jocund atmosphere. Slurred and off-key singing could be heard around the compound and from most dwellings, horns clinked, and palm wine casks were smashed, with the dregs syphoned into the waiting throats of soldiers and civilians alike.

Every so often came the sound of female laughter or the unmistakable grunts of couples engaged in carnal pleasures from dark corners and some, unashamedly, out in the open. There were fist fights and the odd stabbing, but none was fatal. It was as if the town was in celebration, with little moderation on their supply of alcohol being observed. There would be no further supplies making it to this town; the inhabitants didn't know that yet, but it mattered not.

As the night stretched, the guards became more inebriated, with the exception of the garrison commander and a handful of disciplined warriors, who chose to remove themselves from the merriment and take up residence on the other side of the town. This eventuality was also accounted for, and the royal guard had men watching the house ready to storm the premises once the order was given.

During the preceding hours, the royal guard had surreptitiously located the dungeons where the captives were being held. He knew the man that possessed the keys, another drunkard, and from information gleaned from the man, he had a rough idea of what to expect within. The captives' liberation was long overdue, their freedom but a few moments away.

The time had come to carry out Niran's bidding, and there would be no mercy for the perpetrators of the injustice that had befallen the children of the realm. The innocent would of course be spared, but a message needed to be sent. One that was loud and clear, leaving no room to be misconstrued — anyone that stood against the Adelanis or their allies would sooner dwell in the dark halls of Esu's underworld.

The royal guard sought out the stocky warrior, Uzoma, and a few more of his trusted men amongst the bustling townsfolk, and

silently indicated that the hour was upon them. They all inconspicuously detached themselves from the various groups they were engaged with and slowly started to converge near the town walls and the massive timber gates.

'Men, you know your tasks, keep watch while we take out the guards on the wall. If anyone sees us or appears suspicious, kill them, but try to preserve the lives of the innocent if you can. The rest of you, come with me. It is time to fulfil your duty to your prince. May the gods guide you,' said the royal guard, as the men spilt into smaller groups.

Before long, the royal guard and four others were climbing the steps to the ramparts, daggers in hands, as they glanced nervously around. Faint sounds of laughter emanated from the top of the steps, a good sign which meant that the palm wine had made its way to the men on watch.

As they came to the top of the steps, which offered a view of the vast surrounding wilderness bathed in darkness, they were met by the sight of four guards; one lazily leaned on the stone wall, an outstretched arm holding an overflowing horn, which dangled over the wall as if waiting for a bird to come and whisk it away. Two others were seated around a large calabash, the contents of which they scooped and downed in one draught before repeating the process. Seemingly, they were competing to see how quickly they could consume the aromatic beverage; the fourth man had clearly failed at this game.

The approaching men immediately noticed the shifty-eyed guard from earlier in the day, who seemed to be thoroughly enjoying himself; the front of his cotton shirt was soaked from the drink that ran down the sides of his mouth and glistened in the glow of the fires that lit the ramparts. He raised his head at the sound of the men and offered them a wide smile in greeting.

'What are you doing here? I thought you'd be enjoying the events of the evening and be blind drunk by now. To be honest, I'm probably halfway there myself, but don't tell the captain.' He chuckled as he slapped his drinking companion on the shoulder, causing him to spill his palm wine on the ground and look upon the small pool of liquid morosely.

Shifty eyes was about to say something else, but his vision, blurred as it may have been, was suddenly drawn to the blades in the hands of the men before him, sharpened iron catching the glow of the fire that burned on torches hanging from mounts on the wall. The smile he wore fell away instantly as his alcohol-impaired mind slowly began to process the significance of what his eyes beheld.

Before another word could be uttered, the five newcomers set upon the guards. A hand was jammed over the mouth of the man with shifty eyes, and another plunged a dagger into his chest.

The other Three men were taken just as quickly, and their bodies were cast over the walls, instantly swallowed up by the darkness below. As the attackers wiped their blades, ropes were secured to wooden appendages fixed to the wall, tested for resistance, and then tossed over the side. One of the men then blew out a low whistle that mimicked the sound of a bird call.

He repeated the sound once more, this time a little louder, and before long, a similar sound echoed from the dark. The ropes were then pulled taut from below as men began to ascend the *walls. They emerged like apparitions in the night, hooded and grim-faced, ready to descend on the unsuspecting masses below. Once enough warriors had made the climb, with more still clambering upwards, the royal guard relayed his orders, and chaos ensued.*

The festive atmosphere was quickly replaced with one of mayhem as the intruders set about attacking the guards. They were taken completely by surprise and, before long, the air was rent with screams of terror and panic.

The drunken guards succumbed to the blades of the intruders easily enough, and the citizens were sent scurrying away like rats to their dwellings. They were not harmed or restrained, and the royal guard ordered the perimeter around the dungeon to be secured before he unlocked the heavy chains that wrapped around the gratings of the iron doors that had held the prisoners fast for almost a year.

Rotten and termite-infested wooden steps led down into pitch blackness. Torches were lit and swords were held at the ready as the royal guard and a few of his men tentatively descended. A strong scent of unwashed bodies mixed with human excrement and urine assaulted their nostrils, the lower they got, the stronger the nauseating smell became, almost overwhelming the newcomers.

'Chineke's mercy! This place is appalling. How could they possibly hold anyone here? And this is where they have decided to imprison children?' said Uzoma incredulously, as he buried his nose in the crook of his arm and bore a torch above his head with the other.

'In these conditions, I'm almost scared to think what state these children will be in. Come, let's make haste, I fear there is

little time for these poor souls,' prompted the royal guard, as he quickened his steps.

The steps led down to a large room that dwarfed the dwelling above. The earthen walls were packed tight with stones of all sizes in rough haphazard patterns, presumably in a bid to offer some sort of stability, but signs of stress were clearly visible from the cracks that snaked along the earthen walls.

It was obvious that no care, or much else for that matter, had been put into this space, which may have been the intention, considering its purpose. There were metal rings affixed to the walls at various locations; some had chains with hand or leg clamps at their ends. Other objects were strewn about randomly, the soldiers saw as they made their way through the pitiful space; a whip here and there, iron rods, baskets that came alive and shook violently with trapped rats, and cruller items still — an assortment of knives, hammers and other devices; what they would have been used for didn't bear thinking about.

From the torch light that illuminated the space, the men were able to discern areas with dark-coloured patches on the floor and walls. Dried blood. Never a good sign.

The further they walked, the larger the room became, and now, they could make out a series of makeshift cells aligning the walls. The foul scent was much stronger here; some of the men had to force themselves not to gag; and then, amongst the shadows, they saw the children.

They had been herded into the cells like goats, boys and girls together. Some cowered away in fright, others stared with vacant, bloodshot eyes, but the odd child looked on without fear, as if *silently challenging the newcomers. One thing they all had in common was the look of the malnourished and distressed; starved and broken. Some bore marks on their skin, evidence of the wickedness they would have had to endure at the hands of Olise's men. This could not go unanswered, thought the royal guard as he scanned the gaunt, bemired faces before him.*

'Do not worry, young ones. We mean you no harm. We are here to set you free. Soon you will be reunited with your families,' said the royal guard as he moved to inspect the locks on the nearest cell. His men did the same and the sound of metal being struck echoed as locks were broken and chains dropped to the ground.

None of the children made any attempt to walk towards the open doors, as if scared that this was some cruel trick. The royal guard's heart broke to see them in such a state. He gently reached for the closest child, who flinched at his touch. 'Don't be afraid. I promise you no harm, child. What is your name?' he asked, but the boy would not respond.

He ventured again using a different tactic. 'My name is Lanre and I am a royal guard from the Kingdom of Ile-Ife, sent here by prince Niran himself.'

'Is that true?' asked an older boy of about 16 summers; he had been one of the children that had not averted his gaze when the men had arrived. There were many marks on his body and face, which he may have earned from his boldness, but he seemed to bear them almost with pride.

'Yes, I speak the truth. These men are from the Igbo tribe, some of whom may be your kinsmen.' Lanre indicated the warriors who had accompanied him and were busily freeing the

other children from their imprisonment. 'We have come a long way to deliver you and we have made a solemn vow to ensure that you are returned safe. You can trust us.'

The boy assessed Lanre and the other men for a few seconds, before turning to his peers on either side of him almost in reassurance. Finally, he faced the warriors. 'Very well. I give you my thanks,' he said. He then addressed his peers. 'These men seem genuine. Let us put our trust in them.'

Lanre felt a moment of respect for the young man and thought that he must be the child of a chief with a strong bloodline and, most likely, a name to go with it.

'Well said. Come, let us make haste. It is still not safe here. We will set a course for the nearest town to replenish our supplies and establish your respective tribes and provinces. But I assure you that your captivity has ended.'

Now, the children were ambling out of the cells, and only then did Lanre and his men understand the magnitude of the task before them. Some of the children were almost skeletal in appearance, some limped, others required support to walk. Most had injuries of some description, the worst of them already showing signs of infection from the corruption that seeped from their wounds. In that moment, it dawned on Lanre that many would not make it back alive.

Besides the soldiers above ground that they had to subdue, there was still the jungle to navigate, with all its unfriendly inhabitants. This would be by no means an easy task to fulfil, but the stones had been cast, and he was determined to get as many of them as possible to relative safety.

Just then, while most of the children had left the cages, Uzoma called upon Lanre from one end of the room in a distressed tone.

'You will want to see this,' he said as he guided him to the far end of the room. 'What am I supposed to be looking at?' he asked as Uzoma pointed toward the end of the room that was shrouded in darkness, just before he bore his torch over his head, revealing a long passageway with more exits in various directions that extended far beyond their vision.

It was a network of tunnels, in fact, that all led to gods-know where. Then it all made sense. These tunnels most likely ran underneath the entire town, which showed that the occupants were far more than a collective of useless drunks, but resourceful and shrewd. It appeared they had gone to great lengths to conceal their true numbers, which on reflection was understandable, given that they were tasked with guarding Olise's prized possessions – the children. The very thing that would guarantee continued fealty amongst the tribal rulers and maintaining control over the kingdom.

Lanre had thought it had been too easy, but now, he understood Olise's reputation for being a cunning and unpredictable individual. He belatedly realised that the commander of the garrison had disappeared into one of the dwellings and had never been seen exiting it, according to his men, and realised that he'd probably used a similar tunnel to exit at a completely different location around the town.

'This is not good. Get these children above ground now. We need to leave this place immediately!' Uzoma didn't need to be told twice and, for once, he didn't follow up with his usual comedic

remarks, but set straight to the task he was given. He had seen the look on Lanre's face and had correctly deduced the potential peril that awaited them.

Suddenly, one of the tunnels started to emit some light, faint at first but slowly starting to get brighter. Voices followed the light. Men, and lots of them.

'Ogun protect us,' Lanre muttered under his breath, 'they are coming for us.'

The stocky warrior was by Lanre's side, having been alerted to the oncoming threat. 'I can hold them off with a few men. The passage is narrow, so they won't be able to overwhelm us easily. We can take them at the mouth of the tunnel and hold them back for as long as I have strength in my right arm, to give you a chance of escaping this place,' he said in his gruff voice. Lanre saw fear in the warrior's eyes, which mirrored how he felt, but he also saw his resolve.

Before Lanre could respond, the young boy who had addressed the captives and a few other older boys walked up to them. They had armed themselves with objects discarded around the room.

'We can fight. Besides, I'd like the opportunity to pay back these soldiers for their hospitality.' The other boys echoed the same sentiment, and from their expressions, there would be no dissuading them.

'I can't let you throw away your lives so needlessly. I have a duty to see to your safety and—' Lanre began, but he was abruptly interrupted by the lead boy.

'You have done your duty, I am freed. Now let me do mine and sate my wounded pride. There is no time to argue, the other children are in more need of your help.'

The boy spoke true, for there was no time to argue as the voices from the tunnel were growing ever louder and closer. Lanre made a snap decision.

'Fine. I'll leave five of my warriors with you, strong men and good in battle. I'll take the children to safety, but I will return for you. I swear it before the gods. May Ogun *protect you all.'*

He stole a quick look at the stocky warrior and favoured him with a curt nod before turning his back to issue orders and escort the remaining children to whatever chaos awaited them above, taking Uzoma with him.

It was slow going getting the children to ascend the steps, but they moved as quickly as their feeble limbs permitted them. As they left the room, the faint sounds of fighting trailed behind them.

Lanre burst out of the dwelling and was greeted by the warm night air on his sweating brow and the smell of smoke. He had positioned three men at the entrance of the dwelling to guard it and fend off any soldiers that came to investigate the captives, but they were nowhere in sight. He noted a trail of blood in the gravel in one direction, thick droplets, most likely a fatal wound, but no sign of its owner. There was evidence of a fight, a vicious one by the looks of it, as more blood covered the wall of the house opposite where they stood. His men may have given their lives to fulfil his command, but there was no time to ruminate on this, no time to even offer them a silent prayer. They were all in need of prayers

right now, so he pushed the thoughts to the back of his mind and began ushering the children out in small groups.

Stray dogs and goats ran rampant in a bid to escape the madness of the evening, the red-orange glow of fire could be seen reflected on dwellings and illuminating the night sky in several locations.

Faint sounds of iron and bronze clashing, along with the cries of the wounded, drifted through the air. They needed to get to the main gates and out of the town as quickly as they could, even though Lanre dreaded the prospect of travelling through the jungle at night, but in any situation, he'd rather contend with wild animals than with wild men. They then stumbled upon the first body. It was one of the town guards, bent over a calabash with his arms almost wrapped around it, like he was trying to protect the drink. He was run through the back, a sorry sight. Then more bodies came into view. He saw more guards, some of his men and the odd townsman.

Some of the children began to whimper and lament, forcing him to silence them with sharp rebukes. It pained him to do so, but this was not the time for emotions, lest they alert the enemy to their position.

They kept moving, hugging the shadows as best they could, until Lanre spied a large dwelling that appeared semi-secluded and out of sight from the main path through the town. He decided to hide the children there. This would allow him the time to assess his surroundings unfettered and regroup with his men. So far, they hadn't seen a living soul, just the dead and the odd stray animal. But men were close, he could feel it.

Once all the children were secure, he barricaded them into the dwelling with broken stools and timbers, instructing a couple of older girls to keep them as quiet as possible, before he, Uzoma and a third warrior went out in search of the rest of their men.

They moved quickly, staying within the shadows like leopards stalking a prey. It didn't take them long to find the first group of fighting men. From their vantage point, they saw a group of their warriors, perhaps fifteen men, fending off a slightly larger force of men, soldiers mixed with some townspeople. Another bad sign. This explained the dead townsmen they had come across on their way here, and it gave him some relief to know that his men were not just killing indiscriminately. They seemed to have joined the fighting in support of the local guards.

Another unexpected twist in the horribly unravelling events of the evening, a reminder that it was impossible to prepare for every single eventuality.

His men were faring well considering the odds against them. No surprise there, as Niran had specifically handpicked the men for this task. Men that he could rely on in difficult situations. That didn't account for the local militia, who bolstered Lanre's men, but he had enough good men to direct their efforts as one coherent unit.

The defenders were hacking away at Lanre's men with little skill, whist his men pressed their attack, sending the defenders onto the back foot. There were obstacles everywhere; toppled tables, broken stools, shards of broken calabash, and the defenders stumbled over them as they were driven back, only to be impaled by the spears and swords of their attackers.

Lanre gave Uzoma but a glance; he responded with a nod and, without a word, the three men sprang out from their hiding place straight into the melee to join their companions. They were soon parrying sword thrusts and slashing. In just a few moments, the fight was over.

'Where are the rest of our men?' Lanre asked one of his warriors. The man was breathing heavily, and needed a few seconds to catch his breath, adrenaline rapidly seeping out of his system, realising how close he had been to death's eternal embrace.

'I don't know, it was a disaster. As soon as we started attacking the guards, the citizens turned on us. They were like deranged animals; I don't know if it was the drink or Esu that possessed them. The fighting separated us and flowed in all directions. I lost all my orientation, I'm sorry.

'You have done well. We have the children. They are safe for now, but we need to find our men and leave this place,' Lanre ordered.

'Are we not taking the town? Surely, we can't travel back at night with everything out there. We have only just arrived!' said another warrior.

'Believe me, I'd love to take off my sandals and stretch my legs with a horn in my hands, but it's not safe here. I don't think we know the true extent of the force tasked with protecting this town, so the quicker we set about our business and depart, the better.'

The warriors obviously didn't like what they were hearing, but nobody challenged him. Lanre spoke for the prince, and that was all the persuasion they needed.

They gathered themselves and headed off in search of the rest of their men. Along the way, there was the odd skirmish, but nothing that they couldn't handle. They found more men, doing what warriors do to an invaded town, pillaging. Lanre reprimanded them with threats of a formal punishment if they made it out alive, and they all fell in line. Soon, he had enough men at his back to give him more confidence in the success of their mission. That was until his worst fears were confirmed.

As they went about clearing the roads of opposition, they were ambushed by a large group of guards led by the commander of the garrison. It was a desperate attempt to win back the town but, clumsy as it may have been, it had the intended effect of discouraging and setting doubt in the hearts of Lanre and his men. Before they knew it, many more guards and townspeople had heeded the rallying call of the garrison commander, surrounding Lanre's group, and this was where they had to prove their worth.

Stones, pieces of wood and all manner of debris rained down on them from rooftops and windows, while spears and swords were thrust at them at ground level. Lanre's men desperately fended off the attack as best they could, but it was getting hard. They managed to keep a close formation, determined not to get dispersed and become isolated as easy pickings for the town's defenders. One of his men screamed out in pain as he took a stab to the thigh and, a moment later, Lanre was struck in the head by a flying object that drove him to his knees, dazed.

Uzoma grabbed him under one arm and roughly dragged him to his feet while he slashed back and forth, cutting one man across the arm. He pushed Lanre behind him and picked up a discarded spear, which he held mid-shaft under his armpit as he swung it violently left and right.

'I pray we are not out of favour with the gods this night. There is much I am yet to accomplish with my life. I haven't tasted the sweetness of Amaka's lips on mine yet. I won't be pleased if I am to lose her to the local touts!' Uzoma said to Lanre, who was trying to shake off his dizziness.

'Even at a time like this you jest! You won't be tasting anything but a blade in your mouth if you don't focus, for the love of the gods! I may yet kill you myself if we make it out alive!' Lanre shouted back, as he rejoined the fight. Despite Uzoma's inanity, he was a skilled and experienced warrior, and a man you would want besides you in a fight.

The commander of the garrison was now barking orders for his men to close the ring around Lanre and his men, but Lanre sensed a slight hesitation, and that was all the time that was needed for him to know that their attackers were not hardened warriors, but men merely compelled to defend their home.

War cries suddenly erupted from further along the street and more of Lanre's militia came into view, charging down the defenders from the rear position of the commander. Lanre wondered where they had come from and what had taken them so long to arrive, but thanked the gods for their timing, nonetheless. From their eagerness to join the fray, these men seemed enraged by something; maybe they had seen something that had fuelled their anger – the state of the children, perhaps? He'd soon find out, but the fight had finally shifted in their favour.

Taking advantage, Lanre quickly ordered his own men to advance, and they immediately responded, rushing out to take the hesitant defenders that had failed to surround them. The arrival *of Lanre's additional men at the rear of the defenders served well as a distraction, reversing the roles of the aggressors and the cornered. Men were slow to parry a blow here or raise a shield there and the mistakes cost them dear. Within minutes, the ambush was foiled and some of Lanre's men disappeared into the dwellings around them. Fighting could be heard from within, and men were soon sent flying through windows and tumbling from roof tops to their death in the streets.*

Those of Lanre's men that remained on the street drove their attack forward seeking to take out the commander of the garrison, his guards and the townsmen that aided him. It turned out that the commander was not as experienced a fighter as he was an ambitious tactician. As soon as he lost a few men about him, he immediately threw down his sword and pleaded for mercy.

Lanre spared his life but informed him that judgement was reserved for the children, which had the instant effect of sending the commander into tears. He knew what fate awaited him, presumably from the torment he and his men had inflicted on the children, and Lanre thought to himself how satisfying it would be.

'It seems like the gods have destined me to taste Amaka's sweet lips after all! I will kill a ram in honour of Chineke when I return to my village,' Uzoma was saying as he beamed from ear to ear.

'You and this talk of Amaka. Have you forgotten about the snakes and man-eating crocodiles between you and her? Or the children that still need to go back to their provinces with all the conflict in the kingdom? I think you really need to consider your priorities,' Lanre replied as he winced from the pain of the lump

that had now grown on his head where he had been struck earlier. He felt around the growth tentatively.

'After what we have just been through, nothing is impossible,' Uzoma replied. Lanre just shook his head in response and turned away to speak to the other men, not wanting to have to deal with Uzoma's comments.

Shortly after, they rounded up the survivors, bound them in ropes and set off to get the children. Surprisingly, Lanre had only lost four men, but many were injured, and it was decided that they'd stay a while longer before they made the arduous journey back to the eastern province of Imo. Some of the townspeople who had not joined in the fight came out to ingratiate themselves with their new rulers, and they were falling over themselves to outdo each other to the amusement of Lanre and his men.

The children had not been discovered, since they had been barricaded in the dwelling, and they were elated to know that their ordeal had truly come to an end, and they would finally be reunited with their loved ones. Most of them. Those that were strong enough to make it and those that would not succumb to the wild on their journey back. For now, they basked in their newly found freedom.

When the commander of the garrison and some of his guards were brought before them, the children all jeered at them. Some spat, some picked up rocks and hurled them, while some just stood and cried. Before long, more began to pick up stones, sticks and other objects. This emboldened others, even the ones that cried and soon, all the children were scrambling to find things to throw at them. The stones got bigger, and the objects got harder.

The commander and his men begged as they rolled on the floor attempting to turn their bodies away from the objects, unable to protect themselves with their bound hands and legs.

One of the children found a discarded spear, another a dagger, then it turned ugly. Lanre stepped away, no longer interested in seeing the suffering of the commander, just as some of the children were taking turns with the weapons. His thoughts were then drawn to the men and the boys he had left in the cells below the dwellings.

He summoned the nearest of his men to him and ran off to find them. He hadn't seen any of those men in the crowd. His heart lurched, worry slowly creeping up his spine thinking about the stocky warrior, who had been his second-in-command.

They reached the dwelling, and he drew his sword, dreading what he'd find below as he descended the earthen steps. It was deathly quiet, and he feared he would only be met by the dead, but the room was still illuminated. Could it be the flame from a dropped torch that had somehow not been extinguished?

He wasn't prepared for what he did see. The stocky warrior was there nursing a cut on his shoulder, as was another of his warriors. 'You yet live!' Lanre exclaimed when he saw them.

'I had little to do with it if I'm to talk truth,' said the stocky warrior, who was clearly still reeling from the near-death experience he had just escaped.

'What of the other men, and the boys who stayed behind?'

'A few of them are dead but a couple remain.' The stocky warrior lifted his head, indicating towards the far end of the room. Lanre had to raise his torch above him and peer into the gloom.

Walking towards him, unrecognisable from the blood that was splattered across his face and body, was the boy who had spoken to him earlier and had asked to stay. Behind him followed two more, equally drenched in blood. The first boy had a look about him, one that had not been there before. There was an ugliness in his eyes, something dark, deep-seated and menacing, compounded by the sneer that was plastered on his face, the white of his teeth just about discernible from one corner of his mouth.

'The boys fought well. Too well, in fact, but that one killed most of the attackers. I've never seen anything like it. So vicious, so precise. You would have thought he was possessed by some devil,' said the stocky warrior, tilting his head towards the figures that were now emerging from the shadows.

As the boys approached, Lanre studied them intently. 'It seems you are natural warriors. Born killers. I never asked your names or which tribe you are from,' Lanre ventured, now feeling slightly uneasy as he peered into the dark eyes of the foremost boy.

'My name is Etim, heir to the chieftaincy of the Akwa-Ibom province, and first son of Edem. But you might know him as Edem the ugly.'

The boy standing next to him stepped forward and Lanre immediately recognised the features in his face, the muscular physique below the scars of his recent ordeal. 'And I am Obinna, son of Zogo the black and heir to the noble seat of the Igbo people.'

UNREQUITED LOVE

Raucous laughter reverberated off the walls of the great hall. Men cheered and wine flowed freely. Servants scurried about bearing platers and clay pots of an assortment of roasted and stewed meats, boiled root vegetables and exotic fruits. Drinking horns were constantly being replenished, held aloft by unsteady hands of men with seemingly unquenchable thirst, and musicians blared out tunes from three-yard-long kakakis. The polyphony created by the wind instruments was drowned out by the many voices that filled the room, intoxicated not only by the palm wine and ogogoro, but also by the taste of victory.

Every inch of the hall's floor was covered in thick, exquisitely woven carpets, and cushions of animal hide stuffed with fowl feathers softened the saddle-sore backsides of countless men arrayed about the room. Braziers hung from fixtures in the wall, illuminating the hall, a fire hazard most certainly, but each one had its own attendant that took the utmost care to ensure that the fire never waned or was in danger of setting alight the expensive and highly flammable fabrics that decorated the hall. Like most things in these parts, appearance had to be maintained; appearance was everything for the northerners.

No females were present in the great hall, not even servants, just men – princes, lords and chiefs big and small, with their captains and senior members of their retinues, and Toju.

If one thing could be said about the northerners, it was that they knew how to throw a banquet. But this celebration was not without merit, it was in recognition of their military prowess and their successful vanquishment of yet another ambitious tribe that had set their sights on the emir's kingdom. A tribe that had been decimated at the hands of Danjuma, first son of the great emir and the heir to the northern kingdom.

The praise that was lavished on him from the men in the room was unceasing; every few minutes, one of those present would raise his horn and commend him for his bravery, his guidance in the mist of battle, or something or other, and it only got increasingly incessant the more tongues were loosened by the endless flow of alcohol.

Danjuma was seated on a slightly raised dais piled with cushions. His brothers, the other northern princes, were about him, and Toju sat on his right-hand side, in his usual place of honour. In truth, all the praises directed at Danjuma were discreetly and deservedly directed at him. Each time a toast went up, the announcer would favour Toju with a lingering look of acknowledgement, and the brave amongst them would toast him after they had finished their praise of Danjuma.

Men were always cautious in these parts; the emir and his family were always held in too high esteem and the people almost worshipped them as gods for as long as they had ruled. And rightly so. The northern emirs of old had raised the once barren desert settlements into one of the most powerful kingdoms north of the great rivers, and their generosity was never in question. The lords of the north had eaten from the palms of their rulers for generations, and no one would ever even dream of biting the hands that nourished them.

But on this day, no one was more deserving than Toju. He alone had led the vanguard into battle, setting the fury of the northerners ablaze with the desire to follow him into the jaws of death without fear. He had taken his personal army and driven them deep into enemy lines and straight into the heart of the invading army, ripping it out for all to see. He had charged down the man who led them and slayed him with one decisive blow from his grandfather's spear. Before he reached the leader, it was said that he had sent no less than one hundred men down to the dark halls of *Esu's* underworld. This story would have of course been embellished but, in truth, it wasn't too far from reality. And Danjuma knew it. Every time he was praised, he would raise his horn and then incline his head at Toju as if offering him equal amounts of praise. Toju would accept it and return the acknowledgement gracefully, but deep down, he could care less about what the lords of the north thought, or anyone in fact, except for that of Habibah.

She was the only thing that anchored him to this place, a constant reminder of the reason life was worth living, besides the love of one's immediate family. The concept of love, or any strong emotion other than the desire to fight, had always been foreign to him, but the moment he had met Habibah, all this had changed.

Now he likened his feelings for her to going into battle – approaching it with all his focus, passion, and enthusiasm, seeing nothing in the periphery but her. As the gods would have it, and to his utter disbelief and joy, so it was that she saw him. She filled his every thought and was the fuel that drove him to do better, to be better, and raise his status to one that could be looked upon with pride. He would cement his accomplishments in stone and secure an already unparalleled legacy for his name and his future generations.

Despite all this, it was not lost on him what effect his rise in status and favour with the emir had on the lords of the north. He could see it in their subtle looks, the hushed comments and some of the poorly veiled drunken compliments proffered. After all, he would always be a foreigner in their eyes, and was seen as one who was taking the respect that rightfully, or unrightfully, was due them. But he cared not. In his mind, no one could challenge him on any front, be it in arms or in intellect, not even the princes. His arrogance, or self-belief as he saw it, was the one trait that could not easily be shed from his character, and it was one that he was loath to depart with.

Usman, who had been his closest ally ever since he had stepped foot in the north, nudged him, bringing his thoughts back to the room. They had formed a deep camaraderie of mutual respect and trust, which had only gotten stronger through the passage of the many battles they had stood shoulder to shoulder in. Usman was showing off his latest wound, or badge of honour, a half-severed finger on his left hand, which he had lost in the latest battle courtesy of a stray arrow from the army they had faced earlier.

'The women will be falling over themselves to nurse my latest wound, I imagine,' he was saying to Toju and one of his brothers.

'You will get nothing but a cripple's sympathy, dear brother. Besides, how will you shoot your arrows now? If I were you, I'd make plans to concentrate on my skill with the sword from now on. Leave the archery to better men,' one of the princes replied.

'Good thing I only need two fingers to hold the arrow of a drawn bow, and not this finger. Don't you worry, little brother, I will be shooting many arrows tonight but, unlike on the battlefield, I hope these arrows do not hit their mark!' Usman responded with a wink, causing a burst of laughter amongst his siblings.

'Toju, you should be in more of a joyous state right now, you miserable devil. You have yet again proved your worth to your adopted kingdom. At this rate, the emir will run out of gifts to bestow on you! If you weren't my brother-in-law, I'd be very jealous of you right now,' Usman said with a beaming and genuine smile.

'And that is why I will always favour you, Usman. You never fail to speak your truth and are seldom without the right words. I am fine, but these events bore me. I'd rather be on a battlefield, or with my wife.'

'Ah. It seems that you can't get enough of my beloved sister. She may finally crack that hard exterior of yours yet. Soon you'll be putting down your spear and raising babies instead, living a simple life and getting plump off the lands!'

'Do you really see me doing that? I think not. My place is on the field of battle; after all, I am a warrior born, and not even Habibah can change that.'

'I will wager Usman is right,' said one of the other princes. 'I give it another year and you'll be retired from all the bloodshed for sure. Once Habibah is heavy with the first child, you'll not want to leave her side. Take it from me.'

'I wouldn't place my coin on that eventuality if I were you. For one, I don't see that life suiting our dear Prince Toju. His right arm has a mind of its own and will not allow it,' chimed in Danjuma, who was also unusually open on this evening, courtesy of the fine palm wine that constantly found its way into his horn.

'Let us not talk about what I might or might not do if Habibah suddenly finds herself with child. I can't think of anything more terrifying than that. Anyway, what have you heard about these Fulani tribesmen?' Toju ventured, trying to divert the conversation.

The mention of this tribe immediately caused Danjuma's brow to furrow, and the smile he wore slowly faded away. The Fulani were a tribe of nomads who roamed the far northern straits and had already gained a substantial foothold just beyond the limits of the emir's kingdom. They were rumoured to number in the hundreds of thousands, and by all accounts, were just as fearsome and formidable as the northerners, If not worse.

It was said that they had originated from somewhere in the northeast, far beyond the great sea that divided the lands, as a small theological group, travelling north and west, spreading word of their faith. Before long, they had won the hearts of countless regions and had expanded rapidly. At first, they were said to be a non-violent sect, with the sole ambition of preaching peace and the divinity of their one true god. This was a concept that was foreign in this part of the world, where most worshipped a multitude of gods, all of whom were considered to be divine and omnipotent. Nonetheless, the more their word spread across northern parts of the continent, the more their narrative shifted from compresence to control and, with it, the desire to take dominions, first with words and, eventually, by the strength of arms. Now, they were akin to a force of nature, strong, unyielding, and determined to be the one source of power and only voice throughout the continent.

'Now this is something that gives me much concern. My spies have informed me that these Fulani continue to win territories beyond our borders. Many have either succumbed under the weight of their might or have willingly given themselves over just to preserve their provinces and their skin.' Danjuma said, pensively.

'Surely, we have nothing to fear from this tribe. Look around. Every man seated here has at least ten thousand men under his hand, and all answer to the emir. That is not even considering our own armies. Our numbers will match the grains of sand that separate us! And who are more skilled fighters than us, eh? Not even the fabled warriors from the south. No offence, brother-in-law,' said one of the younger princes as he inclined his head to Toju, who simply dismissed the comment with a flick of his wrist. Tonight appeared to be the night of loose tongues.

'You have much to learn, little brother. Regardless of what you have under your hand, you should never underestimate a man who faces you. You would do well to remember that,' Danjuma responded before turning back to Toju.

'I believe that they seek to take the measure of us before they decide to venture across our borders. They undoubtedly would have heard about our strength, especially after what we did to our last enemy, and may simply be probing to see how we react. I am almost of a mind to send an emissary to them directly, to see what type of men they are, and to give them the opportunity to state their intentions,' Danjuma said as he swirled the wine in his ornate horn.

'Why don't we just wait to see what they do? If they cross into our borders without permission, it will be clear that they intend to wage war. Then we have every right to take the fight

to them and crush them,' responded Usman, who had perked up at the possibility of gaining another battle scar.

'No. I'm with Prince Danjuma, we should seek them out first. Show them that we do not cower in the face of the sandstorm. That will force them to reveal their hand. I will go. I've always wanted to visit our far northern borders. Plus, the time away may do me some good,' Toju replied.

All the princes exchanged looks, but none of them was willing to voice their concerns, knowing that Toju never took kindly to being challenged or refused once he was determined to do a thing.

Usman cleared his throat before carefully replying, being the closest to Toju, 'We have people for this role, brother. This is no task for a man such as yourself. A prince of two kingdoms, no less! You give these foreigners too much honour by even entertaining the thought of gracing them with your presence.'

'I agree,' added Danjuma. 'Let one of our trusted men be tasked with this, not someone of your station. You have done too much already. I cannot have you risk your life unnecessarily. There is nothing left to prove.'

At the last sentence, some of the princes winced, while some clumsily turned to join other conversations around them, not wanting to see how Toju would react to the comment. When the words were uttered, Toju had had his eyes fixed straight ahead of him, but now he slowly turned his head to face Danjuma and fixed him with a level stare.

Danjuma saw a glint of something raw and unhinged in Toju's eyes, but he held his gaze. He knew of the pain that persisted deep in Toju's heart since he had heard the news of his father's passing, and the desire to continually throw himself in harm's way to appease a sense of remorse, perhaps. But Danjuma had accepted him as a brother as well as an equal, and would treat him as such by not pandering to his ego as most of the northern lords did, but rather speak his mind.

Sensing the slight tension, Usman gently placed his hand on Toju's arm, which visibly dispelled some of the stiffness in his posture. He looked at Usman almost thankfully, then back at Danjuma.

'I am not trying to prove anything. I do, however, appreciate your concern. But, my prince, I will be the one to deliver the emir's message and see this army with my own eyes. I have earned the right to serve the great emir with my blood, and this I do for him as much as I do for myself. It must be done. I will depart at sunrise. With all due respect, my prince, let us not argue or waste any more time on the matter.'

It was Danjuma's turn to fix Toju with a stare of his own, appraising him. He had to admit to himself, Toju was unlike any man he had ever met. No man was braver, or more arrogant for that matter, but he respected him for that. At the same time, to a much lesser degree, he resented him. No man had ever opposed him or disobeyed his command until Toju set foot in the north. However, he was prepared to let the unintentional slight pass. Maybe it was the palm wine or the fact that this southerner had managed to find his way into

Danjuma's life and somehow change his perspective. Either way, now was not the time or place to address it. That was a matter for another day.

After a few seconds he nodded his head. 'Very well. Go with my blessings; but, Toju, try not to get yourself killed. More 'serving' is required of you by the great emir and I would be saddened to lose a man of your worth, and a brother.'

Toju was gracious enough to produce a rare half-smile and inclined his head in respect. 'Thank you, my prince. Now I must prepare myself. Please excuse me,' he said as he stood from the comfort of the carpet and tilted his head at Leke, his blood-guard, who was seated a few paces behind him. He favoured Usman with another nod and departed the hall, leaving behind the sounds of vivacity, which slowly faded into the background.

Leke had heard the conversation, and was visibly troubled. This was nothing new; in all the blood-guards, he had always been the one to champion a level-headed and measured approach to all things. His persistent aversion to risk had always rankled Toju, but he had since learned to accept it from his protector.

'Do you think this is wise, my prince? You will be travelling completely blind into unknown territory. Who knows how they will react? I would advise you to reconsider,' Leke said as he strolled beside Toju through the high arched hallway with golden painted pilasters and swirling murals that adorned the walls.

'Not you as well! Spare me your thoughts, Leke. My mind is set, so don't try to dissuade me. I must see it done.'

To Toju's annoyance, Leke moved ahead to block his path and placed his hands on his shoulders, halting him.

'I see your demons, my prince. I bore many myself. I still do, but I've learned to suppress them. Some will always be your companions, walking beside you for a lifetime, and some will eventually shed and seek another soul to torment. You could never have influenced the fate of your father; besides, he'd want you to carry his name with honour and dignity. You are, after all, the first prince and true heir to his throne, no matter what has transpired since. So, it's what you do with this pain that matters. How you harness it and temper it until it is as hard as the iron of your spear and sharpened as such.'

Toju slowly relaxed the muscles in his back. No matter how annoying Leke was, he always spoke wisdom, yet again proving his worth as a blood-guard, but Toju could not take back his words, just as the setting sun could not reverse its descent into the distant horizon. The stones had been cast and he would see this thing through.

'I hear you. I truly do, but I must do this, Leke. I do it not only for myself but also for my bloodline. I don't ever want it said that I didn't do enough for this kingdom, so there is no disputing my hard-earned titles and my place here. When I eventually leave to seek out my brother in the east, I want them to say, "There goes a true prince of this land. A warrior. All the lands and accolades he has gained through battle are his and his alone." Only then can my demons be sated.'

Leke finally saw things clearer now that he viewed them through the eyes of his charge. Toju had always been a pompous prince, but that had changed the moment he casted his eyes on his bride and lifted her veil, and further still, following the devastating news from the south. Toju was by no means a perfect man and could never be completely cured of the arrogance that ailed him, but there was a marked change.

'I see,' Leke replied as he lowered his hands from Toju's shoulders. 'That makes it all the easier to ride with you, my prince, wherever it is that your fate takes you.'

'No, Leke. This is something I must do alone.' He held a hand up, not giving Leke the opportunity to respond.

'You have been beside me ever since the day I open my eyes to the world, but I will not have you walk this path with me. I require your protection, but not for me. I want you by Habibah's side. Right now, she is the most important thing to me in this foreign land and I cannot trust any other man to take this responsibility. No one, not even the northern princes with their guards and vast army. If I am to commit my life to the unknown, I will fare better with the knowledge that you will protect her as you would your prince. It must be you, and I will not hear otherwise.'

Leke had his mouth slightly open but resisted the temptation to object as Toju's words washed over him. How could he deny such a request? He knew that Toju had fallen for this exotic princess, but only now did he realise the extent to which their devotion to each other had blossomed. He simply nodded his head, knowing that any further protestation would be a fruitless effort.

'Enough of this sharing of intimacies; I would see my time better spent. Speaking of Habibah, have her summoned to the main courtyard. I will ride with her tonight.'

'Your will, my prince,' Leke finally said as he turned and hurried off to carry out Toju's bidding, leaving him in the hallway staring up at the frescos that almost seemed to dance from the torch lights that clung to the walls, flames swaying from a light breeze that wafted through the large open space. Had he made the right decision? He wondered. He would soon find out. Now, he would fill his mind with no other thoughts besides his wife. Tomorrow's problems would remain exactly as they were – tomorrow's problems.

Habibah stood in the middle of the courtyard wearing a dark nondescript kaftan and matching lengthy head-tie that wrapped around her hair and lower face. She pulled an extra layer of cloth like a shawl about her shoulders to keep her warm against the night chill out in the plains. The temperature tended to drop quite considerably at night, a vast contrast from the sweltering heat of the daytime. She could just about make out the main gates of the palace and heard them creak open. The silhouette of a rider stood tall against the moonlight. Leke, the ever-present blood-guard. She knew what would come next.

She readied herself, tying the shawl into a knot over her chest and pulling up her kaftan slightly, exposing delicate ankles and snakeskin sandals fastened halfway up her calves. She turned away from the gate, facing the other direction, and sure enough, the sound of hooves pounding on the flagstones at a gallop slowly became audible. Within seconds, a horse came into view, the rider sitting low in the saddle with an arm extended reaching out to her.

She put one foot behind her and raised her arm ready to take hold as she was grabbed by the powerful hand across her forearm, which she mimicked on the arm of the rider. Propelled by the momentum of the horse, the rider swung her backwards and up onto the saddle, and she matched the movement effortlessly, twisting her slim body until she was safely seated behind the rider, and wrapped her arms tightly around his waist. She buried her cheek in his back and breathed in his familiar scent, felt the muscles in his back and the motion of his shoulder blades against the reins of his horse.

If there was one thing she was conscious of about Prince Toju, it was the excitement that surrounded him. His actions were always carried out with dramatic effect; even with a trivial thing such as horse riding, he would somehow turn it into a spectacle, and it exhilarated her. She had never expected to fall for a man of his reputation; violent, conceited, and a foreigner no less, but over the last year, she had not been able to imagine herself far from his side. She had studied him like a scroll, as if running her fingers over every word, tracing every crease line

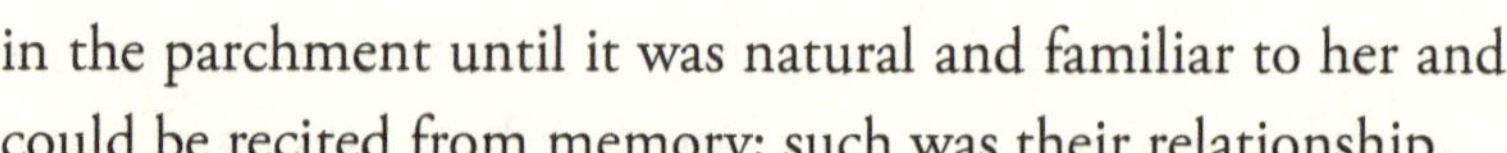

in the parchment until it was natural and familiar to her and could be recited from memory; such was their relationship.

She raised her head to look over Toju's shoulder and saw Leke racing ahead through the gates towards the city beyond. Further back, two more horses took up the rear, the other royal guards from Ile-Ife, Toju's most trusted men. They accompanied the prince everywhere. It was reassuring to know that she was always protected around him. She felt a sense of security that she had never really known before he came into her life, despite the size of her family's considerable retinue. Another reason she felt bound to him.

They rode in silence as they always did, savouring the moment and their freedom from the ever-watchful eyes in the palace. This was their usual escape when the noise got too loud, a time for them to be at peace with themselves and their surroundings.

She closed her eyes, felt the tiny grains of gravel that whipped past her cheeks, the rhythm of the horse and the gentle snorts it made. She felt the pounding of Toju's heart in his chest and the slight gasps he made whenever the horse's hooves touched the ground. He still had not truly mastered his breathing when he rode his mount, but he was a much better rider than he had been when he first appeared in the north. She might make a northerner out of him yet, she thought, and she held him more tightly.

The small group eventually made it out of the city and passed the smaller towns that gave way to villages dotted around the kingdom, mainly keeping to the outskirts to avoid being recognised and accosted by the citizens, who held the royals in almost godlike esteem, until finally they reached the open plains.

Their path was only lit by the crescent moon and the multitude of stars that were scattered in the night sky overhead; otherwise, they were surrounded by complete darkness. There were no torches from dwellings to be seen for miles, but the horses didn't slow. They all knew this path well and it added to the excitement of it all.

With the darkness came the welcoming silence of the open plain. Besides the odd sound of a wild goat off in the distance, nothing was perceptible out here. No hubbub of a vibrant city, no drums pounding, or orders being issued, just the sound of the wind as it swept through the sand and rustled dry bushes and leaves, and the sounds of their horses. Northern horses were especially trained to traverse this terrain and they did so with ease, spraying clumps of sand in their wake.

They rode for several miles and eventually came to a large oasis lined with palm trees and shrubs. The lake here was the only source of water for miles around and, during the day, it teemed with all manner of the creations of the gods; cattle, snakes, rodents, and smaller creatures such as scorpions and insects, all gathered harmoniously to seek nourishment under the unforgiving sun. However, at night, it was a place of tranquillity that served as a sanctuary for those seeking peace.

The group dismounted and walked their horses the last few paces towards the lake. Toju untethered a goatskin water pouch that had been attached to the side of his mount before handing the reins to one of the guards from Ile-Ife, then helped Habibah down from the saddle.

The reflection of the moon and stars helped to illuminate their surroundings somewhat, but one of the guards had already begun to gather pieces of wood and other dry flammable objects to make a fire. Toju walked over to the lake, Habibah in tow, and bent down to fill the goatskin pouch. He stopped halfway through the process then threw his head back and drank deeply from it, before refiling it and passing it to Habibah. She also took a long draught, water streaming down the side of her mouth and soaking her kaftan, before passing it back to him.

'It's all clear, my prince,' came Leke's voice further ahead, who had made a quick survey of the area to ensure that they hadn't been followed or that no one was around.

'Good. Wait for us here, we shall walk over the rise. And, before you ask, I have my sword with me,' Toju replied, tapping the sword that hung from his hip as the gold-plated scabbard reflected the moon's glow. Leke insisted, and always made a point to double check, that the prince never walked unarmed. Toju never did, he always kept at least one blade on his person out of habit, but Leke never failed to remind him, even more so since they set foot in this foreign land, and for good reason.

One of the guards offered Toju a makeshift torch, which he accepted before making his way towards the rise just north of the oasis, leaving the three guards behind.

Toju held the torch over his head with one hand while the other gently held on to Habibah's hand. He sprang onto protruding rocks with cat-like agility and pulled Habibah up to join him, but she never once faltered. She was surprisingly agile herself for a princess that had known nothing but comfort and a pampered life. Growing up with many siblings, most of them boys, she had quickly learned that she needed to be strong enough to match them to be taken seriously. After all, she had come from a bloodline of warriors, and there was no rule against women aspiring to rule despite their seemingly delicate constitution.

Even if there had been, Habibah would have challenged that way of thinking. She was not one to be content with weaving baskets, or sewing dresses, or having the sole purpose of being the subservient housewife whose duty was confined to producing heirs for her prince. No. She would stand by his side as an equal partner in all their endeavours and strive to be of one mind and body with her husband.

Toju accepted her for who she was and loved her the more for it; perhaps women in the south were not as bold? She knew not, but it mattered little. All she knew was that she was bonded to an individual with depth and gravitas, not an average bright-eyed prince with dreams limited to self-advancement and wealth like most of the lords of the north. No. Toju was a rare breed.

Despite the impediment of her attire, which was pulled up and bunched in her free hand, they continued to make their ascent until they crested the rise. The landscape stretched out before them and into the darkness in every direction, moonlight illuminating the peaks and troughs of the undulating terrain, which was framed by distant lights from the city to the south and far off to the north, all accentuated by the dazzling stars.

Toju hastily piled up scattered twigs and branches and put the torch to the pile he made; before long, he had a fire going. He brought along a length of cloth, which had been wrapped diagonally around his shoulder and waist. Untying it, he placed it on the ground for them to sit upon. They sat tentatively, feeling for jagged rocks under the cloth, and took comfort in each other's body heat as they gazed into the darkness.

'Could there be a better place than this? We are truly blessed by the gods to have all of this at our disposal, are we not?' she asked as she peered into the distance.

'You have not seen the beauty of the gods' creation until you have seen the south. There are places that will astound you; great waterfalls completely concealed by unbroken forests of green that you'll only find a path to from following the antelopes, rolling hills that stretch as far as the eye can see, fertile and ripe like a young girl, jungles bursting with vibrant colours, exotic fruits, and plant life. Plus, the odd crocodile or leopard that would eat you alive!' he joked. She giggled and hit him on the arm affectionately.

'You miss it, don't you? It doesn't take a marabu to know it. It is written on your face. I know you will never truly see these lands as your home, but you have found a happy life here, have you not?'

'I have, but it is my duty to return one day. You know this. I have a commitment to my brother and an uncle to kill. Once I have fulfilled these duties, I will be free to live out my days as I choose. Until then, there is no rest for me,' he said, with a hint of sorrow in his tone.

'Not until the next great adventure presents itself or another opportunity to prove the strength of your sword arm. When will it truly ever be enough for you?'

'You know what I am. I have never hidden that from you.'

'I know and I accept that. I just feel that I alone will never be enough for you.'

'Nonsense! You are everything to me. I never thought I would ever utter those words, but I speak truth. All I do is for you. For us and our legacy. My father taught me that much – "Nothing is more important than leaving behind a legacy for your children to follow. More than just a name". That is one of the few sayings of his that I remember. I never understood what it meant. Not really, until now. Our children, if the gods deem to bless us with some, will have a legacy that stretches far beyond these lands, a legacy that no man will be able to take from them. When I achieve that, only then will it be enough.'

Habibah looked at him in the darkness and her love for him grew even more in that moment. She had known his desires and ambitions, but only now did he really articulate them to her.

'Besides, wherever my fate carries me, I can only hope to be blessed to have you at my side,' he said, almost expectantly, as he turned towards her.

'You expect me to uproot my grand life here and follow you to your lands of green and crocodiles?' She paused. 'I will go with you anywhere your fate takes you, my love,' she finally said, and smiled teasingly.

'So why all the suspense, eh? For the love of the gods! You really had me there.' He laughed as he wrapped his arms around her in a loving embrace. She returned his affection and they sat there for a time entwined like two old trees that had grown twisted around each other.

'You see those lights over there?' Toju said, pointing north, 'That is the first place my fate will lead me.'

'Is that not where this so-called Fulani tribe have taken up residence? You can't possibly be thinking about seeking an audience with them, after all the news that filters down from our borders? Ah. I see. You have already decided, have you not?' Habibah asked, already knowing the answer to her question.

'Yes. I ride at sunrise. There isn't anyone willing to confront them.'

'Willing to die, more like it!' she snapped, sounding harsher than she intended.

'I now have interests here to protect, so I must see it done. Besides, do you think they would dare to lay a hand upon me? No doubt by now they too would have heard my name on the lips of all those that have since travelled between these borders, especially after the last conquest. I will stake my grandfather's spear on it.'

'For as great a man as you are, my love, do not allow yourself to be blinded by your own lustre. It is a fool who possesses a blade and holds it by the sharpened end.'

'Good thing I am no fool. I certainly know which end of the blade to hold, and how to wield it. But I assure you, I only go to talk, nothing more.'

'We can only hope that they will listen. I will not try to convince you otherwise but will you swear to me you will return?'

'I will walk through the dark halls of the underworld and strike down *Esu* himself just to be by your side. There is nothing to fear, I promise.'

She looked at him for a long while before she finally responded. 'I know you will. So, I have you to myself for a few hours; we should make the most of this precious time the gods have allowed us.'

'Right now, I am only for you.'

They lost themselves in each other's arms, relishing every second under the night sky, choosing not to dwell on the challenges of the day ahead. The world was lost to them, a distant thing, a blur of distant lights and darkness. Time did not exist in that moment; they were free, unburdened by the responsibilities they carried, the expectations shackled to their station. Nothing mattered, just Habibah, Toju and nothing else.

They eventually drifted into peaceful slumbers, Toju's filled with visions of redemption and Habibah's vivid with her deepest desires – a happy family removed from the trappings of royalty and complete with child. Hours passed and they woke as the temperature dropped further. They gathered their belongings and headed back down the rise to the lake and their waiting attendants.

Leke was awake and alert as he often was, but both the royal guards were dozing away. Leke must have drawn the short straw, Toju mused. They woke the guards and readied the horses for their journey back to the city. Habibah looked back at the rise as they all mounted their horses, and froze the view in her mind's eye, just as Leke's horse spurred into motion, sending sprays of sand in the air.

'Are you ready, Habibah?' Toju asked capturing her attention.

'Yes, my love. I was just wondering when the next opportunity for us to visit this place might be.'

'Soon, Habibah. Very soon.'

With that, Toju turned his horse's head towards the south and dug in his heels. The horse reacted to his touch and immediately set off after Leke's horse, which was already in full gallop. It was still dark, but the sky had already begun to shed some of its blackness.

Sunrise was close at hand and, with it, Toju's destiny.

WHEN DESTINY BECKONS

'This is your chance; take him now!'

Splinters were sent flying in every direction from the wooden practice swords as they met repeatedly. This dance had persisted for some time now, and neither of the two that wielded the training blades seemed willing to relent.

Ayo had been watching over the proceedings for almost an hour, and he was still amazed that the two opponents had lasted this long. But his amazement was mostly directed at one of them in particular, Enitan. The boy was facing a man twice his age and a full head taller, but he still managed to match him with every stroke, every feint, as if he was facing an opponent of his equal.

It was clear that the older warrior was reaching the limits of his endurance and was fighting purely on will power and experience, not wanting to be utterly humiliated by a mere child. Sweat glistened on his arms and torso and ran down his face from his bald head, threatening to obscure his vision. His attacks had long since lost their ferocity and intensity and were only swung to protect himself and seek advantage where none was to be had.

The same couldn't be said about the young prince. He could smell triumph, it was but a moment away, and he chased it like a predator seeking a wounded prey, dogging his opponent, forcing him to make mistakes, backing him into corners, all the while pressing his own attack.

Ayo studied the child that had once been so innocent, so blithe, and marvelled at the young man he was becoming. He watched the way he moved on his feet, the pivots, the balance and shifting of weight, and the speed of his sword arm. It was nothing short of mastery. He felt like a proud father watching his son take his first breath. The boy had clearly been an attentive student, taking to every lesson he had been taught, studied, and practiced every step of this sacred dance, making adjustments of his own to complement his stature. It was a joy to behold knowing that one so young had so much potential and natural ability.

If it were a real fight, the older warrior would have already bled out, having been struck several times, from the marks that adorned his athletic frame; bruising along one of his inner thighs, across one forearm and on both sides of his ribcage.

In contrast, the young prince was as fresh as a newborn, not a mark on his body or bead of sweat on his brow. You would have thought that he had just woken from a refreshing sleep and was simply playing with his peer, the only giveaway being the fortitude that burned in his eyes.

Enitan dodged a swing that was aimed at his head, twisting away from the wooden blade like a masquerade dancer, with effortless dexterity. However, his guard was slightly down, and he seemed to be relying on his speed a little too much as he avoided blows and failed to take advantage of openings created by the missed attacks. But with every swing from his opponent, the young prince inched ever closer, leaving little room for the older warrior to manoeuvre.

'Do not toy with him, Enitan! Raise your blade. One stroke can end it all!' Ayo shouted from his vantage point on a wooden platform overlooking the training compound.

'Our young prince is something with that blade, eh?' Wale said as he came up behind Ayo.

'He is indeed, but he lacks discipline at times. He moves as if he is invulnerable to attacks, so sure of himself. I almost hope he makes a mistake so he can learn from it,' Ayo replied, not taking his eyes off the fight.

'I'll wager you might get your wish yet. I think Enitan's opponent is drawing him in, giving him a false sense of security and just biding his time for the perfect opportunity to strike. He is slowing, but he isn't breathing as heavily as you'd expect from an exhausted man. See?'

Ayo diverted his attention to the older warrior, heeding Wale's words. He was right, the warrior was baiting the prince. He smiled to himself knowingly. A hard lesson may yet be learned today by the young prince.

Just as the thought was at the front of his mind, Enitan moved in and retracted his sword ready to deliver what would have been a fatal blow. As quick as a flash, the older warrior spun away from the thrust aimed at his chest that followed and brought the flat of his sword down hard on Enitan's extended arm.

The slap of the sword as it connected was audible and the young prince let out a scream, dropping his sword immediately and clutching onto his bruised arm. His opponent didn't stop there; he moved quickly around the prince and kicked him behind the knees, causing him to fall to the ground and, at the same time, reached out to grab a handful of the prince's bushy hair, in a bid to pull his head back and expose his neck.

The prince, however, had other plans. As soon as his knees touched the ground, as if pre-empting the follow-up attack, he fell flat on his chest, scooped up a handful of gravel and small stones with his good hand and turned on his back. In the same motion, he flung the dirt in an upwards arc that connected with the face of his opponent. The man hissed and covered his eyes, but by the time he had regained his vision, Enitan had already retrieved his sword and was standing to the man's side with his sword resting on the man's shoulder poised at his neck.

'Do you surrender?' he asked in his high-pitched, innocent voice.

'I surrender, my prince. Well fought,' the man acknowledged, still blinking out the bits of dirt in his eyes.

'Ha! That was brilliant, Enitan! I should have placed a wager with you, Wale,' Ayo said, turning to the commander of the guard, who tried to mask his disbelief and failed miserably.

Ayo was truly impressed. He had not seen that coming and again marvelled at the resourcefulness of his young charge. Enitan was shaping into a fine warrior and would certainly be one to watch when he became of age.

Ayo leaped over the rail that secured the platform he stood on, landing lightly in the compound, and made his way over to the two figures in the centre. He had a goatskin pouch full of water that he handed to Enitan.

'You improve every day, my prince. We may yet have to find you more difficult training partners at his rate.'

'I am still here, you know. You could at least allow me to depart with some of my dignity still intact!' complained the older warrior with a tiny hint of embarrassment.

'Spare me your dignity. You should be proud that our prince has finally beaten you. The others didn't last half as long as you did, so think of it as your contribution to the betterment of your future chief. An honour I would say,' retorted Ayo, not giving the older warrior a second glance. He turned to Enitan and noticed that the bruise on his arm had begun to swell and had taken on a crimson hue.

'You should see to that, my prince, but take it as your first battle scar,' Ayo said.

'It's hardly a battle scar and I don't think it's something I would want to brag about. It really hurts, the bone might even be fractured!' Enitan said, alarm slowly rising in his voice as he touched the bruise tentatively and winced with every prod.

'It's not broken. If it was, you would be screaming your head off right now, and you certainly wouldn't have been able to perform that excellent move you used to end the fight. Good use of your surroundings against an inattentive fighter.'

'Again, I am still here!' the older warrior shouted over his shoulder as he ambled away still wiping his face.

Ayo dismissed the response with a gesture just as Wale joined them in the compound.

'Very good work, my prince. Keep it up and Ayo will soon be without purpose!' Wale said, laughing until he saw the bruise. 'Oh, that looks painful, you should have it seen to straight away.'

'Does it look broken? What will I do if my sword arm is broken? I will be ruined!' lamented Enitan.

'My prince, it is not broken, I assure you,' Ayo replied as he flashed Wale a glare. 'But please go now just to put your mind at ease.'

Without another word, Enitan hurried off as fast as his legs could carry him, leaving Ayo and Wale behind.

Wale stifled a laugh. 'That would almost look comical if I didn't know how much pain he must be in.'

'The pain will serve him well, and the bruise will be a reminder not to take anything for granted. Better a bruise than a missing arm,' Ayo said.

'You push him too hard. He is still a child, don't forget; a prince with responsibilities, yes, but a child no less. He still needs the opportunity to do what children do and have some fun occasionally, no?'

'That is out of the question. When I was his age, I had already killed at least five men and been in one battle.'

'You cannot compare yourself with the young prince. You are modakeke, bred to fight and to serve. He, on the other hand, was born to lead and to rule. And with that privilege comes the opportunity to choose his own path; well, to some extent.'

'That may be so, but the current state of affairs in the kingdom has deprived him of that privilege, would you not agree? If the last year has taught us anything, it is that we all must acquire the propensity for violence regardless of our societal status. Do you think the threat of death at the hands of our enemies affords reprieve for those of rank and high of birth? We unfortunately do not have the luxury of knowing where and when violence will find us. Right now, there is no room for childhood sentiments. He must be fierce and feared. This must be ingrained in him, now, or he will learn a hard lesson, much worse than what he learned today.'

'That is a very bleak outlook on life my friend. I think we need to find you a woman to curb your dark notions and your violent tendencies, justified as they may be.'

'All I need is my blade at arm's length, my friend, and the strength to continually serve the prince. Anything else is a distraction.'

'Are all the modakeke designed so? I always thought your famed temperament and prowess were mere myths. The more I get to know you, the more I'm beginning to think of them as nothing more than myths was to grossly underestimate your people.'

'Ha! I will take that as high praise coming from you, Wale. All the better that we are viewed so. You would be surprised at the number of fights that have been avoided just from the mere mention of my association, or the sight of my tribal marks. But I fear I may be amongst the last of my lineage. It has been over a year, and I've heard little to nothing of modakeke survivors from the war at Benin. It may very well be that the last of the modakeke truly followed the king to the gates of the afterlife. As would have been expected, but…' Ayo trailed off, as he pondered the void the king and his allies had left behind, which was now occupied by snakes and vultures feeding off the people's ever-growing fear and fuelled by the influence of the traitor king.

'Come now, Ayo, do not dwell on such matters, less you fall into despair. If you do, who will be left to guide our prince, eh? I've seen the darkness that surrounds him, even if it is something we are all reluctant to speak of. I fear what he would do, what he would become, if he did not have you to tame whatever it is that consumes him.'

It was true, whatever unknown entity it was that afflicted Enitan, which was prone to surface on occasion, was an unspoken subject around the royal court. Hushed as it was, nonetheless, people close to the prince had started to notice. There had been sparring partners who had sworn that the boy had appeared to be possessed whenever he was angered. Ayo had seen it on several occasions but had always somehow found a way to calm the young prince down before whatever it was spilled forth, but there was no denying that some invisible hand was upon him.

'Like you said, let us not dwell on such matters less we all fall into despair. The prince is fine,' Ayo said in an attempt to dismiss the conversation.

Wale looked at him sideways with a raised eyebrow. 'Fair enough, my friend. I will allow you to convince yourself that there is no issue to address; after all, he is your responsibility, and it is your burden to carry.'

'It is my responsibility, and I assure you that there is nothing to concern yourself with.' Ayo was conflicted with doubt in his own words. He couldn't claim to have the slightest understanding of what it was he was dealing with, but was also unprepared to broach the topic until he had a better understanding.

'How does the old chief fare? I must admit, my focus has solely been on the prince, and I have not requested an audience with the chief, but I hear that there is has been little improvement.'

'It is not good. His health worsens by the day, and I fear it is but a matter of time. None of the Babalawo have been able to provide an effective remedy to his condition, and the chief has now refused to even entertain further medical assistance. Not only that but every day, more of his allies gather to seek an audience with him over some dispute or other. They have naturally been turned away, and tension is building amongst the nobles. I fear the outcome if the worst were to happen.'

The health of Enitan's grandfather, Chief Kola, had deteriorated over the past year from some mysterious illness. Whether it was his age that had finally caught up with him, or some unknown source, no one knew; however, many had attributed his waning health to the demise of King Jide and the guilt that haunted him for not having been there with the full force of the west to stand by the king in his hour of need. However, it was obvious that if he were to succumb to his illness, there was bound to be some turmoil in the west.

Kola could easily hand over the reins of power to Enitan, who by right was entitled to take up the chieftaincy title, being a direct descendant and the only known living male in the family tree, but there were others who thought themselves more deserving, cousins once or twice removed and other distance relatives, who had been born and raised in Ogun. They all saw Enitan as somewhat of an outsider, a child that had no business ruling the west, regardless of his lineage. One that had never set foot in Ogun prior to the events in Ile-Ife, now come to take that which did not belong to him. As far as they were concerned, Enitan's birth right had perished along with King Jide, and he was nothing more than a refugee prince.

However, this was not the sentiment felt by all. There were still many supporters of the old rule of succession and Enitan's right to the chieftaincy in the west and, with time, the throne, being the only known surviving Adelani. However, their support was greatly outweighed by those who opposed what was largely considered to be an antiquated ideology.

They wanted to unshackle themselves from the old traditions and pave way for a new law and regime with fresh blood and new ideas. No one had dared to voice these opinions openly, but Olise's recent conquests had emboldened this growing way of thinking, which had presented them with the perfect excuse to wipe the slate clean.

Enitan had of course stayed well away from all the political wrangling, and had little interest in ruling, but this was not the thinking of Chief Kola, who naturally wanted to bequeath his legacy to his direct bloodline now that he had one alive and well.

'I should see him, and take Enitan too. The prince has been reluctant to visit his grandsire for a time now, but I think it is mainly from the fear of losing yet another loved one. He should not turn away from his duties.'

'I agree. This is one thing that needs to be addressed. The tribes of the west are like hyenas when it comes to power. I can see them circle, awaiting an opportunity to seize control. These parts have been ruled by the same family for generations, and many have long questioned the need to persist with this age-old tradition, albeit not openly. Now that Enitan has appeared, most of their plans have been scuppered. Before his arrival, it was no secret that Chief Kola would have had to nominate one of the tribal leaders to rule in his stead when the time comes, believing that he had no living heir. Enitan has changed all of that.'

'Wait. Were you not the same person saying the prince needs to enjoy his childhood but a moment ago?'

Wale let out a hearty laugh. 'Okay. Maybe I did, but this is something that does need attention.'

'You twist like a leaf in a storm, my friend. I hope I do not have to rely on your decision in the future!'

Just then, their attention was diverted by the sounds of the palace bells tolling. The sound echoed around the training yard and frantic movement was noticed on the battlements. The repeated clanging only meant one thing. The arrival of unknown, and most likely unwelcome, visitors.

Both men looked at each other in alarm, already thinking that Olise had finally decided to cast the stones and set his sights on bringing the west to heel sooner than anticipated, but no word of an advancing army had filtered down from the bordering towns and villages to the east. Surely, they would have been warned. Or had they all pledged their fealty to the traitor king without a fight, or worse still, acceded under the weight of Olise's military might? All these thoughts flashed through their minds without them uttering a word.

Ayo didn't wait to exchange theories with Wale but instead set off in search of the prince. Wale took off in the other direction, presumably to join the household guards and take up the lead as their commander in securing the ailing chief.

Ayo found Enitan soon enough, his arm already bandaged with a poultice over the bruise. Enitan had already armed himself with his sword and was struggling to tie the fastening on the side of his leather breastplate, trembling and clumsy fingers fumbling the leather strings as he tried to pull them taut. It brought a smile to Ayo's face to see that the prince was of a mind with him. After all, he had trained the boy well and had tried to prepare him for this eventuality.

When Enitan saw Ayo, the relief that washed over his face couldn't have been clearer. 'What is happening? Are we under attack? Do you think it is my uncle?' Enitan asked, panic dangerously close to the surface of his voice.

'I know not, my prince, but you are safe behind the walls of the palace, you know that. If by some miracle they are breached, there are two thousand warriors here that will lay down their lives to protect you. Besides, it may all be a false alarm.'

'I cannot be seen to cower behind the walls, I must be seen to be brave. Let us go to the battlements and take a look. Will you escort me?'

'Of course, my prince. You need not even ask. I am nothing if not your shadow.'

Enitan nodded, took in a deep breath to steel himself, picked up his sword and headed to the door. As they both walked through the hallway, the scene was one of chaos; soldiers ran back and forth appearing somewhat disorganised as orders were barked out from various directions and weapons passed around.

To Enitan's credit, he seemed to ignore all the activity around him, head held high and shoulders back as he strolled purposefully towards a staircase that led to the upper levels of the palace. Ayo followed close behind him, not missing a step, but a sense of excitement gripped him. He yearned for a good battle. A chance to display his skill. He had not truly had the opportunity to demonstrate just how much of a fighter he was. Most fights he had been in ended rather abruptly, not giving him the satisfaction he desired, and he had not been in a full-scale battle yet, since he had been tasked with spiriting away the young prince from the destruction of Ife. Maybe now his time had finally come.

Ayo, as it so happened, wasn't like most men. He had been blessed with heightened senses, which had served him well throughout his hard upbringing. It was no surprise that he had been marked to be a blood-guard at the tender age of five, outperforming all his peers effortlessly, and proving himself to be invaluable to the tribe.

King Jide had personally overseen his training and welfare once he caught wind of his abilities. He confirmed that the then unborn Enitan would be his charge, which went against protocol, as blood-guards were normally assigned to the nobles by the council of ten, the elders and highest-ranking warriors of the modakeke, but Jide had overruled them just to secure Ayo to protect his bloodline, a great honour indeed, and one that Ayo had been eternally grateful for.

As they climbed the stone steps to the battlements, the bells rang louder here, almost deafening. The massive bronze features were erected on the four corners of the palace, and it took two men to swing the heavy dangling pendulum back and forth as it struck the inside of the bells. The noise ceased once the guards noticed the prince, and some gathered about him to relay whatever message had caused them to put the residence of the palace on high alert.

The palace was the highest structure in the city, with a panoramic view of the surrounding landscape for miles. Beyond the city, thick forests teeming with game and wildlife buffered the city limits like a mother's embrace. Enitan had envisioned the forests ablaze with plumes of thick smoke reaching for the sky and a flood of people frantically heading towards the palace to seek refuge behind the high stone walls. Instead, he was met by a peaceful scene, complete with clear blue skies and birds gliding above, chirping audibly in the distance.

'What is the report here?' Enitan asked, assuming the role of the noble prince, something he had taken to well. Again, Ayo smiled. Another lesson that the prince had come to be familiar with; always showing an authoritative and decisive exterior amongst those he would soon rule.

'There are warriors approaching, my prince, they are travelling through the city thoroughfare as we speak. One of our guards noticed the column of men approaching the city and didn't recognise them as any of the warriors from the western tribes. He rode here in all haste to warn of their arrival, my prince.'

'He was right to do so. Where would they be now?' Enitan asked as he peered into the distance towards the city.

'They should soon come into view, my prince. Word has already been sent further west to the closest town for reinforcements as a precaution,' replied the guard, who was sweating but managed to keep his composure.

'There will be no need for reinforcement,' Ayo said, as he looked over towards the city. Every man on the wall turned to face him, confused.

'What do you hear?' he asked.

They all just looked between themselves before someone piped up. 'I do not understand, there is no sound to speak of.'

'Exactly. If this was an army bent on invading the city, the people would be in a state of panic, and we would hear their screams for miles. Silence will never precede a raid. Instead, it is almost as if some apparition was visiting, and the people are gripped by fear. I'm also guessing that the gates of the city were opened wide for these visitors, so they can only be allies of the royal court.'

An exchange of looks once again by all on the wall as they took in Ayo's words. No one spoke, all waiting with bated breath for the newcomers to show themselves. Soon enough, a row of dark figures could be discerned in the distance, walking right through the primary path that snaked through the heart of the city. They could also make out the citizens gathering, not running away, another good sign. But who could these people be?

The closer they came into view the more Ayo's heart began to race. With his keen eyes, he had picked out some distinctive features in their attire, the armour they wore almost seemed... familiar. He dared not allow himself to confirm what he was seeing, but rather wait for others to see what he did.

There were about twenty of them, marching in formation. You could tell how disciplined they were from the way they moved, every man among them perfectly in sync with those around them. They brandished long spears that were held upright, none wavering, none at a different angle, all expertly composed.

The one who led them rode a beast of a horse, its black coat browned from the journey but imposing, nonetheless. Its rider sat bolt upright, back painfully straight in the saddle, one hand holding the reins and the other resting comfortably over the pommel of his sword, the tell-tale signs of one who treated his weapon like an extension of his arm. His demeanour spoke volumes without words needing to be vocalised; he was one that was not to be trifled with, a born warrior, leader, and a man to be respected.

The warriors that followed in his wake were no mere rabble either; these were elite warriors, killers, proficient in their work and highly professional. The kind of warriors that any king would be proud to boast about.

'It cannot be,' Ayo whispered, but Enitan picked up the emotion in his voice.

'What do you see, Ayo? Who are they?' Ayo was transfixed on the men and didn't hear the prince until Enitan nudged him in the arm. Ayo turned to the prince as if noticing him for the first time, eyes welling with tears. Enitan asked the same question, but more delicately.

'Who are they, Ayo?'

'Your army, my prince. It is your army.'

'My army?' he asked confused. 'They are barely enough to serve as a household guard. What do you mean?'

'These men, my prince, are all the men you will ever need.'

Enitan turned away from Ayo to look at the men, now almost within a spear's throw of the battlements, and familiarity hit him like a slap in the face. He looked upon the handsome face of the one who led the warriors. Albeit slightly weathered, with a greying beard that engulfed his chin, it was not enough to hide that infectious smile, that air of absolute confidence and authority.

Enitan backed away from the battlement as if he had seen something that had frightened him, then turned without a word and headed for the steps down to ground level. Ayo followed him, still in disbelief.

As they exited the palace, they were met by a group of the guards that had already gathered within the compound, armed and armoured, ready to repel an attack. They stood in close formation, but not as confidently as the men who approached. Beads of sweat ran down foreheads, shields were held shakily, some clattering against their spears, and heavy breathing was perceptible. Their anxiety was palpable. Some of these men had not been tested in battle and some had never fought beyond the training square; newly trained warriors, a testament to the shortage of good fighting men lost in the war. But they were determined and had the heart to fight and die for their chief, a quality that mattered above all.

Ayo took all of this in as the two of them made their way through the throng of men to the front until they stood in the shadow of the towering gates that barred them from the city. Two guards stood either side of the gates and looked to the prince nervously.

'Open them,' Enitan said simply, eyes set beyond the mass of wood, peering through them. The men at the gate looked to Ayo, who gave a slight nod, and they began to heft the solid timber bar that held the gates fast.

A breeze played at their feet once the gates were open wide enough, swirls of dust spiralled and swept through the compound behind them. Enitan walked through and came to stand just beyond the gates, Ayo at his right shoulder, as the column of men came into view.

The man on the horse halted his men about twenty paces away from the prince and leaped from the horse. He landed almost effortlessly, with a slight grunt, causing a puff of dust to rise where his feet had touched the ground, and began to make his way towards the two figures standing in front of him.

Four of the closest warriors in the line behind disengaged from the body of men and followed closely behind their leader. They were all strapping men, exuding youthful radiance, confidence and the unmistakable air of superiority, muscles rippling in their thighs and arms as they moved. Enitan immediately noticed that these men all bore some similarity in features, all unique but discernible, and realised that they must be the sons of the one that led them.

They all walked together and halted a few paces from the prince and Ayo, both sides staring at the other, none of them willing to bridge the final gap, as if a deep chasm lay before them.

'By all the graces of *Oduduwa*, do my ageing eyes deceive me? Can it be that Prince Enitan, the last in the bloodline of King Jide, stands before me so? And Ayo, the gifted protégé? Surely the gods would not play such a cruel trick on an old man.'

'Your eyes do not play you false. It is me, Adedeji,' Enitan replied, struggling to hold back his joy in seeing one of his father's most trusted advisors, a man who had been like an old loving uncle to him and his brothers, and the head of the modakeke. His restraint wavered and his young features broke almost instantly, a wide smile spreading across his face and threatening to split his cheeks, as he bolted forward to clinch the old warrior.

Adedeji lifted Enitan off his feet and clasped him to his chest a little harder than he had intended, all the while laughing with elation at his good fortune. He held him there for a moment and then, as if belatedly remembering etiquette, put him down gently and bowed his head acknowledging him. The four warriors that stood by Adedeji followed his example and inclined their heads, but it was obvious that they could barely restrain their excitement from finding one of their own, Ayo, as well as the prince.

'How are you even here? We have heard nothing for months and assumed that you all perished in the war. What news have you brought from the east? Did more warriors survive?' Enitan rattled off, unable to contain himself. Ayo was also eager to ask questions of his own, but he managed to master his emotions and allow the prince to get the answers he sought.

'My prince. I have much to tell you, but your father, the king, sent us away the night before the final battle. He commanded me to take good men and travel west. I saw no logic in his orders and had thought that the despair of the hard day had robbed him of his reasoning, but now I see that, as always, he saw what we all could not. He said my spear was needed in the west. He needed me to live… he needed me to live for you, my prince.'

As he spoke, his eyes wondered off to a distance place, somewhere far from this land, perhaps still on the soil of Benin and the hill where he had last seen King Jide. Tears began to stream down the old warrior's face involuntarily, running into his beard, but his features remained impassive; however, sadness was unmistakably written behind his eyes as he remembered his king. Some of the tears made it through the entanglement of his greying beard and reached the soil, little droplets parting sand as they landed. Adedeji realised that in his moment of soliloquy, his words and emotions were likely to pierce the fragile heart of the young prince, and he quickly reverted to his usual light-hearted nature.

'Come, Prince Enitan. There is plenty of time to hear about the deeds of your father, plus, I'm sure you would love to hear of the many adventures on my journey, like the tales I told you back in Ife. First, I need to wash the dirt of the road off these old bones, and a warm meal would be most welcome. I have long eaten rodents and small birds, and I would sell my sword just to have some real food in my stomach. And palm wine!'

Enitan's smile came back. 'Of course, my chief advisor, let us rejoice in your arrival. I will see to it that a great feast is held in your name.' Adedeji smiled. He had not missed the title that Enitan had granted him, and a feeling of fulfilment descended on him.

Hours had passed and the warriors from Modakeke became acquainted with their new surroundings. Rested, refreshed and fed, they settled into the household as if they had been part of it from the moment the first foundation stone had been laid in the earth. During the feast, Adedeji had sat with the young prince for hours and regaled him with tales of his father; all the great adventures they had been on together and the achievements he had accomplished over the course of his rule, up to his last days on the field of battle in Benin.

Enitan was completely engrossed as he listened in silence, oblivious to the world around him, soaking up every word. He felt closer to his father through the memory of him and, as Adedeji spoke, he found himself thinking about the short and joyous moments he had spent with him; the sound of his father's laughter, the feeling of his rough and calloused palm in his, the itch he got from the stubble of his father's beard whenever he kissed him on the head. His young heart ached.

At times he would smile when Adedeji mentioned some great deed or feat performed by the beloved king, but mostly he cried silently, tears streaming down his face unbidden as a fleeting image of his father stole into his mind's eye. This did not deter Adedeji from telling Jide's story; he wanted the young prince to surrender himself to his feelings. He had correctly assessed that the prince would have pushed all his grief, all his emotions down to a place beyond reach. He sensed Enitan was in much need of the catharsis, a need to release the deep-rooted despondency. Better the prince dispel all his emotions now and let it be done, he thought. For the days ahead would be filled with nothing but hard choices, and clarity of mind was a necessity. For a mind shackled to anguish and sentiments could only serve as a conduit to poor decisions.

And Enitan seemed the better for it afterwards. He left the feast before long to seek solitude and probably ponder the conversation in his chambers, while Adedeji sought out Ayo. They met outside in the compound, where their words could not be overheard, their only companions being the crickets in the undergrowth, whose sounds filled the night air.

Adedeji got straight to the heart of the matter, no preamble and no pleasantries, simply a commander addressing one of his warriors.

'Tell me, Ayo, who do I need to be concerned about in this place?' he asked. 'I trust that you know the lay of the land well enough to mark those that may not share the best interest of our prince.'

'There are a few of the neighbouring tribal leaders that are simply waiting for Chief Kola to part from this world before they show their hand. I have heard rumours of men who scheme to seize power, seek to assert their independence, or align themselves with Olise. They would never voice their intentions publicly and try to disguise their ambitions, but I see it all.'

'Good, I would expect nothing less from you. You have ever been the diligent warrior. And the old chief? Do you think he has lost his influence on the people of Ogun?'

'He very well may have. He has been ill for some time now, and the change in the city has never been felt more. The people need reminding of who their rightful ruler is, and he has been out of the public eye for a time. Also, attendance at court by the chiefs is not what it used to be. Once the idea of the prince succeeding Chief Kola was made known, it was obvious that the decision galled some of the prominent men in the province. Now, some do not even acknowledge Enitan's summons but instead send their seconds. I believe they are due a lesson in obedience.'

'And they shall have it. We will seek out these so-called men of high esteem and show them the error of their ways. The roots that do not serve the tree are useless and need to be cut away lest they inhibit the growth of the tree. I will see to it personally that every tribe in the west prostrates before Enitan and him alone. I believe this is what King Jide sent me here to do, and I will see it done. But first, I will see a more permanent arrangement settled. Enitan must be formally proclaimed chief before the eyes of all the people of Ogun.'

A smile spread across Ayo's face. Maybe he would see some action after all. Long had his sword been sheathed, calling to him to be released from its bondage. He was suddenly filled with a sense of excitement and could scarcely contain himself.

He told Adedeji all he needed to know about the western tribes, who had the most warriors, whose fortifications were the strongest, who would be likely to yield, their weaknesses, and all other manner of information. Adedeji committed all to memory and planned to seek an audience with Chief Kola at first light. Although he respected the ailing chief as the rightful ruler, he felt it was time to pass that responsibility in its entirety to the prince. If the prince did not possess the title officially, the chiefs would always have an excuse, and persist to conspire and seek an advantage. But once Enitan was named, nothing could be misconstrued, and then, he would have a free hand to bring them all to heel.

The next morning, as the cockerel crowed, Adedeji along with Enitan and Ayo sought out Chief Kola. The old chief was delighted to host them and elated at the sight of Adedeji, who he had not seen in over two decades. They spoke at length and the chief revealed that he had been waiting for the moment to relinquish his title to the young prince, a gift to his only living grandchild. He confessed that before Enitan had arrived in Ogun, he had intended to split the rulership of the province and share it between three of his most powerful allies, since he had no male heir.

However, Enitan's appearance had been a gods send, as the division of the province would have broken generations of tradition and the continuity of a traceable bloodline of rulers.

The day after that, Chief Kola wasted no time in sum-
moning the high priest of the shrine of *Ogun* the god, to
preside over the ceremony of succession. This was highly
unconventional, as ceremonies of this nature had for centuries
been performed in the shrine in the presence of the heads of
the leading families from around the province, but the chief
was too fragile to make the journey, so exceptions needed to
be made, and the palace hall was the substitute.

A handful of trusted chiefs were in attendance, showing
their respect and support, a gesture of immense significance,
especially since they heeded the call at such short notice
with no protests given. Others refused outright to make an
appearance. They would be the first to receive a visit from
the modakeke.

Enitan was draped in a colourful wrapper, freshly dyed
with the royal colours of the Ogun tribe, tied across one
shoulder, exposing an arm. A dead silence was observed as he
walked the length of the hall to the front where the priest and
two of his attendants awaited him. He was asked to turn and
face his grandfather, who was seated rather uncomfortably on
his highchair, Wale and another guard either side of the old
chief ready to support him if needed.

The old man recited the words that had been spoken to
him so many years ago when he had taken the chieftaincy,
a blessing of sorts and words of wisdom to bestow on the
recipient of the title. He struggled at times and was short of
breath, but he was determined to carry out his duty to his
young relative.

Once completed, Enitan turned back to the priest, who in turn chanted sacred words reserved for newly anointed chiefs. He dipped some leaves bound together into a small calabash held by one of his attendants and splashed the contents, some blood taken from a ram sacrificed to appease the gods, onto Enitan's face. More words were spoken, and a set of bright red coral beads was placed around Enitan's neck. Finally, the horsetail regalia was placed in his palm. It was done.

Enitan was now the chief of all the western provinces. He turned from the priest, looked over to his right and beamed at Ayo, who returned the expression. He looked to his left and gave a slight bow to Adedeji, who in turn repeated the gesture, a look of pride plastered on his weathered features. Then he faced his subjects for the first time. His expression changed; he was no longer the scared boy who had arrived a year ago unsure of his place in the world. He was their liege lord and they, his vassals.

He turned once again to Adedeji and gave his first order as chief, his voice stern, almost menacing – 'Send for every chief who has deemed themselves too distinguished to heed my summons and attend me here today. They will prostrate before me or face the consequences of their stupidity.'

SERVITUDE IS RESERVED FOR THE WEAK OF HEART

The carved mahogany throne cut a dark figure in the room. It was placed almost in the centre of the large space and immediately drew the eye of anyone who entered. It was, in truth, a thing of beauty. Hours of labour by a master craftsman had clearly gone into the making of the throne. It had an exceptionally carved backrest with twin figures on each side depicting warriors that brandished swords and royal regalia. The backrest ended in peaks curved and pointed like the tusks of an elephant, and intricate swirling patterns depicting scenes of battles and presiding gods were chiselled into the armrests and legs. The smooth and harsh edges of its dark gleaming wood were polished to a high sheen with animal fat. The seat was also festooned with leopard pelts, adding to its magnificence, and other furs of exotic animals lined the floor beneath the throne, all placed with dramatic effect. And in the throne sat Olise, one arm dangling nonchalantly over an armrest, legs splayed and back arched. This was the ruler of all the southern kingdom.

However, to him, the title was an empty one, a falsehood in some regards. It was a title he would only deem himself worth of once he had secured the lands and provinces to the west and east of him. The very thought embittered him. He had ruled the lands for a year and was still no closer to quelling the troubled east or conquering all the west. His spies and allies offered him nothing but bad tidings and empty promises rather than solutions to his dilemmas, and this frustrated him, leaving a bitter taste on his tongue like bitter leaf.

They were all fools, he thought angrily, and for the thousandth time, he wondered whether he should replace those that he had entrusted to remove the nuisances that persisted to impede his dominance in the realm, like the little stones that found their way into his sandals, hurting his feet. But he was no fool to the reality that replacing his already well-established network and government would be counterproductive, which was bound to set his plans back even longer than he was prepared to stomach. No, he would continue to bide his time and suffer these so-called allies a little while longer, but their time would surely come.

After the hard-won battle with Jide, all the bloodshed, the allies and irreplaceable warriors lost, all he had to show for it was a kingdom in tatters. In his eyes, nothing could be more humiliating. The only comfort was that he sat in the seat of kings, Ile-Ife. The ancient city of the gods and the birthplace of all the Yoruba tribes. That and having sole control of all the major and strategically placed towns that held the wealth of the southern realm – Benin, Ondo, Ilesha, and a handful of others – these were the provinces that kept his coffers full and provided the resources required to sustain his expanding armies and, more importantly, giving him the power to maintain his position and keep his subjects under his hand.

As he pondered his predicament, supplicants were ushered into the throne room one after the other to prostrate before him and place their offerings at his feet. There was all manner of items piled up to one side of the throne from the long procession that had taken half of the day; gold and other precious metals, bolts of fine fabric, jewellery in the form of rare gems and beads – bracelets, necklaces, and anklets – fresh produce, casks of palm wine, kola nuts, cocoa, livestock, held outside the palace by attendants, and much more.

Each of these men had come to renew their vows to their king and pledge their armies and resources whenever they were to be called upon. Olise sat there and waved off each new arrival after they confirmed their fealty, without so much as a word of acknowledgement. His thoughts were elsewhere, contemplating the actions he needed to take, the people he needed to kill, but they were interrupted every time Efetobo announced a newcomer.

Efetobo had done well to survive the sack of the city. He was, in fact, the only royal councillor out of the five that had previously held the title before the city was burned to have made it out alive; the other four had met their fate on that dark day, and none had even been acknowledged.

As for Efetobo, he had been smart enough to take refuge within the grounds of the palace rather than flee with the rest of the citizens, and had only appeared once the town was won, proclaiming himself Ekaete's personal spy and advisor.

He had quickly ingratiated himself with Olise when the then prince had ridden into the city triumphantly with King Jide at his back in a cage bound by chains of gold. Efetobo had managed to worm his way to the head of Olise's councillors, styling himself chief councillor, and personally overseeing the selection of new members to replace those that had perished. He had of course taken advantage of his position and appointed men he could easily influence, and the council in effect spoke with his voice. Now that he wielded some power and finally felt he had achieved what had always been destined to be his, he adopted the arrogance and pomp of a baboon. The double layer of fat under his chin quivered every time he spoke, and his waist had taken on a few more inches, a clear sign of the comfortable living afforded a man of importance.

His voice boomed with every announcement, a new level of authority underpinning his tone, another attribute he had recently acquired, as he asked the next supplicant to step forward and make their appeal to the king.

In truth, Olise despised him. He regarded him as a leech, one whose only purpose in life was to feed off the achievements of others, and was liable to detach himself at the first sign of a better opportunity to advance his position. Olise would sooner have his head adorn the battlements along with all the others that decorated the façade of the palace, if not for the blood he shared with his mother, being her distant cousin. Olise's mood darkened at the thought of such men in his court, but he was obliged to appease Ekaete for all she had sacrificed for him.

Just then, Efetobo was introducing a man that caught Olise's attention. This man was not as well presented as those that had come before him, his kaftan was faded, the ends of the arms and legs were frayed, his sandals were dusty, worn and falling apart, and his face, from the deep lines on his brow and around his mouth, had clearly been no stranger to hardship.

'This man is Goke, an elder from a small village in the province of Inisa, come to pledge his fealty,' said Efetobo. 'What have you brought with you to offer to your king?' he continued.

'Your highness, I am from a lowly village, and we do not have warriors or anything of significance to offer you besides our loyalty and three goats. We have suffered consecutive bad harvests and we struggle to feed our families. I thought… I would like to know… can you aid us, my king?

Now he had Olise's full attention, and he sat up on his throne. 'So let me make sure I completely grasp what you are requesting of me. You want me, the king, to support you, and in return, all you offer me are some goats? Is that correct?' Olise's tone was level, but the look he placed on the poor man was enough to convey exactly what he thought about the request.

The man swallowed hard, his Adam's apple bobbing up and down in his throat, as he realised too late that he had wrongly judged the generosity of the king.

Olise snapped his fingers, and one of the palace guards that stood by the wall came forward, head bowed expectantly.

'Take this man and string him up for a day in the sun. Him and his goats!'

The guard raised his head slightly with a mind to confirm the order he had just received, then promptly thought against it, and remained where he stood. Olise then turned his attention to the man once more.

'You should thank your gods that I don't have you flogged to death for your insolence. After your punishment, you have one moon to return here with an offering that pleases me. Fail to do that and I will descend on your village with fire and burn it off the face of the earth. By the time I am done, it will be no more than a mere stain in the soil, never to be spoken of again. If it does not serve any purpose to me, what is the point of it?'

The man was too shocked to respond and just stood there with his mouth gaping wide. Before he could protest, the guard that had been summoned hooked an arm under his elbow and forcefully dragged him away. Only then did the man find his voice and begin to lament and beg for mercy and the return of his goats, but his voice soon faded into the distance.

'I have seen enough people for one day. Send them all away.' Olise stood and stretched his neck as he turned to Efetobo. 'And the next time you bring peasants before me with their arms out begging for alms, it is you I will have strung up, Efetobo.'

'Forgive me, my king. I assumed that you would be interested in hearing the voices of all your subjects. Maybe they are due some compassion after the hardships they have endured?'

Olise shot him a venomous look. 'Compassion? Please, Efetobo, enlighten me as to what hardships you speak of?'

'There have been famines, my king, that have blighted several provinces, all but crippling some of the small villages. Added to the food shortages, sickness is spreading amongst the peasantry and there have been talks of a curse plaguing the lands ever since...' Efetobo caught himself just before the words passed his lips, suddenly unsure of how he could phrase his sentence without causing offence or rousing the temper of Olise.

'Spit it out, why don't you! Do you think I do not have ears? You think I do not know what they say, what they truly think of me? It means nothing! Does a lion entertain the thoughts of an antelope? He does not. He is the one that determines those that will become his food and those that will have the privilege of life. They should be grateful for their wretched lives with the knowledge that I have not yet decided to feast!'

Efetobo's chins started to quiver once more as he contemplated his next words.

'My king, all I was trying to say is that a small gesture of goodwill would go a long way in the kingdom. These are simple people that do not expect much other than the means to feed their families. And for those with harder minds and wills, a gesture could quench their thirst for rebellion. It could douse the flames of retribution that may still burn in the hearts of some of your chiefs. Many complain that they cannot afford your tributes. Perhaps, if you were to grant them one moon to recover their losses, they would– '

'One moon! Enough of your babbling. Why don't I take some of the wealth you have acquired over the last year to compensate for those that are so poverty-stricken, as you have said, to supplement what I am due as their king, eh? What do you say to that?'

'My king… you would not… what I mean is, I do not think–'

'Silence! That is exactly what I thought. You cannot find the words when it concerns the weight of your own pouch. I do not want to hear any more of this foolishness. If these peasants do not pay their tributes, then they must find other means to serve me. That is all. Now leave me. I am sure that you have more pressing matters to attend to, do you now?'

Efetobo did not wait to respond, but quickly bowed his head and all but fled the room, panting from the effort of lumbering his bulk out of the throne room, swaying from side to side as he walked off.

'I am surrounded by imbeciles,' Olise said to no one in particular, as he rubbed on his temples to get rid of the dull ache behind his eyes. Hearing voices, he raised his head to see if Efetobo had stopped to fray his nerves even more and saw two of his men standing by the archway where Efetobo had hastily departed. They were high-ranking warriors within his army, men he had sent out to gather information and gauge the temperature of his troubled kingdom. He beckoned them forward, eager to learn of more important news besides the governance of goatherds.

These were hardened warriors. Men that had fought alongside him when he won his crown at Benin. He did not trust them entirely, as their loyalties were intrinsically entwined with the promise of gold and power, which Olise was willing enough to pay for their expertise and experience. But more so, because of their lineage. They were from the Calabar tribe, a proud and powerful tribe that harboured a deep contempt for the throne and even more for the man that sat upon it. The Calabar despised him for the dishonour he had perpetrated on them many years ago when he broke the sacred law of guest rights and slaughtered one of their greatest warriors in cold blood in this very city. Having such renowned warriors on his side could only serve to his advantage if he played his hand with care.

'Odafe. Etido. What new developments do you bring me?' Olise asked, forcing a half-smile on his face.

Etido was the first to speak when they came to stand with Olise. He was a tall man, a clear head above most men, and was well defined, his shoulders and arms bulged with muscles, thick veins standing out and snaking across his biceps, threatening to burst from the skin. Coarse dark hair covered his features from his legs and forearms to his chest and face. A patchy and unkempt beard covered his cheeks and heavy-set jawline, matching the knotted and bushy hair that crowned his head. His thick eyebrows were almost joined as one, sitting over menacing, dark, hooded eyes. He had a wide nose and when he spoke, his nostrils flared, reminding Olise of a warthog before a charge.

In stark contrast, Odafe was a reasonably handsome man and appeared to represent the epitome of a warrior, until he opened his mouth, revealing the dark and twisted soul he truly was. Athletically built and compact with ropes of muscle on his arms and legs, unlike the bulging mass of Etido, he was as if sculpted from stone. His dark skin always seemed to glisten with oil or sweat, Olise could not tell. He was clean-shaven, with hair cut close to his scalp and wore a perpetual half-smile on the side of his mouth. His intelligent dark eyes were constantly moving, analysing everything around him, and he spoke with only a hint of an accent when he used the tongue of the Yoruba. Olise had always had an eye on him, for he valued a shrewd mind in a warrior, particularly one that worked to his benefit, but he maintained the knowledge that he always had to keep him close.

'My king, the news is not good. Blood stains the lands in the east, villages are burning, the people are shattered and there are battles in every province. It is difficult to say which way the fighting will go, but at this rate, it could go on for some time,' Etido said, in his gruff and deep voice.

'Is this news supposed to be useful to me? Or is there something I am missing? I asked for an update, and instead, you feed me information that half the kingdom already knows! Today is not the day to test my patience, Etido. I have already strung one man up, do not make me have to repeat the order!' Olise said as the dull throbbing behind his eyes intensified.

Etido looked more sour than afraid of the threat he had just received and was about to make a further comment when Odafe interjected.

'My king, we do have some slightly more favourable news. We have been observing both sides of the fight quite closely and discreetly for a time, seeking a weakness or some flaw we can exploit. Unfortunately, there were none to find. Everyone is tense and sees deception everywhere, and rightly so. However, we thought the next best way to gather information was to apprehend some men and get them to spill their secrets. So, we did, taking men from either side of the battles. And after some gentle persuasion, we were able to extract some details that would be of benefit to you, my king.'

'And by gentle persuasion, I take it you mean torture?'

'Yes, my king. That was the only sure way to make them… agreeable to our questions.'

Etido frowned at that, clearly showing his displeasure with the methods that Odafe had employed, which indicated that he still maintained some degree of honour, arguable since he carried out Olise's bidding. Nonetheless, he believed that warriors should be granted the choice to die as they lived, with a blade in hand, rather than being humiliated and rendered utterly helpless, subjected to having their flesh peeled from their bones like cattle.

Olise noticed the look but chose to ignore it, as Odafe continued to relay his message.

'In fairness, we did not torture the men captured from the Calabar tribe. As I do not particularly find satisfaction in killing my own people, unless it was completely necessary, or the gold was weighty enough. Only the Igbo and Yoruba tribesmen fighting for the so-called prince suffered by my blade. It must be said, however, that both sides shared some interesting information.'

'Will you get to the point already and spare me the suspense! Why can I not seem to get a straight answer from anyone today?' Olise shot out, clearly losing his patience.

'The Yoruba and Igbo fight for a young warrior, a boy really. Some claim that he is one of the late king's sons. We did not have the opportunity to set eyes upon him ourselves, but this information was corroborated by all these we captured, so I believe it to be true. The mere belief in such news is, in itself, as dangerous as the words being true. Warriors flock to him like vultures to a cadaver. Gates are opened to receive him, and the people embrace him. We also discovered that most, if not all, of the Igbo chiefs have sworn to him, and his numbers continue to grow by the day. More disturbing still is that rumours say that he was responsible for the taking of Ada and the liberation of the hostages a year ago,' Odafe finished, and waited for a reaction from Olise.

This was troubling news for the king; his heart was beating faster at the thought of a child of Jide, one of his nephews, no less. Could it be true, could one of his brother's children have made it out of the city alive? His men had assured him that no one had survived the wreckage of the palace and the multitude of charred bones that had been recovered attested to the numbers that had perished in the fire-ravished building.

If one of Jide's sons had indeed survived, his legitimacy on the throne would always be questioned. Furthermore, the threat of a revolt against his reign could easily sprout wings and take flight, spreading across the provinces. This, he could not accept.

'I need certainty of this claim. It could merely be another old wife's tale to keep the seed of rebellion germinating. I need proof before I act. Bring me indisputable evidence of the lineage of this so-called prince; only then can I show my hand.'

'Perhaps it may be worth waiting this battle out. Bide your time for the inevitable outcome. One of the two sides is sure to triumph sooner rather than later, and they would be doing you a favour without you even having to lift a finger. Once a side has proclaimed victory, you can fall on them with spears and clean up whatever remnants remain,' Odafe suggested.

'I see little honour in Odafe's proposal. Why wait like cowards, my king? We have the strength of numbers and the advantage of surprise. I say we sweep through the lands and destroy everything in our path between here and the far eastern borders of the kingdom. We would spare those that throw down their weapons and are willing to swear themselves to you, which will bolster our ranks in the process, but for everyone else, we grant them a swift death,' Etido said passionately.

Olise pondered the words of his commanders for a minute, still reeling from the news that had just been disclosed to him. He grudgingly concluded that he would have to consult with Ekaete, even though it pained him to do so. Jide had always accused him of being too dependent on Ekaete, insisting that he had lost his voice and relied on Ekaete to pull the threads. This was something that he had sworn to change if only to prove to himself that he was capable of ruling the kingdom on his own terms. However, he could only deceive himself for so long. The truth was, he needed his mother's guidance for without it, he would be lost in this world of deceit and darkness.

The silence that followed impregnated the room, and Olise realised that they were waiting for his command. He brought his thoughts back to the present and looked at both men in turn, for a few more moments.

'The men you captured; do they still live?' he asked Odafe.

Odafe looked slightly hesitant for once, the smirk on his lip only dropping for a fraction of a heartbeat before returning. 'They do, my king. The strong ones at least.'

'Good. I will question them myself. Have them prepared to receive me. Once I have all the information, I will decide on how we are to proceed.'

'That may be difficult…' Odafe replied, his smirk dropping once more. Again, Etido's frown returned, a look of discomfort mingled with disapproval contorting his features.

'And what exactly do you mean by difficult?' Olise asked.

'Most of the men that live, well… they are missing their tongues. I thought it an appropriate action to ensure that they do not speak of anything they had witnessed whilst in our… care,' Odafe responded.

'You do mean to dispose of them afterwards, do you not? So, why you see the need to prolong their suffering, is beyond me,' Etido shot at Odafe, who just shrugged his shoulders nonchalantly in response.

'Taking the tongues of some helped to loosen the tongues of others. It was a necessity.' It was not necessary, and it was all too clear that he had done so simply for his own pleasure.

Olise was losing more of his patience. 'Please tell me that you still hold men that have not lost their ability to speak?'

'Yes, my king, but you will not get much out of them now. Shall we say that the process of "gentle persuasion" is taxing on the giver and the receiver alike? The captives are recovering, or better yet reflecting on what little time they have left. I feel it is always good to give them some respite. Time to appreciate the benefit of being forthcoming, before continuing. This will give them the opportunity to gather their thoughts and do what is best for them and provide clarity on a way out of their miserable predicament.'

Despite Olise's rising anger, he couldn't fault Odafe's logic and relented. 'Very well. Send for me once they have "recovered", but do not try to persuade them any further. Not until I have spoken to them. Understood?'

'Your command, my king,' Odafe said with a slight bow.

Olise dismissed them with a wave of his hand as he sank back into his throne heavily. His head was now throbbing, whether it was from his growing concerns from the news, or the actions of his men, he could not tell. One thing he did know was that he needed to find Ekaete straight away. He reached for the horn of palm wine that rested on a wooden stool beside the throne and downed the content in one great gulp, a white line of the beverage running down the side of his mouth.

He again reminded himself that he needed to drink less, he needed clarity, but then resigned himself to the fact that he needed the drink to steel his nerves before he faced his mother. After setting the horn down, he stood up warily and walked towards the entrance to the bedchambers.

The torch wrapped in rags and soaked in animal fat popped and crackled in the fire, sending the faint scent of roasting meat wafting around the room, mingled with the smell of a concoction of burning herbs, making the air heavy. The light from the torch only lit a small section of the room, the rest of it engulfed in darkness. Ekaete sat in a large chair in one of the far corners facing the main door to the bedchamber, elbows resting on the arms and hands steepled together pensively.

She could tell that Olise approached; she felt the vibrations of his heavy footfalls on the timber flooring that lined the hallway, she felt his distress and knew that he must have finally had word from the east. Of course, she had been privy to this information for some time now and had tried to warn him about the threat, but he had dismissed it as rumours. She had long decided to let him hear it from men he trusted, in the hopes that their words would be the catalyst that would spur him into action. Her only hope was that his procrastination did not cost them all dear.

There was a rap on the heavy timber door and, after a moment, Olise pushed it open. He stood in the doorway for a second, eyes adjusting to the gloom, and turned towards the chair where Ekaete normally sat.

'Mother. I will never understand why you enjoy sitting in the darkness so. One would think that the light would cause you harm.'

'Have you finally come to listen to reason, my son? I take it all I have tried to warn you about has now been confirmed?'

'I would not say confirmed. Not entirely anyway, but yes, it appears to be as you said. I am still loath to act until I know for myself. I cannot afford to misstep, not at a time when the whole kingdom is desperately waiting for me to fail. I must move with caution.'

'And it is that cautious approach that will be your undoing. What is it you are waiting for exactly? Do you want this prince to march to your gates with an army at his back and introduce himself? Is that when you will take things seriously? I have not sacrificed so much just to see you squander it away to satisfy your newly found dignity! Right now, you need to assert your rule, rid the kingdom of any threats to the throne and secure your bloodline to ensure a favourable succession when the time comes.'

'If you are suggesting that it is time for me to take a wife and father a child, that will not be happening any time soon. Succession is the least of my concerns right now. This is my time and I intend to wield the power I have to secure my own place, otherwise, all the bloodshed will have been for nothing.'

'Nonsense! Every step we have taken to get to this point has been designed. Every risk and every setback anticipated.

And every drop of blood necessary. Do not ever forget that! What good is a kingdom won if you do not intend to rule it and pass it on to your bloodline? A strong lineage is the very essence of long-lasting power.'

'We see things very differently, Mother. I have almost come to tire of all the threats, the lies, the betrayals. How many more towns must I burn, or heads must I collect before the people know I am not one to be trifled with? And yet, everywhere I look, I see shadows wielding daggers poised to stab me and rob me of everything I am, everything I have accomplished. Not only that but I am also tormented by Jide's face. He resides behind the lids of my eyes whenever I shut them, and now, I hear one of his sons lives. How can I sleep knowing that I must further damn my soul and kill another blood relative? The burden of it all.'

'Olise. The crown is a heavy load to bear and the yoke it is fastened to has many facets. You knew that before it was placed upon your head. But you do not bear the load alone. I am your mother, and I will do everything in my power to lessen the burden that weighs on you. All I ask is that you play the role that has been ordained for you. Seize the respect you deserve from your subjects, or further instil fear in their hearts, but most importantly, never show your weakness. For weakness, my son, is the defining trait of those who must serve, not those who rule. And rule is what you were born to do.'

'You make things sound so simple. If only it were so.'

'It is, or at least it can be. Have I not guided you, held your hand through every twist of fate that has been dealt to us? That is what I was born to do and so it will always be. Now get these thoughts of Jide out of your mind, and if you see shadows, they are the ones that I have put there to protect you.'

Olise did not doubt her words for a second but decided not to explore the subject further. He would never openly admit it, but Ekaete had a way with words that always soothed him, re-instilled his confidence. She, after all, was one of the few people who genuinely had his best interests at heart, so there was no surprise.

'Mother, despite what I have shared with you, do not be mistaken. I do not intend to relinquish my authority or give respite to the peasants I allow to draw air in my kingdom. I only voice my thoughts for you to understand that which disturbs me within. We have come too far, as you have said, and I would rather reduce the entire realm to ashes before I succumb to the whims of those that would sooner see me fall.'

'That is good, and I have every faith in you, my child. We must seek to use the knowledge we have gathered to our advantage. Do not forget that besides the conflict in the east, we still have enemies in the west to contend with. There are many provinces there that still defy you. They must learn who they look to for support. Not to mention the north. Only the fates know of what is brewing beyond the great river. That is one place I have absolutely no visibility or influence.'

'Indeed. However, my eyes are only turned towards our interests south of the river. As for the west, they will soon learn what it means to stray from under the cloak of my rule.

The lesson I intend to impart on them will be one they will not soon forget. I have already summoned all the chiefs in the west that have yielded, to attend me in the village of Iwo three days from now. There, I will inform them of my orders to carry my wrath to any settlements that are yet to pay homage to me. This will also give them an opportunity to prove their loyalty once again. If they refuse, they will share the same fate as those I will destroy. I will see to it personally. Once I am done there, the conflict in the east should be nothing more than mere skirmishes, and I will take what is left. I must say, for all Odafe's questionable methods, I see great merit in his suggestion.'

'I do see the wisdom in this approach, but I am sure there is much that can be done while you settle matters in the west. I will travel east in your stead to see what more can be gleaned about this prince, and anything else that may be of benefit to us. As for the men Odafe captured, do not trouble yourself with them. Leave this to me. I will speak to them and learn of any secrets they have yet to reveal.'

Somehow, Olise felt sorry for the captives. He knew that those poor souls would be better off enduring Odafe's cruelty rather than a visit from Ekaete, but he had no doubt that if there was anything untold, they would offer it all willingly enough. He also realised that he had not mentioned anything about the captives, or his intentions to question them. Another subject not worth exploring.

'As you wish, Mother. I can spare a few men to accompany you. I cannot have you travel alone while the countryside is in

flames and the roads are rife with all manner of delinquents.'
Ekaete raised an eyebrow and one corner of her mouth turned
upwards ever so slightly, clearly amused at his comment.

'Do you honestly believe I require babysitting or think
I am incapable of protecting myself? Your concern is appreciated, but you need not worry yourself on my behalf. You
need men you can trust to remain here while you travel west.
When do you plan to go?'

'I will march for Oyo in a day, there are several stops I
must make along the way and there is much to prepare. I
will leave Etido in command of the city in my absence with
two-thirds of the army. The rest will accompany me.'

'Do you think that is enough men to take with you? A
king should always travel in force to dissuade anyone from
getting the wrong idea.'

'No need. More men are needed here for that very reason.
Besides, I will gather warriors to me along the way, or do you
forget that my forces stretch far across the realm now? Those
aware of my coming will flock to me like bees to nectar from
a sunflower. My orders to ready themselves have already been
dispensed, you have nothing to fear.'

'Let us hope that you are right. Nonetheless, I will watch
over you as I have always done.'

'Even from many miles away? I am truly a lucky man.'
Olise had no doubt that she would do exactly that, and yet
again, that was another mystery that he had no intention of
knowing the full details about.

'I will begin my preparations. Let me know if anything
useful comes out of your meeting with the captives.' With

that, Olise turned for the door and left his mother in darkness, with his mind set on all the tasks ahead of him. He felt a twinge of excitement at the prospect of travelling. He had long been confined within the walls of the city and relished the opportunity to again don his armour and march at the head of fighting men. Nothing set his heart racing more than the thought of contest and conquest, and suddenly, he felt alive again. Maybe that was what he had needed all along, to walk out from the shadow of the ruin inflicted by his ascension to the throne and carve out a new path for himself. It was time for his subjects to witness the greatness of their new king and set an example for those that would sooner deny him his glory. Many would come to rue the day they failed to obey the words of the king of the south.

Parched lips, chafed wrists and aching joints were Obi's new reality. There was no telling the hour of the day, nor did he have any recollection of how many days had passed since he had been held captive and bound like a sacrificial goat in this dark and damp cell that had come to be his home.

There were no windows, the mortar that held fast the stones that formed the shell of the room was home to cockroaches, the ceiling leaked, leaving rancid puddles mixed with human waste in the rough stone floor, the stench was nauseating, and his only companions were rats the size of kittens that constantly nibbled at the dead skin on the soles of his feet. At times, it felt like the ropes around his wrist had loosened, only for him to struggle against his bondage and be rewarded for his efforts with spasms of pain that shot through his arms and legs. Everything hurt and he pitied himself for getting into such a sorrowful state.

He was a noble warrior, one who had fought for what he believed to be the good of the kingdom. He had taken up his spear to stand beside his chief, beside his prince, son to an honourable and just king who had fallen to the cruel ambitions of a man who sought absolute power. But most of all, he had fought for a dream of a better place for his family and the generations that would follow behind them. None of that mattered now. He had no grand illusions of a fair outcome. No hopes of a saviour that would break his bondage and spirit him away from this place of misery. No chief or prince running to his aid. All he had were his thoughts and the rats.

He had been captured with a small group of warriors sent to scout enemy lines. They had been set upon by men who overwhelmed them and beat them unconscious before hauling them off to wherever it was that he was being held. His initial thoughts were that he had been taken by the river tribes, the very men he and his companions had been sent to spy upon, but it soon dawned on him that he was greatly mistaken. He had vague recollections of being transported across faraway lands, the scent of the rivers was replaced with that of forests, trees, plants, moist soil, and then waste, excrement, urine, and dampness.

He had woken a few times, but his thoughts were muddled, his vision cloudy. How many blows to the head did he take? His whole body ached, and then came the screams. Men, oddly familiar voices. His companions. Their anguished cries filled his ears, the room rang with their sounds, tormented, and tortured souls begging for respite and telling all that was asked of them.

Eventually, the screaming had subsided, and was replaced with something far more disturbing, unintelligible moans, humming noises as if from mouths that had been sewn up, no longer able to string words together. Was it from the pain? He could no longer tell. All he could do was wait and keep the rats from feasting on his toes. He kicked out every so often whenever he felt them bite him, but he soon tired of this, deciding to conserve his strength for whatever lay beyond the cage that held him captive. He knew something was coming and again felt an overwhelming sense of hopelessness.

He was determined not to surrender himself to his anxieties, not to allow his fears to possess him, consume every fibre of his being. He would tell them nothing of whatever they asked of him, even if it meant not seeing the sun again. Was that not what it meant to be a man of honour, a true warrior? To stand by one's vows of loyalty despite the horrors that one may have to endure. No amount of pain inflicted, promise of water to quench his thirst or food to quell the pang of hunger that stabbed at his stomach would make him betray his chief and his prince.

He rolled over in that foul space, surprising a rat that must have been feasting on him and sending it screeching into the darkness. His eyes had long become accustomed to the dark and he could make out the caged door of his cell. It was open. That was impossible, it had always been locked, coiled with chains, but as he gazed at it in the gloom, he realised that his eyes did not deceive him; the door was wide open, invitingly.

He was certain that it had been closed but a moment ago, or did he imagine that? Had the water and food deprivation finally caught up with him, playing with his thoughts and his ability to see with clarity?

He closed his eyes and tried to focus on something else, anything else, and then he heard a noise. It was faint but clear enough for him to know that it was no imagined sound. He sat up, leaned forward, and twisted his head so his ear was facing the door to the cage. There it was again, like the sound of eggshells breaking under the weight of feet. Only a few minutes ago, the only sound that had existed in this place had been the squeaks of rats and the occasional moans from the others who dwelled somewhere in the darkness.

He turned his head and tried to peer through the gloom, squinting as if the action would improve his vision. Only blackness lay beyond, and then he caught a movement. Something or someone was there; he felt the presence deep in his bones, his skin prickled, his heart began to beat faster, and his breath came in short bursts.

'Who is there?' he called out, but he had been so long not talking and without water that his words came out in a croak. He tried again.

'Show yourself. Only a coward would hide in the shadows from a man bound in ropes!'

Nothing. And then his eyes began to register something, faint at first, slight details, slowly forming as if the very darkness itself was taking shape, manifesting, coming to life. A figure began to materialise. He could just about make out a silhouette, someone tall, slender, curved at the hips. A woman. Then a face emerged from the darkness, that face. Ekaete.

Obi's eyes went wide, tongue and throat taking on a new level of dryness, skin prickling, hairs standing on his arms and legs. A heart-stopping chill overcame him and he shuddered like he had been plunged into iced waters, he began to shiver and yet he was sweating, cold, every sense screaming in unison. The cell had suddenly become too small, he felt claustrophobic, suffocated in that small space, and then a warm sensation began to spread on his thighs and under his backside. A part of him realised that he had urinated on himself, but the rest of him was rooted to the spot, paralysed with fear, eyes beginning to water, heart now pounding in his chest and the shivering becoming more violent. He tried to move backwards but his bondage would not permit him. There was nowhere to go.

'You know why I am here. Do not make me ask you more than once. Tell me everything I need to know about this prince.'

Obi could not speak. He tried but he only blathered, unable to articulate his thoughts or convey anything of meaning, mind solely filled with the urge to scream as loud as his lungs would allow and run as far away as he could, but there would be no running from this nightmare. She came closer, too close. He could smell and feel the darkness oozing from her like water evaporating from the heat of the afternoon sun.

He found his tongue then and sang like a sparrow, words spilling from his lips uncontrollably, ceaselessly. No stones were left unturned, and no secrets were left unspoken.

HARD CHOICES TO BE MADE

A plan of the entire southwest, pinned down with daggers on all four corners, was etched in exceptional detail on the large cowhide that dominated the table. The work had clearly been undertaken by someone meticulous, with a keen eye, and that took great pride in their work. Perhaps it had been intended to festoon the hall of a wealthy merchant, or the throne room of some chief or king. Instead, it was being viewed for the sole purpose of formulating stratagems and battles.

Several men, battle-hardened, grim-faced, and tense, huddled around the table peering down at the map. Despite their many victories, there was no sense of jubilation here. No fanfare or pats on the back, just the anticipation of the battles that lay ahead of them and the nagging thought of more bloodshed to come.

The one thing that was shared in the room was the sense of respect, familial bondage almost, and unyielding loyalty. Loyalty to themselves, and most especially, loyalty to their prince and potential heir to the kingdom, who stood foremost by the table with his arms outstretched, palms resting on the rough wooden surface. Every man here would die for him and the man that stood beside them. All willing to lay down their life without a moment's hesitation, despite their difference in station.

But Niran was undoubtedly revered above all. His coming to the east had been seen as a gift from the gods, if anyone was asked. He had singlehandedly restored the balance of power in the region from the Calabar to the Igbo, wresting lands and provinces that had been disputed and the object of many a bloody battle for generations.

With his influence, he had sworn the Igbo to him and rekindled a desire in them to rule the lands of their forefathers, as they once were hundreds of years ago, before the tribes of the Calabar grew in power.

Over the past year, many battles had been fought in his name and he was yet to concede a single defeat. He was a master tactician, a marvel for one so young, brave, choosing to fight alongside his people, and wise, which only gained him more respect from those already sworn to him, and attracted more spears to march at his back.

What had initially started off as a group of four warriors now swelled in the thousands and stretched across most of the eastern provinces, with great cities and towns answering only to him. There was no denying that he had accomplished much, in such a short space of time. His deeds were spoken about as if things of legend, but none more than his audacious action of rescuing the children that Olise had taken hostage for insurance. The citizens were still in awe of this feat, that against all odds, he had perpetrated such a bold plan under the noses of everyone and succeeded, choosing not to take any glory from it.

Perhaps it was because not all the children had returned from the perilous journey to their families, and he had felt personally responsible for this failing. However, the families of the unfortunate ones held no contempt in their hearts towards him. In fact, they loved him the more for his intentions, as no one else in his position would have performed such a selfless act just to restore the morale of the people and reunite long-parted families.

Now, the next course of action was being deliberated. Although the Igbo had gained plenty of ground, the Calabar continued to resist further advancement, bringing both sides to an impasse. Heavy casualties were being inflicted on both sides, with each desperately seeking the advantage.

The room Niran stood in held the very power of the east, all the ruling chiefs of the Igbo people, with the head of the tribe amongst them, Zogo the black, one of the few men of note to have witnessed the battle for Benin and yet lived to tell the tale. Zogo had been determined to die beside his king on the field, had fought to within an inch of his life, and was defeated not by the foes he faced but by the limitations of his mortal body. He had fought against impossible odds in a desperate attempt to reach his king, when Jide had been captured, knocked unconscious and his body dragged from the field by Olise's men to be paraded as the greatest trophy of any battle.

Zogo had continued fighting for hours after Olise had taken his prize and left the field to be swept clean by his warriors. He was fatigued, bleeding, but inching ever closer to the walls of Benin, only to be pushed back by wave after wave of fresh warriors seeking to claim his head. Yet he did not fall.

The Igbo and Modakeke warriors that had survived the onslaught fought beside him but, one after the other, they fell to the spears of Olise's men. And yet Zogo fought on; sword broken, struggling from a multitude of wounds, but still with unwavering resolve, he pushed on.

When the Modakeke and the Igbo numbered but a handful of fighting men, the highest-ranking Modakeke warrior implored Zogo to flee. He begged him to live, to raise support and come back to rescue Jide. He told him that if every man were to die there in the shadow of the walls of Benin, no one would take the burning indignation of what they had witnessed on that day to inflame the hearts of the people in the kingdom. If that very fury was not taken away from that field of blood, all hope of igniting the desire for justice by the people would be snuffed out like the light of a candle in a breeze and replaced by fear. The fear of what Olise would do since he had the audacity to take the crown.

Zogo saw no reason to act on the speech of the Modakeke warrior; rather, he was determined to heed the final words of Jide before he was struck down and taken. "Fight for your kingdom!" Jide had cried out.

His mind was set, until the Modakeke warrior convinced two of Zogo's axe-wielding guards to drag him away, while the rest of the men covered their retreat. Zogo had to be forcefully manhandled away from the battle, literally kicking and screaming, just before the massacre of Jide's warriors was complete.

He was then made to travel east to his homeland, the only safe place left for him to go, utterly exhausted, defeated, and unable to offer any further resistance. Along the way, he had consoled himself with the idea of rousing his people and the warriors who had not heeded the call to arms, to build an army and take back their kingdom and their king, but when he arrived, he was met with turmoil. The ripples from the war in the west had spread far, like tentacles reaching to all the corners of the kingdom. Olise had people scouring the countryside, burning, pillaging, and claiming lands in his name, proving yet again just how ruthless and thorough he was in his quest to secure the kingdom. If one thing was to be said of Olise, he was not a man to take half-measures, and when he committed to doing a thing, he did it to the best of his ability.

To further compound the woes of Zogo, the Calabar tribe had taken up arms against the Igbo, destabilising the region even more. They had seized the opportunity of unrest in the kingdom to stake a claim to lands they had been contesting for centuries. What better opportunity would they have to assert their authority and fortify their position before Olise set his sights further east, which would dash their hopes asunder for all eternity? Most of the Calabar held no love for Olise, apart from a few minor provinces that had familial ties with Ekaete, so their actions carried the blessings of the ruling classes of the Calabar.

Now, battles raged over large areas, boundary lines shifted constantly and Zogo would be plunged into yet another struggle for survival. But his homecoming had not been all bitter. He learned that Niran, second son of the man he had been willing to follow to the dark halls of *Esu's* underworld, not only lived but had managed to consolidate the power amongst the Igbo, uniting all the tribes of these people, including those that had previously sought to break away and seek their own independence. Now they all fought under one name: Prince Niran.

Niran had held lands for these people, set up networks of communication across the region and brought order to the tribe. He had defended their borders and gained lands of his own, dealing devastating blows to the Calabar.

Zogo's first-born son and heir to his titles had been amongst the many sons and daughters Niran had freed from Olise's clutches, and had survived the journey to their kinsmen. This act alone had bonded Zogo to Niran, and he would stand at his shoulder until the gods themselves decided to part him from this world. Now, Zogo served as one of Niran's chief advisors and had sole command of all his Igbo kinsmen, under Niran's rule.

'Is it necessary to capture these patches of swamplands?' said Ikenna, a respected but ageing chief from one of the eastern provinces. 'We hold most of the land worth taking, including the supply routes and passages further east, thanks to your decisive actions. Given time, I'm sure we can starve these river men,' he continued, prompting some agreement from the gathered men.

'And why do you think that has not already happened? After all, it has been over a year since we started this campaign and still we seem to lose almost as much territory as we gain, the river tribes continue to trouble our less protected borders, but they do not appear to be lacking for provisions and their moral is intact,' Niran said.

He waited for a response, but no one spoke up.

'It is because they are true masters of their environment. Every major harbour and coastline in the south can be reached from the rivers, provided men are willing enough to brave them,' Niran said as he used his finger to trace the lines drawn on the map before them. 'And what better incentive do they have to use the waters to their advantage than to have the threat of losing their lands altogether? These waters are as well connected as any land route in the south, and they are relying on us to overlook this factor.'

'That may be so, but some of these rivers would take days to traverse, and they are linked to the great sea! Small vessels would be pulled out and destroyed by the current!' said another chief.

'Agreed. But they know these rivers as well as they know the faces of their children. They are fishermen first, warriors only out of necessity. Do not forget. Do you really think they would not know the nature of the waters they have lived beside for generations? We have only been here for a year, and they all their lives. That is the only logical explanation for their continued survival. Adapt to their environment or perish.'

'So, what do you propose, my prince? There is no way we can stop them from using the rivers. Unless we take away their canoes,' said Adebola, one of Niran's loyal high-ranking warriors and former commander of the guards in the Ondo province, under the late Chief Olusegun Lawal.

Niran was silent for a moment, which was unusual for him, as he nearly always had an immediate answer for all things, as if he possessed the power to read one's thoughts before one gave voice to the words. All the men present turned to him now hopefully, sensing the delay in his response.

'I see no other way,' he finally said. 'We will have to take the fight directly to them. We must meet them on the rivers and take away their advantage.'

Seun raised his eyebrows at Niran's words, but the blood-guard chose to hold his tongue and listen silently to the full plan, as did several of the other men present. However, some did not feel the same obligation, and immediately voiced their concerns.

'My prince, I trust your judgement unequivocally, however, this is one that bears considerable risk, which many may not be able to stomach,' said Achike, another Igbo chief.

'I would like to hear how you propose this action, my prince. For one, we do not have the vessels, nor do we have the experience to navigate those rivers,' Zogo added, which drew more nods of agreement.

'That is not entirely true. We hold the province of Warri, which is almost entirely surrounded by rivers, and a lot of its inhabitants migrated from the River-lands years ago. I remember my father holding court with their elders, who petitioned to settle in those lands with his blessings, wanting a peaceful place away from the troubled province, but also with the desire to stay close to the waters. Besides, they are expert boatmen and fierce warriors. Have you forgotten that they were among the first provinces that initially offered resistance when I began this campaign? They will spearhead our attack on the rivers.'

'That may be so, but we will need many vessels to take across an army that will be considerable enough to inflict a significant blow to our enemies,' said Ikenna.

'We are in no short supply of carpenters, and all we require are a few canoes to take a handful of men over a period, say a day or two, and strategically place them in advantageous locations to lie in waiting.' Now, they all leaned in to listen.

'We simply need to ferry our warriors to all the major rivers that border Calabar territories.' Niran indicated on the map for clarity. 'I suspect that this is where they would deploy their canoes from. From these positions, we can take them with spears when they are on open water. And for the ones that make it through, the Warri canoes will sail upriver to confront them and cut off their escape.'

The men processed the plan for a few moments, seeking the likely pitfalls before anyone spoke.

'That is a bold plan indeed, but our warriors on these strips of land will be cut away from the main army and can easily be set upon if word gets back to the garrisons near the shore,' Adebola observed.

'That is a possibility, yes. But they will remain concealed until the canoes are well clear of the shoreline. Besides, we will require a diversion and a reason to send them running to their vessels. Our main army will attack from the land, spreading their lines across the border in this direction to force the Calabar warriors to abandon their posts, which should hopefully send them straight into our trap. From what I have gathered, this location is where the largest group of warriors and their supplies are located, and that is where we can inflict the most damage,' Niran finished.

The men contemplated Niran's words further, some looking between themselves for approval. In the end, they all acknowledged that the potential reward of taking such a strategically located and vital position outweighed the risk.

'I am in agreement with your plans, my prince,' said Zogo. 'As am I,' said Ikenna, and this was echoed by the other chiefs in attendance.

'Very good. Zogo, I would like you to lead the main army in the attack. Adebola will lead the men that will spring the trap on the islands.'

'And you, my prince? I trust that you will remain here with our reserve warriors just in case we require support?' asked Achike.

'No. I will sail with the Warri boatmen.'

That drew everyone's attention, but none as much as the tall blood-guard Seun, who turned his head sharply with a look of concern distorting his features.

'Is that wise, my prince? We cannot afford to leave our position here unprotected and without proper leadership. I think you should remain with a force strong enough to hold this town lest the Calabar are plotting an attack of their own,' Zogo pleaded, not even attempting to hide the apprehension in his tone.

'That will not be necessary.' Niran turned to Ikenna. 'I would like you to remain here and lead the men while we are gone.'

Ikenna looked pained as he responded to the command. 'My prince, I cannot stay idle while men fight in my place. These are the lands of my forefathers, and I should have the opportunity to defend them.'

'But you have been doing just that, Ikenna. Now, I would have you stay your spear. The people here look to you not only as a chief but as a father. Who better to guide and reassure them at a time like this?' Ikenna could not fault Niran's argument. After all, the army were currently stationed in his hometown of Aviara, which was the closest town to the borders of the Calabar, and one that had suffered a great deal since the battles had started a year ago, with its borders constantly being challenged.

'Yes, let the young men do the fighting. You have already proved yourself a hundred times over, Ikenna,' Achike said, in an attempt to console his old friend, and received a displeased look in return from Ikenna.

'It is settled then.' Niran turned to the royal guard that stood closest to the entrance to the room, one of two that had accompanied him from Ife, a year ago. The other had led the daring rescue in Aba. Both men that he trusted unreservedly, besides Seun, his blood-guards, Adebola and a handful of Adebola's men, who had been the first group to swell the numbers of his followers and helped him gain his foothold in the east.

'Take my message to Warri. Tell the chief of my plans and have him prepare fifty warriors and eight vessels ready to sail in five days from the rivers west of the town of Irri. We will meet him there. This message is only for the ears of the chief and no one else.'

'Your will, my prince,' the royal guard said as he bowed his head and ducked under the timber lintel of the room.

'There is much to prepare. Please, see to your people. We will resume once our allies in Warri confirm they are ready.'

With that, all the men started to disperse, talking amongst themselves as they left the room. Seun, however, stayed behind, as he was never far from Niran's side. The tall warrior obviously had doubts about the plan but had chosen not to voice them in the presence of the gathered chiefs and warriors.

'What is on your mind, Seun? I can sense your trepidation. Please, speak freely my friend,' Niran said without taking his eyes off the plan before him.

'My prince, surely you cannot lead the attack on water. I of all people know the fear you hold in your heart. Let one of the other warriors stand in your place. It would be far more reasonable for you to lead the attack on land,' Seun ventured.

It was true. Niran had an innate fear of large waters. He was the only one amongst the princes that could not swim and had had a near-death experience when he was but a boy in the streams back in Ife, leaving a scar within him that ran so deep that he had never recovered from the trauma. Despite his valour, intelligence, compassion, and gods-given natural ability to be a leader of men, he had always held a feeling of ineptitude hidden in his heart caused by his inability to master the skill of something that came inherently to his siblings. He had found distractions in the pursuit of knowledge and training to mask his fears. But now, he felt that he owed it to himself and the people he may very well come to rule, to be a leader in all things. To face his demons unflinchingly if he was ever to walk in his father's shadow.

He had battled with this for most of his adolescent life and was determined to overcome it and prove to himself that he was worthy of the title he held. Of course, no one except the blood-guards and his siblings knew of this, and he had determined to keep it that way.

'I hear you, but I feel that this is something I cannot shy away from. If I do so now, I will never be the leader I am destined to be. I appreciate your concern, I really do, but do not argue with me on this matter. I have made up my mind, and so it will be. Besides, you are one of the strongest swimmers I know, so what do I have to fear?' he said, favouring Seun with a nervous sideways smile.

Seun stood there for a time and studied the prince, knowing well enough that any protestation would be wasted breath, for he knew that not even the gods could deter Niran once he set his feet on a path.

'Very well, my prince, but I would have you accompany me to the river now. Let us take one of the fishermen's canoes upriver to better see our defences along the coast. If you are to face your fears, what better time to do so than now, eh? It would go some way to easing my tension if you were to experience some of what you will encounter when we do sail into battle. Once you are onboard, you will see that there is no place to run to, or much room to move, for that matter.'

Niran smiled again, knowing Seun always had his best interests at heart. 'What you really want is for me to use the opportunity to make a more informed decision, to see if I can be deterred! A cunning plan, but do not think I will go back on my word. I will accompany you nonetheless, as I cannot deny that the experience would serve me well. But first, I must finish my work here,' Niran replied with another smile.

The chiefs and favoured warriors left the townhouse that Niran had commandeered as his quarters, to enter into a bustling square filled with a multitude of people. There were soldiers and townspeople in every direction going about their day unhurriedly; however, behind the façade of what appeared to be a harmonious community, there was undeniably a sense of tension just beneath the surface.

Ever since the battles had started, the town of Aviara had borne the brunt of the initial and failed invasion of the Calabar. Chief Ikenna had done well in repelling the attack, which most had agreed was down to nothing short of the luck of the gods.

Soon after, Ikenna sent word to Prince Niran, who immediately recognised the importance of securing the strategically located border town and led a contingent of his warriors and some Igbo chiefs to reinforce the borders. His arrival had been greatly received by the townsfolk, and he would soon have no end of people accosting him for all manner of subjects. This did not trouble the prince, as he genuinely cared for the people, happily sharing his time freely whenever he was approached, a trait he had inherited from his father. But many of the chiefs had advised that he become less amenable, knowing that his presence could potentially draw the attention of those that would wish his demise, or seek to use the information of his location to their benefit.

Besides the men that had accompanied him from the start – Seun, two royal guards from Ife, and Adebola and his men from Ondo – each chief had sent their best warrior to join the prince's retinue, for fear of his safety, and he was never left unprotected. Men guarded his every movement from sunrise to sunset, and nothing escaped their observation.

And so it was when one of these guards noticed a woman who had been lingering about the townhouse just as the chiefs had left for their respective dwellings. There was nothing particularly unusual about her, although her attire somewhat stood out; she favoured a dark iro and buba and matching head-tie, dissimilar to the lighter colours worn by the other women in the town in the oppressive afternoon sun, but there was something about the way she sauntered passed him and effortlessly blended into the crowd. He had felt a moment of unease, a brief shiver that passed as suddenly as it had come, so he decided to follow her.

He couldn't take his eyes off her, the way she whisked through jostling warriors hauling weapons and supplies and townsfolk labouring with carts and livestock. It was almost as if she knew where they would place their feet before they did so, and she would move into the openings that they created as though it was something she had practiced.

She was clearly light on her feet, slight of build and energetic. The guard quickened his pace, trying to walk alongside her to glimpse her face, but she always seemed just out of reach, and the throng only seemed to hinder his progress further. Then, she turned her head, as if knowing she was being followed, and looked directly at him and straight into his eyes.

Her gaze stopped him dead in his tracks and his heart almost ceased to beat in his chest. He was suddenly filled with the urge to turn and flee in the other direction, but felt as if invisible hands held him fast to the spot, as her dark eyes tore into him with a look that screamed wordlessly, conveying a silent message that his mind could not quite comprehend.

They both stood there watching each other for the briefest of moments, but it felt like an eternity to the guard, and his throat felt bone dry of a sudden. The woman then began to turn her head, deliberately slowly, all the while watching him under the dark folds of her head-tie, almost as if warning him to abandon his curiosity before she continued on her path away from where he stood.

The moment they broke eye contact, it was as if he was released from bondage, and he knew then that the prince was in danger. Without thinking, he began to shout out and point in the woman's direction. 'Stop that woman! She is a spy!' he shouted as loudly as his voice would allow, then unthinkingly, he shot forward and began to give chase.

No one around him seemed to take heed of his rants at first but people cautiously moved out of his way as he darted past them, shoving, and leaping over obstacles on the ground. He glimpsed the woman turn the corner between two low dwellings and moved quickly in that direction. Other warriors had now noticed the commotion and began drawing weapons as they ran after the guard, calling for others to follow for fear of an attack by the Calabar.

When the guard reached the two buildings and turned the corner, the woman was standing a few paces in front of him waiting, and he almost careened right into her. He desperately tried to avoid her, leaning backwards, and ended up slipping, but quickly gained his feet. She had not even flinched.

'Who are you, woman?' he demanded as he levelled his spear in her direction. She did not utter a word but fixed him with a cool stare. Up close, he could see that she had striking features, beautiful but haunting at the same time, a slender face and piercing dark brown eyes, and the same feeling he had felt but a moment ago started to take a hold of him once again.

Her lips moved slowly, but he heard nothing, as she slowly began to lift her right hand. His mind screamed again, the noise filling his thoughts, but he was unable to move, utterly defenceless like a calf in the presence of a lion, vulnerable, powerless.

She raised her hand to her face, fist clenched and palm facing upwards, then opened her hand and blew at it. A white powder-like substance shot into the guard's face, temporarily blinding him, and he howled out in pain. Just then other warriors arrived to find him rolling around in the gravel, hands pressed to his face and screaming incoherently as if his face had been doused in burning oil.

Some of the warriors tried to comfort and subdue the thrashing man, others searched around the dwelling, but the guard kept repeating that the shadows had come alive and were trying to take him away – the beginnings of the ramblings of a mad man. Only he could see his fears manifested so vividly behind the lids of his eyes.

Besides the guard whose cries rent the air, and the warriors that had followed him, there was no one else around, and the woman he had spoken of was nowhere to be seen.

A BLIGHT ON THE LAND

Toju traced his fingers over the faded inscriptions on the shaft of the spear he had carried along with him from Ife. It was the only reminder of home that he possessed and the only connection he had with his bloodline. The spear had been owned by his great grandfather, King Kayode, and would have seen many a battle and reaped countless souls from the earth if the legend of the man who had first wielded it was to be believed.

Although Toju was never given to sentimental values, he secretly cherished this item, as it was a reminder of who he was and where he came from, a concept that could easily be lost to him in this distant land miles away from the soils of his forebears.

He spun the shaft around in his hand once, enjoying the balance of it, before hanging it up gently on the mounts created to hold it on the wall. He stood there a moment and adjusted its position, so the inscriptions faced him and the broad head caught the light of the morning sun just so.

He had decided against taking it with him, not wanting to appear overly threatening when he treated with the Fulani. He would, however, carry his sword and a small axe, which were lying on the bed behind him. He donned his leather breastplate, which had been cleaned to a high sheen with animal fat, taking great lengths to ensure that all the fastenings were tied just right, before testing the restraints and making sure it was not too tight over his torso.

This was his usual routine on the eve before a battle, and he would prepare for this meeting no differently. Discipline and dedication to his craft were two things that Toju would not, under any circumstances, take for granted.

'Are you ready, my love?' Habibah walked into the room looking every bit the northern princess. She wore a long length of linen kaftan tied at the waist, accentuating her slender but curvy figure. Thick gold bracelets jingled as she walked, and her hair was styled into two thick braids wrapped around the sides of her head and bound at the nape of her neck with thin beads. As she approached him, the rays of the sunlight that filtered through the room struck her, making her dazzle, and Toju could not help but break the sombre expression he had worn just before she entered with a half-smile.

'You are truly a sight to warm the heart,' he said as she came to stand in front of him. He could tell that she was nervous, despite her attempt to mask her fears with a smile of her own. He cupped her face in his hands and lifted her chin to his face.

'There is nothing to fear, Habibah. We have gone over this. I only intend to reason with these people and extend the branch of peace that the emir offers. Nothing more. They would be foolish to bite the hand that bears fruit.'

'Let us hope so. I would only ask of you one thing,' she replied, looking deep into his eyes. 'Promise me that if things do not go to plan, you will flee. Do not follow the voice of your ego. Think of me and all the people that love and depend on you. Promise to come back to me, my love.'

He held her there for a moment, taking in her beautiful features and freezing them in his mind before he spoke.

'I promise you that I will do everything within my strength to return to you. Gods willing, I will have no cause to draw my blade, but know this. If I am threatened, I will not hesitate to defend myself.'

Habibah looked into his eyes, saw the conviction in them and, scarier still, the undeniable spark of excitement deep in those dark pools. She knew that he relished the prospect of riding over the sand dunes to confront this horde, she knew he yearned for it.

She would never understand men of his kind, warriors, always so eager to prove themselves – to be viewed as the strongest, the fastest, the most skilled at arms, the one that others would look to with admiration, envy, or fear. Or could it be that the challenges they set themselves were the only things that filled them with the desire to live? She would never know. What she did know was that she was bound to this man and had given her vows to support his every endeavour, be it ill-conceived or otherwise, and she accepted that.

'That is enough for me,' she said finally and, without another word, she backed him towards the bed until he sat down, then bent to help him tie the loose leather straps of his sandals around his ankles and muscled calves.

They remained in a comfortable yet familiar silence while he finished preparing, then they both stood and walked towards the door. Just as Toju reached the threshold, Habibah grabbed him by the hand and pulled him towards her for a long embrace. They held each other tightly for a moment, and when they disengaged, he took her face in his palms and planted a tender and loving kiss on her brow, before exiting the room, leaving her behind with the ghost of his warmth and his scent. As she watched him leave, she placed her hands over her stomach protectively.

A clear blue sky, without the slightest hint of clouds, filled Toju's vision as he stepped out into the courtyard of the palace. The bright disc of the yellow sun that hung overhead cast its rays on everything around him, making inanimate objects look magnificent as they caught the light. He stood there for a short while and closed his eyes, taking it all in. He took a deep breath, which was chased by the smell of palm trees, fermented milk from the goats and cattle, and leather hides drying in the morning sun. The smell of the north.

He had come to appreciate these scents, although somewhere hidden in his subconscious, he yearned for the smell of home, but he pushed that thought even deeper to focus on what was ahead of him.

'My prince. Your men await you at the gates,' came the voice of Leke, who came to stand beside Toju along with the two royal guards from Ife, and handed him a plain white cloth, the sign of peace, which Toju would tie to the scabbard of his sword.

'Thank you. They did not need to gather on my account. Gods willing, I will only be gone a short while,' Toju replied as he took the cloth and began to tie it around the end of his scabbard.

'Are you really surprised? These men adore you and would sooner go in your place. The least they can do is to see their prince off. The other princes are also waiting for you.'

'This is quite the send-off. I should be honoured,' he said with only the slightest hint of sarcasm.

'They are the ones that should be honoured, to have a man of your status represent them in what could potentially be a pivotal moment for their tribe and, perhaps, their future.'

'We are all honoured, then,' Toju mused as he faced the main gates, purposely choosing not to place too much emphasis on the enormity of his task. He then turned to look at Leke, and his eyes flashed with a gravity that reminded Leke of the man the prince had been before he had taken his bride.

'Stay close to Habibah. I am depending on you. If I have not returned by sunset, take her and my men southeast to my brother Niran. I will still honour my vow to my brother with the support he needs, even if I am no longer here to witness it. Swear this to me, on all the gods, that you will see my wishes fulfilled.' He waited for Leke to acknowledge the command and did not break eye contact.

After only the briefest of pauses, Leke replied. 'I swear it, my prince. I will keep the princess safe and deliver your men to Prince Niran as you have asked.' Deep down, Leke knew that this would be a hard ask. For if Toju did not return, Leke would more than likely find himself convincing Toju's men not to storm the camp to seek the prince's rescue, or join him in his fate, not travelling hundreds of miles away to a foreign land. However, he would honour his prince's command and see it obeyed no matter the cost.

'Good. Now let us see this display of northern might. Nothing fires my heart more than the sight of a formidable army displaying their military splendour!'

Outside the main gates, the northern princes and their personal guards sat their mounts in ceremonial robes, flowing babarigas with intricate stitching detail on the neckline and sleeves and headgear that wound around their heads and loosely over their shoulders, all white fabric against the heat of the morning sun. They all carried long curved swords and daggers, and the younger princes had their bows strapped to their horses in leather pouches. Beyond the princes, in perfectly still and disciplined lines of horses, sat Toju's army, resplendent in full armour, awaiting the arrival of their commander and hero.

As soon as they spied him, a collective war cry pierced the air, the northern warriors' signature sound, and one of the reasons they were often referred to as the screamers by the southerners. Toju's skin prickled with excitement, overwhelmed with pride at the sight of the men that had followed him into many battles over the year he had been in these lands.

The emir had presented him with two thousand men as part of his wedding gift for Habibah's hand, and within a year Toju had increased that number by another thousand or so northern warriors who had voluntarily requested to join the ranks of his army on the back of his repute alone.

As Toju looked on at his men beaming with pride, Usman guided his horse away from the other northern princes to stand next to Toju.

'Are you certain you would not take some of your men with you? A prince should always have an emissary that proceeds him for meetings of this kind, not to mention a reasonable escort. You must take your southern guards at the very least...' Usman implored.

'There is no need for that. Let us not cover old ground, my friend, it has all been decided. Besides, my guards have their orders, so they will be otherwise engaged.'

'I will come with you, then, let us do this together, brother.'

That was the first time Usman had referred to Toju as a brother, and the words truly moved him. He turned to look at his friend's concerned face.

'Come now. Do you have so little faith in me carrying out such a simple task? I seek to deliver a message and gauge the temperature of these people. Nothing more. You almost sound like your sister. But I sincerely appreciate your concern... brother.'

Usman managed a sad smile, just before their attention was drawn to the sound of horses galloping, followed by a cloud of sand. Danjuma and five of his personal guards brought their horses to a screeching halt a few paces from Toju and Usman. Danjuma rode a magnificent black stallion with a shining coat that looked just as majestic as its rider, who also wore a matching black danshiki, a vast contrast to the white attire worn by his brothers.

The future emir of the Hausa cantered towards Toju and Usman. He gave his brother a friendly nod and then turned to Toju with an approving look in his eyes.

'Prince Toju, the emir sends his best wishes and a prayer to the gods to make this a peaceful and swift meeting.'

'You have my thanks, Prince Danjuma. Please extend my good wishes to His Eminence and tell him that I hope to bring good tidings on my return.'

Danjuma inclined his head in acknowledgement. 'Go with the gods, Prince Toju. Let us hope that we will have cause to raise our horns and feast in your honour when you return.'

'As do I, my prince. As do I.' Toju then pulled on his reins, guided his mount through the lines created by his warriors and set off to the border at a gallop, without a backward glance.

Toju had never ventured this far north in all the time he had been in this foreign land, but he felt a tremendous sense of adventure as he spurred his mount further away from the place he had come to know as his second home.

The terrain here was different, still sandy but hillier with spatterings of large rocks that jutted out of the ground like grey giants emerging from the earth. The sand soon gave way to gravel and there was more vegetation dotted around with large, twisted trees that stood like sentries, dried, and withered in the blazing sun.

He passed a few villages, but each time he rode by, the inhabitants scurried away and hid in their dwellings like rats fleeing the paws of a cat. Poverty was evident here, and fear was palpable. Solitary rams stood in open fields, disease-ridden beasts, starved, tracked by multitudes of flies, and ribcages protruding under tightly drawn skin. Broken ploughs lay discarded without the field hands to operate them and the odd goatherd, group of children or mothers with babies tied to their backs under folds of wrappers, roamed the plains with vacant and bulging eyes staring back at him with a mixture of fear and curiosity.

These people had obviously lived with the threat of the Fulani but were clearly not seeking to relinquish the lands that they had once worked, probably for generations; but now, they were too scared to work them. In truth, Toju cared little for them or their plight, but part of him wondered why they had not departed these forsaken lands in search of better opportunities. He could never bring himself to understand the ways of the peasants. So, he rode on without a second thought.

The sun had now reached its highest point in the sky and the temperature soared. Sweat glistened on Toju's brow and arms, and he felt beads run down his back soaking his undershirt. His horse fared no better, sweating profusely from muscled flanks and shiny neck, working tirelessly under Toju's weight. He had pushed the beast hard, not giving it any respite. He wondered whether he should stop to rest his mount but was too eager to reach his destination, and he dug his heels in the flanks of the horse, willing it to move faster.

More time passed and, in the distance, he finally caught sight of a sprawling camp that stretched far beyond the reach of his vision. He had reached the Fulani people. He decided to stop for a while before continuing, to water his horse and gather himself in final preparation for whatever lay beyond. He checked his weapons and made sure that the white cloth was still fastened to his scabbard, while his horse rested, snorting appreciatively as it nibbled on some dry shrubs.

His heart was beating faster now, and he could feel the blood circulating in his veins, while all his senses came alive. He also felt a twinge in his stomach, the same feeling he got just before riding into a wall of spears, and he smiled to himself. His destiny awaited him; this is what he repeated in his head as he observed the camp from afar. Before long, he checked his armour once again, using a rag to wipe away some of the dust from his travels in an attempt to look a little more presentable, before mounting his horse to ride down the last stretch of land between him and the camp.

As he got closer, he observed that the camp was scattered over a vast area of land. There were two hills separated by a deep gorge that had a stream running through it. Tents were spread across both hills in a random pattern of stretched animal hides and colours, interspersed with what appeared to be a network of brown veins, pathways, between sections of tents. Perhaps these people were more organised than they initially appeared. He would soon come to learn this.

Closer still, he saw a cluster of tents at the bottom of the gorge, much larger than the ones above, with rows of large timber stakes angled diagonally outwards. The hills on both sides of the gorge sloped down to level ground towards the mouth of the gorge, and pathways snaked down to intersect at this point. Men could be seen all along the paths, glints of sunlight reflecting off the metal they bore. Whether by coincidence or by design, the camp layout and location were perfectly situated, offering protection and a view in every direction.

As he approached, he discerned men on peaks of protruding boulders dotted about the site. He caught the sounds they made, sharp blasts from horns, which seemed to be repeated by others. Sentries, passing messages on the wind to warn of the presence of an intruder.

He was too far away from each one he passed to make out any discerning features, but he at least saw that they carried longbows. This confirmed that these people were a well organised and cautious people, so he would approach them in a similar vein.

He loosened the straps of his scabbard and raised it above his head, showing the white cloth attached. He had hoped the wind would carry it and let the material flap in the breeze making it more visible, but it drooped limply down to his arm instead. He could only pray that an overzealous scout would not decide to send him an arrow in greeting, making this trip a very short one, but it was too late to turn back, so he urged his horse forward.

The gradient of the terrain he rode on began to slope towards the mouth of the gorge, so he decided to make for the larger tents nestled there, as that was where he suspected the ruler of this tribe would naturally choose to reside, but he slowed his mount to a trot with his white cloth held high to avoid looking threatening.

A few moments passed and he saw columns of men jogging down from both sides of the hill, keeping good order as they converged to the crossing of the two paths. He was much closer now and could make out more of their features. He saw that the men wore short tunics and leather belts, footwear that appeared to be a mix of fabric and leather covering their entire foot to ankle height. Some had greaves on their shins; thick cloth fastened around the legs with a thin plate of metal protecting the shin, and some wore plates of metal across their chest, held in place by the same type of cloth tied behind their backs.

Most carried small circular shields of metal and elaborately large, curved swords, while a handful carried bows with unpleasantly crude-looking barbed arrowheads, nocked and ready to fly.

When Toju was within one hundred paces of the gathered warriors, he brought his mount to a halt and decided to wave his scabbard, letting the white cloth sway from side to side, so there was no mistaking his intent. He repeated this action, but the men ahead of him stood still, unmoving, watching. Perhaps they were waiting for him to bridge the gap, Toju thought. So, still with the sign of peace held above his head, he spurred his horse forward slowly.

About thirty or so paces out, a tall warrior disengaged from the line of men and stepped forward. He was clearly an officer of some rank judging from his bearing. The clothes he wore were like those of the other men but of much finer quality. Leather straps held his chest armour in place, which extended down to his groin and was accessorised with other pieces for protection; connecting plates of armour over his shoulders, thin plates of metal on his arms, and a cap that was wrapped in cloth around his head.

Toju saw that all the men, although dark skinned, were of a much fairer complexion than his people and their hair was curly and fine, rather than thick and knotted like every man and woman he had known. Beards and thick moustaches seemed to be favoured by these men, making them look more imposing, but none of that mattered to Toju. As far as he was concerned, they were but men and they would bleed just the same if the atmosphere were to take a sudden turn for the worst.

The man that stepped forward wore a long, curved sword on the left side of his hip, right arm across his body and his hand gripping the hilt poised to draw as he walked forward. He stopped some paces ahead of Toju and began to speak in a tongue that Toju did not recognise. His tone was clearly hostile, and it appeared he was gesturing with his head, issuing a command of some description.

'I do not understand you, but I come in peace,' Toju replied, pointing to the cloth on his scabbard. The man did not seem to take any notice of this and continued to bark the same word in his guttural tongue. Finally, he took his hand away from the hilt of his sword and gesticulated in an up-and-down motion, pointing at Toju.

'I see. You want me to dismount? As you please,' Toju responded as he swung out of his saddle and landed adroitly on his feet. He stroked his horse on the head down to its nose, stripped the cloth from his scabbard, which he held in one hand, and started to walk towards the warrior.

'Who rules here? I come on behalf of the great emir in the north. Does anyone speak Hausa or Yoruba?' Toju asked, but his tongue was clearly as foreign to this man as the language he was greeted in had been to Toju. Toju had started to lose patience and his exasperation grew further with the threatening tone of the warrior before him, who had now returned his hand to the hilt of his sword and raised his tone. He had also changed his stance; feet apart, one in front of the other, knees bent ever so slightly, back arched forward, ready to lunge at the slightest provocation.

Toju recognised all these signs and willed himself to remain calm and approach the situation rationally, choosing to heed the words of his wife that persisted in the back of his mind.

'See this?' he held the cloth aloft. 'It is a sign of peace! No fighting. Here to talk,' he ventured, but the warrior must have taken Toju's tone and gestures for insolence, and he turned to his men and barked out a series of urgent commands. In an instance, the men started moving to either side of Toju, sword tips pointing in his direction, a message that needed no translator to decipher. There were probably around thirty warriors, teeth bared, and some clearly issuing insults.

"You see how they treat a man such as yourself? They are but lambs before a lion ready to feast. Show them the grave error they have made on this day." The voice whispered in his head.

'You dare to threaten me?' Toju seethed, as he looked around at all the twisted faces now berating him in unison. He could only tolerate so much before the red mist of violence descended over him, but he had the presence of mind to hear Habibah's words deep within – 'Refrain from bloodshed if you can avoid it!' However, her words were drowning in the much louder, more overpowering voice of the god that compelled him to spill blood. *"Show them. They are insignificant pests. Show them so they will forever speak of your name in awe."*

'So be it, you peasants. Let us see if any of you are worthy to stand against me,' he spat, all the while assessing weak spots in their armour, where each warrior stood and how long it would take for them to be within striking range, the most advantageous spot to make a stand. There was no turning back now, and a cold feeling of rage mixed with excitement began to surge through his body. He drew his sword, *"Yes. cover the soil in their blood."*, dropped his scabbard on the ground, and pulled out the axe on his belt. *"They will learn of your name today. Show them!"* The sun on his blade dazzled the closest warrior to him, and he saw the horror in the man's eyes, the sudden recognition that the person who stood before him was not one to be taken for a cornered lamb before slaughter, but a hyena amongst hens.

The tall warrior had the same expression on his face as he drew his own sword, pointed it at Toju and shouted out something that Toju presumed meant "kill him" or "apprehend him". So, he gave in to the voice in his head and proceeded to do what he was made for, hoping that his work would be pleasing to *Ogun,* the god of war.

Voices rang out all around him, as men began to step forward toward him. Being the astute student of combat that Toju was, he had anticipated where the first threats would come from and how he would react, and his instincts had never failed him.

The first two men that came for him acted out of nervousness rather than any real intent to commence the proceedings. The one in front swung from a high stance, long blade slicing through the air diagonally towards Toju's head. He sidestepped almost into the swing, ducked under the falling blade, and used his left hand holding the axe to smash into the back of the sword as it swept harmlessly away from him. The momentum of the warrior's swing and the assistance from Toju's counter caused the heavy sword to continue in its path, which ended up across the knee of the man that came in behind the first, who screamed as the blade bit into his leg and shattered the bone on impact.

The man who had swung the blade, still in shock at Toju's speed and the fact that he had just crippled his companion, now stood with his side exposed to Toju, who wasted no time in bringing his other hand with his sword down into the man's neck, dropping him quickly. Without a moment to lose, Toju darted forward; there were many men to kill, and he had to take down as many as he could before he was overwhelmed by their greater numbers.

He came in high at the next man, leaped as he extended his sword into the man's neck in mid-air, landed and swept low, turned one hundred and eighty degrees, axe above his head, blocking a strike and hacking at a leg on the other side. Spinning back to the sword he had blocked, he drove his own sword upwards, underneath the armour. *"Yes! I will drink of their souls and bathe in their blood!"*

He kicked the dead man away from his blade into another, dodged a wild swing, hacked with his axe at the hand that held the sword, moved sideways, parried another blow, but caught the edge of the sword with the bottom of his hooked axe head and controlled the wrist of the man that wielded the sword, causing him to swing his sword towards another, while slashing him below the beltline.

Within the blink of an eye, the peace had been shattered. The fight was fast-paced and brutal, and no quarter was given. Toju suddenly remembered the archers. He parried another swing from behind him and quickly scanned the tangle of men. Luckily for him, when the fight had started, the men had come at him without a sense of order, all discipline lost. Many had run across themselves to reach him, which served him as a shield against the archers, who had not moved from their original position since the fight started.

Toju kept his eyes on them and tried to remain outside of their line of sight, as they were clearly waiting to get a clear shot at him. He continued to move around so that men were always positioned between him and the archers and continued to cut them down one after the other, all the while, slowly inching toward the archers. *They are no match for a true warrior. A fitting sacrifice you have provided.*

There were two men with shields that now stood between him and the archers, the others were circling, choosing not to attack recklessly after witnessing so many of their companions fall under Toju's blades. One of the archers had an arrow drawn back halfway, ready to shoot, and Toju decided to act. With cat-like speed, he darted to his next opponent and feinted to his right for long enough to cause one of the shield bearers to stumble in the opposite direction, leaving a clear line for the archer to make a shot, which he did. The arrow narrowly missed the man who had stumbled with the shield, and he knew it as he took his eyes away from Toju for a moment to yell over his shoulder to the man that had taken the shot.

Toju was on him in an instant, crashing his shoulder into the first shield and sending the man sprawling backwards, then spinning away and towards the archer. He ran at him at full tilt, almost in a crouched position, both arms extended to his sides bearing his bloodied weapons. The man was halfway between fitting another arrow onto his bow when he spotted Toju and clumsily dropped the arrow in horror. Before he could react, Toju's axe came chopping down on the man's exposed forehead.

The next archer was also caught in a paralysis of sorts, between fear and indecision, which made him pay dearly. Toju swung for him, and the man raised his bow to defend himself out of sheer instinct and the innate characteristic of self-preservation. The bow snapped in half and the sword travelled on to slice across the man's sternum. None of the archers wore breastplates like their companions.

The blow was not hard enough to cause a fatal wound, the snapped bow had taken the brunt of the attack, but it was enough for the man to roll away and flee, both hands clutching tightly to his bloodied chest. The rest of the archers took a cue from their companion and dropped their bows in fright, leaving the bloodshed on the plains behind them.

Toju paid them no further attention and immediately spun around to the remaining warriors behind him. They were not as confident as they had been earlier, seeing that this one man had killed more than half their number in mere moments, but the commander of the men now stepped forward barking out orders to his warriors, spittle flying from his mouth as he spoke like a man deranged.

It was too late for them now. *Ogun* was amongst them, and he would have his fill of blood through the hands of his vessel. Toju was oblivious to the hesitance of the men, all he saw were blades pointed toward him with the sole intent of doing him harm. And he would return the favour in kind. Gone were any notions of diplomacy and reason. In its place, the wrath of a god and the pride of a deadly warrior.

The commander was clearly urging his men forward, which they were reluctant to do, but some had begun to shuffle forward tentatively, shaky swords held before them. It was obvious that these men were not used to the skills of their opponent, perhaps men had always run before them. Not anymore. Never had they witnessed a single warrior of such skill oppose them so belligerently, showing no regard for who they were or what they stood for, a lesson only a few of them would live to learn from.

Toju was moving again. He had always been one to take the initiative and push forward when others pulled back, and this was no different. Now, he aimed for the commander. A swift decapitation of the head that controlled the body was always a sure way to completely extinguish the flame that fuelled a group of warriors' resolve.

As he dashed towards the commander of the warriors, he pulled his arm back and threw his axe, which spun in the air at chest height. The warrior's eyes went wide as he saw the axe hurtling towards him, but he reacted surprisingly well. He immediately took a step back and brought his sword up and across his body, just in time to deflect the axe at the mid-section of his sword, sending it spinning away harmlessly to the side.

It took a skilled swordsman to pull off such a manoeuvre, but it was his last time demonstrating his skill. He had focused on the axe far too long, watching its trajectory as it flew to his far left, but this was only a distraction. The real threat came in much quicker than he had time to fully react to. As he turned to face Toju, the prince was already a pace or two in front of him, coming in fast.

Toju thrust his sword forward, aiming at the man's ribs, the gap between the armour, since the warrior's body was still half turned from his earlier stance. In the same instance, the commander turned to face Toju square, which granted him a few more moments on earth.

The sword just scraped the armour of his breastplate and travelled down towards his thigh, slicing through it, and leaving a gaping wound that spilt an unusually large amount of blood on the ground. The blow was clearly mortal, as the bleeding could not have been staunched in time by any healer. The man fell on his back, crying out in agony and terror. Toju stood over him for a moment, *"This one must suffer!"*, but decided to leave him where he lay as he was no longer a threat. He then turned to the remaining men now visibly trembling. *"No one should be left alive. Kill them all!"*

'I came to you in peace, and yet you chose to insult me. Now you must all follow this road to wherever it ends. Time to face your gods like true warriors,' he said, as he started to walk slowly towards them, leaving a trail of blood that dripped from his sword.

Without warning, a booming voice issuing a series of commands in the same foreign tongue echoed across the field. Loud, clear, and permeating with authority. Toju spun round ready to defend himself against another attack and saw that more warriors were racing down the slopes on both sides, and from the larger tents further behind, all converging on his position. It seemed hopeless. There was no way he would be able to defend himself against so many. He would inevitably be taken, or killed in the process, but strangely, he felt nothing. No fear, no anxiety, no great sense of impending doom, just peace.

"Their numbers mean nothing. I will guide your hands to victory, as I have done before now. You have nothing to fear. We will reap these mortal souls from the earth, together!" whispered the voice in his head.

Toju had to suppress the voice that dwelled in a deep corner of his mind. He could not allow himself to utterly succumb, as he feared he would travel down a path that he was not willing to place his feet in. But it was always a challenge. Much easier to embrace his darkness, especially when the red haze of battle was on him; however, Habibah's words floated somewhere deep in his subconscious, like the flickering light of a candle in a sea of shadows.

He forced himself to focus, to be guided by his rational mind and not by his blades. He then saw the man who had spoken the command and caught everyone's attention. At the head of the warriors, who had now amassed in Toju's path, stood a man of average height. His facial features were hardly impressive or as imposing as his voice had suggested. In fact, he seemed to have an air of genuine kindness about him – warm eyes framed by delicate wrinkles and crow's feet, upturned thin lips parted in a subtle smile, and a well-groomed and oiled beard that hung down to his chest. He was clearly a man of status from his attire – he wore a long flowing gown of good quality, which reached down to his ankles, tied at the waist with another length of cloth. Even from where Toju stood, he could tell that the fabric of his attire was expensive from the way it shone when the sun hit the ripples it made from the light breeze that swept through the path.

The man also wore an elaborate cap that was bound in more swirling cloths, not too dissimilar to the head wrappings of the northern lords. However, the main distinguishing feature was the gold he wore – rings embedded with rare stones and bracelets that matched the colour of the sun.

This man was not only wealthy but bold, as he proceeded to walk towards Toju with the confidence of a man that knew that the presence of the warriors at his back was more than enough to deter an irrational decision from being made. Little did he know of the man he was attempting to negotiate with. He at least had the decency to raise his hands at shoulder height to show that he was unarmed and meant to treat peacefully, which Toju granted.

'Greetings, great prince. It is an honour to make your acquaintance,' he said in perfect Yoruba with only a hint of an accent. Toju was taken aback by his fluency and grasp of his mother tongue and could not help but feel a pang of nostalgia for his homeland hearing this man speak.

'You speak my language well for a foreigner. What is your name?' Toju asked, still brandishing his bloodied weapons before him.

'My name is Hassan, emissary and chief advisor to the shahbanu of these great people and fearless warriors. We were informed of your coming and hope to treat with you regarding the future of our peoples,' he said as he inclined his head slightly.

'So, is this how you *treat* with all your guests, or only the ones of note? I must say that I am not impressed by your hospitality. Sending men to accost me before I even have a chance to hold court. Or was this some sort of test?' Toju asked with an edge of steel in his tone. His blood was still up, and even the hint of a slight was enough to tip the balance of violent darkness that was slowly receding from him, but the outcome of this discussion hung on a thread, and Hassan sensed it. Toju thought absently that it would be a pity to get blood on this man's fine attire.

Hassan looked around at the carnage Toju had left in his wake, the bloodied corpses of warriors, the commander who desperately clung to his wounded leg, hopelessly trying to staunch the bleeding as he groaned in a low consistent murmur, the warriors that stood like scared goats with relief and fear plastered on their pitiful faces. He then turned back to Toju with a look that conveyed a multitude of emotions – wonderment, fear, and genuine regret.

'The legend that precedes you is not a thing of falsehood. Great prince, I assure you that this is not how we treat guests.

There obviously has been a misunderstanding, some error of judgement that I can only apologise for. Our men would have simply been carrying out their duty and perhaps felt threatened by your actions'

'Threatened by my actions? By all the gods' mercy, I flew a white cloth! Do your people not acknowledge this as a sign of peace? Or perhaps, the only colour you recognise is the colour of fresh blood. Please tell me!' Toju demanded, the earlier sensation of violence slowly rising in him again.

'No, no, great prince. I do not mean to offend you. Please accept my sincere apologies. Allow us to receive you in a proper and appropriate manner. One that befits someone of your status. Please, come with me. I assure you that no further harm will come to you. And I most certainly do not intend to damage our reputation in your view, any further than we may have already done. I swear it on the one true god.' Hassan had his head bowed as he spoke, with his hands held forward almost in supplication.

Toju considered him for a few heartbeats before he replied. 'Very well. Take me to this shahbanu at once. I have already spent much more time than I had intended here, and I will not waste another moment.'

Hassan looked up with an expression like he had been struck across the face as he eyed Toju's blood-spattered armour and the weapons in his hands with already congealing blood clinging to them.

'Apologies, great prince, but you must be bathed and presented as your status demands before the shahbanu.'

Hassan looked pained to speak but continued awkwardly. 'A certain level of… decorum must be observed. No offence intended, great prince, but I hope you can understand.'

Toju could not help but be amused at the man's discomfort, but he had a point. After all, this was what the northerners practised. They believed that cleanliness was next to godliness, and the emir would never admit anyone to his presence unless he was made to be clean and presentable.

'Fair enough. I accept. I make it also my policy to have a clean blade when I am in the presence of great lords, and matching clothing would be welcome. Lead the way, Hassan.'

Hassan cringed at the response, but visibly let out a breath of relief, and his next few words stumbled out of his mouth like goats suddenly set free from a locked gate.

'Yes, of course, great prince. I will have servants and a warm bath drawn for you at once. Please, please, this way.' He indicated in the direction of the large tents.

He made a flick of his wrist, and the warriors that stood barring their path immediately parted as if a stampeding elephant was about to come charging through. Toju realised that this man, as awkward as he was, possessed considerable power amongst these people, and made a mental note to remember this, as he may yet call upon the man's influence in the future. They both started making their way towards the tents.

THAT WHICH
IS LOST

The melodic sounds of scores of talking drums and agogô bells heralded the procession that came through the streets of Ogun. Women, festooned with anklets and bracelets of cowry beads that chimed as they danced, and children added their voices to the beaten-out tunes, singing songs of jubilation that created an atmosphere of pure euphoria. The streets were awash with a kaleidoscope of bright and vibrant colours; swirling fabrics, dyed clothing fashioned from animal hides, beads, feathers, and masks donned by almost everyone in sight. Even the low-born and beggars were gifted new clothing for this special occasion, not to be left out of the celebrations that had infected the community.

There was much cause for rejoicing in the city of Ogun. Not only had the gods seen fit to bestow twenty of the realm's fabled warriors and the last of the once-thought-annihilated Modakeke tribesmen, on the people, augmenting their growing military power, but they had also been blessed with a new chief. A young and noble chief from an unquestionable bloodline to usher them into a new era of prosperity and good fortune. *Ogun,* the god, was surely smiling down on them.

Enitan, the often reserved boy, had not wanted any elaborate ceremony as tradition demanded, content with the small observance he had received when he was anointed chief, but as soon as word got out that the old Chief Kola had handed over the reins of leadership to his only living grandson, the people demanded to celebrate him, to show him their loyalty and gratitude and welcome him into the bosom of Ogun officially.

Surprisingly, many of the chiefs of the western provinces had accepted him without question, all too eager to extend their vows of fealty and pledge their spears to Enitan. But there were still a few that loathed the idea of a boy chief that had appeared from nowhere and now wielded more power than he had any right to, or knew what to do with.

The lords who refused to recognise Enitan's rule were from the most prominent families in the west. Their bloodline was pure and could be traced back in history almost as far as Enitan's ancestors, who had ruled Ogun for centuries. They had hoped that the province and, along with it, the chief-taincy, would be evenly split and passed to them, since the chief apparently had no heirs to speak of, and now their plans had been dashed to the wind with the arrival of Enitan.

Adedeji had sent out contingents to each family, giving them the opportunity to accept the hand that fate and the gods had dealt and to submit to their new chief, but he soon found out that with ancient bloodlines came deep-rooted pomposity and an innate sense of entitlement that he could scarcely fathom. These men had made their position clear, and in so doing, all but spat in the face of their new liege lord. Adedeji had informed Enitan that he would need to set an example. He could not be seen to entertain dissent from lesser men. Ogun was watching. As was being displayed today, he would have to put on a show, one that his enemies would not soon forget, and show the people that he had what it took to rule.

But today was a day of celebration, no politics, no plots. It was about the people, and nothing would be allowed to taint the festive occasion.

Enitan sat on a throne atop a raised dais that had been erected in the town square, in the shadow of a mighty mahogany tree that offered a respite to the blistering sun. Under the tree had recently been home to a mentally challenged vagrant; however, the man had not been seen around these parts for some time now. Adedeji and Ayo stood at either side of Enitan's shoulders, with the Modakeke warriors arrayed about the dais in full, newly made armour, each looking resplendent as they held their spears, and with expressions that gave nothing away other than the clear message that the chief was not to be approached without prior consent.

'How long do you suppose the ceremony will last?' Enitan asked as he adjusted his grandfather's ceremonial cap, which rested on his head awkwardly. It was a cap made for a grown man, far too big for his small head, but Enitan liked it just the way it was, fancying himself more regal, but most of all, honoured to wear the accessory that had rested upon the heads of his ancestors.

'It is hard to tell, my chief. We, unfortunately, are at the whim of the people today. It is them who have organised the proceedings. So, I am afraid we can but indulge them with smiles and words of encouragement,' responded Adedeji, who was enjoying the celebration; a welcome sight to him, far from the bloodshed he had witnessed for so many years.

'I hear that there will be wrestling. I am told that many contestants have travelled from all over the western provinces to compete, and you will honour the winner with those tubers of yams and palm oil,' said Ayo excitedly as he jerked his head in the direction of the neatly piled root vegetables and large calabashes that had been placed at the foot of the dais.

'Ah. So that is what all the food is for. I was thinking someone was going to offer them to me as a gift. I could have at least been informed that I would need to make a speech!' Enitan said, with a little concern in his voice.

'No need to overthink it. You just say whatever comes naturally to you. A good chief must learn how to improvise and how to address an audience at any given moment. What better opportunity would you have to practise, eh?' replied Adedeji.

'I suppose you are right, but it does not make the prospect any less daunting.'

'Bah. It is nothing, just smile and offer them praise for their performance. Also, try to make it personal and genuine.

Speak on something you noticed about their skill or strength. I'm sure the words will come to you.'

'I hope so.'

Just then, the drummers and other musicians entered the square, drowning out the chatter and diverting the attention of all the spectators that had gathered around. The drummers were followed by the dancers – the women and children – then finally several strapping young men. They wore only cloths tied around their waist and groins, but they were all fine specimens of men in their prime. Their bodies were oiled to accentuate their physiques, pects bulging, biceps and thighs knotted with muscles and veins, rippling with every movement as they flexed and walked along to the music and the adoration of the bystanders.

There were only twelve of them, a far cry from the number that would normally have participated, which tended to be several scores. This was another reminder of the devastation wrought by the war of the tribes a year ago, where so many men, young and old, had needlessly lost their lives, ripples of which were still being felt, as Enitan saw the odd man or woman look on solemnly, some shedding silent tears, presumably remembering a son, brother or husband that would have competed today, but had marched out to the drums of war, never to return. Called upon not only by their duty but by the gods themselves.

The procession made its way around the square, making a show of just how skilfully the participants danced or played their instruments of choice, before coming to a halt some paces away from the dais. One of the lords from a neighbouring town stepped forward. He wore a flowing agbada with multiple patterns embroidered on it – the sign of a wealthy man – folded up on each shoulder, revealing his hairy arms. He cleared his throat before addressing Enitan.

'Prince Enitan, son of King Jide Adelani. Thank you for granting us the opportunity to rejoice in your name on such a monumental occasion. We are truly honoured to have a living child of the late king amongst us and to take up the mantle of chief of all the western provinces. May your reign be long and prosperous. May the gods *Olorun* and *Ogun* bestow their blessings on you and guide you as you embark on this sacred journey of leadership. May they blind the eyes of your enemies and bind their hands, so they will not see or seek to raise weapons against you. *Olorun*, we call on your name,' he finished, and everyone around intoned the god's name in unison. '*Olorun*, we give praise to you.'

'Now, without further delay, I would like to present to you the wrestlers, fine and strong young men from all over the region, here to fight in your honour for the privilege of joining the ranks of your great army, my chief.'

Enitan surreptitiously looked sideways at Adedeji. Another detail, which he had failed to be communicated to him. Hopefully, there would be no further surprises. The spokesman continued in his booming voice, now turning to address the people gathered in the square.

'We must thank our new chief for his great generosity and the bounty he has provided to all the peoples of the west.

There is no better way to show our appreciation than to put on a great show, a display of our talents as a people, our strength, our resilience, and our courage! Let us begin.' He finished just as women appeared and started to hand out local produce and other items of food stock. Before long, the air around the square was permeated with the smell of cooking; an assortment of meats spitted and grilled, corn and ground nuts roasting over open fires, soups and vegetables stewing; no mouth would go unfed on this day.

Enitan's nostrils caught the whiff of a mixture of aromas that made his stomach growl. 'When he said, "my great generosity", does that mean I am the one feeding the people today?' he assumed aloud.

'Indeed, you are, my prince. Though all the prominent families in the region donated something or other, the bulk of it would have come from the palace. A good chief must also be seen to be generous,' Adedeji said with a wink, which made Ayo let out a chuckle at Enitan's surprised reaction.

'Well, if I am contributing the lion's share, then I must have first choice of all the prime cuts!' Enitan said with a broad smile as he patted his stomach. Ayo could only smile at his young charge, finally seeing a glimmer of the carefree child he had always been before destiny had altered his life. He just hoped that the prince's mood would remain so for the rest of the day.

A large area had been cleared to serve as the ring where the wrestlers would fight. They were then made to draw marked sticks from a leather sack. The men with matching symbols on their sticks would be paired up to fight.

'Care to put a wager on one of these fine young men, my prince?' Ayo asked with a raised eyebrow 'I hear the local favourite is that one over there. He goes by the name of "The Cat", as his back has supposedly never touched the ground in any contest,' he continued, pointing at an athletically built man shredded with lean muscles.

'I am not one to encourage gambling but, given the occasion, my coin is on the brute over there. Look at the size of him! It would be a short contest for any man he lays his hands on, surely,' Adedeji cut in, pointing at a massive man with bulging muscles who rotated his shoulders back and forth and eyed up the competition.

'I think I will go for him.' Enitan pointed to an average-sized man who was not as muscular as his counterparts but stood confidently appraising the men around him. There was nothing remarkable about him, besides the swollen antihelix on both ears, but it was more the look he had in his eyes, as if the competition had already been won and he was just going through the motions for the sake of it. 'Yes. That is who I pick.'

Adedeji and Ayo both looked at each other and then back to the man Enitan had singled out.

'Are you sure, my prince? I would hate to take your coin so easily,' Ayo said, only half expecting Enitan to change his mind.

'I am sure. Shall we say two gold pieces?' Enitan replied confidently, all the time never looking away from the man.

'Fine by me,' Adedeji said.

'Me too!' agreed Ayo.

The first few elimination matches were uneventful, the competitors grappled and struggled with themselves, the aim being to successfully pin down their opponent with their back to the ground before they were declared the winner and moved on to the next round. Men were thrown, tripped and tackled, each exhibiting their strength and cunning, all to the cheers from the crowd that steadily got intoxicated from the palm wine and food that was shared amongst them.

The brute made easy work of his opponent, slamming him on the ground with such force that he had to be carried out of the ring unmoving, but otherwise had no life-threatening injuries. The Cat was nimble and lived up to his name, dancing around his opponent and performing acrobatic feats, which set the crowd roaring with excitement, before throwing the man he faced over his hip and rolling on top of him to make sure his back was flat on the ground. The people cheered even more loudly; he was clearly the favourite.

Then came Enitan's pick. He seemed to struggle with a man that was a clear head taller than him, and the fight went on for longer than most. There were times that he was thrown, but he always managed to find his feet when he landed and never let his back touch the ground. His opponent soon became impatient and tried to perform a diving tackle to take him to the ground, but Enitan's wrestler seized the moment. He expertly spun away and positioned himself at the man's back, wrapped his forearm around the man's neck pulling him backwards, whilst extending his leg behind him to complete the trip. The man came crashing down to the ground in a puff of dust and Enitan's wrestler, still moving, came in front to place his knee on the man's chest to make sure that his opponent's back was flat on the ground. The crowd went wild, cheering their appreciation for the display of mastery of technique.

'Did you see that? Enitan said enthusiastically, as he bounced up and down in his chair, hardly able to contain himself.

'Do not get too ahead of yourself, my prince. Even if he makes it past the next round, that monster over there just has to grab him, and it will be a very quick bout indeed,' Adedeji said, also thoroughly enjoying the contests. Nothing pleased him more than to see men in combat of any form.

'He would have to catch him first. Did you not see how he moved?' Enitan replied.

Ayo just laughed at Enitan's reaction, his heart lifting further to see the elation in the young chief. Maybe the contest is exactly what Enitan needed, he thought, and decided to talk to him about making these types of competitions a regular occurrence, and not only for celebrations.

The next rounds saw more men eliminated. The brute ended up getting disqualified, to Adedeji's displeasure, for throwing a man clear from the ring and almost into the crowd. He had initially tried to throttle the man he fought after he took him to the ground face down from a devastating throw, earning him a warning, before flinging him so high that he dislocated one of his shoulders on impact with the hard ground. The crowd loved it, cheering, and laughing uncontrollably, but this went against the strict rules of the contest; for contestants to engage each other within the confines of the ring, not to gouge at the eyes, strike the groin, intentionally break bones, and not to deliberately try to kill opponents. The injured wrestler won the fight on this technicality, but he was clearly unfit to continue and ended up retiring shortly afterwards.

The wrestler called The Cat and Enitan's warrior made it through their own fights and to the final bout, bringing the event to a climax. Everyone around the ring, including the prince and his retinue, enthusiastically cheered them on, chanting their names like heroes of a thousand battles.

The Cat came swaggering into the ring like he owned it, all teeth and playing up to the crowd. The other contestant was the complete opposite, with no fanfare, just a calm and serious expression, focusing on the man that stood across from him on the gravel.

Enitan rose from his seat and raised his hands, signalling for calm, while the Modakeke warriors began to thump the ends of their spears in the ground to draw attention to the prince and bring the people to order.

'You have both displayed a tremendous amount of skill here today, and your places in this final event are well deserved. I have really enjoyed watching and learning from you, along with all the other contestants. Fight with honour and may victory favour the better man!' Enitan said loudly to more cheers from the crowd.

'What did I say? I told you that the words would come to you. That was exceptionally done, my prince,' Adedeji offered with a bow, which was rewarded with an excited flash of teeth from the young prince, just before the drums began to beat indicating the commencement of the final bout. A deadly silence soon befell the square, and most were on their feet, some craning their necks to get a better view.

Both men circled, watching each other, waiting for the opportunity to strike, then in a blink of an eye, they both lunged, almost at the same time, and they were in a clinch. The noise that followed from the crowd was deafening.

Both men struggled, arm over arm, trying to secure a firmer grip, muscles straining, teeth gritted and grunting with every effort. The Cat managed to hook both his arms under his opponent and clasp his fingers together behind him, aiming to lift the man from the ground and throw him from the side with a twist of his hips. The other man anticipated this move and immediately sprawled, kicking his legs wide behind him and dropping his hips.

They struggled in this position for a heartbeat and then the other man got The Cat in a tight headlock, trying to drag him to the ground. They both crashed to the floor on their sides and The Cat instinctively curled his body towards the other's, so as not to give him leverage to tighten the lock further. The Cat managed to pry himself free, and they were on their feet again, instantly colliding back into a clinch.

A quick turn of the hips and a throw saw The Cat hurled over, but he landed on his feet with the skill of an acrobat, to more cheers. He then ducked under an attempted grab, went for the waist of his opponent with both arms wrapped around him and quickly placed himself behind him. Again, he tried to throw the man backwards, but the other saw this coming and again spread his legs wide to anchor himself to the ground. They strained against each other, panting, chests heaving, sweat dripping, and limbs slippery, making it difficult to maintain a firm grip. The other man suddenly twisted his body within the grip of The Cat, so they were facing each other. He shifted his lower body to one side and managed to hook a leg behind The Cat, tripping him. Again, both fell to the floor in a tangle of limbs, each man trying to roll on top of the other until they were both coated in gravel and dirt all over.

The other man managed to mount The Cat, who arched his back, so it wasn't flat against the ground, while using his hands to try and smother the man on top of him, but it was futile. The other man swept both of The Cat's arms away violently and hooked both of his feet behind the shins of his opponent, kicking his legs out and spreading him flat on the gravel.

'We have a new champion!' roared the man in the agbada, and the crowd exploded with a mix of emotions, some jubilant while others lamented in disappointment and rage, clearly having backed the wrong fighter, and paying for it in coin.

Both fighters got to their feet and The Cat was gracious enough to raise the hand of the other man and display him to the crowd, followed by an embrace in recognition of his strength and a sign of respect.

'It seems our prince has quite the eye for untapped talent. A very good choice indeed!' Adedeji said as he clapped his hands at the performance.

'I cannot believe I won! I must be favoured by the gods today.' Enitan laughed, still amazed at his good fortune.

'Favoured by the gods or an extremely lucky choice! But I refuse to be seen as a sore loser, so congratulations, my prince. And a perfect addition to your growing army,' Ayo said with a smile accompanied by a half bow.

'I think both will make fine additions. Even the brute that was disqualified earlier,' Enitan replied with a wink at Ayo, who responded with a conspiratorial smile as if he had known this would be Enitan's decision all along.

'Are you sure about the brute? A man that cannot follow simple rules in a fair and bloodless contest may lack the discipline required to stand within a wall of spears and follow orders. A warrior without discipline is not only a burden unto himself but also, even more, for those that stand by his side,' Adedeji remarked.

'We all saw him fight and there is no doubt that his raw strength and brutality would serve well in battle. His skill would be wasted tilling a field or hunting wildlife. I would rather put him to better use. Maybe becoming a warrior would give him a purpose, don't you think? Also, I know that the day will come when I will eventually have to face my uncle in battle. When that day comes, I would like to have warriors like him at my back,' Enitan finished and received a surprised look from Adedeji.

'I agree with the prince. We need strong men to defend our land. Men that will strike fear in the enemy and will have the courage to do the things that most will not,' Ayo added.

'You continue to amaze me, young prince. It seems that you have inherited some of your father's wisdom. If this is your wish, I will see to his training personally. Maybe we can make a fierce warrior out of him yet,' said Adedeji.

'I am glad you agree, Adedeji. Can we now conclude our business here? I am not sure how much longer I can bear having to smile, wave and give good speeches, and the noise here is starting to give me a headache!' Enitan beckoned the man officiating over the event and hastily whispered some commands into his ear.

The man then turned back to the crowd with raised arms, motioning to the crowd for calm, with the assistance of the modakeke, who again thumped their spear ends into the ground.

'Townspeople. Friends. We have a winner!' More roars from the crowd. 'These men have fought with honour and grace, well, most of them did.' Laughter and jeers from the crowd. 'But fought they have, and they have proved their worth under the eyes of our great protector *Ogun,* god of war, and our chief, Prince Enitan. Now the time has come for the winner to claim his prize and the coveted title "onija nla", the greatest wrestler of the tribes. Step forward.'

The man who had won walked towards the dais, head bowed as a show of respect, with dust still coating his features and his hair. Enitan stood to address the man.

'What is your name, great wrestler of the tribes?' Enitan asked.

'My name is Dami, my prince.'

'Dami, you fought with bravery, almost as if the gods themselves lent you their abilities. I was particularly inspired by your fighting spirit and determination, and I can only hope that the example you have set here today will be noted by all the warriors and people of Ogun. As your reward, I grant you the honour of joining my royal guard and a place in my army. I hope you will serve well.'

Dami was clearly astonished by the honour granted him and could only look at his feet in shocked silence as he pondered his response. He had expected that his prize would not go beyond the food stock that had been neatly stacked next to the dais.

'My prince. My chief. I am at a loss for words. I am eternally grateful for your generosity, and I will serve you with honour and pride until the gods deem it time for me to pass from this life,' he replied, with his head bowed even lower to emphasise his gratitude.

'Of that, I have no doubt. Please, take these gifts as a token of my appreciation for your acceptance,' Enitan replied, indicating the provisions that would go a long way to feeding Dami and his family for at least one moon. Enitan then addressed the crowd, raising his voice until he was almost shouting, his high-pitched, boyish voice coming out as a squeak, not having cracked as yet.

'I would also like to honour some of the other men that have shown their strength and skill today, who I feel must be rewarded. The wrestler called The Cat and the big fighter over there. Please, step forward.' Some of the crowd booed the big brute as he shuffled forward to stand beside Dami in front of the dais.

'Both of you deserve to be rewarded for your display today and you will also be granted places in my army as spear bearers.' They both thanked Enitan profusely, clearly showing their surprise at being given an opportunity of such magnitude.

Enitan then turned to the brute. 'You, however, will need to prove that you are worthy of the position granted to you. I would see much more restraint and willingness to accept the rule of command. Do not make me regret my decision here today.' The big man bowed his head as much as his thick neck allowed, swearing to uphold the honour bestowed on him.

The crowd cheered once more, and the serving of drinks and food resumed as people began talking amongst themselves about the great competition they had witnessed and the generosity of their new chief. Just then, two royal guards came to stand by Adedeji and hurriedly relayed a message that appeared to trouble the old warrior. Once they had passed on their message, they headed off back in the direction they had come, towards the palace.

'My prince, there is news that awaits you at the palace. We should return with all haste, as it is of some importance,

I am told,' Adedeji said to Enitan, who began to feel slightly anxious at the change in tone of the old warrior.'

'Please lead the way,' Enitan replied, as the Modakeke warriors formed up behind the prince, who marched off after Adedeji and Ayo.

When they arrived, several of the guards they walked past had peculiar looks plastered on their faces, which was deeply unsettling, but Enitan chose to ignore them and head towards the bedchambers of his grandfather.

In truth, he had feared the worst for the old man for some time now and prepared himself for whatever greeted him behind the large iroko doors. He had known that this day would come sooner rather than later, but the reality of losing his only blood relative would still be a great personal loss, and would be no easier on his emotions regardless of how prepared he felt.

There were more guards outside the doors to the bedchamber, Wale among them, as he stood with his arms crossed and spoke to a man that was dressed in weathered armour and a rag for a cloak. The man had a shock of unruly hair and an unkempt beard interspersed with iron grey.

There was something vaguely familiar about him, something in his eyes and the way he looked at Enitan when he noticed him. The sight of this stranger stirred a suppressed emotion, a distant memory, like a hazy dream that you desperately try to recollect the details of, once awoken.

Enitan did not allow his gaze to linger but immediately turned to Wale, who broke away from his conversation as soon as he noticed the prince flanked by Ayo and Adedeji.

'What news? Is my grandfather...' Enitan could not bring himself to finish the sentence.

'No, no, my prince. Your grandfather is fine, but I think you need to go inside at once. And it would be best if you entered alone.' The last words were uttered oddly, which made Ayo and Adedeji steal a quick glance at each other. Enitan had also picked up on it and turned to look at both of his most trusted men.

After a split second, Ayo nodded and placed his right hand on the hilt of the long blade he always carried on his waist, and then rested his left hand over the wrist of his right. Enitan understood the gesture from his time spent with Ayo traversing the unforgiving landscape of the west a year ago when they were forced to flee Ife. They had devised a series of hand signals and gestures to be used when speech was not an option. A secret language only they understood and still practised. The sign meant that Enitan was to move with caution, to take stock of anything and everything around him, but most importantly, it meant that Ayo would watch over him and would leap to his defence if he felt that the prince's life was threatened.

This reassured Enitan. He turned to face the timber doors, swallowed hard, and pushed them open.

Old Chief Kola's chambers was spacious, with two large windows that offered plenty of natural light, which filtered through the room, painting it in a reddish-orange hue from the setting sun, as if the room was ablaze with fire. Beautifully crafted pieces of furniture and bronze sculptures filled the corners and shields, spears and swords adorned the walls.

Underneath the east-facing window was the old man's bed, draped in animal furs and soft cloths to keep his shivers at bay. Kola lay peacefully on his back as he always did, but there was someone sitting next to him on the side of the bed with their back to Enitan.

Enitan could hear their whispers, which sounded urgent and heavy with emotion, and felt a pang of guilt, as if he was intruding on some confidential discussion that was not meant for his ears. However intrigue, as was always the case with him, had a strong pull. He moved closer. He walked slowly, trying not to make too much noise on the straw mats beneath his feet, which was almost impossible.

When he was just a few paces away, the old man turned his head slowly towards him, alerted by the sound of his steps, and he visibly brightened, a wide but pained smile spreading across his face. Enitan noticed that Kola's cheeks were wet with tears.

'Enitan, my beloved grandson, and chief of the west. Come, come. See who the gods have delivered to us? *Ogun* has taken pity on a dying man and truly granted me the peace I yearned before I depart this world of hardship,' he said, waving Enitan over with a quivering hand.

The person who sat beside the old man rose, deliberately taking their time, began to turn around. Enitan was breathing faster now, his ears filled with the pounding sound of his heart.

'Enitan…'

That voice.

'Enitan. My sweet, sweet boy.'

This could not be happening. Was this some sort of dream, some cruel trick of the eyes?

'Mother?'

They were all crying now, no shame, no restraint. Just overwhelming relief, uncontrollable love.

Enitan could not recall how he had cleared the space between him and Queen Lara, but he was cocooned by her embrace. He felt utterly vulnerable, laid bare but protected by his mother's love. It hit him like the waves of the ocean, disorientating him, engulfing him, but at the same time cradling him. Soothing him.

He breathed her scent and pulled himself away just to peer into her eyes, only to bury himself in her bosom once again. He did not know how long they had stayed there, but the room was dark now, no longer aglow with the light from the sun. Fires would need to be lit.

All the while they had embraced, they had not uttered a single word; everything that needed to be said had transpired between them in those moments, and they had seemingly forgotten about Kola. Realising this, Lara gently guided Enitan to her side and leaned over towards her father with an outstretched hand.

His eyes were shut but he had a warm smile across his face, cheeks still wet from the tears of seeing his only living daughter after so long. But he was unmoving, and he would not open his eyes again.

MISGUIDED AMBITION

Heavy footsteps echoed in the long hallway of the palace, turning the heads of the sentries that lined the walls sharply towards the noise and back just as quickly to avoid making eye contact with the approaching men. Subtlety had never been one of Etido's strong points, rather he preferred to wear his emotions like his armour, visible for all to interpret. And his emotion presently was incandescent rage.

Not long after Olise marched with his retinue to the western provinces, the dust from their sandals still heavy in the air and unsettled, Efetobo had called a secret meeting with the council to discuss the governance of Ile-Ife in Olise's absence, blatantly ignoring Olise's express commands for Etido to preside over all matters concerning the kingdom in his stead. Word had reached the ears of the bulky warrior, who was now on his way to express his displeasure at not being consulted. Etido only saw things in black and white and nothing in between. He had always despised men of the court, likening them to vipers, prone to using their venomous tongues to slither to the top of society, rather than using the strength of their hands, and they were always ready to strike when an opportunity presented itself. Efetobo's actions confirmed just that.

On reaching the closed doors to the hall of councillors, he chose to overlook the guards on duty and forgo the appropriate manner of announcement, instead kicking in the doors with one large-sandalled foot, etiquette being another trait far from his strong points.

'What is the meaning of this intrusion?' demanded Efetobo just before he saw who it was and wilted like a flower deprived of water under the murderous glare of the imposing warrior.

'Are you so in a hurry to have your head decorate the ramparts, Efetobo? How dare you call a meeting without my knowledge?' came the booming voice of Etido.

Efetobo tried to compose himself in the presence of the other councillors and restore his authority in the room. 'I believe this meeting was called for the councillors of the city. The last time I checked, you were not a councillor. Or am I to believe that Olise granted you this title without our consent, the very men responsible for appointing people to this office?'

'Do not play the fool. We both know I am no councillor, but I am in command of the city by order of the king, which grants me the privilege of overseeing everything that pertains to the city, including matters concerning the council. So, let us not pretend that this is news to you.'

'That may be so, but some discussions require… refined minds to engage in intellectual discourse,' Efetobo replied as he looked around the room at the other councillors, silently willing them to present a united front and not be intimidated by this scary individual.

Etido gave a short knowing laugh and simply strolled to the nearest seat and fixed his dark eyes on the occupant. The look was enough to send the man almost toppling over in his haste to relinquish his seat and scurry to stand beside Efetobo, who just watched on with mounting contempt.

Etido took his time to make a show of sitting down askew in the wooden chair that creaked with effort under the bulk of the massive warrior. He took in the frightened and indignant looks of each man seated, one after the other, before fixing his glare once again on Efetobo.

'So, what exactly do "refined minds" talk about behind closed doors away from the ears of the throne? This all sounds extremely suspicious, with the distinct hint of treason.' Etido's expression was stern, leaving no room for his words to be misconstrued, and the two warriors who had accompanied him reinforced the severity of his inference in the way they visibly tensed, as if waiting for the order to seize the first person to talk out of turn. How quickly the atmosphere in the room had changed from an air of pomposity to one of palpable terror.

'No, no, Etido. There is no talk of treason here. Please do not get the wrong impression!' replied one of the councillors, just before another added, 'We are simply discussing the interests of the city and its people. No one in their right mind would dare to defy the king!'

'And yet it appears that this was the very intention. Why else would you fail to inform me of this meeting? Please, explain why whatever words that pass here should not be shared with the king? Or do not the interests of the city concern the king?' Etido asked, nostrils flaring as he spoke.

'I see now that we have started this off on the wrong foot. Please, Etido, there are no conspiracies to be found here. We only gathered to review the city finances and think of better ways to utilise the king's taxes. There is much advice we can give as to how the king can better direct these funds to benefit the city. Especially now, in these times of unrest and famine.' Efetobo's jowls quivered as he spoke, clearly trying to diffuse the tension and knowing when he needed to swallow his pride.

'The king will of course have the final say in any matters brought up here, but it makes no sense to bring him ideas in their infancy. We are merely exploring the best possible options first, and eliminating those that may not be favourable,' chimed in another councillor.

'Then what need is there for secrecy? Let us hear these ideas of yours. As the king is not here, I will judge whether they would be of any value,' Etido replied as he looked between the men.

They all turned to Efetobo, who passed a fat finger across his brow to wipe away a bead of sweat before clearing his throat.

'As we said, these ideas still need to be thought through. But while you are here, there is a matter of some concern that we would be interested to understand your thoughts on. The king is… how can I put this… not acting himself lately.'

Etido leaned forward with his elbows on the table between them with his fists closed under his chin. 'Go on.'

'Well. Some of his actions are considered by some to be somewhat… cruel. He punished a wretched farmer the other day. Had him strung up like animal hide in the sun waiting to dry, and he did the same to the poor man's goats, for the love of the gods! He wasn't even permitted to take the carcasses for his trouble, instead, it was shared amongst the guards. The poor man also suffered from severe heatstroke. Only the gods know if he survived. The last I saw he was being carried out of the gates by his distraught relatives.'

'Truth be told, the people are suffering. The lands are rife with famine and disease, and they are still squeezed for their taxes. Some have had to sell all they own and have been reduced to beggars with arms outstretched on the roads seeking alms. Only to be mistreated for their misfortune like pests,' added another councillor.

Efetobo continued, 'Rumours are being whispered that the gods have forsaken us, and we are being punished for the desecration of this once sacred city. We need to appease the gods, make sacrifices, build more shrines in their honour, anything other than carry on in this fashion.'

'This is the very reason King Olise put a warrior in command and not one of you with your empty words and misguided ideas. There is no curse here, the lands were razed, or have you forgotten? It will take time for the soil to replenish sufficiently to yield good crops. We need to secure more fertile lands to be cultivated and livestock to graze, which is exactly what King Olise is doing, while you warm your seats and make yourselves feel important in your secret meetings,' said Etido with unconcealed scorn directed at the men before him.

'And who will cultivate these lands, eh? Will it not be the people? The same people who are oppressed and starved. They would not have the strength to lift a hoe, let alone toil in the fields for days under the hot sun. We need to provide them with the resources to sustain the lands they have or seek assistance from outside Ile-Ife. If we were to attract and encourage more trade across the provinces, that would go a long way to restoring our bleeding coffers and improve relationships,' suggested Efetobo.

'Etido, you mentioned fertile lands, but where will these lands come from and what of their owners? Do you expect them to simply hand it over or will they be forced out of their inheritance and be displaced, adding to the multitude who have already lost everything? This cannot be the solution, surely,' another councillor remarked.

'What nonsense! The people will do as they are commanded and give what is asked of them or face the consequences. They should be grateful that they are allowed to live under the protection of the king!' snapped Etido, clearly losing his patience.

'I do not think the people will see it as such and I fear that this very way of thinking will only lead down one road, more unrest, uprisings and rebellion,' Efetobo said frustratedly.

Etido rose from his seat, sending the chair he sat on sliding backwards across the tiled floor. 'Enough! You people do not have the liver to do what is necessary. Open your eyes and look around. If you have not noticed, we are still at war. There are battles being fought across the realm, tribes vying for power, thieves and marauders roaming the lands preying on the weak and you want to improve trade? What is needed is a strong hand, someone to sweep the land clean of all those that infest it. Someone to put an end to the fighting and restore order. To do this we need armies, weapons, supplies, and the king's taxes are the only solution. It will benefit the people in the long run, but it is a necessary evil, and no one is in a better position to accomplish this than Olise. From now on, there will be no more conspiring, no more secret meetings. Am I understood?'

As Etido looked around the table, he was met with sour and deflated looks, except for Efetobo, who stared back with an expression of pure venom, but he begrudgingly nodded his head slowly, accepting that there was no reasoning with this man, as did the other councillors.

'Good. Now let that be the end of it.' Without waiting for a response, Etido turned and walked towards the kicked-in doors of the hall and ducked under the lintel with his men in tow.

'These so-called men of violence are so narrow-minded. They are cursed with not seeing beyond the length of their spear, completely missing the wider view. I refuse to let every-thing I have worked so hard for turn to sand just to be blown away in the wind,' Efetobo seethed.

'Be careful, Efetobo. You do not want to provoke the anger of Etido. I agree, he is narrow of mind, but I fear his judgement would be rash, swift and unforgiving if we were to defy him. Besides, he speaks with Olise's voice, and we all know what would become of us if unfavourable words were to reach his ears,' replied one of the older councillors called Boniface.

'Your fears are not without merit, but that is exactly what men such as them want, for us to bleat like goats to their bells. To kneel before them and eat whatever excrement is given to us and be thankful for it. Well, I for one will not. Olise would never have taken this great city if it was not for my assistance, and what gratitude did I receive for it?'

'Please, Efetobo. Remember your place and where it is you stand. Etido commands the warriors left behind to protect the city and at this moment, our influence barely stretches beyond these four walls. And are you forgetting Ekaete? She may have ears everywhere. No more of this talk before you land us all in boiling water. If not for yourself, think about our families,' said another councillor as he looked about the room nervously.

'Very well. There is nothing more to be said. We will adjourn this meeting to a more peaceful time if ever one comes about.'

All the men stood and filed out of the hall in pairs bent over in hushed discussion until the muttering faded into the distance. Efetobo was left still at his seat at the head of the table, mind deep in thought as he pondered his position in Ife and the best course of action to take. Whatever he decided was bound to antagonise someone's inflated ego, but he had little choice. One thing he did know was that he could not bear to sit idle; as the old saying goes, "Idle hands do *Esu's* work", however, in his case, the hands that cease to remain still were the very things that would lead him to the path of *Esu*.

'We have rounded up all the villagers, my king. What are your orders?' asked a black-clad warrior of Olise, who sat on a tree stump surrounded by the glowing orange hue of the village he had just put to the torch, as he casually gorged a mango, the nectar running down his arms and dripping from his elbows onto the ground.

'For one, can you get those women to be quiet? All this sobbing is ruining my appetite,' he said, not even bothering to look up at the man he spoke to as he slurped the fruit noisily and licked his sticky fingers.

A few paces away, a group of villagers were huddled together and made to kneel in what used to be the centre of their small community, about forty of them; men, women, and small children, frightened, with ashen faces, as they watched their houses and everything they owned burn.

Olise had marched his men west, making frequent stops at towns and small settlements to rest and replenish his supplies, taking whatsoever he desired with no resistance. He was the king, after all, and he expected to be revered as such. That was until he came to Iwo, a village a few miles east of the province of Oyo, where he had summoned the loyal chiefs of the region.

The people here had been reluctant to hand over all the food stock they had laboured to produce. The rock-strewn gravel here was difficult to cultivate and riddled with invasive species of plants that absorbed the little nutrient in the soil needed to turn over a good harvest. The meagre produce that the village inhabitants had managed to grow would only go so far to feed them but not quite enough to sustain the whole community. And now, this king with so many ravenous mouths behind him demanded they give up everything and be left to starve.

Some of the elders and younger men in the village had stood up to their king and refused his commands. Now, the whole village was being punished as an example of what it meant to deny the king his due.

'You should be ashamed of yourself for treating your own subjects like untamed animals. How can you leave us with nothing? Have you no mercy in your heart?' asked one of the elders before he was struck on the side of his head with the shaft of a spear by one of the warriors that guarded him.

'No, let the man speak. If you wish to endanger the lives of your people further, please carry on. Let us all hear how a king should appease his subjects. But I must warn you, choose your next words wisely because starving could soon be the very least of your concerns, old man,' Olise replied as he casually tossed the seed of the mango into one of the burning mud huts and began to stroll towards the kneeling villagers.

The old man looked around at the people that knelt beside him, his people, all with pleading eyes, silently beseeching him to spare a thought for their lives. But pride is a curse that afflicts many men, even to the point of detriment to those that they love.

He turned back to Olise, gathered as much phlegm as his sinus and throat could muster, and spat a huge blob that landed inches from his feet. 'Do your worst, false king. You have already destroyed our homes and taken all that we have. Without the precious little food you have robbed from us, we are all dead anyway.' Women began to lament, and children began to wail.

Olise looked at the terrified faces of the women, saw the defiance in the eyes of the men and had a moment to calm the anger that rose in him. Over the past year, he had learned to curb his violent and impulsive tendencies, trying to practise some measure of leniency. But most times he failed. He was by no stretch of the imagination a perfect man.

'Brave speech, old man, but now you must bear the consequences of your words.' He turned to one of his warriors. 'Kill all the men but spare the women and children. They will live to carry my message to others who may have a notion to oppose me.'

Without warning, some of the younger men leaped to their feet in a burst of rage, refusing to die without a fight. They rushed the armed warriors that surrounded them, kicking, using their fists, and attacking them with anything they could lay their hands upon. Most were cut down before they could make a meaningful challenge, but a few managed to put up a good fight and disarm a warrior or two, taking their weapons.

One of these men landed a sickening blow to the head of a warrior with a discarded piece of wood. The warrior dropped to the floor like a rock, unmoving. The man then snatched the spear that had fallen from the warrior's lifeless fingers and charged towards Olise, spear point angled towards his chest. Some of Olise's men dashed to protect their king, but the man was too quick, and they would never reach the king in time.

Olise saw the man coming and stood firm, not even attempting to defend himself, rather opening his arms invitingly as if to welcome a friend.

A moment later, the spear rammed dead centre into Olise's chest with such force that Olise had to take a step back to brace himself from falling backwards, sandals skidding in the dirt. Although the thrust was slowed somewhat by the quality of Olise's armour, there was enough momentum and ill intent behind it to rip through the leather and crack his sternum. However, only a finger's width of the spearhead made it through, underneath unyielding, like iron.

The warriors that rushed to protect him stopped in their tracks gasping in disbelief, but not as much as the man who wielded the spear. The point was still wedged into Olise's chest but had failed to penetrate the skin. Now a deadly silence befell the scene; everyone watched in horror, frozen on their feet as if witnessing the passing of an apparition.

Olise's face twisted into a snarl just before he grabbed the shaft and yanked it out of his armour and from the hands of the man that held it, who just stood there with his mouth open wide and his eyes threatening to burst out of their sockets.

'A skilful thrust, but you would dare strike your king! I will make an example of you. Seize this man and put him in ropes.' Turning to some of his warriors, he added, 'Are you not supposed to be protecting me, and yet you allow a peasant to unman you and attack me? I should have you all stripped of your privileges and flogged raw! You had better thank the gods that I need every warrior at my disposal right now, but do not for one heartbeat think that I will let this matter pass unanswered. Be done with the rest of the village men now, you fools,' he roared.

The little fight that had just infused the men of the village seeped out of them as quickly as water held in a woven basket after what they had all just beheld. They dropped their weapons, defeated, some muttering silent prayers to their gods and others cursing the name of the king for an eternity, just before Olise's men went about slaughtering them indiscriminately. A moment later, the only noise to be heard were the cries of the women and children, punctuated by the sounds of the thatched roofs of the burning dwellings collapsing.

Olise turned away from the scene of carnage, rubbing his sore chest, and walked towards the threshold of the village where most of his retinue had camped, shortly followed by his men, who wiped their blades clean of the villagers' blood. Some of them looked to him in awe, others in fear, all concluding that their king was more than a mere man of flesh and bone, but something else. Something much darker than they could begin to comprehend.

The incident with the villagers had darkened his mood. He had hoped that he would not have to burn yet another village and send more souls to *Esu's* dark halls, but it was clear that many still opposed his rule and he could not be seen to turn a blind eye to such an affront.

'Any word from the scouts?' he asked as he approached one of his commanders who was speaking to a group of warriors.

'No, my king, but they have been gone long enough and should return presently. We saw the smoke from the village. I take it that they refused to submit willingly, am I right'

'Indeed, they did. It surprises me how some people are so quick to throw their lives away for a principle, especially one that does not benefit them. We shall see if the next town feels the same way after they learn of what has transpired here.'

Just then, there was some commotion away to their left, and loud chattering from many of the warriors who stood around the camp, straining their necks to catch an eyeful of something. A moment later, some of the warriors parted to reveal four men pulling on ropes and struggling to drag along something that had no place amongst civilisation. Odafe appeared beside these men and seeing Olise, came straight over to him.

'My King, you will not believe the gift I found for you while we were out on the hunt,' he said, eyes wild with excitement.

The four men came more into view, dragging between them the biggest hyena Olise had ever seen. The beast was huge, almost the size of a calf, as it struggled against its bonds. Its black snout had been muzzled with a thick cloth, securing its powerful jaw, while ropes wound around each of its spotted limbs. Every so often, muffled yelps escaped its mouth whenever one of the ropes was yanked.

'Where on the gods' green earth did you find this beast?' Olise asked, impressed.

'It was sleeping under the shade of an iroko tree next to the carcass of an antelope. It had obviously eaten its full and decided to take a nap. Good for us, as I hate to imagine what that thing would have done if the circumstances were reversed. I thought you could do with a pet. I can certainly think of ways to put it to good use,' Odafe finished with a wolfish smirk on his lips, noticing the young man tied up from the village.

'You are truly a depraved soul, Odafe. Have you ever contemplated consulting with a healer? Though I fear there is little hope for you. However, I appreciate your consideration, and this beast may yet prove useful.'

'I live to serve you, my king. Are there any questions you would like answered by that young man over there? I would be glad to oblige,' Odafe said.

'Perhaps. But for now, we need to make ready to move to the next town. This province is proving more stubborn than I had hoped. There is much to do here, and the people deserve to see their king in the flesh. No point in ruling the realm

from the comfort of one city. I need to look them in the eyes and weed out those unwilling to serve me, just like those from this hovel of a village.'

'I could not agree more, my king.'

More noise drew their attention and the commander Olise had first approached stepped forward. 'My king, some of the scouts have returned, the men that ranged further southwest of our position. They have some disturbing news.'

'Send them to me at once,' Olise commanded, already dreading what information he was about to receive. A group of dust-caked men walked up and took a knee before him.

'King Olise, we have just returned from the town of Ibadan. There we heard reports from several merchants that a new chief has taken the seat in Ogun and is amassing his support with all the major provinces in the west.'

Olise's mood darkened further on hearing this news. Normally, his first instinct would be to change course and march his army with all haste to confront this chief and demand his homage or raze the city to the ground, but he could not afford to alter his course, especially when he had men awaiting him in Oyo. He would learn what he could from there and decide on his next course of action. So, he was changing after all, and he even surprised himself at how rational thought prevailed; seldom as it was, surprising, nonetheless.

'Every time I blink, someone new is taking up a title somewhere in the realm without seeking my blessings. I will deal with this in time but, for now, we will stick to our plan and march onwards to Oyo. I am sure I will glean all the information I need before I fall on this new chief and ask him to prostrate at my feet or decorate the city walls with his head. The fact that he has not sent word to his king offering his hand in fealty is insult enough, but I will give him the benefit of the doubt, for now.'

'And the prisoner, my king. What would you have us do with him?' asked one of the warriors that had accompanied Olise to the village.

Olise looked at the young man for a moment, and the man met his with a level stare of his own. There was no sign of fear, more of respect, admiration even, but also a look of acceptance of whatever fate awaited him.

'Bring him along. Maybe this one will be useful for something,' he said as he turned away and headed towards the rest of his men, followed by Odafe and a few of his senior warriors.

Before the sun disappeared behind the horizon, Olise's retinue marched into Oyo. The city was once a thriving agricultural hub, being a major producer of crops such as maize, cassava, yams, and palm produce, which was transported across the region. Almost all its inhabitants were farmers, with a handful of elders that presided over the people. During times of peace, the region was famously known to be a haven for anyone who sought work as a field hand and was willing to contribute to the machine that fed the kingdom.

The soil here was fertile and said to be blessed by *Oko*, the god of farming and agriculture, who was believed to visit the land once every year on the night of a red moon, leaving behind a harvest that could feed a generation.

But ever since the war of the tribes a year ago and the growing famine that now swept through the kingdom, the demand for Oyo to produce and export crops quadrupled. It remained one of the largest cities to provide supplies, which also made it a target for local bandits and thieves seeking to rob the food supplies and sell them at extortionate rates across the regions.

Olise had put a stop to that by setting up a garrison in the city as well as building a wall around it to deter would-be perpetrators. Anyone who was caught attempting to steal faced the harshest of punishments; beating to within an inch of their life then stripped and tied to poles dotted outside the city perimeter, left to be picked at by the crows and vultures. The remains of many desperate men were still visible on the landscape around the city, acting as silent sentries. Mostly ragged clothing still tied to the posts and some just bones, if they hadn't already dropped to the ground to be taken by feral dogs or other wild creatures.

Although Olise's decision to deploy an army to secure the city was initially viewed as an act of strong and considerate leadership – aiding the people in their time of need – it had really been a decision motivated by self-interest and enterprise. With his command of the city, he now had full control of the management of the supplies, which were mostly diverted to Ile-Ife and sparsely shared with the rest of the kingdom. He had designs to further exploit his position by being the sole source of food supplies across the realm, charging them whatever he felt like, and doing exactly what the common thieves would have done, but on a much larger scale.

As his men marched through the thoroughfare of the city, Olise cast an appraising eye over the many food stores, the security, and the people. He liked what he saw and was satisfied that his interests were sufficiently protected. The workers quickly averted their eyes as he passed by, confirming their perpetual submission to the laws here, and each warrior he passed bowed his head or prostrated in reverence to the king. A heartbeat later, a group of warriors intercepted him with orders to guide him to the meeting place, where all the chiefs he had summoned were gathered.

It was a large structure; timber framed but sturdy, with a great length of thatched roof that hung down to head height on all sides. Rather than a door, patterned straw mats hung from the opening, which was parted by two guards as Olise approached, both bowing their heads to their king.

The sweet aroma of burning incense wafted through the air, faint smoky trails swirling mesmerisingly through the rays of light that pierced the building at varying angles. The scent was not solely to create a pleasant atmosphere, but also to mask the scent of nervous sweat, unwashed bodies and, more importantly, the stench of fear.

Olise, flanked by Odafe and a handful of his commanders, took up half of the building across from several minor chiefs and citizens of high standing from the western province – wealthy merchants, elders, and the odd warrior with a name that preceded them. They stepped forward one after the other and prostrated before him, apart from two of the elders, to Olise's irritation. However, he was willing to let it go if they could offer him information of value, but note their names he did.

'Enough with all the pleasantries. What is this I hear about a new chief in the region? Does the right of kingship not demand that any such anointing is done only with my express blessings, and why has one of you not seen fit to inform me sooner?' Olise asked as he eyed the gathered men.

No one answered immediately, all carefully and nervously weighing up their thoughts on an appropriate response that would not provoke the wrath of Olise, until one man summoned the courage to step forward.

'My king, please accept our apologies but our hands have been bound on matters relating to the region. Not long ago, a group of Modakeke warriors arrived in the city and swore themselves to the boy chief. The man that leads them is an unyielding and unscrupulous old warrior. He immediately went about putting all the prominent families in the region under watch, with orders to arrest anyone that appeared the least bit suspicious or was perceived to harbour any ill intentions towards the boy. We have come here at great risk to ourselves and our families, but felt compelled, no, obliged to inform you as soon as word reached us of your intended visit,' said the man called Tunji, one of the heads of the leading families from Ogun.

Olise's throat suddenly felt dry. 'Did you say modakeke? That cannot be so. I wiped the soil clean of those wretched warriors. They are nothing but bones scattered across the fields of Benin! How are you certain?' Olise asked, rage steadily building inside him.

'It is true, my king. I have seen them myself and they all bear the tribal marks on their cheeks that attest to their breeding. There is no mistaking these men… my king,' said another prominent man called Dotun, also head of a high-standing family in Ogun, as he came to stand next to the first man who had spoken.

Dotun continued. 'There is more, my king. Rumours suggest that the boy chief is a direct relative of the late Chief Kola, hence the reason he was so quick to surrender his titles and not pass them down to the families that were promised to succeed him when the time came. Some say he is the grandson, child to the late King Jide…'

A cold chill crept up Olise's spine and his skin began to prickle. How could it be? First, he heard that one of Jide's sons had possibly survived and was waging war in the east, and now he was confronted with the news that another supposed son had taken up the mantle of power in the west. Not only that, but he also had Modakeke warriors with him, the most renowned and feared fighting men ever to walk the soils of the tribes. He refused to believe the words that resounded in his ears.

Without even realising it, his fists were balled up at his sides, face contorting in waves of rage, distress, anger, and emotions that could not be described. He needed to direct these feelings at someone, anyone. Efetobo came to mind, the fool that was tasked with securing the city, seeing to it that the queen and the princes were taken during the sack of Ife. He had failed, and this oversight could not go unpunished. He would pay with his life, the bloated bastard. But he was miles away, nestled in the bosom of the wealth and comforts he had acquired through his false service to the throne, thought Olise angrily.

He made a mental note to make sure that seeing Efetobo suffer would be his first order of business on his return to the capital. He had never liked the pompous bureaucrat and now, he had the perfect excuse to see him removed permanently, relative of his mother or not.

He looked up at the anxious faces that stared back at him. Expectant faces, awaiting the commands of their king. Now more than ever, he had to exhibit firm leadership, decisiveness, and ruthlessness.

'It concerns me not whether this boy is a relative of the old chief, more so that he had the audacity to elevate himself without my approval. For that alone, he must die.' Olise's words were severe, devoid of all emotions. 'If the boy is truly aligned with Modakeke warriors, I will require all your men of fighting age at my disposal. Every one of you. I expected a leisurely visit to my kingdom. Now I find myself potentially having a battle on my hands.'

'Battles are what we live for, my king,' said Odafe from beside Olise with a twinkle in his eye.

'Yes, but why bloody my hands when I have such loyal subjects ready to do the work for me?' replied Olise, as he looked back at the men that stood before him.

'It would be our pleasure to rid you of this nuisance, my king. We had already begun to make arrangements but only needed your blessings to cast the final stones,' responded Tunji with nods from Dotun and another one of the prominent figures of Ogun.

'I can field fifty warriors and summon more men from the neighbouring towns and villages that remain loyal to the throne. Within a few days, we could be outside the city, besieging it and cutting off all their supplies, along with their hopes of reinforcements, while the men from Ogun here today can strike from within like a poison until the boy and his allies throw themselves at our mercy. It would be an easy victory for you, my king,' said one of the other chiefs, called Goke.

The usual self-satisfied smile returned to Olise's face. 'That is all pleasing to hear; I expect nothing less. You have my blessings to resolve the matter however you see fit. In the meantime, I think I will remain here in Iwo with my men. It has always fascinated me how crops that feed our kingdom are cultivated, and this is a rare opportunity for me to observe the process in person,' Olise replied.

Odafe looked disappointed at the prospect of watching farmers and not putting his skill to good use, which was not lost on Olise. 'Do not worry, my friend. I am sure we will find ways to keep ourselves entertained, Odafe. Maybe we could use that beast you captured. Its appetite must have returned by now and I am sure that some fresh meat would not go amiss.'

Odafe perked up a fraction as his colourful imagination ran wild with all manner of dark and disturbing thoughts on how to best utilise the animal.

'I would say that that concludes our business here, good men of the west. Now, bring me the head of this boy chief. I would sooner look upon the dead face of my kin if he truly is who he claims to be.'

With that, all the gathered men began to disperse to carry out their king's wishes.

FORSAKEN PRIDE

Good palm wine always made a bad situation better. There was nothing quite like that sweet milky taste, and the warm sensation that washed over the body and dulled one's consciousness when the beverage started to take effect. Palm wine was simply the drink of choice when you wanted nothing more than to crawl into a ball and hide under a rock, never to be disturbed again. This was the resounding sentiment that overwhelmed the chief of the Calabar tribe.

Essien had tried to be a good leader; respected, loved and objective. All that had slowly begun to erode once the drums of battle sounded across the River-lands, and that was the beginning of his unravelling.

His father, the late chief, had borne a deep-rooted antipathy for the Yoruba royal court that had all but consumed him. It had stemmed from what were believed to be the unlawful killings of a father and daughter of Calabar blood; one a stunning girl, the envy of every woman in the tribe, the other a great warrior with a name that echoed far beyond the imaginary lines that marked the realm.

Their deaths had taken place while supposedly being under the protection of the then king many years ago, and the perpetrators of these crimes had seemingly avoided the deserved sentencing, denying the Calabar of the retribution they demanded, a slight on their pride that they would not soon forgive or forget. Essien had been no more than a babe in arms when the infractions occurred, and some of those involved were more than likely ghosts by now but, amongst the tribes, grievances were inherited, passed down through the years like an ancestor's old spear, and the late chief made sure that his enmity would live on in his offspring.

Essien had wanted nothing to do with this burden of hatred. He had always planned that once his father departed the world of the living, he would wipe the slate clean, form new alliances, open trade to other regions and start afresh with his people. But the old guard from the Calabar courts would not allow this. They pushed him into seeking disengagement from the kingdom, for Calabar to be recognised as a sovereign nation, not to answer to a Yoruba monarch that sat miles away on a throne built on the backs of the people, something that had not been done in centuries.

And independence from the kingdom was all but proclaimed by the late chief, though unofficially, but more through rebuffed extensions of amity from the Yoruba monarchy and failure to heed the call to arms when the war of the tribes had erupted a year ago. The late chief had planned to send a message to King Jide personally informing him of the Calabar's position, but dysentery had robbed him of the opportunity, leaving the decision in the hands of his heir, Essien, who had an entirely different vision for the people of Calabar.

Essien had at least honoured his late father's wishes in death and had not partaken in the war of the tribes, choosing to remain neutral, a decision that was mainly influenced by the elders of Calabar; they could not fight for a king they did not respect or recognise as their sovereign, nor could they fight alongside the very man who was said to have wielded the spear that spilt the blood of their tribesman and created the chasm that spurred the wheels of hatred in motion.

Now, a year later, there was a new face that demanded their subservience. One that, unlike King Jide, did not offer a hand of peace or reconciliation but saw it as his right to rule them. This man claimed to be from the loins of the great King Jide, and had adopted an approach that was not dissimilar, driven by an ideology of tribal unity, and one king. It was clear that he was unwilling to compromise with a misaligned kingdom, half of whom accepted him and the other half against him, rather, he simply demanded absolute fealty. It was claimed that this man was Prince Niran, a name that had already sent ripples through the provinces and was chanted in equal measures of respect and loathing in the River-lands.

The prince's campaigns had resulted in his taking many of the prominent towns and villages in the region, and he continued to sweep through the lands, gaining more ground in his pursuit of conquest. More astonishingly, not all his victories had been through force of arms, many had opened their gates to him willingly and he was famed to be a man of great honour and dignity, guaranteeing and ensuring the safety of those that had turned to him, and even going as far as to welcome them unreservedly into his growing nation.

Essien could only admire a man of such qualities, a view which could not be shared openly. His council of elders, however, were hell-bent on ridding their lands of this outsider, and they held sway amongst the warriors of Calabar, who outnumbered the average civilian at least three to one. So, resistance and war were the only responses to be expected from the heart of the River-lands. Essien's hands were tied, and his fate, it would appear, preordained.

As he sat in his chambers draining the last dregs of palm wine from his horn, his thoughts sank deeper into melancholy. He could not help but think of all the bloodshed to come, the innocents that would be forced to suffer from the decisions that they had no choice in making. Decisions made by men who supposedly had their best interests at heart, but were really driven by self-advancement, disingenuous principles, and a grievance that should have perished with the late chief.

From somewhere to his rear in the large quarters, he heard crunching noises. He at first thought it was his imagination, induced by the palm wine, but the sound came again, much closer this time and unmistakable. It was the sound made when eggshells were crushed under the weight of a foot.

He spun around just in time to see a slender woman emerge from the shadows of the room, tall and mesmerising with dark eyes and a ghost of a smile playing about one corner of her mouth. His initial thoughts were to dash the horn he held at this person and run out of the room screaming, but something held him fast to his chair. He felt as if he was in a trance, and he was simply observing this whole scene play out from afar, outside of his own body.

The woman slowly walked towards him, almost as if she glided across the floor, so smooth was her movement, like a dancer, the gentle sway of her hips, the rhythmic motion of her arms; he was powerless to turn away. With every step she took towards him, he fell deeper into this state of paralysis. He willed his muscles to react, but they failed to respond, as if they did not belong to him. His tongue was dry, he was unable to speak, and his thoughts clouded. 'Am I dreaming?' he said to himself blearily.

The horn he held slipped from his fingers and hit the floor with a loud clatter. The spell was broken. His muscles came alive, and he instinctively kicked at the table next to him, sending the calabash that held the rest of the palm wine tumbling. It shattered when it hit the cold stone floor, the white beverage leaving a pattern on the slabs. Then Essien found his voice and shouted out to alert his guards.

No sooner had his cry for help left his mouth, than the door burst wide open. His personal guards, who were always stationed outside his chambers, spilt into the room, five of them with swords in hand. They scanned the room for the source of the noise and saw their chief reeling beside the upended table and broken calabash. Following his gaze, their vision then settled on Ekaete. She hadn't moved when the guards rushed into the room, but stayed in the same position, as rigid as an old tree, imposing, confident.

Two of the guards immediately moved to either side of Essien, while the others took up the front, forming a barrier between their chief and Ekaete. She did not appear to be rattled by the sight of the men and sharpened iron trained on her, and that ghost of a smile remained as if challenging them to make the first move.

'Who are you and how did you get past all my guards to find yourself in my private quarters?' Essien commanded in his native Calabar dialect. He had tried to sound authoritative, but the note of anxiety was evident in his voice.

'My name is Ekaete. Tell your men to lower their weapons. I mean you no harm. I only seek to warn you,' Ekaete replied coolly in the same tongue, never letting her eyes stray from Essien.

'Chief, do not trust this... woman. We have heard her name spoken in whispers; she is a witch!' one of the guards replied. Another took a surreptitious step back, another swallowed hard.

That smile remained. 'Call me what you must, but you would be wise to heed the message I bring to you. Do not allow your fear of me to cloud your judgement. As I said, I do not wish to cause you harm,' she replied.

Without warning, the guard who had spoken dashed forward, spurred on by nervousness, eager to detain the intruder while he still had a molecule of courage residing in him. The point of his sword extended, intending to deliver a wound to incapacitate Ekaete, but he only split the air.

One instance, Ekaete was there, standing in front of them as clear as day, the next she was not. They had all seen it, and yet they had seen nothing. Their eyes could scarcely comprehend what had just occurred; she had vanished right before their very eyes.

The guard spun around frantically, searching the room, and looking to the others to confirm that he had not just imagined it all. The frozen faces staring back at him in utter horror were all the confirmation he needed.

Just as quickly as she had disappeared, she returned, this time standing beside the man who had been bold enough to attack her. He was slow to turn to face her and although the others now saw Ekaete standing beside him, they could not give voice to warn him, their mouths open wide in terror and their tongues stolen from them in disbelief.

Ekaete reached out and merely brushed her fingers across the shoulder of the man, and that was all it took. He dropped his sword, which clattered to the floor, the sound unusually loud in their ears and causing some of them to flinch. The man's head inclined upwards, and his eyes rolled back to the roof of his skull revealing the sclera. His jaw dropped, sagging, and a thin line of saliva began to dribble from one corner. He stood there in a vegetative state, unmoving, as if in a deep sleep on his feet.

'I will forgive your insolence only the one time and grant you another chance to heed my words. The next attempt to be foolish will have irrevocable consequences for every one of you in this room. Are you ready to listen to me now, or do you yet wish to provoke my anger?' she asked Essien in a tone that was delivered calmly enough but weighed heavily with the thinly veiled threat.

Essien tentatively stepped from behind the men that protected him, coming to stand across from Ekaete. One of his men tried to restrain him, but he simply raised a hand stopping him. If one thing could be said about the Calabar chief, it was that he was no coward. A drunkard, maybe, but he had learned to face his fears a long time ago and was determined to show his mettle, despite every fibre of his being currently threatening to betray him. The effect of the palm wine had evaporated, and he was now faced with the cold, sobering reality of the situation.

'I find it hard to believe that any message from you, especially if it is one that is of benefit, as you would have me believe, will be imparted without a cost. Tell me what it is that you want from me first and I will judge if it is worth the knowledge of your message,' he said as he looked from Ekaete to the guard who stood like a living statue, silent and oblivious to his surroundings.

'How very perceptive of you, Essien. You are indeed wiser than most would regard you. I was right to seek you out and not one of the elders of your tribe. I only ask one thing – put aside this enmity you bear for King Olise and accept him as your sovereign ruler. With him, much can be accomplished, and I will see to it personally that Calabar will be a servant in name alone. You will be free to rule over your people as you see fit. But you will pay your share of the king's taxes and come to his aid when summoned.'

'That is everything my people fight to oppose! They would rather die than serve a man that has no regard for our tribe and traditions. You underestimate the gravity of the hatred borne by my people. It is as entrenched in their blood as the roots of the oldest trees that spread deep below the earth. To most, ignoring or setting aside this desire would be akin to losing a part of themselves, like the loose soil that clings to the roots when it is drawn forth from the earth and exposed to the sun. I fear that you ask too steep a price.'

'And is this how you truly feel, Essien? You have been at war for the best part of a year. You lose ground every few moons and your people continue to suffer. How long do you think it will be before the young prince and his allies march to the heart of your city and take everything from you? Would it not be more prudent to preserve the lives of as many of your people as possible, if it meant putting aside your pride? And this pride you so dearly embrace, it is an immaterial thing, something of no measure, no true value. Lives, on the other hand, are not, especially the lives of the innocent, those whose only crime is their choice in following their tribe blindly, even though they are led unknowingly straight into an abyss?'

'What I want for my people is irrelevant. I am but one person. A commitment as grave as you ask requires the consent of the council of elders. Such is the way of our tribe.'

'But you are the chief, and they are your subjects, or am I mistaken? This is your chance to seize the respect you deserve and assume your role as the only voice of authority in the River-lands. All you need is to prove yourself invaluable and deliver them one decisive victory against these invaders, and this is exactly what I offer you.'

Essien pondered these words. He was being presented with the solution to all his problems, one that would turn the battles in his favour, preserve the lives of his people and see their morale soar. Not to mention the opportunity to be recognised as the only Calabar chief to ever defeat the great monarchy of the Yoruba, assuring his place in the scripts of history.

He would, of course, be required to forgo his father's dreams of sovereignty, which would undoubtedly leave a bitter taste in the mouths of the elders to see him prostrate himself at the feet of Olise. However, would that not be but a small price to pay to accomplish all his forebears had only ever dreamed of achieving? At that moment, the choice was abundantly clear to him — the risk of annihilation of his tribe, or victory with reasonable concessions on his chieftaincy? The latter was certainly more appealing and a chance to break from under the shadow of his father and his loyal supporters. He could be his own ruler and govern the people as he had always intended.

After a few heartbeats, he levelled his gaze at Ekaete, peering into those deep dark eyes. Her smile broadened. *I have him*, she thought satisfactorily.

Turning to one of the men at his side, Essien issued an order, 'Summon the elders to me at once and prepare the warriors. There is much to discuss, and we have a battle to win.'

'Yes, chief,' replied the man as he backed away to the entrance, keeping an eye on Ekaete before disappearing through the door of the royal chambers.

'It is time for Calabar to take its rightful place in the tales of our history. Long have your people deserved this moment, and long will your name reign in this region, Chief Essien,' Ekaete said.

Essien could not help but smile. His time had finally come and now he would go forth towards a decision that would alter the course of many lives for years to come.

THE RIVER
WHENCE WE CAME

The bows of the canoes parted the waters like sharpened blades through tender meat, sending ripples before them into the open waters like the vanguard of an invading army. Before their voyage, maps of the vast network of rivers that spread like veins through the River-lands had been committed to the memory of every man on board the vessels of Niran's modest fleet. This precaution was a necessity in the event of the canoes being separated during the fighting, although this eventuality was one that they prayed would be avoided at all costs in this unfamiliar and hostile environment.

The silence of the river was almost deafening, save for the gentle lapping of water against the vessels and the occasional birdsong carried on the wind, no sound could be heard, accentuating the eeriness of the scenery. Niran had insisted on launching when the moon began to descend beyond the horizon to allow his men sufficient time to traverse the length of river between him and the Calabar and to get them all into position.

What he had not accounted for was the dense fog that heralded the harmattan season, clinging to the river's surface like unruly clouds refusing to take to the skies. Visibility was restricted to but a few paces, which meant that the vessels had to travel in tight formation for the occupants to stand a chance of seeing the faces and hand signals of those that manned the crafts and, if necessary, to be within earshot once the chaos of battle descended on them.

The impaired vision brought on by the fog was both an advantage and an impediment. The fog offered them the benefit of masking their advance if lookouts were stationed on the strips of land adjacent to the river's route; however, they would also be blind to any vessels that could potentially be coming towards them from the other direction, making this whole endeavour more perilous than at first anticipated.

The fog rolled over the river like a life form; twisting, turning, and spiralling in an almost seductive and spellbinding manner, only to be sent into multiple directions once it met solid objects.

As was expected of a warrior prince's vessel, Niran's led the silent procession along the waters. There were five men in each of the streamlined vessels and the fleet numbered twelve. The crafts were designed mainly for speed with a width that did not permit the occupants to sit side-by-side, but rather in a line spread from bow to stern. Niran travelled with his closest companions; Seun, who never left the prince's side, and three of the royal guards that had been with him since he fled Ife a year ago.

Two earlier boat runs had already preceded Niran's fleet, ferrying Adebola and some forty Yoruba warriors to the narrow strips of land that ran parallel to the rivers. These warriors would lie in wait and alert the fleet of any movement in the water with horns fashioned from either goats or antelopes, and once both sides were engaged, they would aid the fighting from land, hurling spears at the rearmost enemy vessels. They too, however, would be hampered by the elements, and would thus need to be eagle-eyed to spy on any movement that threatened the prince's advance.

Zogo, on the other hand, led the assault on land, moving in from the southeastern border with his Igbo warriors. Their attack would commence at the sound of the first cockerel proclaiming the arrival of dawn. If everything went as Niran had planned, the Calabar boatmen would appear on the waters as soon as the fog was dissipated by the first golden fingers of sunlight. This was all he could hope for, but, as with all things, their fate was in the hands of the gods.

Niran could not dispel the tension he felt in his muscles, nor could he release his grip from the sides of the canoe. His palms ached and yet he did not feel comfortable enough to relinquish his hold. He was sensitive to every pitch and roll of the vessel, which he felt in the pit of his stomach, accompanied by a cold shudder that ran down his spine. Despite the chill in the air, a sheen of sweat coated his brow and his exposed arms, beads ran down his back and chest under the light leather breast armour he wore and, as hard as he tried, he simply failed to master his pounding heart.

For all his composure and level-headedness in all the battles he had been in, this was by far the most petrified he had ever been – a battle to conquer his innermost fear. Seun's reassuring hand reached out and weighed heavy on his shoulder, seemingly sensing the turmoil raging in the prince's mind, and Niran looked back to acknowledge him with a curt nod.

Before today, Seun had taken him on several boat rides to get him more attuned to the waters in an effort to quell the prince's fears. This had helped to some degree, but only a fraction. It was one thing to board a vessel for leisure and another to be floating towards uncertainty and perhaps impending doom. However, he knew that his people looked to him for confidence and an iron will to persevere through whatever the gods had laid before them. It was his duty and, at the core, the very essence of a ruler of men. With this added pressure in mind, he clenched his teeth and was determined to show the face of a fearless warrior, regardless of what he felt deep within.

He told himself once again that this had been the only viable course of action to secure the heart of the River-lands and that every other alternative would have yielded the same results – a protracted battle that saw no victors but rather lasting consequences to the innocent people of the province. People who had already been forced to endure immeasurable anguish. This, he simply could not allow.

A low hiss sounded ahead of him; the man at the front of his canoe was gesturing towards the other vessels on either side of him, a gesture that was then replicated by others and silently communicated across all the crafts. Niran squinted his eyes and strained his neck for a better view. He knew the sign well; the enemy had been sighted.

The pulsation of his heart picked up in pace and he had to close his eyes and slow his breathing to steel himself. He then reached for the blade at his hip to loosen it from the scabbard, and all his men did the same. They had decided to leave their shields and spears behind, choosing to take swords, daggers, and axes to travel light and unencumbered, so it was no surprise that some of the warriors felt a little vulnerable. They had no choice but to depend on the spears of their companions to cover them from land.

Everything was silent, too silent in fact, and Niran could not help but feel a sense of foreboding. Suddenly, a black crow cawed and burst through the fog overhead, flying in the direction from which they had come. Every man saw it and the same thought was at the forefront of their minds. This was not a good omen.

Lights appeared in the distance, one or two at first, then a multitude of them, casting an orange-reddish hue across the river. Fires held aloft by the hands of many men. 'It is an ambush!' someone yelled, but it was too late. Spears ripped through the fog, fast and deadly like the black talons of eagles seeking unsuspecting prey.

Men began to scream out in pain as the missiles struck flesh, loud splashes could be heard from men falling into the river, presumably with fatal wounds, and the distinctive sound of disarray was all about Niran as he looked around nervously, bending as low as he could within the confines of the vessel.

'Spread the line and secure our flanks!' commanded Niran out of pure instinct, and the drivers of the vessels at the sterns summoned every ounce of strength they could muster as they dipped their long bamboo poles into the water to guide their vessels wide and away from the centre of the river.

Turning back to the royal guard that steered his craft, Niran sought eye contact with the man. 'Stay our course. We will take them head-on.'

Seun flashed him a quick glance, knowing that this would be Niran's command, but was surprised nonetheless to know that, despite the imminent danger, his prince was still willing to put his life in the hands of fate. Without thinking, Seun rose from his position, moved forward and leapfrogged over the prince, landing with an awkward thump in front of him.

'What are you doing?' Niran roared angrily.

'To serve as your shield, my prince. If you would go headlong into the jaws of danger, do not expect me to stand idle,' he replied as he drew his sword and a short axe from his waist and settled in a crouched position, looking forward and waiting for the next volley of spears to appear.

Every warrior on the vessels, those that were lucky enough to have escaped the tips of the spears unscathed, now had blades in their hands, faces twisted in anticipation and eager to pay back their attackers in kind.

The fog had started to clear and just ahead of the canoes was a series of makeshift wooden platforms lining the river's edge. Several Calabar warriors occupied them brandishing spears and crude blades, and more warriors occupied the river ahead in wider boats of their own, over a score of them, all brimming with warriors, the vessels bobbing up and down under the weight of men.

An order went up in the native Calabar tongue and the men on the platform hurled their spears once again, being able to aim more accurately with the lifting fog. More men were struck, some splashing into the murky waters to a certain death, but nobody changed their course or slowed the pace of their vessels.

The boats that carried the Calabar warriors started to advance, seeing that the westerners were not deterred by the two attacks. They could not allow them to progress deeper into their territory and were determined to stop them there and then. As no party sought to yield, both sides braced themselves for the unavoidable collision that would begin the bloodletting.

The time that it took for both sides to bridge the now churning river felt like the longest wait Niran had ever experienced. It was no more than a few heartbeats, but in that moment, it felt like an eternity. Men were already on their feet, eager to be the first to leap onboard the enemy's vessel to strike the first blow. Weapons were poised ready to deflect or strike the men opposite them, then a low murmur began to resonate from both sides, like a herd of elephants stampeding in the distance, slowly increasing in decibels, and growing in intensity. The murmur, now the voices of scores of men, grew into a dramatic crescendo, just as both sides collided.

Splinters flew as the canoes and boats crashed together, destabilising men, and sending more into the rivers. Blades began to swing, axes cleaved, and knives jabbed in a sudden burst of violence that coated the surface of the river in red.

The royal guard at the bow of Niran's boat was down from the force of an axe that had found the gap between neck and shoulder, and his blood was already pooling under their feet. Seun wasted no time in leaping forward and onto the boat they had collided with, parrying, and stabbing with the skilled precision of a Modakeke warrior, almost clearing the wider vessel singlehandedly. Niran was right behind him, as were the remaining royal guards.

The boat was rocking wildly under the prince's feet, and a pang of fear took him, but the royal guards at his side braced themselves against him, affording him time to regain his balance. He was silently grateful to them as they had obviously deduced his tentativeness and chose to support him without making their intention obvious.

He could see Seun ahead fighting two men at once, meeting one of his assailant's blades, bending low and hacking at the exposed leg of another. A boat came up beside them and three men jumped onto the boat they stood upon. Niran had no choice but to act.

He dashed forward, momentarily forgetting how unstable the decking under his feet felt. The first man saw him coming, turned and swung his blade at waist height. Niran took a quick step back, almost colliding with the royal guards behind him, then brought his sword up, deflecting the blade off centre, and immediately twisted his wrist to bring his sword back in a sweeping downwards angle to strike the man across the chest. His attacker wore no chest armour and Niran's blade ripped through him, leaving a deep gash that induced a shriek of pain.

The man dropped his weapon, both hands now clutching his chest. Niran pulled his sword back fluidly, drove it into the man's stomach, stepped forward and shouldered him off his blade and into the river. The next man, hearing his companion's scream, spun round to face Niran, while the third advanced on Seun's rear. Niran had not stopped moving forward and he kicked out at the man's shin, which sent him toppling forward and onto the waiting tip of Niran's short blade that he brought upwards in his left hand. The blade took the man under the chin, stopping him instantly, and Niran sidestepped away from the falling warrior, who landed face-first on the deck.

He had to reach the third man before he managed to get close enough to Seun, who was oblivious to the threat behind him, still clearing a red path before him. The man was raising an axe, aiming to bring it down on Seun's head from the back, but he stopped dead in his tracks with a grunt, turned and desperately tried to remove the blade that Niran had thrown perfectly, and was now embedded between the man's shoulder blades, his fingers failing to grasp the hilt that was just out of reach.

His eyes went wide, seeing the prince lunge for him just before he was impaled. The man dropped to his knees dragging Niran's blade down with him. Another war cry sounded and a Calabar warrior was running towards him from the other side, about to clear the distance between the two boats. Niran let go of his sword and dove backwards, the spear of the warrior narrowly missing him. Before he even hit the deck, one of the royal guards behind him was already leaping over Niran, thrusting, while kicking back one leg in mid-air, putting more force behind his attack. The Calabar warrior never saw the strike coming and he was dead in the blink of an eye.

The second royal guard, called Lanre, helped Niran to his feet while the other one covered him from the front. 'Thank you, but do not waste your time on me. Aid Seun,' Niran roared over the din, and Lanre dashed forward without thinking.

Niran retrieved his sword and took a moment to assess their situation. There was fighting everywhere. Most of the canoes and boats were close enough to form walking platforms, with some not holding their original occupants, the warriors having leaped onto opposing vessels. One or two canoes were ablaze, and a number were sinking, either from the weight of the men on them or from the spears that had pierced the deck. He watched the bow of one of them disappear beneath the darkened water, and there were bodies everywhere, some bobbing up and down lifeless, others strewn across the crafts in all manner of positions, trampled by men desperately trying to reach their next victim or move to a more secure position.

He quickly scanned the shoreline and was pleased to see that his warriors were engaging the men that stood on the wooden platforms, but there was no sign of Adebola and the warriors he had sent along with him. Could they have fallen foul of another trap? He wondered. It was as if the Calabar warriors had been privy to every detail of his plan and anticipated every strategy they had so painstakingly prepared for. How could this be possible? Now was not the time to dwell on the matter. Now, they needed to fight and, above all, survive.

He brought his thoughts back into focus and swept his gaze over the boats closest to him, saw some of his men struggling against Calabar warriors on both sides of them and decided to assist them. He sprang into action, disregarding the rocking vessels under his feet as he leaped from boat to boat. One of the royal guards followed close behind, determined not to leave the prince unprotected.

The canoe was wedged between two of the enemy boats, and being attacked from both sides. Three of his warriors stood side by side and fended off assaults from either side, but they were clearly losing as two of them fought off three warriors while the other fought two. One of the warriors that faced three had found a discarded shield and was blocking several blows that came in quick succession, whilst the man at his side thrust his blade as fast as he could without finding much success. The canoe his men fought from was too narrow for Niran to make any meaningful contribution, so he made a snap decision.

He turned to the royal guard that had accompanied him: 'Make your way to the rear of those two, and I will do the same on the other side.'

'My prince, there are three men on that side, let me take on those men. You risk too much as things stand.'

'There is no time to argue. Please, do as I ask. They will have their backs to me, so do not worry yourself, just take out those men,' Niran replied, pointing to the other side of the boats.

'Your will, my prince.' With that, the royal guard began to make his way to the other side.

Luckily, this group was the closest fighting knot of men to the prince, so he was able to creep up behind the line of three Calabar warriors without being confronted by others. They were still hacking away at the westerners on the canoe in front of them and did not see the prince slowly edging towards them from the rear.

As soon as Niran was in striking distance, he drove his sword into the lower back of the man closest to him, intending to pull it free in time to strike another before they had time to react; however, the man he stabbed yelled out and turned suddenly and violently towards Niran.

As the man turned, Niran's sword was again ripped from his grip, and he found himself unarmed. The wounded man, blood gushing from his open mouth, lurched forward, one hand cupping the blood that spilt from the protruding sword, and the other holding a machete. He raised his hand weakly as if intending to strike Niran, who stumbled backwards, tripped over a corpse, and landed awkwardly on the deck of the boat, but the man never made it. The machete dropped from his raised hand, and he pitched sideways, falling into one of the other men he fought with.

Pulling himself up on his elbows, Niran searched desperately for a weapon, anything he could use to protect himself, and then saw a spear just out of his reach. One of the other two men had abandoned his fight, seeing his companion drop, and was now coming towards Niran screaming obscenities. He brought his axe down hard, and Niran just managed to roll free of the black iron axe head as it split wood within the boat and bit into the decking, which held the axe fast. Fortunately, Niran had fallen into one of the enemy boats, which offered some room to manoeuvre. If it had been in one of the canoes, he would have been missing part of his anatomy, but the threat to his life was far from over.

His assailant heaved on the handle of the axe several times as he looked over at Niran, eyes wild and spittle flying from his mouth as he cursed in his native tongue. Niran had mere moments to react as he propped himself up on his elbows and knees to regain his feet. He saw a broken shaft of a spear by his feet and snatched it up, charging towards his attacker.

Just as the man pried the axe from the deck, the wooden shaft in Niran's hand smashed into the side of the man's head, then across his exposed thigh, followed by a savage kick to the side of his ribs. As Niran kicked him, he reached out for the axe in the man's hands and yanked it from his grasp, just as the man toppled over into the river.

Axe in hand, Niran ran straight for the third man who was still hacking away at the men stuck on the canoe and decapitated him in one swift swing. He dropped the axe, seeing the man that held his sword, placed his foot on the limp body and retrieved the sword.

The royal guard that followed him had managed to kill both men he faced and now, Niran had four men about him.

'We need to move to secure ground. Head for the shore on the west, tell as many men as you can. We will regroup there and make our stand,' he managed to say through deep breaths, chest heaving and muscles burning in his legs.

The three men started to clamber out of the canoe and head towards the west shoreline. Niran and the royal guard took up the rear. The fog had begun to lift and the sight that greeted Niran filled him with despair. The Calabar clearly outnumbered them, with boats still coming through the narrow pass ahead brimming with warriors. Out of the twelve canoes that Niran commanded, only three or four still held a full complement of warriors. The rest of his men were scattered across the open waters, desperately fighting for their lives, dead or on the cusp of making their final journey to the dark halls of the underworld.

Without the reinforcements expected from Adebola, there would be no escaping the inevitable. Should he sound the retreat and save the lives of the few that remained, or maintain his decision to make for the shoreline and stand to face the

enemy, risking more casualties and potentially condemning his men to a certain doom? Both options came with their perils, but one of them could give them a chance of survival. It then occurred to him that he had come too far to turn and flee. What would the people think of him? The people who so desperately looked to him to serve as the catalyst of change in the realm. How long would it be before all the hard-fought alliances decided that he, after all, was unworthy of the legend that was so quick to be bestowed on his name? At that moment, he realised that he would rather stand and die facing his enemy with a sword in hand, as any true warrior would. It was the only path destined for him. His decision was made.

Suddenly, one of the three men ahead of him cried out in anguish, tumbled from the boat he had just boarded and fell into the river. No one had seen what happened, but a heartbeat later, spears started to rain down on them, like blades delivered from the heavens seeking death. The Calabar warriors that held the platforms along the shoreline had defeated the men they fought and were now reinforced by more men ferried from the boats that persisted to fill the narrow waters.

Spear after spear was hurled with deadly intent, seeking victims as if they played a sport of target practice with the men onboard the boats, carefully taking the time to avoid their countrymen and finding great success. The screams of the westerners soon rent the air, but more were now trying their best to retaliate, taking discarded spears and sending them back as quickly as they could.

With mounting horror, Niran saw that there was no cover in sight and the shoreline was still several precarious boat lengths away. If they stayed on the boats, they would soon be plucked from the vessels and skewered like chickens ready for the roasting fire. They had to keep moving to stand a chance.

'Keep going! Aim for the shore, that is our only chance of survival!' Niran roared at the royal guards and the two warriors ahead, who had slowed amidst the chaos. However, all was not lost. Two canoes that held Niran's men had noticed the prince and begun to turn their vessels to reach him in a bid to place themselves between him and the line of spears. The drivers strained against the long poles that manoeuvred the vessels, cords of muscles in their arms tensing with the effort.

One of the drivers suddenly flew backwards and disappeared into the river, impaled by a spear to shouts of encouragement and jubilation from the Calabar warriors. The men in the canoe started paddling with their hands, swords, anything that would create sufficient momentum to turn the craft. Their effort appeared to be hopeless.

Seun continued to wreak havoc deep into the bowels of the enemy's advancing lines. He had lost all sense of order the moment he had seen the number of boats that were heading towards their small fleet. His only thoughts were to prevent these men from reaching the prince and salvage their waning plans, which were all but in tatters.

Some of the westerners, inspired by the sight of him and the damage he inflicted, began to congregate about him, adding more pressure to the unrelenting Calabar warriors. The fighting became even more savage and desperate. The environment in which they fought did not offer any opportunity for a disciplined assault, men simply jumped between boats, fought to clear them of their occupants and moved on to the next boat. This pattern was repeated for what seemed an age.

Seun's arms were slick with blood as he swung his sword and axe. A spear came darting towards him, which he sidestepped. Using the short-handled axe in his left hand, he deflected the shaft further away from him and, with a back-handed stroke, slit the throat of the man that attacked him. Another came in with a sword, swinging downwards at him. He crossed both axe and sword to take the strike and brought both downwards in an arc along with the enemy's sword, leaving the man exposed to take the point of Lanre's sword, who fought at his shoulder.

Then they heard the commotion and saw the rain of spears that ripped through the men further back along the mingled boats and canoes. His heart almost stopped in his chest; the prince was nowhere in sight. He swept his gaze over the carnage and saw two canoes frantically trying to turn with men pointing towards something. He followed their line of sight and spotted a group of men moving as best as they could towards the shore opposite the Calabar spearmen, but they were still within range of the spears that continued to rain down. 'Niran!'

'The prince is in grave danger and needs our protection. We must reach him before it is too late!' Seun said to Lanre, before turning to the other western warriors in close proximity. 'Your prince requires your swords. If he falls, all we have fought for will count for nothing and the kingdom we all yearn for will be carried away on the breeze and lost to us forever. We cannot allow this to happen. Fight for your prince!' he roared, and the men about him responded vehemently 'For the prince!'

That brief speech seemed to have breathed new life into the men as their blood-churning war cries resounded causing all the Calabar warriors within earshot to pause for an instant, which was just enough time to allow doubt to slowly poison their resolve.

If the westerners had fought savagely earlier, now they fought with the wrath of the gods, all in the name of Prince Niran. Even the fatally wounded amongst them were compelled to summon their last ounce of strength to take at least one more victim before they allowed the darkness to overcome them.

Seun wasted no time as he raced towards Niran, leaping from boat to boat in single bounds and killing men effortlessly as he went. He would land on a boat, dodge an attack, slash, leap to the next boat, sidestep out of the path of a swinging blade, thrust, parry, slice, and so it went. Every strike he performed found its mark and he left nothing but corpses in his wake as he desperately charged onwards to stand beside his prince.

The Calabar warriors on the timber platform had now realised that the prince, the highest possible prize to claim in this gods-forsaken river of sorrow, was within sight, and they doubled their efforts to be the one to bring down the man that had been the scourge of the Calabar tribe for so long. For they knew that fame, wealth, and the eternal gratitude of their chief awaited them if they were successful.

Seun did not slow but tried to quicken his pace; despite the multitude of obstacles to contend with, from the men eager to kill him to the unstable boats beneath his feet, he pushed himself onwards. He heard Lanre's panting just over his shoulder and was thankful that the royal guard had managed to keep up with him.

He killed another man as he dashed forward, pivoted on the ball of his front foot, and brought his sword upwards under the man's armpit, then he stole a quick glance at the prince, still making his way towards the shoreline. In a moment of horror, he noted that out of the three men that had been running with the prince, only one remained. The others must have been struck by the falling spears, which had slowed somewhat, because one of the canoes that had rowed to the prince's aid had now reached the far end of the platforms, and the warriors onboard were engaging some of the spearmen. But the platforms on that side of the shore were numerous, manned by many Calabar warriors. Some were engaged in fending off western warriors in general, while others still had their eyes on the prize, the very means to bring the battle to a decisive halt.

Seun stopped and looked for the platform closest to the prince, as that would be the biggest and most obvious threat. His eyes rested on one that held four men, a spear each in their hands and more spear bundles at their feet. One of them took aim at the prince, hurled his spear but missed. Seun's heart leaped. He had to reach those men at once but there were no boats or canoes close enough for him to use to bridge the gap between them. He would have to swim across, which would take too long, and worst of all, leave him vulnerable to a carefully aimed spear.

'Look, over there. We can make that boat, it is closer,' shouted Lanre at his back, seemingly having the same thoughts as Seun. Without a second thought or another word, they both set off. Seun went first, taking a couple of steps back in the large boat, then shot forward to build enough momentum and took one long leap. He flapped through the air for a split heartbeat then slammed into the side of the boat, winding himself in the process, but still managing to grab a hold of the side and drag himself up and into it. The boat rocked under his weight, and he saw two dead men onboard, both Calabar. One had a spear jutting from his back and the other was missing a leg below the knee and would have bled out. He turned towards Lanre, who was already running to the edge of the other boat, about to jump.

Lanre fell short and plunged straight into the river, but Seun reached out to grab his flailing hand and hauled him into the boat. They were now within a spear's throw of the platform, and this was as close as they could hope to get to those men. If they were to attack, the spearmen were certain to divert their attention to them, potentially sealing their own fate, but allowing the prince time to make it to safety. It was a gamble they were both prepared to take; after all, what was their purpose in life other than to protect their prince, even if it hastened their own demise?

Seun fixed Lanre with a knowing look and then nodded, which was returned. Both men understood what needed to be done without the need for words. Seun then took careful aim and threw his axe with a grunt. The small axe spun through the air in a blur of grey iron and caught one of the spearmen in the side of the head, splitting bone on impact. It was by no means an easy throw, and looked as if it was guided by the hand of some god, but it evoked the intended response. When the axe struck, Lanre could not help but let out a cheer, which died in his throat as quickly as it had come, as a spear was sent back to them in response. One, then another, the spearmen now seething with bloody murder at the sight of their tribesman with an axe decorating his features.

Seun and Lanre avoided the first volley easily, as they were thrown in anger with no skill behind them. Seun then yanked the spear out of the dead man's back. 'Is that the best you can do, you cowards? Try again, I'm right here!' he roared over the river, but the spearmen would not have understood him anyway as they only spoke their native tongue. Lanre snatched up one of the spears that had missed them and landed in the boat. 'Now we shall see who the better spearmen are,' he said with a smile.

The majority of the Calabar warriors on the platform then took turns throwing their spears at the boat, realising that they needed to take their time, but the last warrior still sought out the prince. He would not be robbed of this opportunity, so he slowed his breathing, stretched out an arm in front of him, pulled back the other until the spearhead was level with his eye, and let it fly. He watched as the black shaft soared through the sky, began to arc, and came down hard, his efforts rewarded with a satisfying bellow of pain. He had hit his mark.

A pain that Niran had never experienced in all his years seized him and he was thrown forward and spun halfway around at the same time. He crashed down into the deck, striking his head on the side of the boat on his way down, dazing him. He was not sure what had happened but, subconsciously, he knew he had been hit with a spear. He struggled to raise himself, head pounding, and his vision blurred, then pain lanced through his left side, sending him back down hard on his stomach.

He raised his head, tentatively looking over his shoulder, and saw a long shaft protruding from his back. His fear was confirmed, he had been struck by a spear. Despite the agony he felt and the haze of his concussion, he still possessed the presence of mind to know that he had to keep moving. His position was too exposed, and he needed to make it to safety. He gritted his teeth against the pain, pushed himself up on his right arm and slowly made it to his feet.

The pressed layers of leather armour he wore had saved him from any lasting injury, absorbing most of the spear's momentum, but about three finger widths of the sharpened iron head had made it through and was embedded in his back near his shoulder blade. As he stood, the weight of the shaft caused the spearhead to dislodge, ripping through more of his flesh as it fell from his armour. Niran cried out in pain and suddenly felt lightheaded, just before he toppled over the side of the boat and into the murky water.

The cold sensation from the water engulfed him like icy fingers wrapping around his every extremity, coupled with a jolt of fear that overcame him as he plunged deeper. He was disorientated, unsure as to whether he was upright or upside down, and he began to kick and beat his arms vigorously. The pain in his back was gone, as was the grogginess he had experienced but a moment ago. Both were replaced by pure terror as he twisted and turned in the dark waters.

He gasped for breath and took in a mouthful of water, lungs burning, eyes bulging and stinging, the sounds of his muted screams and thrashing water deafening him. Bubbles, flailing arms, heart beating three times as fast. The darkness was coming. His lungs felt like they would explode, burning pain in his chest, fingers raking at his throat, reaching upwards or downwards, seeking something to grasp. Anything.

There were bodies everywhere, performing 'death dances' in the water, the pirouette of the drowned, slowly twirling, arms and legs splayed, lifeless faces, eyes white, vacant expressions. He reached out and tried to grab one of them and use it as a support to propel himself upwards to the salvation of air, but it only dragged him down further into the darkness below that claimed everything here.

Panicked thrashing, utter helplessness, realised hopelessness. *My dreams, everything I have strived for, bled for, die with me. Here. Now. In this cold, dark place,* he thought despairingly. His heart had begun to slow, lungs full of water, limbs too heavy to move. Not long now.

Vision beginning to fade, body spasming, yearning for the respite of oxygen. The darkness was close at hand.

Something moved in the murkiness below him, rising, rhythmically like an eel. The bodies about him were slowly travelling downwards, so why was this one moving in the opposite direction, towards him? *My final moments are upon me,* he thought, convincing himself that his rational mind had fled just before the darkness consumed him.

He glimpsed black hair, long braids like snakes trying to escape a basket, slithering in all directions, inching closer still. His vision came into focus, and he could make out the outline of a face, dark eyes, delicate features, and a warm smile. A woman's face, iridescent, enchanting, stunning but haunting and yet, compassionate. He saw cowrie shells decorating her neckline and both wrists. Her dress was the colour of water, shimmering, blending into the surroundings and somehow outlining her slim figure vividly. Her hands reached out to him, pulling him close, cradling him, soothing him.

This was unfathomable. *What do my eyes behold? Have I already crossed into the world beyond that of man? And who can this woman be? Perhaps she is the keeper of the gate come to lead me on my final journey through the dark halls of the underworld,* Niran thought to himself. Nothing made any sense.

'Do not fear, son of King Jide. You still remain amongst the living. The hour for you to walk through the halls of darkness is yet to come, for you have much to accomplish in the world of men, my child. I will lead you to the path you must take, just as I did your father before you. But you may never speak of this, lest you wish to dwell in the depths of the river and have the fish pick upon your bones.'

Niran could only listen transfixed, but he knew that everything he heard and witnessed, despite his rational mind still struggling to comprehend any of it, would follow him to his grave. Then the realisation hit him like a slap across the face. *Yemoja*, the goddess of the rivers. This was no dream, no distorted image flashing before his eyes in the face of death. This was his reality, and he was truly in the presence of divinity.

Everything from that point on became a blur and, moments later, he was on the shore convulsing and spewing water. There were shadows about him, slowly taking light like the sun clearing a dark cloud. Faces slowly took shape, some familiar, then voices, people he knew, his people. Adebola was amongst them with a look of concern, looming overhead with a handful of warriors gathering about him. 'The prince lives!' someone shouted out to cheers.

'What happened?' asked Niran in a trembling voice as his nostrils were tickled by the metallic scent of blood, burning wood and plant life indigenous to these parts.

'We were ambushed, my prince. Somehow, the Calabar warriors knew we were coming. They were waiting for us, concealed in the shrubs and bushes. It is only by *Olorun's* divine mercy that we made it out of there alive. We fought a bloody battle and, unfortunately, there was no escaping a significant number of casualties, on both sides, but we persevered and overcame them. We even managed to capture a few of their warriors, who told us about the trap that was set for you, my prince. So, we came to you as quickly as we could,' Adebola explained as he rushed through his words, clearly trying to articulate all that had befallen him and his men before the adrenaline that coursed through his veins fled from him.

'We won, my prince. I am unsure how, but despite all the impediments we faced, your plan worked. The rivers belong to us now. It is only a matter of time before all the river tribes fall before you and beg for your mercy!' Adebola finished, eyes bright with excitement.

Niran closed his eyes and took in a long breath of air and held it in for a heartbeat, savouring the moment, then let it out slowly. He looked around at the smiling faces about him, took in the scenery beyond, the wreckage of vessels, the mixture of warriors, allies and foes, in varying states – triumphant, despondent, wounded, or dead.

He pondered how the Calabar had been able to anticipate his strategy and stay one step ahead of them. Could he have been betrayed by one of his own? The implications of this would be catastrophic, as only the most senior people in his purposely small circle were party to the full details of his plans. But there would be time enough to deliberate and solve that riddle. Now, he needed rest and wanted nothing more than to close his eyes and sink his head into the soft wet sand at his feet. And that is exactly what he did.

A FLIGHT
OF COWARDS

'Something does not appear to be right about this scene. There should be nothing short of an army here if the knowledge we possess is accurate, and yet, all I see is a handful of men idling insouciantly like this was some common village,' Zogo said as he peered through the bushes that concealed him and his Igbo warriors.

They had travelled under the cover of night to the bordering town on the threshold of the River-lands, to observe the settlement that was thought to house supplies and the Calabar's first line of defence. However, as dawn approached and sunlight washed over the landscape and the dwellings, all they saw was a handful of guards warming themselves at the fading fires from the chill that had accompanied the night. There were no defensive walls to speak of, no ditches or sharpened stakes in the ground to serve as a deterrent to would-be attackers, and the men did not appear to be alert in the slightest. It was as if they had been burdened with a task that they had no choice but to obey.

'It could still be a trap. Maybe they anticipate an attack and expect us to be drawn in by this façade,' whispered Zogo's son, Obinna, in their Igbo tongue.

'I doubt that very much. I have seen the look and demeanour of men plotting a ruse, and these pitiful excuses for warriors do not appear to possess that quality. Unless they are excellent actors. But I am willing to wager my spear that they are not,' Zogo replied, still squinting through the leaves, taking in every detail of the town's surroundings. He was an old warrior with a keen eye, and he had experience enough to trust in his instincts.

'What are your orders, my chief?' asked Obinna.

Zogo looked to the skies and gauged the position of the raising sun. 'The prince should be in position, or close enough by now, so we follow through with our plans. Ready the men, we will advance on my signal,' Zogo responded, as he checked his spear and looked at the imposing figures of the two axe-wielding bodyguards that were always at his side. He nodded to them, raised a fist in the air, stood from his crouched position and started to creep through the bushes.

The Igbos emerged from the vegetation like lions silently stalking their prey. They chose not to announce themselves, no war cries or shouts, just the sound of rustling leaves disturbed by a multitude of men and the odd dull metallic clink of weapons.

The men at the fires were none the wiser, too preoccupied with dispelling the lethargy that preceded the light of dawn, but suddenly one of them caught movement out of the corner of his eye. He slowly looked up, his features registering the surprise of seeing so many men converging on their position. He raised his hand to warn his companions, but before he had the time to utter a word, a spear came flying through the air to silence him.

The other men around the fires jumped up in shock, scrambling to arm themselves, but it was too late. The Igbo warriors were upon them so quickly that it was over before any of the unfortunate guards even had a chance to put up a fight.

Using hand gestures only, Zogo instructed his men to advance on the town. Even though he sensed no threat, he was not prepared to take anything for granted and would proceed with caution.

A group of warriors remained by the now diminishing fires to serve as lookouts, while the rest made their way into the haphazard network of pathways created between the dwellings. They moved quickly, still maintaining their discipline, and silently but methodically went through the dwellings. It was clear that this had once been a fishing village from the equipment and wares sprawled about the compounds – nets still hanging from bamboo posts, upturned boats in various states of disrepair and construction, baskets, and stacks of palm leaves for weaving. But there were also the tell-tale signs that a large contingent of men had recently occupied this place, and not just locals, but warriors. There was a blacksmith's workshop, the furnace still warm, with an array of unfinished weapons in view – spear and axe heads, machetes and daggers, weapons clearly not designed to gut fish. There was leatherwork – scabbards, fastenings and the like. Food stores brimming with vegetables, salted fish and meats, enough to feed more than just a few town dwellers. It looked as if the place had been abandoned in haste and very recently.

How could that be? thought Zogo with mounting dread. It was almost as if they had been forewarned of an imminent attack. And if they knew to expect them, they must also know of the prince's plans, which was even more troubling. The prince was a prized target, so there was merit in believing that the Calabar warriors would focus all their resources on his capture or elimination at the risk of losing a town. He was suddenly filled with the urge to head to the coastline with all alacrity to ensure the safety of the prince. But his first objective was to secure this town and hold it. That is what the prince demanded, and those were his orders, so he was duty-bound to see this task through.

After a short while, some of his warriors returned, dragging several men between them. The men had obviously been beaten and had to be hauled by their elbows, and held upright in the presence of the Igbo chief.

Zogo looked over the captives; they appeared to be dressed in nondescript clothing, faded kaftans and other pieces of rough-spun materials, but they wore good quality leather sandals, which were not congruent with the rest of their attire. 'And what do we have here?' Zogo asked, arms folded in front of him and raising an eyebrow.

'We found a few men in some of the houses, my chief. They are Calabar warriors attempting to pass as townspeople, and I believe you would be interested to hear what they have to say; well, the ones that decided to talk,' replied one of Zogo's men as he held up a captive by the crook of one of his arms.

'I trust that you do not intend to waste my time. Where are the townspeople or, better still, the warriors that occupied this town?' Zogo asked one of the captives.

The man closest to him looked up from under his swollen eyebrows and spat in the dust beside the chief's feet. One of the axe-wielding guards at Zogo's shoulder immediately stepped forward and drove the butt of his long axe handle into the stomach of the man, which prompted a bout of strained coughs.

'I will tell you what you need to know, but I require some guarantees.' This was spoken in heavily accented Igbo by one of the other captives. The man seemed to have some authority amongst them just from his confidence and his bearing.

'And what guarantees do you seek?' Zogo asked.

'I only ask that you spare my life and those of my men. We were only following orders, as I am sure you are. Grant this request and I swear never to raise arms against you and your tribesmen, as all the gods are my witness,' the man beseeched.

'You cannot seriously believe the words of this traitor. Any man willing to betray his tribe so quickly can never be trusted.

The moment we release him, he will forsake his vows and seek the first opportunity to stab us in the back. Men such as this should be made an example of,' said a young warrior, whose face was twisted with hatred.

'That decision is not yours to make, young man, and a true warrior is nothing without his word.' Zogo then turned to address the captive: 'If the information is useful, I will consider your life, though I cannot guarantee the same for all your men.' The young warrior who had spoken earlier kissed his teeth in disgust, which earned him a stern look from Zogo and the men at his back.

'That is good enough for me,' the prisoner replied after a moment's thought. 'Your intuition is correct; this is a stronghold held in chief Essien's name, but we received orders yesterday to move the army to the coastline to prepare for an attack. We were told that the prince himself would be there, so every able-bodied warrior went for an opportunity to be the one to capture or kill the most renowned name in all the eastern provinces. Only a few warriors were left behind to guard this town.'

Zogo's fears were confirmed – Niran was in grave danger. It seemed that he had no choice but to go against the prince's wishes if it meant potentially saving his life. He took a moment to think before turning to one of the men that stood beside him.

Turning to Obinna, 'Summon Uzoma to me at once. We will take some of our men to the coast to aid the prince. The rest will remain here, and Uzoma will see to it that the town is secured,' Zogo said. The warrior beside him inclined his head and hurried off in search of the named man.

Turning back to the captive who had spoken, Zogo watched the man intently. 'I will spare your life and that of all your men, for now, but I will not set you free. You will remain our captives until I return. If the prince lives, he will be the one to pass judgement on you, but I will stand in your favour for the information you have provided. However, if the prince has been taken or, worse still, fallen...' Zogo let the unspoken words hang in the air for emphasis; he needed not comment any further.

The captive seemed to accept the terms begrudgingly, but the look of relief on his face was visible as he translated the words to the other prisoners.

'Chief, I do not think this is a wise choice...' said the young warrior but was cut short by a raised finger from Zogo as he addressed one of his other men.

'Find a suitable place to lock them up, but I will not have them ill-treated any further. Provide them with water and food if they require it,' he said, finger still raised at the young warrior.

'Yes, my chief,' the man replied as the prisoners were taken away.

Once they were out of earshot, Zogo turned to the young warrior with the look that had earned him the name *the black*. 'Never again challenge me in front of our people, or anyone else for that matter. Have you lost your senses? The only reason you are even allowed to stand beside me is out of respect for your father's memory. I will not repeat myself. You will remain here with the men. Do not make me regret my decision to take you under my hand, Etim.'

The young warrior held Zogo's gaze as if he was about to voice his own vituperation, muscles in his forearm tensing as he clenched his fists, but he decided against it and instead inclined his head. 'Apologies, my chief. I spoke out of turn, and it will not happen again.'

Zogo only flicked his head upwards in response, dismissing the boy, who stalked off after the captives, leaving Zogo with one of his guards.

'I see so much of his father, Edem, in him, and there was nothing good about that cold-hearted bastard. The temperament of the boy is uncanny. His solution to almost everything is to shed blood like there is not a single rational bone in his body. It is a wonder that people have not started calling him Etim the ugly,' Zogo said as he watched the boy disappear behind a house.

'He is still young and encumbered with the burden of a marred ego from being locked up for so long and losing his father to such unfortunate circumstances. Mind you, he certainly does not lack in ambition, and it is only a matter of time before he stakes his claim on the chieftaincy title of the Akwa-Ibom province,' replied the guard.

'Oh, I am counting on it. And I would give it to him gladly if I was convinced that he would be a man worthy of the title, but I just do not see it. It seems his only purpose in life is to prove that he is a fearless warrior with a heart of stone, but a leader must exercise restraint when it is needed, compassion, and understanding. He cannot comprehend, let alone possess any of these qualities, gods help us.'

Just then, the man known as the jester came bounding in. 'Chief Zogo, how can I be of service?' he asked, full of enthusiasm.

'Must you always be so annoyingly cheerful, Uzoma?' Zogo asked shaking his head.

'To spread cheer is one of the little pleasures in life, my chief. One can so easily fall into darkness considering the lives we live, after all,' Uzo replied.

'As long as your cheer does not prevent you from carrying out your duty.'

'Ah, but you should know that my vivaciousness only conceals the head of my spear, my chief,' Uzo said with that infectious smile of his, and it was Obinna's turn to shake his head.

'If you say so. The Calabar warriors that manned this town were ordered to ambush the prince. Somehow, our plans were uncovered. Prince Niran will need reinforcements at the coast, and we must march to his aid immediately. I will lead a few of our warriors, but this place must be held for the prince.'

Uzo rubbed at the stubble on his chin in thought, and his smile now turned into a frown. 'This is grave news indeed. So, what would you have me do, my chief?'

'You will remain behind and see to the defence of this town, should the Calabar decide to return. Dig trenches around the perimeter and send out scouts to man all the paths that lead here. Do whatever you must to hold it. We cannot afford for this place to fall back into the hands of the Calabar. The prince will be depending on it.'

'Your will, my chief. But my first task will be to rid this place of all the rats. It is infested, and some of them are huge!'

'I do not care about the rats, just carry out my orders. I want this town completely fortified before the sun reaches its peak. Understood?'

'Yes, of course, my chief. I will see to it.'

'Good. And get that furnace fired up. I am sure there are some men amongst us that have the skill to work metal. We may come to need it. Now go.'

Uzo inclined his head to Zogo and hurried away, issuing instructions to some of the men. Before long the Igbo were hard at work about the town, dismantling boats and using the material to erect barricades, sharpening wooden stakes to be hardened in fire and driven into the ground behind the freshly dug trenches, gathering pitch, oil and other combustible materials, and placing men at all the locations of vantage around the town. More Calabar warriors were discovered hiding amongst the dwellings, and they chose to surrender without the slightest resistance. They were joined with their companions in a shed that doubled as a makeshift prison, and held under guard.

Zogo had selected thirty of his best warriors to accompany him on his task, leaving some forty men behind to defend the town, a gamble if the Calabar did return in force, as the men left behind would be spread thinly defending a town of this size, but they had prepared as best they could, and would give their lives to fulfil their vows to the prince.

Just before Zogo marched, he gathered his warriors about him to give them some final words of inspiration, when he spied a plume of smoke rising a few paces away from where they stood. They raced to the source of the smoke, spears in hand, fearing that the Calabar had somehow gotten past or overcome their lookouts and scouts without an alarm being raised.

They then came upon several men standing outside one of the smaller dwellings now completely engulfed in flames. Standing closest to the fire with a look of smug satisfaction was Uzoma.

'What is the meaning of this? I leave you in command for five heartbeats and you have already managed to set the town ablaze. What if the flames spread? And do you not think that the sight of a column of smoke on the horizon would not attract the eye of everyone in the surrounding area?' Zogo roared at Uzo.

'My chief, it could not be avoided. Some of the men found a nest of the biggest rats I have ever placed my eyes upon. The house had to be torched immediately,' Uzo replied sheepishly.

'Rats! For the love of all the gods, Uzo!' If this town burns before I return, I will have you flogged raw! No more foolery and put the fire out at once!' Zogo did not wait for a reply and walked off angrily with his chosen men in tow ready to depart the town and head for the coast.

'At least we have solved the rat problem. Now we can concentrate on more important things,' Uzo said to no one in particular, as he shrugged his shoulders and turned away from the fire.

Etim was standing close by, eyes fixed on the dancing flames as they rose above the dwelling. As he watched, he could not help but think that the flames mirrored what he felt deep in his heart – a desire to consume everything that stood in the path of his destiny and leave nothing behind but ashes.

WINDS OF CHANGE

'I could get used to this feeling,' Toju said as he reclined in the tub filled with steaming hot water. This was a new experience for him. The people of the tribes were content with bathing in the lakes and rivers or drawing pails of water from wells to throw over themselves. Heating water to bathe in was seen as a waste of time and effort. This was one thing that Toju could honestly say was an oversight by his people and one that he would seek to rectify in the future.

There were several female servants draped in thin, almost see-through clothing that didn't leave much to the imagination. Their soft linen attire clung to their slim physiques, accentuated at certain body parts that would draw the eye of even the most pious of men, as they went about replenishing his tub with steaming water to keep the temperature consistent, whilst serving him sweet beverages and fruits. Toju knew that this display was nothing short of a deliberate attempt to lure him into a false sense of ease and comfort, but they were gravely mistaken to think a man such as he would be so inclined.

He did, however, indulge in the proffered pleasures, not wanting to cause offence, although his sword was beside him leaning against the side of the tub, with his hand firmly wrapped around the hilt, so he was not entirely naked.

Another steaming calabash was emptied into his tub by one of the attendants, whose eyes lingered on Toju a fraction longer than was necessary, seeking reciprocation, but Toju only offered a curt smile in response before turning away. He was obviously the object of all their desires, this rough foreigner that came down from the hills and slayed a dozen men demanding an audience with the shahbanu, which was granted without the threat of reprisal despite his insolence. Such a man was a rarity in the lands of these people, and certainly one to be revered.

Toju's mind, however, was firmly focused on the meeting ahead; everything else was a mere distraction as the dirt from his travels was washed away, leaving him with a feeling of rejuvenation. The curtains that covered the entrance to the tent suddenly parted and Hassan strolled in with a warm smile plastered on his face.

'Great prince, I trust our hospitality is to your liking?' Hassan's eyes moved to the sword beside the tub. 'Really, it is not necessary to have a weapon here. You are a most welcome guest of the shahbanu. No harm will come to you, that I can assure you.'

'It was not necessary to make an attempt on my life, so forgive me if I do not feel entirely comfortable, guest or not,' Toju replied.

'Understandable, but I can only offer our humble apologies again for our minor… indiscretion.'

'Minor indiscretion? Forgive me, but I fail to see how an assassination attempt can be remotely perceived as minor. Would you consider it minor if I decided to take your head? Anyway, what is done is behind us now. I believe I am pampered sufficiently enough to address your ruler; do you not think?' Toju asked as he stood up, having no shame in exposing himself in front of all the attendants in the room.

'Very good, great prince. However, no one is permitted to bear arms in the presence of the shahbanu. You will have to leave your sword with one of the guards.'

'That, Hassan, is not going to happen. My sword will remain on my person, but no harm will come to the shahbanu, that I can assure you.'

Hassan's smile faltered, and for a moment he was, for once, lost for words.

'Great prince, I am afraid… I must insist…'

'And I will humbly decline. Let us not waste any more time on this charade. I am cleaned, and I am appeased from your earlier welcome, but I am a man of some status and cannot afford to put my life at risk again.' He stretched out his free hand to an attendant who hesitated before reluctantly passing him a cloth. Two more attendants hurriedly went to him and began wiping him down, taking their time to surreptitiously admire his seemingly sculptured figure.

'I will inform the shahbanu of your… request, but this may be displeasing to our great ruler. Forgive me, I will allow you to dress and return for you presently, great prince.' Hassan bowed briefly and then disappeared through the curtains. Toju could only smile to himself at seeing the man's discomfort, but he cared not. All he knew was that nothing would part him from his blade, no matter how nicely, or forcefully for that matter, they insisted.

The servants had laid out a long flowing kaftan of white linen for him to wear, but Toju decided to don the cloths he had arrived in, now cleaned and polished, feeling much more comfortable in his armour. He did, however, decide to wear the kaftan under his fighting leathers to show that he was willing to make some compromises.

Not long after, Hassan returned and could not help himself from scrutinising the prince from head to toe, making sure that not a stitch was out of place, and that he was presentable to stand before this ruler of vast tribes.

'The shahbanu has granted you to carry your blade, great prince. This is indeed a significant concession, one that I personally have never seen granted even to great lords. This should go a long way in proving that you are held in the highest of esteems.'

'Should I have expected anything less?' Toju responded with a hint of arrogance that was not lost on Hassan, who only inclined his head gracefully, not wanting to provoke the prince's anger. He needed to placate Toju and ensure that he was in a calm state of mind before he was admitted to stand before the shahbanu. The last thing he wanted was for emotions to overshadow any negotiations, which would not bode well for any of the parties involved and certainly have wide-reaching implications. To all intents and purposes, Hassan hoped for nothing more than amicable discourse between two great nations in the hopes of discovering common ground but, deep down, he could not help the scepticism he concealed within his heart.

Hassan held open the curtains for Toju and indicated for him to pass through respectfully. Once they were outside, Toju saw that even more guards were stationed around the camp. This was unsurprising, as he would have done the same if he had been in their position. A leopard walking amongst goats was the image that came to his mind, and he smiled to himself.

Hassan led the way along a path that snaked between the large tents, each manned by at least three guards. Toju did not fail to spy the odd looks that were directed at him as he walked by. Many quickly averted their gaze, but some looked on as if silently challenging him to confront them.

Let them look. It is unlikely they will ever see a greater warrior in their lifetime, he thought pleasingly. Perhaps he was not far wrong, as the unmistakable glint of veneration was written in every glance, even those that attempted to appear intimidating.

They came to a very large tent nestled in what seemed to be the centre of the camp. An awning was attached to one side of the tent with a few wooden stools neatly arranged beneath it. Perhaps this was a waiting area of sorts for the many supplicants that sought an audience with the shahbanu.

Toju concluded that this was no ordinary horde rampaging across the lands, but a well-organised and ordered civilisation with structure, policies, protocols and, most of all, discipline. He began to reassess his opinions towards them and decided to change his approach and restrain his arrogance and sense of entitlement. Self-effacement had never been his strong suit, but diplomacy was his main objective, after all, and he was determined to settle on an outcome that benefited his own interests and, by extension, those of his adopted people and these foreigners.

He could not help but notice the sheer number of guards dotted around the tent. There must have been at least thirty warriors strategically positioned. Five manned the entrance to the tent, and it was clear that these men were the elite from the quality of their armour, weapons, and the battle scars they wore just as proudly.

Hassan approached the lead guard, who stood with his arms crossed, faint white scars zigzagging around his forearms. The guard did not take his eyes off Toju, and there was nothing but hostility behind those dark pools. This man was a killer, nothing more. Hassan, despite his obvious status, still looked uneasy as he talked in hushed tones with the battle-hardened warrior.

The man only grunted, looked over his shoulder at the four men that stood behind him and flicked his head. They parted and stood at attention in unison, exposing curtains of exquisite artwork. The stitching was extraordinary, intricate swirling patterns in perfect symmetry in a multitude of colours, truly the work of a master. The curtains alone could easily fund a small army, giving Toju a sense of the wealth this ruler possessed.

'Please, great prince. The shahbanu awaits you inside,' Hassan said gently.

'Will you not be accompanying me to stand as a translator?' Toju asked.

Hassan laughed quietly, 'The shahbanu does not require my service in this, great prince. She is well learned and speaks the tongue of every land and people under her vast rule.'

'She? Are you telling me this shahbanu is… a woman?' Toju asked in surprise.

'Oh yes, great prince. It is in the name. A shahbanu is a title for a female ruler. Forgive me, I should not have assumed that you would be familiar with our terminologies.'

Toju was now the one to be lost for words. He could not even begin to comprehend what he had just been told. In his world, leadership in any form was a title solely reserved for men. There were queens and consorts, of course, but they only ever played a minor role in the hierarchy of power. This concept of a female ruler was as alien to him as the language they spoke and he was suddenly more intrigued to meet this shahbanu, ruler of this conglomeration of nations.

Without responding to Hassan, he took a step towards the curtains, stole a brief look at the leader of the guards, who narrowed his eyes and produced a half sneer, then walked through them.

The tent appeared to be larger within than it had seemed from the outside, and as suspected, it spoke of great wealth. A long timber post was erected in the centre that held up the roof, with several more around the room all wrapped in soft fabric. Cushions of all sizes with similar patterns to the curtains were spread around, and the entire floor was covered with animal furs and carpets. Tapestries adorned the walls of the tent, all masterfully crafted and telling a variety of stories – battle scenes, beautiful landscapes, palaces, animals, and much more. A delicate floral and welcoming scent tickled his nose, which he inhaled deeply as he closed his eyes.

'You are the model of the picture I had in my mind's eye, great prince of two nations. Come. Sit with me and share in my wine,' came a soft voice in flawless Yoruba that had not a hint of an accent.

'I must say that you are nothing like what I had imagined, Shahbanu,' Toju replied with a smile as he walked over towards the figure reclining on a couch laden with cushions.

When he got closer, he almost faltered at the sight of her striking features; although she lacked the natural beauty of Habibah, she made up for it in several ways. She was probably of middle age, but he could tell that she possessed a strength about her and the vitality of a young maiden.

She had a sharp-angled jawline framing a delicate nose and full lips. Almond-shaped dark brown eyes were accentuated with dark liner, which added to her mystique. Her eyes were piercing, and exuded intelligence as she watched Toju who quickly regained his composure. A ghost of a knowing smile played on her pink lips.

Toju stood before her and drank in every detail; the texture of her skin that appeared darkened by the kiss of the sun's warmth, her slender neck down to the intersection of her collar bones, wrapped in many thin ropes of gold hanging down to her bosom, the curves of her hips under the flowing clothes she wore. He saw that she was tall, a head shorter than he by his reckoning, from the way she took up most of the length of the couch. A thin cloth covered her hair but failed to hide its voluminousness, unruly black strands escaping from under her head covering, cascading over her shoulders.

Then he saw the raised calluses on her palm as she reached for the beaten copper cup beside her. She was no delicate flower. What did he expect of a woman that ruled such a vast people? She would have to be as ruthless as any male ruler, more so in fact, to be able to maintain her grip on the reins of power under her possession.

'Please join me. I have taken the liberty of ordering some palm wine from your lands, and wine from my homeland, processed from exotic grapes, should you wish to partake. Do you have a preference?' she asked as she returned his gaze, obviously impressed at the image of the man before her.

'Thank you, but I think I will refrain from drinking. For now.'

She inclined her head in acknowledgement but poured herself a glass from a bejewelled copper decanter, which must have cost a fortune. If her intentions had been to display wealth, she had made her point.

'Great prince, my name is Amina Rabiu, the shahbanu of these people. I must say that the manner in which we received you on your arrival was most unfortunate. I would have you know that this was not my command, but a man of your status would have been expected to travel in a large contingent and with an advanced party heralding your coming.'

Toju shrugged. 'Please, Shahbanu. It is of no consequence now. Besides, the men responsible have paid for their transgressions adequately, with their blood. We need not speak of the matter further.'

'Indeed, they did. Your reputation does not do you enough justice and your name has risen much further amongst my people. I dare say that every warrior of renown in my service yearns for the opportunity to cross swords with you, if only to prove themselves.'

'I will accept that as a compliment, Shahbanu. There have been many men with similar ambitions and none of them has ever lived to fulfil that dream. These men would be wise to seek other means of proving their skill. Nothing but death awaits them should they insist on pursuing such a fruitless cause.'

The shahbanu had a playful smile that was most pleasing to see. 'I see you do not lack confidence. I do admire a man that has absolute certainty in his ability, and his place in this world. It is quite refreshing.'

It was Toju's turn to incline his head in acceptance of the praise. 'So, tell me, Shahbanu. How is it that a woman has come to rule over such a great number of nations? I must admit that I am truly impressed and eager to learn of your story.'

She smiled and took a sip of her wine before she replied. 'I was told that you had a bold tongue, and I can see that those words are true. No one else would presume to be as direct with me as you have, but you do possess a rare quality and a way about you that is most becoming. So, I will grant a deviation from formalities on this occasion. My father was the shah of our people. Feared and loved in equal measures. He had the greatest army that stretched beyond the raging seas and conquered many kingdoms. His name soared across the lands far and wide, and he had wealth enough for several generations. The only thing he lacked was a male heir. He was blessed or, in the eyes of some, cursed with only daughters, and I was the eldest. So, when he passed, I inherited everything. However, it was by no means an easy ascension, and there were many civil wars between our people to take the late shah's seat, but through the blessings of the one true God, I had the support of his armies and the most powerful lords of all our conquered kingdoms to crush those that opposed me.'

'That is fascinating, to know that the people supported you. Where I am from, the seat of a king would pass to his oldest male relative if the king was to have no male issue.'

'I am aware of the laws and traditions of your people. I take it as a necessity to learn all there is to know of those that

I intend to rule. Or destroy.' The last word hung in the air like a black cloud.

'I must compliment you on your grasp of my tongue. It is without fault, and it tells me much about you. But must we talk of conquering nations? I am here to extend the hand of friendship from the emir of the Hausa people. The north is vast and much of it remains unclaimed. I see no reason why we cannot agree upon some arrangement, one that is mutually beneficial and fosters harmonious co-existence.'

'Are these your words or those of the emir; or, more to the point, his heir, Prince Danjuma? Your bloodline does not truly belong in the north with these people, and I am certain many of the Hausa lords would not hesitate to rid you of the favour you have been privileged to receive from the emir. Some may think that you have denied them the favour that should, by rights, be directed towards them.'

Toju was taken aback by the shahbanu's perceptiveness and how well informed she was. He assumed that she had spies that had infiltrated the very institutions of hierarchy in the north. It would not surprise him if the northern lords of whom she spoke were the ones whispering in her ear and feeding her with the vision of northern conquest. He understood in that moment that she was not only ruthless but also calculating, and she rose further still in his estimations.

'That may be true, but I have taken a Hausa princess to wife, as I am sure you are aware, which binds me to the Hausa. Besides, if my dear wife and I were to be blessed with children, they would have the blood of Hausa royalty and the birth right to northern soil and everything that sprouts from it. So, regardless of what any lord thinks, my fate is entwined with that of my adopted family, just as it is in the land of my father.'

'Noble words, but are you willing to risk the life of your wife for people who do not truly accept you? You could easily ride south with her, claim the crown that is rightfully yours and live a fulfilled life. You have no real loyalties to these people.'

'But I do. I swore an oath to my wife to protect her and all that she loves and holds dear for as long as I draw breath. I am many things, but an oath breaker is not one of them. And I am quite fond of the northern princes, they are like brothers to me. Besides, how long will it be before you decide to turn your sights south to conquer the lands of my birth?'

'At this moment in time, I have no desire to ride south. The north is enough land for me to get to grips with, for now. But you surprise me, Prince Toju. I did not believe you to be one given to sentiment.'

'Neither did I. I never thought I would favour anyone outside of my immediate family. Besides my brother, Prince Niran, the rest of my family are gone, taken from me most cruelly, which I will address in time. Now, I must look to find some measure of happiness for myself, and I did not know just how much I needed that until it was practically forced upon me.'

The shahbanu watched him intently for a moment, then took a long draught from her cup. 'I would never have expected to discover such depth in your character. This is most enlightening. Speaking of your brother, do you not wish to aid him? I hear that there are many battles in the south.'

'My brother is one of the most intelligent people I know. I have no doubt that he is resourceful enough to maintain his hold on the regions he has conquered until I am able to return to our homelands and lend him the hand that is needed to cleanse the besmirchment on our family name that is our dear uncle. Until then, he understands what must be done here, and he would expect nothing less of me. Now, we both have our paths to tread and our destinies to fulfil, until a time when our paths inevitably converge once again as, so I believe, has always been written.'

'I admire your devotion to your brother, and to your wife. It is rare to find a man of such virtues. However, that will not change, as you say, the inevitable. You have your destiny, and so do I. Mine being the eventual rule over all the lands of the known world, as was the late Shah's ambition before his untimely demise. I too am destined to fulfil a legacy, a noble one and one of divine justification; to spread the word of our God, the most high. There can be no greater calling.'

'Now we expose the roots which lie beneath. If the message you wish to spread is truly divine, would it not be more favourably perceived by your god to grant the rulers of the people you intend to conquer the choice to judge if this word is indeed meant for them? Or does your god not recognise the free will of men? You could send your priests to spread the teachings of your belief and see if it would be accepted before you act, no?'

'We both know that this would be a futile endeavour. The traditions and customs of the tribes of the lands south of here are too deeply rooted. They will not soon accept the true path unless the choice is taken from them and they are forced towards it. Ultimately, I seek to save them from their ignorance. These false gods you worship will not grant you eternal salvation but rather lead you to damnation.'

'And what makes you believe that your god is any different or superior to the gods of my people? What proof do you have of this claim?'

'There are many miracles that attest to His divine presence. Some I have witnessed with my very eyes.'

'I could argue the same. It is well known that many generations ago, our gods built some of our great cities with their own hands and walked amongst us freely. You can see their influence all around us. And I am sure that you may argue the same of yours. Maybe both our gods exist, and the choice of who we choose to devote ourselves to is up to each person as they desire. Why must one be superior or more revered than the other? Why must there be a right or a wrong in this?'

'There is logic to your reasoning, but that does not change the fact of the matter…'

'Which really boils down to the fact that you have the most nations and the power under your hand, and your vassals continually implore you to spread your preaching to the masses, all under the guise of expanding your territories, which in turn grants them more freedoms and wealth from the fertile pastures captured, which of course, will need to be governed by appointment.'

The shahbanu only smiled. This told Toju that he had the right of her intentions and those of the vassals behind her. She took another sip of her wine.

'How most perceptive of you, Prince Toju. There is some truth in your words, many lords under my command have unfettered ambitions to see their powers swell, which can only be granted through my decision to increase our dominance over far-reaching regions. They will, however, shed their blood for me in taking these lands, so it is only fitting that they are rewarded for their loyalty. In conjunction, if I can win more souls over to the true religion along the way, then the scales are balanced. In the end, we all have our agendas, whether they are cloaked or worn proudly. Denial of this fact is to deny the true nature of humanity.'

'I understand human behaviour all too well, and that is why nothing I have learned here today comes as a surprise. But you must know this; the Hausa are not like any people you would have ever come across. Their power does not only lie in the strength of their many armies, which could rival even yours, but in their bond with the people. I did not understand it myself, coming from a kingdom where there is a distinct line between those of title and those without. This was something that my late father, King Jide, and my brother, Niran, fought to abolish. I was always against their ideas but, having lived amongst the northerners for a time now, I see the value of having those lines blurred. The Hausa aristocracy loves their subjects just as much as they love those amongst them with a name or strong bloodline. And for that, the people reciprocate that love tenfold. If you choose to progress with your plans of advancement in the north, you will not just be facing the emir and all his vassals, but the strength of all the north, every man, woman, and child old enough to wield a sword.'

The shahbanu pondered Toju's words for a moment undoubtedly reevaluating her designs. This was one factor that she had overlooked and one that not even her spies had deemed important enough to disclose. It could very well make the difference between a successful conquest and one destined to fail.

'This is all very interesting but, as I have mentioned, regardless of how you may view my intentions, they are ultimately larger than any one person and in the hands of God. I did note that you failed to mention another seemingly advantageous factor the northerners have. One that is so glaringly obvious. Besides their military strength and their people, they also have you. Perhaps the most fearsome and blessed warrior that I have ever come to know.'

Toju smiled and bowed his head low, a rare gesture of both respect and acknowledgement.

'I do not suppose I could persuade you to abandon your loyalties and side with me instead. I could grant you wishes beyond your wildest imagination – riches, lands, titles, all your heart desires. I would place you above all men under my hand and you would only answer to me. I would even consider giving you… my hand.'

'Shahbanu. I am deeply touched that you would even consider me for such honours. Any man would be a fool to refuse your generosity and your... love. But I am not any man. My spear and my heart belong to those across the sands that lie between us. I can only offer you my sincere apologies.'

'I see. If that is what you wish, I can do nothing but accept your choice, although, it would have pained me not to have asked the question.' The shahbanu looked away with a sad smile. She was obviously not accustomed to her proposals or demands being denied. Toju noticed the slight awkwardness and attempted to lighten the atmosphere, surprising himself as the sentiments of others would usually be of no concern to him.

'Maybe I will have that drink after all and raise a cup to you, a woman to whom there is truly no equal.'

Their conversation stretched until the disc of the yellow sun started to fade behind the horizon. They spoke about their childhood and upbringing, their love of horses, battles, weapons, the beauty of their homelands, and they comfortably shared some of their innermost feelings and fears. They ate heartily, served on platters of silver, delicacies that Toju had never heard of, let alone seen before, and they drank more wine, heady and rich, from bejewelled decanters that were replenished by female attendants summoned by the chime of a bell at the shahbanu's side, whisking away empty platters and replacing them with full ones, then vanishing through the curtains of the tent as quickly as they had arrived.

There was no denying the intimacy that blossomed between them, like two kindred spirits. Besides the social constructs that moulded and define them as people, they were of one mind, similar in more ways than either of them would wish to admit. However, as much as they chose to express themselves with each other, much more remained unspoken between them.

Evening fell and servants came into the tent bearing torches to fend off the darkness.

'It may be safer to travel with the sun to light your path. You have a long distance to travel, and who knows the perils that lurk in the darkness beyond the plains? I can have a tent prepared for you, one that befits your station. Or… you could find all the comforts you require here.'

'If only I could stay, but my people will already be concerned for my wellbeing. Besides, I would not have them send out a search party on my behalf. And the darkness has long been a companion of mine. I have no fear of it, or that that dwells within it. But thank you for your offer and your hospitality. Who would have thought that I would have both an attempt on my life and the offer of a hand to a great kingdom in the same day, eh?'

The shahbanu laughed pleasantly. 'Very true. You are the first to experience many things, prince. I have enjoyed our time together. A pity I do not possess the power to suspend this moment. Maybe in another life things would have been different.'

'Maybe. But unfortunately, these are the lives the gods in their infinite wisdom have seen fit to grant us. We must be grateful and make the best of that which has been given to us.'

They both came to stand across from each other, eyes locked together and unwavering.

'Prince Toju, you do understand that I will ride north with the full force of all my nations behind me bearing swords, bringing nothing but fire and destruction. I will seek you out on the fields of battle, and I will kill you.'

Toju took her hands in his gently and felt the hardness and the calluses on her palms against his.

'I would expect no less from someone as great as you. I will wait to meet you on those very fields of battle, Shahbanu. And I will show you no mercy.'

They stood for a moment longer, not uttering a word, choosing to savour this very moment in time. They had come to appreciate each other's honesty and accepted their vulnerabilities. At that moment, they both felt content, memorising the image of each other as it was now, peaceful and sincere, before the ugliness of war, which would consume that which stood before their eyes and replace it with blood.

She leaned over and planted a soft kiss on Toju's lips that seemed to convey a host of emotions, but was undeniably overshadowed by that of sorrow and loss. This was farewell. When she eventually pulled away, Toju opened his eyes and gave her a sad smile, just before he turned to the entrance, parted the curtains of the tent, and walked into the gathering darkness.

BIRTHED
FROM FIRE

'Revered god of our beloved city, please accept these humble offerings,' Lara said from her kneeling position, with outstretched hands bearing a basket filled with an assortment of items; smoked fish, tubers of yam and cassava, kola nuts and a calabash filled with palm oil, which she placed at the feet of the bronze statue of Ogun, the focal feature in the shrine at the top of the hill on the outskirts of the city of Ogun. Behind her, Enitan and Ayo stood silent with their heads bowed respectfully. Between them was a large ram oblivious to its intended purpose.

'My lady, please bring forth the sacrifice,' said a priest that stood to the side of the statue next to the steps of an altar, dressed in a plain white kaftan that flowed down to his ankles, exposing his bare feet.

Enitan yanked on the length of rope that was fastened around the neck of the ram, bringing the beast forward a few steps. It was a huge ram and Ayo's assistance was required to move it closer still before handing the ropes to a waiting attendant. Lara stood from her knees, briefly glanced at Enitan, and favoured him with a quick smile, before she turned back to the priest and produced a sheathed dagger that was tucked inside the folds of her wrapper, which she presented to the priest.

He accepted the blade, raised it to the statue and intoned some words in the Yoruba dialect of the people of Ogun. He then beckoned to three more of his attendants, who came to stand on either side of the ram, the front two grasping the large, twisted horns. The priest walked up to the ram, knife held behind his back and out of the ram's view just in case the poor creature was frightened by the sight of it and decided to kick against its restraints. It was said that the more willingly a sacrificial animal accepts the blade, the more pleased the gods will be.

The priest continued to chant as he walked over to the side of the ram, and with a swift and practiced movement of his hand, the blade was drawn across its throat, leaving a red line that slowly began to seep blood. Before long the trickle turned into a gush, the legs of the ram buckled and it collapsed to the stone floor.

The attendants dragged the ram by the horns and laid it across the steps of the altar, its blood slowly running down to pool at the base of the steps.

'This sacrifice will be most favourably received by the gods. A clean kill that will surely yield good fortune to your household in the times ahead. You have been blessed here today, my lady and my chief,' announced the priest in a satisfied tone of voice.

'I am glad. We are in much need of good fortune, which has been in short supply for some time now,' Lara responded. 'You have my thanks, priest. I will return to lay another offering with the passing of the next moon, as custom demands.' She bowed her head to the priest, who gave her a prayer and blessing, which he extended to the prince and Ayo. The priest then looked to one of his attendants, who produced a skin of water, which was poured over the bloodied blade and then wiped clean with a square of cloth before the blade was handed back to Lara.

Moments later, Lara, Enitan and Ayo were descending the rise, leaving the shrine and their sombre mood behind them. Enitan had to help his mother down, as she still limped from the wound she had suffered in the leg during the sacking of the citadel in Ile-Ife over a year ago.

Their escort awaited them at the base of the hill – a contingent of Modakeke warriors led by Adedeji's eldest son and Ogogo, former commander of the royal guard in Ile-Ife, now Lara's protector.

'I take it the sacrifice was well received?' Ogogo asked as he extended his arm to assist Lara down the final length of the slope.

'Indeed, it was. We can only hope for the blessings of the gods, as we are, of course, at their mercy,' Lara replied. Ogogo nodded as he guided her to a horse held by one of the warriors and helped her up into the saddle, gently placing her foot into one of the stirrups.

Enitan was handed the reigns to the second horse, which he mounted with ease. He did not often travel on horseback, much preferring to use his feet, but it had become a necessity when travelling with his mother. Besides, his recently earned status required a change in protocol, which he was still adapting to. Everyone else fell in on either side of the horses and marched along in formation, with Ayo and Ogogo flanking their respective charges.

'Riding favours you, my son. You look every bit the young chief you have become,' Lara said.

'It does not feel that way, Mother. Sometimes, I cannot help but think that I am not deserving of the titles bestowed on me. There are more experienced and noble chiefs in the province that would be better suited. If not for the accident of my birth right, I would be nothing but a happy boy without all these responsibilities hanging over my head,' Enitan replied.

'Nonsense. You are most deserving of everything that has been granted to you and I will not hear otherwise. After what our family has endured, this is the least of what you are entitled to. Never forget that you have the blood of generations of Yoruba royalty coursing through your veins, mixed with the blood of the descendants of the gods. No one can ever take that away from you.'

'I know, Mother, but not everyone in the province sees it that way. Despite Adedeji's best efforts to shield me from the politics, the whispers of those who begrudge me are never far from my ear. I do not know if I can be the ruler that can win their respect and their trust. I know it is hard for some to see beyond my age and I fear that they will always consider me to be nothing but a fortunate child.'

'No man is born with all the required tools to rule over men. The experience will come with time, but you will learn. It is your duty as a prince of the realm and now, as chief in your own right. Regardless of who owns that title, there will always be those that bear resentment in their heart. They will learn to fall in line with time. The weight of the horsetail regalia is no easy thing to wield, my child, but you have me at your side to guide you for as long as the gods deem it so. I lost you once before and I do not intend for that to be repeated any time soon.'

'I just want to be accepted. I want to be a ruler that is loved, not one that rules with fear or is ridiculed behind closed doors. Adedeji advises a firm rule, to show strength and the will to do what must be done, even if my decisions are unfavourable to those in power. I do not know if I can rule in such fashion, maybe for a time, but that is not how I wish to be perceived by my subjects.'

'Adedeji is from a different generation. A generation that knew only hardship and war. Men of his time had to show strength or risk being devoured by the hyenas that prowled and fed off weakness. This style of leadership, although seemingly effective, will only breed fear and eventually lead to dissidence. There are other ways to rule. Your father, for instance, took a very different approach. He sought to earn people's respect and elected to govern them with love and compassion, empowering them to make their own decisions, provided it aligned with the rule of his house, and his peace was never broken. In as much as I loved and adored his thinking, this approach also left him vulnerable at times and was viewed by many as overly conciliatory. Ultimately, it contributed to the demise of our kingdom. I know this is discomforting to hear, but you are almost a man grown and you need to understand the intricacies of leadership to equip you with the knowledge to navigate this path with both eyes open.'

'So, what is the answer? It seems that both leniency and a show of too much strength will inevitably lead to disaster. Am I destined for doom like Father?'

'You, my child, will seek a path that is suited to your temperament. Perhaps striking a balance somewhere in the middle – firm but reasonable, harsh in your judgement when circumstances demand it, but compassionate when required. Most importantly, never show the hand that you intend to use to cast the stones; that is for you alone. Take advice from those that you trust but also keep your own counsel. The truth is that there is never a truly right or wrong way to go about it, all you can aspire for is to rule justly. That, I have no doubt you will manage to achieve.'

'I hope so, Mother. But sometimes I feel that I have no choice but to show strength, especially towards those that have openly refused to acknowledge me as their chief. If I am to turn a blind eye to their insolence, how long will it take for them to push the boundaries further? In this, Adedeji has the right of it, I believe.'

'And I would agree. These men would most likely seek to take advantage of your inexperience, now more than ever, while you are still learning to adapt to your new power. If it is left too long, they risk missing an opportunity that may never again present itself. For all we know, their plot to overthrow you, or worse, may already be in motion. But men such as these are only truly governed by their greed and their sense of entitlement. They place reputation above everything, which makes them predictable. You could try to appeal to their pride by offering them something that they covet. Land, title, a seat at your table, perhaps? You could establish a council of chiefs and elders, and grant them authority over matters of little concern within the province, things that would have no bearing on your rule. In doing so, this would bring them closer to you, unknowingly under your influence.'

'And what if that is not enough? What if the power they seek is my seat?'

'Then, they must be destroyed. For they could become the poison that seeps into the well that nourishes the people. But I would also advise that you stay your hand until you are certain they harbour seditious intent, for unjustified actions based on unproven suspicions could as easily have the same effect on the people.'

'How am I to know which path to take? The fact that they did not even bother to attend grandfather's funeral in person was insult enough. This only tells me that they never truly respected his authority in life, just the advantage that was to be gained from being in his confidence. Any true servant of the old chief would have at least put their grievances aside for one day to show their veneration for everything he did for them and the region. If they could so openly disrespect his memory, they must surely be plotting my downfall.'

'You may be right, but they did send envoys in their place, lesser men of their households, true, but their representatives, nonetheless. If they truly wished to offend and show their hand as treasonous, they would not have sent anyone. But I understand and agree with your suspicions and would advise a period of close monitoring before you act. Better to be thorough in your deeds and leave no chance of reproach. The entire province is watching you, waiting for you to stumble. Every choice you make should be calculated. Have these men followed, learn their routines, see who they engage with, understand their strengths and weaknesses, so you can exploit them if necessary.'

'This is already being done, mother. Adedeji has placed people in their households, servants that we can trust. They will inform us of any transgressions, which I feel will only be a matter of time.'

Lara looked over at Enitan admiringly. 'My child, you surprise even me, O. And you say you do not know how to rule. Nonsense. I am sure you will be the greatest chief this region has ever seen!' Lara said as she moved her horse closer to Enitan, then reached out to stroke the nape of his neck as she had always done since he was a babe in arms.

'Mother! I am not a child anymore. You embarrass me in front of our men!' he said in feigned anger as he twisted his head away sharply whilst concealing a smile. He then turned back to her and broke into a wide grin, which she returned lovingly. In that brief exchange of affection, the dark clouds of Lara's thoughts momentarily broke, allowing a ray of happiness to filter through, taking her back to a simpler time of laughter, love, and peace. Then her thoughts drifted to her other children and her beloved husband, and the deep pit of sorrow she harboured from their loss. A pit that could never again be replenished. Gradually, the dark clouds in her mind returned, and her smile slowly ebbed away.

They continued to talk until one of the warriors pointed out a snake on the side of the road that was coiled around a large bush rat with its fangs deep in the rodent's rump. A couple of warriors stopped to pick up stones to throw at the snake in a bid to scare it away. It was too late for the rat as the poison had been delivered and the onset of paralysis was already taking effect.

'Life can be cruel, my son. Do you see that snake? Do you believe it attacked the rodent just because it is higher on the food chain? No. It did so because, just like the rodent, it has every right to survive in this unforgiving environment. If survival means feeding on those that are weaker, then that is what must be done. The only difference between men and that snake is that men are not only driven by their need to survive but also by their greed, their pride, and their desire to conquer. If anything of worth is there for the taking, then taken it will be. You, my child, must show them that you are willing to be a reasonable ruler, but you will not suffer the pride or ambitions of lesser men. More importantly, you will not endure those that seek to question your authority, or your gods-given birth right. Your justice must be swift and without mercy, as remorseless as that snake, when your survival weighs in the balance.'

'So, I must follow the path of reasoning, strength and brutality?'

'You must show that it is you who wields the horsetail, and they that must bow before it.'

'I think I understand, Mother. I am eternally grateful to the gods for preserving your life to be at my side today. Your presence fills me with strength, more than having a thousand warriors at my back,' Enitan replied, his voice breaking slightly as he turned away from her to hide the welling of tears that threatened to spill from his eyes.

'I need to relieve myself; riding on horseback always seems to upset my bladder. Can we stop for a while? I fear I will not be able to restrain myself long enough to reach the palace. I will be as quick as I can,' he said, feeling the urgency to urinate more now that he had voiced it.

'Yes, a short break would be welcomed. I also feel the need to stretch my legs. These uneven roads do my aching thigh no favours.' Lara replied, rubbing the old wound she had sustained over a year ago.

The column of warriors and two horses came to a halt. Ogogo helped Lara off her steed and guided her to a large rock at the side of the path, sending orange-headed lizards scurrying away. He unrolled a cloth that had been tethered to Lara's horse's flank and threw it over the rock to offer some comfort and to keep her clothing free from the dirt. Enitan, followed by Ayo, then waded into the thicket to find a spot away from the men.

Enitan, although a newly anointed chief, was still a shy child at heart and found it difficult to urinate in front of an audience, an idiosyncrasy he had been unable to outgrow, so he needed to venture further into the forest away from the eyes and sounds of his men. Ayo, knowing too well Enitan's insecurities, kept a reasonable distance but kept him within sight.

Once Enitan felt he had enough distance from the crowded path, he relieved himself. He felt much more comfortable after emptying his bladder, and let sound a satisfying moan. Just as he finished, he thought he heard a gentle humming somewhere off to his right. He turned his head to the side and listened; there it was, faint but unmistakable. He stole a glance in the direction from where he had come and where he expected Ayo to be, but did not see him. He continued to sweep his eyes over the verdant forest, but Ayo was nowhere in sight.

The sound came again, low, melodic, and inviting. He had always been an adventurous child, but there was something about the murmur that pulled at the strings of his curiosity. It almost sounded familiar, like a song that haunted your dreams but always managed to elude you when attempting to conjure it from memory in the cold light of day. Then came the overwhelming desire to seek out the source of the sound.

He took another quick glance towards the path, then began to move through the forest, just as he had learned to do when he hunted with Ayo and his brothers as a child. He had a natural ability to blend into the surrounding forest as seamlessly as any of its wild inhabitants, creeping through the foliage, taking his time to place his feet soundlessly, contorting his slim body as he moved to match the shapes of the trees, avoiding branches and other obstacles with the elegance of a leopard.

The sound grew louder and more serene the deeper into the forest he went. Then, through the bushes and entwining branches festooned with varying hues of leaves, he discerned a figure sitting on an old tree stump some paces away, swaying gently to the hummed tune. Enitan stopped, crouched low making sure he was well concealed by the foliage and decided to observe the stranger.

Enitan could see that it was a man from the rough and knotted style of his greying hair. He wore a plain off-white agbada, with embroidery on the frayed hems. The material appeared creased, with the wide-open arms rolled up over his shoulders exposing frail, liver-spotted arms and gnarled hands. One of his hands was coiled around an improvised walking stick of twisted wood like the branches that surrounded them. The stranger had his back to Enitan, so he could not make out the man's features, but he appeared harmless enough, judging by his fragile façade.

There was something mesmerising about the stranger's movement coupled with the mellifluent tune he hummed that softly danced on the wind, and Enitan subconsciously found himself swaying along to the rhythm. He felt as if he was listening to a lullaby that lured him into the clutches of sleep. His eyelids felt heavy of a sudden, and he forced himself to blink repeatedly in quick succession to ward away the weariness that had unexpectedly befallen him.

The stranger abruptly ceased to hum and just sat there, as still as an old tree, and then an unnatural quiet descended on the forest. It seemed like life stopped at that moment – the rustle of leaves, the birdsong, the small rodents that scurried through the undergrowth, nothing but absolute silence.

'The shade from the leaves cannot hide your curiosity, young man. Come and join me, you have nothing to fear from this old man. Besides, a view as beautiful as this is meant to be shared with all who are blessed with the gift of vision to really appreciate the work of the gods,' said the stranger without turning to look at the prince. Enitan's heart almost burst through his chest on hearing the man address him in that raspy voice, which matched his wrinkled attire, but there was undeniably a hint of affability about his tone, like that of a father to a loving child.

Enitan remained where he crouched for a few heartbeats, then tentatively stood, and pushed through the branches towards the man. As he walked, he surreptitiously brushed his finger over the hilt of the blade at his waist, which gave him some comfort knowing that if he needed to defend himself, he had a weapon close at hand. He felt a twinge of fear the closer he got to the stranger, but he reminded himself that he was lord of these lands, and a chief must master his emotions.

Enitan came to stand three paces in front of the man, who looked up to appraise the young prince. Just as Enitan had suspected, the stranger exuded warmth. He had a benign smile framed by a greying beard that was neatly trimmed, in contrast to the hair that crowned his head. Crow's feet escaped the corners of his eyes, and his brow and face boasted a network of wrinkles and deep ridges, but not suggesting a hard life, more a life of happiness and laughter. Given his aged appearance, his eyes were oddly deceptive and not congruent with his outward image. They were bright and vibrant, emanating intelligence with a hint of mischief, a shade between hazel and dark brown, which instantly reminded him of his brother Niran, who was known for the unusual tint of his eyes.

'Had I known I would be in the presence of a prince, I would have made myself more presentable,' the stranger said, with that disarming smile that played on the corners of his lips.

'Good day to you, baba. I could not help but listen to your tune. Where did you learn it? It sounds oddly familiar and yet, I cannot seem to place where I have heard it.'

'If you have heard it then you must be an old soul, for it is not a tune that is commonly known by the people of this region, nor has it been sung in a generation. I knew of it when I was but a boy, probably of an age as you are today.'

'That is odd. Perhaps it stirred up the memory of a similar tune I have come across in the past,' Enitan replied.

'Maybe. Or it could be that you have tapped into some recessive memory of a life once lived. Who knows? Anyway, it is nice to make your acquaintance, young prince.'

'I take it that you are from the city of Ogun or one of the neighbouring towns or villages?'

'No, young prince. I am but a lowly traveller whose only aim in life is to see as much of the gods-created world. I prefer to think of myself as the wind; free to travel the lands at will, swift and fleeting but, more importantly, not being constrained by the laws of any land or person.'

'So how, may I ask, have you come to know of me? You referred to me as a prince, but if you are not from the city, how could you have known that?'

That smile flashed again, but this time there was something different about it, as if it were a gateway to many untold secrets just waiting for the right question to be asked to set them free.

'Young prince, when you have the privilege of living for as long as I have, knowledge will undoubtedly seek you out, provided you are of a mind to learn. Besides, with time you will learn that the world, despite appearing so vast and unending, really is quite small, and all its inhabitants are connected in some fashion.'

Enitan did not quite understand the stranger's meaning but decided against delving too deep into conversation, remembering the convoy he had left behind on the road to Ogun.

'Do you have any family? Any children perhaps? A baba such as you should not be travelling alone. These lands have been unsafe in recent times, there have been reports of skirmishes in different parts of the province and rumours of bandits that are said to skulk the lands preying on the innocent and vulnerable. It would be remiss of me as the ruler of this region not to forewarn you, baba.'

'And a fine and dignified ruler you are, young prince, but you need not worry about me. I am well-travelled in these lands and know where I need to avoid. As for children, I have plenty, all grown now and following their own paths. Unfortunately, I am not as close to them as I once was. Many still stand with me and abide by the rules of their father, while others are stubborn and feel they have outgrown the need to heed my words, going against my wishes and choosing to interfere with matters that are better left untouched. They will answer to me in time but, for now, all a father can do is allow his children to make their own mistakes in the hopes that a lesson will be learned.'

Enitan was completely lost and failed to make heads or tails of the stranger's words, before concluding that these were just the ramblings of an old man.

'As it so happens, I believe that you are acquainted with one of my children. One that I would sooner wish you had not come to meet. Be wary of him lest he darkens your incandescence. When you come to find yourself lost and surrounded by nothing but gathering shadows, listen to the voice loudest in your head and walk towards it.'

'Okay, baba… but I am not quite sure I understand…'

The old man cut him off mid-sentence. 'Oh, how these old bones ache. Help me to my feet, young prince. I think it is time I stretched these old frail legs. If only I was young again. Alas, age is a coin that we must all eventually pay to be admitted through the gates of time.'

Enitan hooked a hand under the proffered arm of the old man, gently raising him off the tree stump. His mind was racing from the words the old man had spoken. Who was this man's son that he supposedly knew? He had purposely kept his circle small, but that did not stop him from running through the list of all the men of note that he had encountered over the past year that could be the likely candidate. He was suddenly filled with a barrage of questions and knew not where to start.

'Thank you, young prince. I think it is time for me to continue my journey as I still have a long road to travel. You must also be on your way. Your mother awaits you. The journey here was hard on her and the sooner she is within the comfort of the palace, the better for her.'

'Wait, what?!' Enitan stared with wide eyes hearing the words of the old man. How could he have known any of this? Before he could interrogate the man further, Ayo's voice drifted through the forest calling after him. His tone was urgent with a slight tinge of concern underlying every word.

Enitan turned his head towards the sound for the briefest of moments, but as he turned back to the stranger, the man was gone, as if he had never been there to start with. Enitan frantically swept his gaze about him and saw nothing but trees and bushes swaying in the breeze. The noises of the forest had returned and, along with them, more unanswered questions. Enitan was truly perplexed at the encounter he had just had and began to question whether any of it had even occurred, or whether it was all part of his active imagination. He stood there for a moment more, still searching the treeline, before deciding to run off in the direction of Ayo's voice.

'There you are. I was beginning to worry when you disappeared from my line of sight. Come, we must make haste back to the convoy. This is no place to linger, my prince. The gods know of what could be lurking within these bushes.'

Enitan was too distracted and only managed a feeble nod of his head, still deep in thought, but he allowed Ayo to direct him back to the line of waiting warriors and his mother.

When he mounted his steed and the journey recommenced, his mother looked over at him noticing his pensive disposition. She studied him for a moment, and when he turned to face her, feeling her gaze bore into the side of his head, she simply nodded and offered him somewhat of a conciliatory half-smile, as if she could tell that he was battling with something that weighed heavy on his mind. He returned the gesture and went back to his thoughts, lost in a cloud of oblivion.

By the time they reached the city and the gates of the palace, Adedeji awaited them in the courtyard, flanked by some of his warriors. Enitan noticed that all the men were fully armoured, and a couple of horses were held by attendants in the wings, saddled and ready to be mounted. A stern and unyielding look was plastered across Adedeji's face, and Enitan dreaded the news he was about to receive.

'What has happened, Adedeji?' Enitan asked without preamble.

'I received a message from one of the servants that we placed in the homes of the prominent families. It appears my initial thoughts have now been confirmed. A treacherous hand is at play. The servant swears to *Oduduwa* that she overheard talk of one of the family elders sending word to gather the strengths of his allied houses to march on the palace.'

'Are you certain of this?' asked Lara, concern etched into her features as she turned to look at her son.

'I am. As soon as I heard, I reached out to the servants I had spying on some of the other houses and they returned with no news of talk of fighting, but reports of suspicious activity; closed meetings with men of note in the city that carried on into the dead of night, smiths forging more weapons than any chief has the right to own, and preparations being made for their personal retinues to guard their houses, which is highly unusual, unless you are preparing for something. They seek to harm you, my prince. There can be no mistaking their intent,' Adedeji finished.

Everyone in the courtyard turned to Enitan, who digested the reports conveyed to him. His mother had been right. How coincidental that they had just been speaking of this very matter, only for it to be so quickly confirmed. The chiefs had finally revealed their hand, leaving him without a choice.

He was now duty-bound to address the matter swiftly and decisively. There would be no opportunity for reasoning, that option had been blown away on the wind. Now, examples were required to be made to show that his authority could not be impugned, and to serve as a deterrent for any future ideas of insurrections.

He looked from his mother to Ayo then finally at Adedeji.

'It seems that these men have made the decision for me. I never wanted it to be so, but they have forced my hand.' He glanced at his mother, then addressed Adedeji, his expression now impassive. 'Take half of the Modakeke warriors and thirty of the palace guards. Bring me these traitors. If they resist, give them swift justice, but I would prefer to follow the threads of this plot to its source. Everyone involved must be held to account. Send scouts in advance of your men to forewarn you of anything awry. We cannot afford for them to discover that we have foiled their plans, lest they decide to flee from my justice. I want this intervention to be as bloodless as possible.'

Adedeji beamed as if he was told of the arrival of his first-born child. 'That is exactly what I had in mind, my prince,' he said, sweeping his arm towards the waiting horses. 'You see, I told you that you would take to your role, for you are a true son of King Jide. With your permission, I will take some of the new recruits along with me – the wrestlers. What better way to test their resolve and offer them a chance to prove themselves worthy of their positions?'

'You have it, Adedeji, but Dami will remain with my personal guard,' Enitan replied.

'Very good. I will leave my eldest son, Femi, in command of the remaining modakeke. I have no doubt that he and Ayo will keep you safe until my return.'

Before long, the mounted scouts cantered through the gates of the palace, followed by a column of marching warriors with Adedeji at their head. The mood in the courtyard was sombre, and Enitan could not help the ominous feeling that descended on him as he watched the line of men fade into the distance before the gates of the palace were sealed shut.

'You made the right decision, my son. It is now in the hands of the gods. All we can do now is to wait and see where this road leads. Do not be hard on yourself. Whatever the outcome, none of this is your doing.'

'I know, Mother. I had only hoped that we could enjoy some more time of peace, but I see now that there can be no rest for a ruler,' Enitan said sadly.

'That may be so, but you have good people surrounding you that are here to bear the load with you,' Lara responded as she squeezed Enitan's hand reassuringly. Just then, Wale appeared at the entrance to the palace with two of the palace guards in tow.

'My chief, apologies for the interruption, but there is a matter that requires your urgent attention within the palace,' he said, as he strolled towards the gathering in the courtyard. He offered Lara an apologetic bow when he noticed her standing amongst the men.

'What is it and why are you perturbed so?' Ayo asked as Wale came closer, noticing the sheen of sweat that coated his brow and the slight display of agitation that was out of character for the commander of the guard.

He lowered his tone slightly as he addressed Enitan and Ayo in turn. 'My apologies, but I cannot talk about it here. It is somewhat of a… delicate matter. Please, my prince, you must come with me.'

Enitan felt a mixture of annoyance and intrigue at the interruption, but nodded, knowing that his position often demanded that his attention would be pulled in all manner of directions. He briefly turned to his mother, kissed her gently on the cheek and told her that he would seek her out once she had rested, before turning to Wale.

'Please, lead the way,' he said as the groups separated – Ogogo, Taiwo and a few guards departing with Lara, while Ayo and Adedeji's son walked ahead and behind Enitan respectively.

Wale led them urgently through the palace, offering no more information than he had previously. They passed through the long narrow corridors festooned with tapestries and bronze sculptures of chiefs and lords long gone, before exiting into the open-air training ground towards the rear of the building. As they had walked, Wale had glanced over his shoulder several times as if to make sure that the prince followed him, and he continually fidgeted with his sword as he walked. Ayo sensed something was amiss, and he could not help the foreboding feeling in the pit of his stomach. He knew that whatever Wale intended to reveal to them could not be anything good. Had he discovered yet another subversion to add to the troubling news that emanated from Enitan's supposed subjects in the west? His mind was rife with images that did nothing to still his nerves, but they would soon find out.

As they walked, Ayo suddenly heard sandals scraping on wood scattered with grains of sand, moving purposefully. The sound came from the timber platforms erected at the height of a man, a level above the court that encircled the training grounds. He could tell that there were several of them, and then he discerned the unmistakable sound of leather slapping against thighs – scabbards. He looked at the prince behind him and Adedeji's son, but they were oblivious to the noise. Ayo's senses had always been as sharp as a knife's edge and his intuition had never failed him. He briefly wondered whether the palace was under attack and the guards were hurrying to man their stations, but there was no alarm, no tolling bells of warning announcing the approach of foes. Then it hit him.

He stopped suddenly as they reached half the length of the training ground, and put his hand out to halt the prince, who had a surprised look at Ayo's abrupt and unexpected reaction.

'Wale, where exactly do you lead us? Speak the truth,' he said as he narrowed his eyes at the guards' commander.

Wale turned to face them and had a strange expression on his face. He briefly glanced upwards towards the timber platforms before responding. 'I am sorry, my friend, but please know that everything I do is for the better of the kingdom.'

As if planned and with impeccable timing, several men appeared on the platforms brandishing weapons. A few held

spears that pointed down to the men below, but most had swords and cutlasses. Ayo noticed that some wore the colours of the palace guards, while others wore nondescript, worn leather armour.

'I hope for your sake that this is but a jest, and one of foul taste, Wale. Please, do not tell me that you have allied yourself with those that would seek harm to the prince, your chief?' Ayo asked. His tone was low but even, infused with an undertone of utter disappointment. He had considered Wale a trusted companion over the past year he had known him, and it stabbed at his heart to learn that one so open and jovial could turn out to be so duplicitous. A stark reminder that in this cruel world of men, one can only turn within to seek trust, as you can never truly know that which lies within the hearts of others.

Some of the men on the platforms moved to the ground, clearing the wooden bannisters with practised ease to surround the three men. However, the men holding spears remained where they stood, not wanting to lose their position of vantage.

'The prince is not truly a son of Ogun and would never be accepted as one. He has not bled for this land, nor has he endured our sufferings. He cannot be allowed to simply swoop in like an eagle only to capture a prized prey and feast upon the seat of antiquity, not even if he bore the same blood as the old chief.'

'So, you would deny the prince his birth right. You would join those that vie for the horsetail regalia? And what is it that they have promised you, eh? Do you think they will elevate you beyond your station once they have used you to further their aspirations? Are you such a fool that you would allow yourself to be blinded by your own ambitions, Wale?' Ayo seethed through gritted teeth, his anger steadily rising.

'You are mistaken. I am a relative by marriage to chief Dotun, one of the oldest families in the region. I would have been a councillor, a man of substance, if only the prince had not shown up here a year ago forcing the old chief to abandon his promise to split the rule of the province between the deserving families, condemning me to remain a servant under the heel of a boy chief, forever scraping at his feet and taking orders. Well, I cannot continue in this fashion.'

'So, betraying your gods' appointed ruler is the alternative you have decided to seek? You speak of condemnation to servitude, but you have ultimately committed yourself to a path that only leads to one place, servitude to *Esu* in his dark halls,' said Femi with unsheathed venom.

All the while, no words had passed Enitan's lips. His expression was that of stone, harsh and unyielding, but inside he was petrified. He could not control the trembling in his hands, and he felt once again like the scared child that had fled Ile-Ife a year ago. That feeling of being hunted and marked for death was the worst experience he had ever been subjected to in his young life, and now, it all came rushing back as he stared down the blades aimed at him.

Anxiety tightened his chest, and a feeling of claustrophobia almost sent him into panic, as though the walls of the court were closing in around him and there were no means of escape. He began to perspire and felt the sudden urge to urinate, to the point that he feared he may wet himself. His eyes darted around frantically, tracking the locations of his assailants, the gleam from the edges of their swords and cutlasses, the unimaginable pain those blades would inflict; he searched for an opportunity to flee and seek refuge in a corner of his chamber and curl up like an infant. But part of him was enraged. Angry at having lived through the ruin of his home city, the peril of Olise's blades, then to find himself in the seat of his forefathers, all for it to end here with his blood spilt on the gravel? This could not be the sum of his destiny. The gods could not be that cruel; or could they? Then his thoughts flashed to his mother, Lara.

'What of my mother?' he asked in a voice that was intended to sound full of authority, but came out somewhat shakily, betraying the façade he desperately tried to present.

Wale looked over at him with genuine pity in his eyes. 'No harm will come to the former queen, that I swear before the gods. She is no threat to us so, provided she makes no trouble, we will let her go free.'

'Save your words, traitor! How do you expect us to trust anything that spills forth from your mouth? You have said your piece, now all that is left is for you to die. And you will die by my sword,' Ayo barked as he ripped his sword from the scabbard at his waist. Femi did the same.

The men that circled them took a hesitant step backwards, unsure of how to proceed, some looking to Wale, who raised a hand pleadingly. 'It does not have to be this way, Ayo. It is the boy we are after, you need not die here, my friend. I will ensure that there is a place for you at court, one of honour that befits your status. Do not throw your life away for that of this boy. You must know that you cannot win here, there are many of us and only three of you. The lustre behind a name is not enough to save you here.'

'And that is where you are wrong, friend!' Ayo spat back with unfettered anger in the last word. 'Do you think that the modakeke would ever forsake their duty for worldly possessions or titles? You will learn today what it means for us to bear that name. The next words out of your mouth should only be the order for your men to fight, anything else and I will strike you down first instead of saving you to the end.'

Femi laughed, loud and full of malice, then pulled a dagger that had been sheathed at his back, now armed with two lengths of iron, before getting into a fighting stance. The talking was over, now was the time for the blades in the hands of all those within the compound to sing.

Resignation washed over Wale's face as he turned to one of his men and gave a slight nod. The man barked out 'Take them!', and the men surrounding the prince and his companions surged in with their blades before them.

In the blink of an eye, Ayo darted closer to Enitan and parried a sword thrust that was aimed at him. His movement was exceptionally fast as he countered, jabbing his sword, and retracting it almost simultaneously. This blade came away with a line of blood that ran down to the hilt and one of their attackers dropped dead in front of Enitan, who stood there with his eyes wide open, shocked at the speed at which the situation had descended into chaos.

The men on the platform began to throw their spears and Femi used his sword to swat two of them away from him in quick succession mid-flight, as if it was the easiest thing in the world. Now he was running towards the platform, switching his path from side to side as he dodged more spears sent in his direction. One came close and he rolled across the gravel, the spear narrowly missing him, got to his feet and leaped towards the edge of the footing of the platform.

He rammed his dagger through the underside of the timber, and it burst through the top, nailing one of the man's feet to the wood. The warrior howled out in agony as Femi, leaving his dagger in place, hoisted himself up and onto the platform to face three men that stood there, momentarily stunned by the speed at which the young warrior had reached them. They thrust at him ineptly with their spears one after the other, but the young Modakeke warrior moved like a dancer; sidestepping, twisting away, pivoting, all as he moved forward to within his assailant's guard. Then he was amongst them. His sword swirled, cutting shapes in the air traced by their blood, and the men screamed.

Enitan had not even pulled out his dagger; he was frozen to the spot as Ayo fended off four men at once. He heard someone cry out off to his left and saw a man fall from the platform and land awkwardly with a sickening thump in the gravel. He looked at the open-eyed corpse that had a clean laceration starting from the side of his neck and snaking round and down to his chest, blood gushing out of the open wound. Movement flashed in his peripheral vision, and suddenly jolted him back into focus.

He reached for the dagger at his side, just as two men moved to sweep around him. He could smell their unwashed bodies and the fear on them, perhaps they smelt his own fear, but none of that mattered. Right now, his only purpose in life was to survive for the next few heartbeats and avoid getting himself run through.

One of the men lunged. Enitan spun away from the blade with ease and without thinking, but he had mistakenly spun towards the other man, who brought his cutlass down with a savage two-handed stroke. Enitan raised his dagger, met the dropping cutlass in mid-air and used the man's momentum to arc the blade harmlessly away from him towards the ground. Muscle memory had saved him; he fought instinctively, just as Ayo had trained him. The repeated drills and hours of painful sparring had all come down to what he did at this very moment.

Letting his instincts guide him, as his attacker's blade bit into the gravel, he moved to the side, placing the man between himself and the first assailant, fouling his advance and, with a reflex that surprised even him, jabbed twice with his blade, hitting the man in the thigh and exposed ribs. The man dropped his cutlass, grabbed his wounds, and fell to the ground, shouting at the top of his lungs. His companion, however, was not deterred and leaped over the fallen warrior straight at Enitan.

This time, Enitan was ready. The man came in high with a thrust but Enitan, being the smaller and nimbler one, crouched and weaved to the side whilst reversing his grip on the dagger he held, so that the blade ran along his forearm. He tapped the sword at mid-length, deflecting it further away from him, and tried to bring his blade up to stab the man underhanded, but his opponent sensed his intention and leaped backwards, harmlessly away from the extended tip of the dagger.

He now circled the prince, watching the blade in his hand, the placement of the prince's feet, reading him, trying to anticipate his move, knowing that the boy had some fight in him. Enitan did the same and tried to stay aware of his surroundings. Without warning, the man sprang forward, catching Enitan off guard. Enitan stumbled back, lost his balance and began to fall backwards, panic gripping him as he watched the man charge towards him, sword ready to skewer him.

Enitan fell onto his elbows hard, numbing one of them on impact, but immediately rolled away just as the sword pierced the gravel where his head had been a moment ago. As he rolled away, he swung his blade backwards in desperation. Luckily, he slashed the man's calf, which slowed his next attack, giving Enitan the chance to regain his feet.

'You will bleed for that, runt!' the man growled, spittle dribbling through his clenched teeth, clearly in pain. He began to limp towards Enitan with murder in his eyes. The prince knew that he could not continue to fight with a dagger. He needed a sword fast or the next attack may be a painful one for him. He looked around and spied the cutlass the first man had dropped, its owner still on the ground moaning in agony as he attempted in vain to staunch his bleeding.

Enitan threw his dagger at the limping man and made a dive for the cutlass. His throw had been rushed but it still managed to strike the man, hitting him with the hilt rather than the sharpened end; however, the distraction gave him just enough time to reach the cutlass. It felt awkward in his hand, a crude weapon with an uneven handle, bulky and unbalanced compared with a sword. It was a tool more suited for cutting grass, but it was a better length of iron to fight with than a dagger.

This time Enitan took the initiative and ran at the limping warrior. He slashed wildly but with purpose from left and right. The first strike was blocked but the second not as well defended, forcing his attacker off balance. Enitan then lashed out with a kick, catching the already wounded leg, and was rewarded with a yelp. The man's guard dropped to reach for his leg as Enitan struck again, cleaving the man between the shoulder blade and neck. The man's eyes went wide but he made no sound as he dropped to the floor.

Enitan watched him in his final death throes and could not turn away. This was the first life he had ever taken, and he was not prepared for the emotions that arrested him at the enormity of his actions. He looked at the blood that ran down the cutlass onto his hands and dropped the weapon. He looked back at the man on the ground, who shook violently once more, then was still. He could not believe that this was the work of his own hands, and felt the urge to burst into tears.

A hot flush washed over him, and he began to have heart palpitations, his breath reduced to short bursts, gasping for air. His vision started to blur, and his whole body shook. *What is happening to me?* he thought fearfully. He turned towards Ayo, seeking the reassurance of his presence, but Ayo was too engrossed in the fight, having downed three men and currently pressing his attack on three more. Now, more men were coming forward, seeking to encircle Ayo, and cut off any options of retreat.

One of the men looked in Enitan's direction, then another, evidently deciding that the young prince was a far easier target. They started to walk towards him, beckoning another of their companions to join them in fulfilling the objective they had been tasked with. Enitan knew then that he would be taken, for he had not the will nor the strength to face three more men, and the knowledge of his impending demise released a raw terror that started in the pit of his stomach and spread through his body as quickly as the blood pumping through his veins. In that instance, he felt every nerve ending, every pore within his skin, every sense amplified by the very air that surrounded him. The edges of his vision began to darken, slowly closing in on the light that filtered through his cornea as if his eyes were being forced shut, and then the world around him burst into flames.

A few paces away, Ayo was lost in a haze of blood. He had downed a few of his attackers, his blade moving as quickly

as a viper, deflecting, parrying, and striking at three men in succession, but he knew that the odds were not in his favour, which made it even more exciting and terrifying in equal measures. Through the men that attacked him, he glanced at Wale, who had chosen not to engage, but rather observe from a distance.

'The coward!' he said to himself and decided that he would make sure that the traitor suffered an exceptionally unpleasant death; then his thoughts turned to Enitan. He countered a strike, fatally wounding one of the men he fought, and half-spun towards the prince to see him just standing there unarmed, staring vacantly down towards his open palms. Then he saw three more men moving to intercept him. He was about to shout a warning to the prince but, in the same instant, within the blink of an eye, the skies were bathed in darkness, interspersed with streaks of lighting that flashed in brilliant whiteness.

Everyone in the compound noticed the sudden change in the atmosphere and looked towards the heavens fearfully. Without warning, a bolt of lightning struck with a loud boom, hitting the ground, and igniting scatterings of dried hay about the compound. The bolt had struck the men that had been advancing on the prince, setting them aflame instantly. Another bolt struck, even louder than the first, scorching the earth, and flames rose from the ground followed by thick plumes of black smoke, impairing everyone's vision.

The scent of burning flesh was heavy in the air and Ayo heard tormented screams somewhere up ahead. He cried out Enitan's name several times, knowing that the bolts of lightning had struck close to where the prince had stood but a moment ago, and he started to wade through the smoke, sword before him ready to defend himself.

A body came flying through the plumes, narrowly missing him, and landing no more than a pace from his feet. The sight that filled his vision was grotesque – flesh burned to a crisp, twisted limbs, fingers splayed in a permanent claw, eyes melted away in empty sockets but, oddly, white teeth revealing a skeletal smile, contrasting with the blackness of the charred skin. Then he heard movement ahead of him.

Out from the smoke and fire stepped a boy in the image of a man. Ayo took a step back, bringing his sword up defensively, blinking the wetness from the smoke out of his eyes. He looked at the figure before him and was immediately filled with dread. The facial features of the man were menacing, one that held no mercy, only destruction. A crooked scar crossed an eye that glowed white like the lightning that had set the compound alight with flames, and the other was like a black pool with a depth that no one could escape from. A set of thick red coral beads adorned his wide neck and rested on chest muscles that bulged like slabs of sculpted granite under a leather breastplate of exquisite detail. The designs on the man's armour moved constantly, like living creatures, glowing with every step that he took. The black jaguar head and pelt that covered his muscled shoulders was just as menacing as the face of the man, teeth showing as if the large cat would come to life any moment.

The man emanated heat and the air around him shimmered, like the warmth of the sun, causing Ayo to sweat despite the chill of dread that ran down his spine. He was huge, at least a head taller than anyone Ayo knew. His exposed arms bore rippling muscles with veins that stood out like the vines on a tree, and in his hand was a monstrous axe with a long wooden handle covered in ancient hieroglyphics that glowed white along the smooth wood. The head of the axe was alight with fire that danced about the curved edge, but the flame did not possess the orange hue of fire, but rather a bluish-white glow.

Ayo's mouth and eyes could not get any wider as he stood there rooted to the spot, mesmerised, terrified, in awe and with a plethora of emotions that his brain could not articulate at that moment. The man looked directly at him and for the briefest instant, the image of the man's face was that of Enitan's, eyes squeezed shut, frightened and innocent as if looking upon an ancient tree split in half; one side rough-textured, darkened and weathered, the other smooth, light and sheltered. The realisation hit Ayo immediately and, without a second thought, he dropped to his knees then prostrated himself, face kissing the gravel and arms outstretched. This figure was no mere mortal of flesh and bones. This was something more, one that you would stare upon at your peril. One that you cower from, show reverence to or run from, the last being the most foolish option as there was no escape once you laid eyes on those who should not be seen; this was *Shango*, the god of thunder. Ayo chose reverence and hoped to all the gods that his actions would be sufficient to preserve his life.

Shango's gaze lingered on Ayo for a few heartbeats, then turned to the remaining men in the compound. Femi, who had come down from the platform and had headed towards the prince to make sure he was safe, saw Ayo's reaction, and without thought followed suit and prostrated himself a few paces away from the blood-guard, face pressed to the ground. The rest of the men just stared, open-mouthed and dumbfounded.

Ayo and Femi felt a sudden intensity of heat as *Shango* walked past them towards the remaining men in the compound. The sensation was almost unbearable, singeing the very hairs on their skin, but they dared not flinch, nor breathe for that matter, just lay on the ground in silence, hoping not to draw attention to themselves. The heat passed over them as *Shango* got further away, and still they lay there unmoving.

The other men in the compound started to shout in terror and one of them foolishly threw a spear at the god, which bounced off his immense chest like a chewing stick thrown by a toddler. *Shango* looked at each of the recoiling and pitiful figures one after the other, then hefted the axe in his hand. The flame that danced about the head burned brighter the higher he held it. He then brought it down fast in a diagonal chopping motion, and from the axe's head shot a bolt of white flames that spread out before him and engulfed every one of the men.

Their screams pierced the air simultaneously. Their tormented cries were terrifying, filled with pure agony mixed with naked fear, not the sounds ever expected to be heard from hardened warriors. Some cried out to their deities, beseeching them for mercy, others called out to their mothers, but most just shouted incoherently as they burned from the white flames that consumed them. Before long, the sweet aroma of charred flesh wafted through the air even more strongly than before, and then all the screaming ceased, leaving behind the sound of skin and fat crackling from the fire.

Both Ayo and Femi stayed where they were, with their faces boring into the ground, not willing to see the horrors that had befallen their attackers until they heard voices accompanied by the sounds of heavy footfall from a multitude of people pounding towards them. The doors of the palace that opened out to the compound burst open and a group of armed warriors appeared. Dami was in front, spear in hand, followed by Ogogo, Taiwo and a few of the palace guards and Modakeke warriors.

The new arrivals all stopped dead in their tracks, most skidding to a halt in the gravel, as they took in the scenery that would forever haunt their dreams, gasping or making the sign against evil. Then came the wail of a female voice, screaming hysterically and calling to her child. Lara.

'Do not look upon his face! Avert your eyes and kneel!' Ayo shouted from the ground, fearing that would turn his wrath on the newcomers, but the scene before them was enough to induce paralysis fuelled by dread, taking away the ability to rationally comprehend what they saw or heed the warning shouted at them.

As all the men looked on in shocked silence, Lara continued to call out to her son while simultaneously praying that Enitan was not amongst the blackened things that bore no resemblance to actual people, now decorating the training ground like burnt and misshapen trees after a forest fire.

'Enitan! My son, where are you? Oh, gods. Enitan. *Ogun,* please spare my child! Enitan!' she pleaded repeatedly as she dropped to her knees, unable to carry herself any further for fear of what she might discover. Tears were streaming down her face, collecting at the base of her chin, and dripping down to the ground, mixing with the dirt and ashes.

The imposing figure of the god still had his back to the gathered people and did not turn immediately. When he did, his movement was slow and ominous as if he was about to unleash his fury upon them for having the audacity to interrupt him as he admired the work of his hands. Many of the warriors audibly lamented in panic as they took in the full image of the foreboding figure of the god with his piercing eye and severe expression. Some dropped to their knees or prostrated themselves, just as Ayo and Femi had instructed, but the odd individual just stood there transfixed in the shadow of the god of thunder and destruction, awaiting their fate.

Shango raised the axe in his hand once more, and the axe head began to burn with intensity, the image of the flame mirrored in the eyes of everyone brave, or foolish, enough to stare upon it.

'Enitan? My son... is that you?' Lara asked as she stared up at the deity, relief, bewilderment, and distress contorting her face. Ayo realised that Lara must have caught a glimpse of the boy, just as he had, and he prayed that her presence would be the thing that would awaken the boy and drag him away from the subconscious state he was in. However, it was not lost on him that *Shango* could decide to burn them all for their insolence. His mind was racing but the thought that came to the forefront of his mind was to protect the former queen. He had failed to protect Enitan from the hands of this god, so the least he could do was attempt to protect the prince's mother.

Before his courage fled from him, he dragged himself up from the dirt and slowly walked towards Lara, all the while with his head lowered in supplication, not daring to look in the direction of the god, until he came to stand by the former queen. Femi, understanding Ayo's intentions, did the same.

Lara continued to call to Enitan, this time softly, pleadingly, trying to coax the boy forth, and at the same time, beseeched the god that held him hostage. 'Enitan... please come back to me, my child, for my heart cannot bear to lose you again. Most revered god, please spare the life of my child... take my own if it is a life you demand, but please release my child, I implore you. He is but a scared boy... let me be your vessel... let me be the one to serve you.'

The flame from the axe continued to grow as it was held aloft, and then the dark clouds overhead began to circle. Streaks of lightning flashed again, and the speed of the wind rose around the compound, sending dirt and ashes swirling in the air. *Shango* had an almost pained expression on his face, as if battling against his will to strike. No one noticed as they all had to protect their eyes from the debris sent flying from the sweeping winds. Suddenly, there was a loud boom as, once again, a bolt of lightning struck the ground, and then all went quiet.

The skies began to clear, dark clouds receding and rays of sunlight filtering through to bathe the compound in the reddish-orange hue of dusk. Then came the sobs of a child, gently at first, then slowly starting to build. Lara and Ayo looked up tentatively, only to see Enitan on the ground, legs folded underneath him with his elbows resting on his lap, palms open and facing upwards. Lara was on her feet in an instant, racing towards him without thinking, arms outstretched, heart pounding and eyes streaming. As soon as she reached him, she dropped to her knees and folded him in her arms in the tightest of embraces. They both wept now, not caring about the people around them while relishing the comfort of each other's warmth.

IDLE HANDS
DO THE DEVIL'S
BIDDING

'For the love of all the gods! Look at the state of me!' Efetobo complained as he stepped into another squelching puddle, coating afresh the hem of what had been a fine long kaftan before he set off, now mired from the mud, and ripped in several places from catching branches and thorns among the foliage in the forest. He had failed to put much consideration into the appropriate attire to wear for this terrain and could not help but feel despondent about his oversight.

He had expected a leisurely and uncomplicated journey, but the heavy rainfall the night before had turned most of the forest into a marsh, making it perilous underfoot. To worsen matters, he had lost a sandal in a mud pit and was forced to abandon it and continue with one bare foot, as his servant was unable to retrieve it. Caked in mud, soaked to the bone from the rainwater retained by the leaves that dripped overhead whenever they disturbed some of the vegetation, and miserable summed up his temperament.

In contrast, his servant was finding their predicament all too amusing, a sentiment he had no choice but to hide from Efetobo unless he wanted to find himself condemned to cleaning the public latrines in Ife for the rest of his days. So, he offered a helping hand when required, and the odd piece of advice to navigate an obstacle whenever the pompous Efetobo would listen, but mostly he bit his tongue and accepted the vituperation or grumbles from the councillor, as was expected of him.

It was obvious that Efetobo was not accustomed to travelling in such conditions or environments, being more suited to journeying on horseback or carried in a litter by his servants accompanied by a retinue of guards. This trip, however, required the utmost secrecy, especially as he was not just putting his reputation at risk but also his head. The delicacy required for this trip demanded that not even Efetobo's closest allies within the royal court could be trusted with the information Efetobo carried in his head. So, he was forced to confide all the details to his long-time servant, who now accompanied him on his travels, and no one else, hence depriving him of the comfort of a full complement of travelling companions to wait on him hand and foot.

'How much further do we have to go? We have been walking for an age now and you swore it was just beyond the last few lines of trees! I'm not sure how much more of this torture I can endure,' lamented Efetobo.

'It is not far, councillor. It is just over that rise towards that line –'

'If you dare say "that line of trees" once more I will have you posted to one of the mining labour camps at the edge of civilisation! I want to know exactly how much longer I will need to suffer in this undignified manner. Look at my feet, for the gods' sake! If anyone were to see me in this state, I do not think my reputation could ever recover from it!'

'No one will see you, councillor. I will make sure of it.'

'And how exactly will you do that, eh? Do you forget that we still need to make our way back to the city, or will you spirit me to my townhouse in a cart covered with palm leaves?'

'I will find a way. Ah, look! Do you see the markings on that tree?' the servant said, pointing excitedly to a large iroko tree with some words of an old Yoruba dialect scratched into it and painted in white.

'Can you read what it says?' Efetobo asked. For all the time he spent in Ife, his grasp of the Yoruba tongue was nowhere near as good as it should have been, as he mostly preferred to speak to his peers in his native Calabar tongue.

'I believe it says, *"he who seeks"*, or something like that. We are very close,' the servant replied, looking around for more clues and then, almost immediately, saw another tree a short distance away with a similar marking. He ran to it and traced his hands over the inscription, lips moving silently as he attempted to decipher the wording.

'Well? What does this one mean?' Efetobo asked expectantly as he dabbed at a bead of sweat that ran down his forehead with a dirty square of cloth he pulled from his waistband. While most men carried weapons on their belts, he armed himself with cloths of fine material, fancying himself more civilised and a man of more refined tastes, a class above the brutish warriors of whom there was no shortage in the realm.

'I can only make out a few words. This one says something about *"the path walked"*. I am not entirely sure, but we are certainly heading in the right direction,' the servant replied, as he began to scan the tree line for more inscriptions. As expected, they found a few more, which they followed until the trees that surrounded them began to thin, and a patch of cleared land came into view. In the middle of the clearing stood a large mud hut with a thatched roof littered with palm tree branches. It was eerily quiet here; the sounds that made up the forest earlier seemed to have ceased, which only unnerved them the more.

'There it is, councillor. I will wait here for you,' the servant said as he nervously looked around.

'Will you not accompany me? I may require you as a translator. Who knows what dialect of Yoruba these... men will speak?' Efetobo said almost pleadingly, obviously uncomfortable at the prospect of engaging with the occupants of the dwelling alone.

'Please, councillor. I have no desire to be involved with men such as these. You asked me to bring you here, and I have fulfilled my obligations. I will await you and see you back to the city safely, but this is as far as I will go. I am sorry, councillor.' The servant was clearly timorous, prompting Efetobo to question his decision about coming here in the first place.

Efetobo's double chins began to quiver, but he was a man of high standing in these parts, so he refused to show any sign of weakness. 'Okay, just make sure you stay here. If you have thoughts of fleeing as soon as I turn my back, dispel those thoughts immediately, or else there will be no hope for you in Ife.'

The servant nodded absently, evidently not even paying attention, too preoccupied with not wetting himself out of fright. With a last dab at his forehead with the cloth, Efetobo passed the threshold of the forest and quickly crossed the ground leading to the hut. He reached it and hesitantly rapped on the wooden door, which creaked open a crack. A few heartbeats went by with no response, and then he swallowed hard and pushed the door further inward before taking a step inside.

The servant watched Efetobo disappear into the dwelling and could not help making the sign to ward off evil. He crouched down amongst the foliage and made himself as inconspicuous as possible. Now, he would wait, until he had cause to flee.

While Efetobo's eyes took some time to adjust to the gloom, a voice startled him from somewhere inside the hut. 'Councillor, what finds a man like you here?' came a croaky voice that sounded like the owner had inhaled smoke for a lifetime.

'I… I am in need of your… assistance… on a matter that concerns the very survival of our kingdom,' he replied, rubbing his eyes and squinting into the darkness.

'And what matter do you speak of, councillor? We seldom interfere with matters of politics. Particularly when it involves the current monarchy. I think you have come to the wrong place,' replied another voice, this one deeper, with a hint of annoyance.

'This matter… may have wider ramifications that could stretch even to this solitary part of the kingdom. I have had to endure the perils of the forest to seek your help… at least let me unburden my concerns.' Efetobo's voice lacked his usual confidence, compounded by the fact that he still could not see the faces of the men he spoke to.

'Perils? Well, apologies for the hardship you have had to tolerate to reach us. Who would have thought that a few thorn-filled bushes, rats and antelopes could be considered perilous?'

This prompted a laugh from another voice from the other side of the hut, a dreadful sound, throaty and grating on the eardrums. 'State your business, councillor. We will determine if what you say is worth any of our time,' came the voice.

Efetobo nervously cleared his throat. 'I am sure that you are aware of the situation in Ife – the king's taxes, the famines, the abject poverty, the disorder, the thievery and butchery on most of the frequented roads between the provinces. The people have an unsalvageable distrust in the current leadership, and they are yearning for a change. All the councillors and high-ranking officials agree but no one will stand up to the king.'

'What is it that you are asking for exactly, councillor? You have travelled this far, so speak your mind.' This came from another voice somewhere else in the room. Efetobo felt like talking shadows surrounded him as he clutched the cloth in his hand against his chest.

'The king and his allies in Ife must… must be… removed…'

'Removed, you say? Am I mistaken in thinking that you were instrumental in the downfall of the last monarchy? That you, Efetobo, conspired with Ekaete to rid the realm of King Jide and his bloodline? Now you seek to undo the labour of your own hands.'

'Yes… but I thought that my actions then were for the greater good of the kingdom. I was misguided, coerced… I… I only acted for the people…'

'For your own advancement, more like it. And who do you see replacing the king, eh? I suppose you think you will do a better job of it?'

'No… I… I would never be so bold as to consider myself the one… the next ruler must be elected by the council…'

'The council which you control? Is that not so?'

'Yes… well, no… it is controlled by all those chosen to represent the people, the appointed house of councillors–'

'Even you do not believe the words that fall from your lips, Efetobo. You would have us deceived as you have deceived your obsequious followers?' This voice was harsh, and admonishing, laced with antipathy. The darkness of the room was suddenly chased away by the light of several candles that flared up around the room simultaneously, revealing four figures seated about the room, the shadows behind them dancing on the walls from the flickering flames that burned the wicks. Efetobo squealed and shrivelled like a leaf deprived of water as he stared open-mouthed at the stern faces surrounding him. All were wizened, weathered from hard living and whatever black magic they dabbled in. One had milk-white pupils oscillating in shrunken sockets, some had markings on their forehead, and they were all missing half of their little finger on their left hands, confirming that they were the fabled seers, or *Babalawo*, as the people of these parts referred to them.

'Please... I do not mean to cause offence... I am just seeking a way to better the kingdom and help the people... If the situation does not change, we will be sentencing ourselves to impending doom...'

'Save your breath!' bellowed the last seer to have spoken. 'We will take no part in whatever plot you intend to carry out. Besides, the king is protected by forces that you cannot even begin to comprehend. Only a fool would willingly risk the wrath of the king and his mother, Ekaete. And are you not related to her?'

'I... I am, but she is the source of all the misfortune that has befallen the realm, and I would sooner renounce any blood ties I have with her...'

The edges of the seer's lips slowly turned downwards as he shook his head, an expression of deep loathing plastered across his grizzled face. 'You are the lowest type of creature, willing to betray anyone for your gains. Leave here at once and never return. You should be thankful to the gods that we are but impartial observers in the realm and not ones to spread the secrets that are whispered between these walls, otherwise, who knows what ill fate could possess you? And ill fate, dear councillor, may yet find you. Now leave!' The last words were shouted with the venom of a spitting cobra.

Efetobo stumbled and fell backwards onto his rump, letting out another squeal as he hit the straw-strewn floor. Not pausing for a instance longer, he scrambled on his palms to right himself and fled from the dwelling as if pursued by *Esu* himself.

The servant watched from the bushes in dread as he witnessed Efetobo tumbling out of the wooden door of the hut in as much haste as the man's bulk permitted. He blundered about running unevenly, fell several times without caring to adjust his kaftan or clean the dirt that smeared his features, and lost his remaining sandal in the process. Gone was the pompous bureaucrat too preoccupied with his appearance, confirming that, within the walls of the mud hut, he had come to meet true fear. As soon as Efetobo reached the tree line and spied the servant, he collapsed in a heap on the ferns, panting and sweating profusely, with a terrified look in his eyes.

'The gods' mercy! I have never been so frightened in all my life. Let us leave here at once,' he managed to say through rasping breaths, as his sizable stomach moved up and down under his dirt- and grass-caked attire.

'What happened back there? What did they say? Will they aid you in your request?'

'They most certainly will not. It was a mistake coming here, and the sooner we put some distance between ourselves and this gods-forsaken forest, the better!'

Shortly afterwards, they were making their way back through the forest to the city, with the councillor complaining each time he stepped on something discomforting to the soles of his soft, meaty feet. As they walked, they were alerted to rustling in the bushes behind them and they both froze in fear.

'What was that?' asked Efetobo in a panicked tone, thinking how convenient it would be to get attacked by some wild creature, completing what had turned out to be a miserable and disappointing day. He then slowly moved to position himself behind his servant, whilst pushing him forward to investigate the source of the noise. The servant was no warrior, but he had the presence of mind to pick up a felled branch and shakily took a step towards the bushes with the intention of poking at whatever lurked behind it, then belatedly thought of what a stupid idea it was, to come armed with a stick if in fact there was a wild creature waiting to pounce on them.

As he got closer, purposely taking his time to approach, a figure emerged from the bushes, which made the servant jump and let out a squeal of his own that bested Efetobo's in pitch and decibels.

It was an old woman, short and crooked, wearing a dark brown wrapper the colour of gravel. The wrapper was wound around her chest, folded tight under her armpits, and flowed down to her ankles. She wore a head-tie of a similar colour, with no other accessories or ornaments. Her feet were bare, and her skin appeared dried and cracked. She had evidently lived a tough life from the look of her gnarled hands and feet, and from the deep lines and wrinkles across her cheeks and brow. But when she spoke, her voice was clear and powerful, as one accustomed to demanding authority.

'Councillor, I presume your visit with the seers was unfavourable? Those old cowhides are charlatans and will do nothing but lead you down a path of misfortune.'

'How… do you know who I am? Who… are you?' Efetobo asked from behind his servant, who had quickly come to stand close to him.

'Who I am is not important but what I can do for you is the wiser question to ask. I know of what you seek – you yearn to rid the realm of Ekaete's influence and restore the kingdom to some of its past glory, is that not so? I may be willing to help you achieve this.'

Efetobo was taken aback by the old woman's words and was for once robbed of speech. His mind was awash with questions, the foremost being how she knew of his intentions. He had not uttered this to a soul besides his servant, who would not have informed anyone. He then thought that this must be some sort of trap. Maybe Ekaete or, more likely, Olise had sent this woman to tease the notion of treason out of him just to have an excuse to see him removed. He concluded that he needed to be guarded with his answers and tread lightly.

'What makes you think that this is my desire? I am a loyal subject of the throne and all I wish is for our nation to prosper…'

'And prosper it will, under a deserving leader. Do not be alarmed, I do not seek to entrap you, and neither Ekaete nor Olise has sent me to test the lengths of your loyalty.' There was a look in the eyes of the woman, one that spoke of a depth of knowledge and understanding. It unnerved Efetobo to his core to think that she had literally read his thoughts, and he was instantly convinced that she spoke truth.

'I… I do not know how you have come to know my thoughts and intentions… and I feel that I cannot deceive you if I were to speak a falsehood… so, I will speak truth. The kingdom is in dire need of a change in governance. Nothing of good has come from the current ruler over the last year, only ill fortune, and more suffering. No one has been left unscathed, and yet the king's power and wealth continue to grow from the toil of the people and everyone beneath him. This cannot go unanswered. Forgive me, but I must admit that I have never known of anyone to offer a hand willingly, without concealing a motive.'

'I agree that the injudicious affairs of the throne cannot go unanswered, and I would be disappointed if a man such as yourself was not suspicious, considering the means by which you have come to hold the seat you possess in the royal court.'

Efetobo had the decency to appear abashed under the weight of the old woman's words, knowing that she had his measure, for he also had blood on his hands. He nodded silently, waiting for her to continue and to reveal the sting in the tail she was bound to deliver.

'Since you have given me no falsehood, I will grant you the same, councillor. My, or should I say, those to which I belong, have grave concerns with Ekaete. She intends to break a covenant of sorts, one which is bound in blood. With our teachings, she has proven herself to be more than naturally gifted, and her aptitudes have excelled to a height which would never have been thought fathomable by one so lowly as she. This threatens the very existence of our… society. One that has managed to remain behind the sight of the world for decades. Now, we risk exposure and the erosion of our very foundations. This cannot be allowed to happen. Her influences must be curtailed at once, but we no longer have the means to reach her. She has acquired ways to obscure her movement from our eyes, which again proves the extent of her growing power. So, we must seek other alternatives to weaken her. Starting with the people around her. This, Efetobo, is how you can help us, and we help you.'

As the woman spoke, Efetobo's anxiety had steadily risen and threatened to induce a nervous breakdown, but he forced himself to appear to be a master of his emotions, even though

he wanted nothing more than to run as fast as humanly possible in the opposite direction. Who was this strange woman with talks of a hidden society, covenants, and powers? Was this all some sordid jest at his expense? He knew of every tribe, group and sub-group that inhabited the lands south of the great rivers, as was his job, and he had never come across anything or anyone remotely close to what this old woman described. The more he listened, the more he concluded that this was something he should have no part of.

He glanced at his servant, who looked ashen. He stood as still as a bronze statue; head bowed to the ground refusing to look up with his eyes firmly closed. He had his hands pressed tightly to his chest and one of his hands repeatedly fidgeted, making the same gesture over and over. Efetobo stared at him for a few heartbeats, and the hairs on the back of his neck began to rise.

'Well, Efetobo. Would you like to have the freedom of choosing the next monarchy, or perhaps, become the next ruler of Ile-Ife yourself? This very moment will come but once in your lifetime, let it pass and you will find no solution to your predicament, which I trust you may have already gathered, judging from the outcome of your earlier encounter. Turn your back now and forever wallow in the shadow of your betters. Who knows, those old crows may yet break your confidentiality and inform Olise or Ekaete of your visit, and then your life would be forfeit. From what I see, you hardly have a choice in the matter.'

Efetobo began to perspire more than he had earlier. There was a practical logic to her words – there was no way of knowing whether the seers would hold their tongues, and even if they did, what hope was there of changing his circumstances? However, if he accepted this stranger's hand, what would he be getting himself into? He could not dispel the thought that there was some missing information that would later come back to haunt him, but could he really afford to squander an opportunity like this? He looked to his servant again, who still hadn't moved and repeated his ridiculous hand gestures, prompting a twinge of annoyance. He would deal with that later.

'How do you expect me to aid you? What would you have me do?' he asked, hoping for a clear instruction to better inform his decision.

'Your task is a simple one – you must take Ife, the seat of power in the tribes, and everything else will fall into place.'

'Take Ife? You talk as if that is a task a child could accomplish! The city has a garrison full of warriors loyal to the throne and under the control of a ruthless general, one of the king's most trusted men, who already suspects me of treason and will not hesitate to mount my head upon a spear to decorate the ramparts. Believe me, I have already attempted to use the power of my position to influence the council to sway opinions on the governance of the realm in a way that would avoid unnecessary bloodshed, but this is futile against men who command with fear.'

The old lady had a smile on one side of her face. 'You are oblivious to the way of things. Politics holds no water in matters concerning real power over the populace. Politics is but a performance staged for the benefit of those outside the circle of true influence, a notion conceived to appease the peasantry and appeal to their sense of order and justice, but it is nothing short of an illusion. I think, over time, you have come to that realisation. Why else would you have sought aid from the Babalawo?'

'That does not give me any confidence that I can fulfil that which you require of me. How do you propose I take the city?'

'This general you spoke of, start with him. He will be the catalyst that begins the process, for he is the stone laid at the base of the dwelling that holds the weight of the structure above. Once removed, all that stands will be compromised and will topple down to the earth.' The woman reached down to retrieve an object that Efetobo had not noticed was there earlier. It was a small calabash that held a piece of cloth wrapped around the rim. She walked over to him bearing the spherical object before her.

'Take this. Go back to your city and seek out this man. When you are in his presence, call his name three times, then smash the calabash on the floor. Heed my words carefully – only call his name three times, no more, then break the calabash. When you drop it, leave the vicinity immediately; do not stay to see the outcome, just leave.'

Efetobo felt the earlier sensation of rising hair all over his body, as he accepted the calabash. All the while, his servant had refused to raise his head or move from the spot he was rooted to.

Etido cast an approving eye over the great walls that encircled Ile-Ife. Before the sack of the city a year ago, no physical boundaries had ever marked the perimeter of these hollowed grounds, as it was thought that no one would ever dare to march on the ancient city of kings, the land of which was once walked by the god *Oduduwa* himself.

Olise had changed that, sending fire and spears to ravage the city and burn it to the ground. Every stone had been torn down and the entire city levelled to pave way for a new city, built from Olise's vision, eradicating all vestiges of what had once been. No expense was spared in the redevelopment, all paid for by the sweat off the backs of the city inhabitants and the oppressed peoples of the kingdom.

The result was nothing short of magnificent – all the hovels had been replaced with solid stone and timber structures of varying heights, shrines and monuments worked in polished bronze were erected, paved roads with large stones embedded into the soft gravel snaked through the city leading to the palace, garrisons rose on every corner of the city, and a vast marketplace dominated the centre, intended to promote commerce and serve as the focal point for all trade in the kingdom. The city had also been divided into quarters, each meticulously planned and designed to separate class and rank amongst the citizens, which created a short-lived storm of controversy. The city now boasted a series of engineering feats that further attested to Olise's vision of greatness – deeper wells, yielding an abundance of clean drinking water, and self-sustaining irrigation systems and aqueducts connecting to water supplies from the rivers miles away, which served designated sections of farmland within the walls. This system also helped to nurture the biodiversity of the city; livestock thrived and mighty iroko, tall palm trees sprouting coconuts and other exotic species of plants and flowers flourished.

The once welcoming and smooth edges of the city had been chiselled down to expose a harsh and jagged exterior that spoke of military might and dominance, a not-so-subtle statement to all would-be invaders. Most of the citizens who had survived the invasion had been left with nothing and had been forced to work as labourers and field hands, building the city and working the farmlands, the harvested produce mainly feeding the palace and the ever-growing army, leaving the labourers with the remnants to feed their families, while those that had allied themselves with the king reaped the benefits. Better opportunities had been afforded the men that made up the armies of the tribes that had aided Olise in winning his wars, many of which had resettled in Ife. Now, the city was diluted by a mix of cultures from across the realm, making up the middle and upper classes, while the natives of Ife were condemned to the lower classes of the newly established society.

The natives still outnumbered the new arrivals, but their courage and dignity had been stripped from them under the yoke of Olise's new regime. They now walked the city like ghosts, invisible, forced to work menial jobs, and were treated like dirt by the other classes. Such was the reality of the true people of Ile-Ife.

Etido was not oblivious to their plight, but he was a warrior and knew all too well the consequences of being on the losing side of a war. However, he owed these people nothing and turned a blind eye to their misfortunes. His only concern was to ensure that Olise's interests were protected, and that the king's peace was maintained in the city.

He walked around stone-faced, inspecting the walls, checking for weak points, but found none. He had no reason to think that the city was under threat, since the battles in the east could potentially last years and the west was all but pacified, or would soon be now that Olise had decided to march there personally, but preparation for the worst was always expected from a diligent warrior.

The poorest quarters of the city were closest to the walls, purposely planned for the weakest in society to bear the brunt of an invasion, if such an event were to occur, and Etido had to endure the despondent looks from the families he walked by. The essence of a thriving community was lost in this part of the city – no laughter or children playing in the streets, no gatherings of women or elders engaged in jovial conversations, no open-air cooking and sharing of food, no sense of unity, just a feeling of hopelessness and vacant stares, half-naked children, bedraggled men, begrimed and miserable faces.

The buildings here were of fairly good quality, but Etido could not help but think that they would soon fall into disrepair, since the inhabitants lacked the means by which to maintain them to the standard expected. Olise would probably have them all evicted and sent beyond the limits of the city to fend for themselves just to uphold his perceived image of perfection, should the whim take him, and Etido would most likely be the one tasked with casting out the people, he thought sadly.

Having satisfied himself with the state of the walls, he began making his way back towards the palace. The path he took gave way to larger buildings, cleaner streets, and a hubbub of animated conversations spoken in a multitude of languages from the more affluent tribes occupying the better quarters of the city. Several of his guards walked alongside him and they soon had to shoulder their way through the throng of people that jostled about on what promised to be another sweltering day in the capital.

Etido was an easily recognisable figure owing to his height and bearing, which naturally commanded attention. His gait was purposeful and those that noticed him immediately stepped aside to allow him through. Some of the warriors amongst the citizens called out to him respectfully, which he acknowledged with a curt nod, while others just bowed in his direction when eye contact was made.

He was happy to see so many fighting men in high spirits and good health, knowing that they would need to be in their best condition once Olise decided to march east and confront this so-called prince of royal blood that threatened to destabilise the balance of power in the region. In truth, he relished the opportunity to bloody his blade once again. Olise had kept them out of any serious fighting for the best part of a year now, and he was a true believer that a warrior with a blunted spear was as useful as a birthing wife on the field of battle. True warriors needed to be tested regularly, their spear tips keen and their physique in prime condition. He had no care for using politics and bureaucratic wrangling as a tool for settling regional disputes or resolving conflicts. For him wealth, titles and lands were won by the strength of one's right arm, no other way would suffice.

He despised pestilent rats like Efetobo and his cronies, with their covert meetings and fancy words, thinking themselves the better men. It would be a joyous day to see the fat councillor's head mounted upon the walls and a council of warriors presiding over matters of state in the name of the king. He amused himself with the thought of sitting at the head of the council as a spokesman and warrior. That would be a befitting role for someone of his talents. Alas, it was nothing more than a dream, but a dream that he could work towards. He was suddenly filled with new purpose, and he held his head a little higher, this time favouring those that called to him with not only a nod but also a smile. He needed to act the part he aspired to achieve, to show that he could engage with people on a human level and was not just a spoke in the wheel of Olise's army, a tool used only to deliver death. He decided then that he would broach the subject with Olise, and he pondered ways in which to persuade him.

The group of warriors was now closer to the palace, walking the final winding length of stone-paved ground that led to the inner wall of the heart of the city. The dwellings along this route were assigned to soldiers only, and the sounds that dominated this section of the city were of a different nature to the other quarters; commands being issued, the rhythmic stamping of many marching feet, and the clashing of iron as men trained or weapons were forged.

More men called out to Etido as he walked past, which was expected here as everyone knew the unmistakeable commander, but then, he heard his name shouted out somewhere off to his right. There was something about the tone of the voice that made him stop and seek out the source of the words. It was a tone he was familiar with, slightly shrilled with an undertone of... fear.

He searched the many faces around, seeking one focused in his direction until his eyes rested on a slight figure, not a warrior but a peasant or servant. He narrowed his eyes as his mind tried to process where this familiar face was from, and then it dawned on him. This was a man he had often seen in the company of Efetobo, yes, he was a servant. Efetobo had probably sent him to relay a message. Then the servant called Etido's name once more.

What is wrong with this fool? He can clearly see that I have noticed him, so why must he shout my name again as if I am short of hearing? Etido thought angrily as he changed his course and started to walk towards the man. However, as he closed the distance between them, he could not help but feel a sense of unease. Etido was no expert on people but the body language and the look he saw upon the face of the servant was one that he had seen on countless occasions from his time conducting raids or fighting in battles. It was the behaviour and the look of someone that sees their greatest fears manifest before their eyes.

Closer still, he noticed that the man was quivering, his hands trembled, his footing was unsteady as if standing on the edge of a precipice steering into an abyss, and he was sweating like a festive goat being led to slaughter. His tongue constantly flicked out to lick dried and cracked lips and his throat moved up and down ceaselessly as he swallowed nervously. He then saw that the man was holding something in his hands, a pot of some kind, or calabash, that he cradled in his arms as delicately as he would a newborn child.

'Do you have some message for me, or are you just going to stand there like an imbecile? Well? Spit it out, boy!' Etido demanded in his deep voice when he came to stand opposite the servant.

The man looked around fearfully and then called out Etido's name once more, just as loudly as if he were calling to someone some distance away; he then unexpectedly raised his hands and threw the calabash to the ground, shattering it into pieces.

'Are you soft in the head? What is the meaning of–' Etido started, just as the servant turned his back and ran off as fast as he could without uttering another word. Some of the warriors close by noticed the commotion and began to gather, while others called for the servant to be apprehended, and then all the focus was shifted to the mountain of a warrior as his bellow captured the attention of everyone around.

Etido's initial thoughts were to discipline the servant for wasting his time unnecessarily, but then the calabash hit the floor, and Etido watched as a puff of smoke rose from the broken shards of the pot, like granulated, sun-dried cassava, but instead of the smoke dissipating into the atmosphere, it rose to the height of a man and began to take shape. The smoke-like substance shifted and turned while expanding in size until it took up the full scope of his vision.

Now faces were emerging from the substance, misshapen, agonised, tortured faces, calling his name, hands forming and reaching out to grab him. Some of the faces he recognised, old faces, men he had killed in the past. Not only the brave warriors he faced down in battle, but mostly the ones that haunted his dreams, those that had fled from him in terror, those that he had cut down as they ran, the weak, the defenceless, the innocent. These were the faces of the men he had been ordered to murder when he was but a young warrior, those he had struck down to prove himself worthy of wielding a spear and leading men into battle. Some were men he had killed in raids on the order of past commanders, wicked men like Olise, others were those that saw his spear on the bloody fields of Benin. The vision of the victims materialised before his eyes as they begged for mercy, another chance at life, or worse, to spare a child, all cut down by his hand.

The faces wailed at him, their ghastly wounds sharpening in vividness, taking on colour – split skulls, broken and hanging jaws, stove-in faces, all calling to him, pleading for mercy still. Their noise was deafening, filling his ears, crawling into his head. His nostrils were filled with the scents attributed to battle, burning flesh, human waste, and foul bodily fluids. The image stretched further, revealing heaps of bodies in a trail that stopped at his feet, a banquet for the carrion birds, dark wings beating the air, razor-sharp beaks pecking, ripping, tossing meat up, and swallowing it down their long gullets.

The images were unbearable. Etido's cheeks were wet with tears as he screamed out for the apparitions to cease. He tried to flee but the images followed him everywhere he turned. He cried for forgiveness, knowing that there would be none for his past deeds. The hands were touching him now, grabbing at his arms and his legs, jagged nails digging into his flesh, pulling and scratching.

Etido screamed louder now, reached for his sword, and drew it desperately. He swung it frantically around, cutting through the images only for them to reappear whole. He continued to slash about him, recklessly, aimlessly, all the while screaming for the images to leave him be.

His arms were now slick with blood, heavy from the wielding of his weapon. His fear slowly changed to anger, and now he raged, shouting that if they would not leave him, he would kill them all over again. He continued to cut through the ever-shifting figures, the broken bodies, until he could swing no more. He dropped to his knees, exhausted, fatigued, defeated.

'You will not take me! I refuse it. I will *never* be taken!' he roared defiantly, and with the last ounce of strength he possessed, he drew a dagger from his belt and drove it deep into his temple, before falling face-first into the dirt, freeing himself from the deeds of his past and the ghosts that tormented him, in this life at least, for who knows what awaited him in the next.

There had been many witnesses to Etido's descent into madness, he had been fine, conducting a routine inspection of the city, and then in a heartbeat, all had changed. He began to scream obscenities, cowering from imaginary shadows, and acted wild and deranged, before drawing his sword and attacking the people around him. The first victims had been the guards that had accompanied him. They had tried to calm him down, then restrain him, but not even their numbers could contain the bull of a man that was Etido.

He had made swift work of them, effortlessly hacking them down like plant stems. More men had tried to intervene, but they had all met the same fate. In the end, close to thirty corpses littered the road to the palace, none of them whole, their blood bathing the gravel in red. All the other warriors had backed away in fear and horror, just before Etido had claimed his own life.

The tale of this tragedy spread like wildfire, while the bodies yet cooled in the morning sun, and a multitude of conclusions were drawn, but the most resounding narrative that filled the lips of those that saw the carnage or heard about the gory details second-hand was that the gods had finally exacted their revenge for the sins of the usurper King Olise – a recompense for the disrespectful treatment and execution of King Jide and the desecration of the ancient city of gods.

It was said that a curse was laid on the city the moment King Jide ceased to draw breath, and it was now destined for destruction unless one of noble blood and spirit retook the throne, and even then, penance would be demanded of all those who had had a hand in elevating Olise, their blood being the only thing that could appease the gods. Thus began the mass exodus of the city, people seeking to distance themselves as quickly as possible before Olise's curse befell them, and they suffered the same fate as Etido.

It started out with small numbers, which slowly increased until people fled the city in droves, abandoning most of their possessions. By the morning of the next day, most of the foreign tribes had left the city, leaving behind a handful of loyal warriors, guards, councillors, and the natives of Ife, who were all too eager to reclaim their city and proclaim the name Adelani in the streets, a name that struck fear into the hearts of those that remained within the confines of the walls of the palace.

NO BETTER CURRENCY
THAN FEAR

'You have quite the turnout, my king. It was only a matter of time before the islanders came to their senses. Proving my point that you can never underestimate the value of having unseen hands that work from within the shadows, despite Etido's misgivings,' Odafe remarked as he and Olise peered out of the first-floor window of the commandeered townhouse overlooking a compound that gradually filled with nobles and their retinues from across the southwestern province.

Over the past few days, more dignitaries had flocked to pay homage to Olise once word of his arrival in the west had spread through the provinces. Most had come bearing gifts and renewing vows, with their arms out in supplication, but a small fraction saw the opportunity to decry the king's policies and handling of the affairs of the realm, expressing their disappointment in his lack of support in dealing with the widespread famines and diseases that ravished the lands and left so many affected. Those people had been foolish to believe that they could speak so freely with the king and had soon come to rue the day.

The outspoken were imprisoned, with the extremely unfortunate ones being fed to Olise's pet hyena, which had become somewhat of a regular feature at Olise's side and served exceptionally well as a deterrent to broaching politically sensitive issues. It was clear that his rule over the region had not waned and the fear he instilled reigned, however, until recently, two of the largest groups in the kingdom had eluded him. The first was the province of Ogun, which was under the influence of this new chief, but plans had already been set in motion to bring that city and region to heel. The other was the island provinces of Lagos, of which the ruler and nobles were now gathered to attend him. The Lagos islands had always been a coveted region and one of great importance due to its strategic location and potential for inter-tribal trading, being a coastal province. It was therefore no secret that whosoever held the islands held the key to securing the entirety of the southwest. So, diplomacy rather than egos needed to dictate the impending discussions.

The former ruler of the islands, Chief Dare, who was allied with King Jide, had perished during the war for Benin, and without any issue of his own, his nephew had ascended the steps to the title of chieftaincy. The new ruler of Lagos had so far refused every summons to formally pledge himself to Olise, but at the same time, he had not denounced Olise outright as being his liege lord.

Knowing the significance of securing the islands, a different approach was taken to pacify the islanders. As a show of goodwill, Olise had elected to send back the remains of the former chief to allow his family the opportunity to carry out the traditional burial rites for their slain chief. This was a gesture that had not been afforded to any of the families of the men that had fought against him and was mainly done at the behest of Ekaete. If it were left to Olise, he would rather have descended on the islands with his armies to force them into submission, but his mother had warned him against such actions, arguing that the alternative would demonstrate his capacity for magnanimity and go much further in unifying the kingdom and strengthening alliances.

Following a series of clandestine exchanges of messages via envoys, briberies, and negotiations between representatives of the palace and the islanders, the chief had finally decided to pay his respects in person and had now journeyed to Oyo with a large contingent of his warriors, who were gathered in the king's temporary lodgings.

'Well, it took them long enough. I should have this chief punished for his tardiness in coming to show me the reverence I deserve, but I am willing to put that aside if the outcome of this charade is… favourable,' Olise responded as he eyed up all the warriors that had accompanied the young chief, begrudgingly appreciating how resplendently they presented themselves. It was well known that after the modakeke, the island warriors of Lagos were considered the best fighting men amongst the tribes, and their display of discipline attested to that knowledge. Perhaps he was wise to follow his mother's advice on this matter, after all, he mused.

'Come. Let us see what these men have to say for themselves,' Olise said, sliding his sword into the scabbard that hung from his belt, before making his way towards the steps that led down to the compound below.

A mixture of excited and anxious muttering filled the air as the gathered men awaited the arrival of the king. The islanders took up most of the grounds, easily distinguishable by rank and status – the nobles and the chief stood out with their pristine and rich attire along with their assortments of gold and silver accessories, high-ranking and renowned warriors noticeable from the quality of their armour, and the lesser warriors from their rigid postures and emotionless expressions. However, the main indication was where each of the party of men had chosen to position themselves within the confines of the ground, which was clearly by design. The lesser warriors formed an outer shell that cocooned those of rank protectively, unsurprisingly considering no weapons had been permitted around the king.

All the talking ceased the moment Olise's guards walked out of the arched stone entrance to the townhouse. Warriors clad in black armour filed out in pairs and spread out in a line before the islanders, all bearing spears and stern expressions, as Olise followed with his hands clasped behind his back, displaying all the superciliousness that was expected of a man who had conquered half the kingdom. The king then swept his arms open with a flourish and broke a smile that never reached his cold eyes.

'Welcome, men of Lagos. I was beginning to wonder when you would grace me with your presence, for it has been long overdue. I must say that this is a grand display, just as I expected it to be. I pray that the tributes you have brought to me are just as grand,' Olise finished, with a raised eyebrow.

There was an awkward moment of silence and inactivity as both groups stood across from each other before the foremost island warriors parted for a young man wearing a blood-red agbada that was tailored in a slim style, dissimilar to the overflowing fashion usually worn by other regions. It was evident that the stitchwork on his clothing would have taken several painstaking moons to complete and it was done masterfully, giving the wearer a regal appearance. The bracelets of gold around his forearm and thick coral beads that swung from his neck only accentuated the image of the man as he glided forward on soft close-toed leather slippers.

The difference between the two leaders could not have been more discernible – Olise, the warrior king in his leather and beaten bronze armour interspersed with interlocking rings of gold and silver, sword at his side, and the chief of Lagos in his traditional stately attire. This man was no warrior, Olise thought distastefully. He put more effort into his appearance than into the ability of his right arm. Olise loathed such men, deeming them weak and having no place amongst the ruling class. Olise had pondered why a man of fighting age had not heeded the drums of war and marched with his old chief. Now he had his answer.

'King Olise. I am Idowu, chief of Lagos and nephew to the late Chief Dare,' he said with a deep and respectful bow. 'I apologise for not coming sooner, but I hope that you can appreciate and forgive our delay in travelling here to attend you.' Before Olise could respond, Idowu turned and beckoned some men forward. Two strapping warriors bore a large wicker basket between them covered with a thick piece of cloth in the same colour as that of the chief's attire, which was then placed on the ground with an audible thump a pace away from Olise's feet.

'Please accept this as our tribute, which should more than compensate the overdue taxes that our region has owed you. As was agreed,' Idowu said with another slight bow.

One of Olise's men stepped forward to uncover the basket, which revealed a pile of gold ingots of varying sizes, rough and unmoulded, some pieces with dirt and dried gravel still clinging to them.

'It gladdens me to know that you pay your debts. Now, all that remains is your fealty, and I will have it now, witnessed in the eyes of all these fine men.' Olise set his dark gaze on the young chief seeking to intimidate him, and as if by summons, Odafe appeared at the entrance to the townhouse followed by two more of Olise's guards pulling a chain wrapped around the thick neck of the monstrous hyena. A thick piece of wood held in place by leather straps had been used to muzzle the beast, but it still snarled and yipped while dribbling elongated strands of saliva from its powerful jaws as it tossed his head back and forth against its restraints. The two men that dragged the chain were noticeably struggling but managed to bring it forward.

Gasps could be heard from the islanders and several of them took a step back in shocked fear of the sight that filled their vision. All but a few of the high-ranking officers and the young chief. Idowu had not even flinched as he stood there watching the animal tossing and clawing at the ground. His features registered fascination with a hint of apathy, but the warriors that had now come to flank him had grave expressions, as if expecting to wrestle the monster with their bare hands.

Perhaps this man is no coward after all, Olise thought with a smirk as he studied the chief. 'Ah, let me acquaint you with my pet. An exceptional specimen of a beast, do you not think? It has become somewhat accustomed to the taste of human flesh, which has not been in short supply. However, it has yet to try the meat of a highborn…' Olise let that last sentence hang in the wind.

Idowu took his eyes away from the hyena and looked directly at the king. There was something in his expression that captured Olise's attention, something almost primal, just like that of the beast.

'King Olise, do you mean to… threaten me? That is hardly necessary. I believe that there is nothing more sacred than the word of a man, this is something that our custom holds dear. You have been given the tribute owed and I intend to fulfil that which I imagine holds more value to you – my pledge, my spear and those of my people. I will pay this debt, I only expected more... formality to be observed. Had I known you are a man with little interest in fanfare, I would have dressed more appropriately,' Idowu replied calmly with a smirk of his own.

Olise could not help but admire Idowu's candour and realised that there was much more to the flamboyant chief than initially assumed. 'Well said, chief, but I much prefer for my intentions to be known early, to avoid any misunderstanding,' Olise replied as he looked on expectantly.

Idowu took the hint and looked to some of the noblemen and elders behind him, silently encouraging them to follow his lead without uttering a word. He then lifted the hems on both sides of his agbada, folded them against his chest and lowered himself onto his knees, before prostrating flat on the ground, actions which were mirrored by all the men that had accompanied him into the compound. They stayed in this position for several heartbeats before Idowu raised his head.

'King Olise, I pledge my fealty to the true-born ruler of Ile-Ife, king of our great kingdom. With my pledge I give my spear and those of every man sworn to the ancient chieftaincy of Lagos, to heed the commands of the king.' In unison, all the islanders repeated the words, "We pledge to the true-born king."

The words spoken and the act of supplication seemed to satisfy Olise and he indicated they all rise with a wave of his right hand. Idowu rose and meticulously began to brush off the dirt from his now-stained clothing. 'I trust that we are now able to share in some palm wine and break kola nuts in friendship. Let us put all matters of the past aside and look to the future of our kingdom,' Idowu said hopefully.

'I would not go so far as to call it a "friendship"; more like the understanding between a master and servant, but I will allow the palm wine and kola nuts. After all, it would be rude to forsake all of our traditions, eh?'

Olise sat at the head of the table on an ostentatiously carved wooden chair draped in furs as he used a crude butcher's knife to cut and toss joints of meat at the hyena tethered a couple of paces away from him. The beast was evidently comfortable in Olise's presence, as was he, almost as if there was some unspoken bond between man and beast. The interaction between the two fascinated Idowu, who sat to one side of Olise, as he raptly watched the huge animal gnarl and snap through bones as if they were as soft as tubers of yam. A feast of sorts had been put together in honour of Idowu, and the hall in the townhouse was brimming with men that indulged themselves in a continuous supply of an assortment of food while most of the kingdom starved. The atmosphere was somewhat subdued, lacking zeal or the feeling of merriment that would have been expected for this kind of gathering.

Most of the nobles and elders from Lagos refrained from drinking, preferring to sit in small groups and huddle conspiratorially as they spoke in hushed tones around the tables that outlined the hall. None of this escaped Olise's attention, and every time he made eye contact with one of these nobles or high-ranking warriors, they quickly averted their gaze to anything else in the room.

'Never before have I seen a hyena of this size and so amenable to the commands of men. If I had been told that such a thing existed, I would not have believed it without setting eyes upon it myself. What is it that you possess to make this beast so docile in your presence, King Olise? I must know your secret,' Idowu asked, distracting Olise from his thoughts.

'There is no juju here. Most animals respond to those that treat them with respect and offer them that which they seek, be it nourishment or protection, not too dissimilar to people. All creatures have an innate nature to survive, and this one has realised that its chances are far greater under my hand. It need not hunt nor scavenge, but only obey the orders of the one that feeds it. That is basic animal instinct,' Olise replied as he tossed another strip of meat in the animal's direction.

Idowu could not help but think that somewhere in between Olise's words, there was a message meant for him, but he chose not to ponder on it. 'Nonetheless, I think it is an impressive feat to command the loyalty of such an animal, which only adds to your legend,' he replied with a slight bow.

'Ha. A feeble attempt at ingratiation. This does not suit you, nor does the feigned display of devotion towards me from your people. Tell me, Idowu, what grievances do you hold in your heart?'

Idowu was about to deliver a speech of his own coated in honey, then caught himself before the words escaped his lips. He paused, looked at the faces of his people, then turned back to Olise, deciding at that moment to spare him the pretence.

'King Olise, my people may have laid their spears at your feet, but they will never forget the hand of fate you dealt King Jide and my uncle, Chief Dare. Both men were loved and respected almost more than life itself, and they were slain like common animals, robbed of their dignity. You see all these noblemen and warriors breaking your bread? Every single one of them bears the scars of your war from the loss of a son, a brother, or a father. There are no more families left whole in Lagos. The ripples of the war for Benin swept through every household, regardless of whether they chose to pick up a spear or not. Now, most are left with ghosts and haunted by memories. No amount of succour can extinguish the grief my people have had to endure, and having a figure to direct all that accumulated anguish, anger and hatred goes some way in helping them to cope with the pain. I for one have lost more than most. Not only did I lose my father and uncle, but I also lost my younger brother. He heeded the summons of war in my stead and marched with the chief, while I was sent away on a diplomatic assignment to garner the support of neighbouring tribes beyond the borders of our kingdom. That is something that will haunt me till the end of my days. King Olise, we are a warrior tribe, we understand the nature of war, for we are accustomed to it, but I have too long seen the sorrow in the eyes of our wives, our sisters, and our mothers. I have seen the pain that is wrought from the inside, how it consumes them and leaves them empty, and I do not wish for my own mother to bear any more grief on her fragile shoulders, for the weight of it will crush her. So, I made the difficult and highly unpopular decision to sue for peace, despite most of my people's desire to seek blood.'

Olise had listened intently to Idowu's impassioned speech, and he even felt a tinge of compassion knowing the courage it would have taken for the young chief to go against the wishes of his people, but the fact remained that these men had stood on the opposite side of the battlefield from him, and he had shown mercy and restraint by granting them the grace of a whole year to come to the conclusion that they were better off pledging their fealty to him, a privilege that no other tribe could boast. Goats do not bargain with leopards, and Idowu needed to be reminded of this fact.

'That was a touching tale, but the reality is that in war, only one side can triumph. Your people had chosen to ally themselves with the losing side, and this is the price you all must bear. I was of a mind to visit fire and death upon your entire region. To wipe out your people's very existence and cleanse the lands of every remnant of the old alliances. I am still of a mind to do just that, but I see that you, at least, the people's representative, are of a sound mind and, like this hyena, you understand that survival outweighs the need for retribution.'

Idowu had a sad smile. 'In my opinion, no one is ever truly triumphant in war, the repercussions tend to spread far and wide like the roots of an invasive species of plant, burrowing deep into the soil. It could take several years to remove all traces of it and even then, some residues will remain that will eventually give life to new plants. King Olise, the kingdom weeps, famine and disease are rife, and battles continue to plague our lands. All I aspire for is an end to the bloodshed and to seek a way to bridge the chasm that divides our great kingdom. There is much more to be achieved in times of peace, for a nation is only as strong as the many hands that bind together to uplift it.'

'Now I see why you were sent to forge alliances rather than being sent to the killing fields. You are a man of thought, Chief Idowu, and not just some blunt object to be discarded.' Olise took a moment to slice a chunk of meat from his plate before spearing the offcut with his eating knife and shoving it into his mouth. He relished the taste for a few heartbeats before turning once more to Idowu.

'I find you quite refreshing, and your way of thinking very different to the archaic ways of those I have given leave to govern. I could do with a man of your… prestige. So, I am willing to grant you a seat on the council of Ile-Ife. Those old bureaucrats could do with some reinvigoration. Maybe that would help to assuage their incompetent tendencies and give them the motivation they lack.'

Odafe, who was sitting on the other side of Olise, raised his head sharply on hearing Olise's proposition, but he chose to hold his tongue. Idowu, on the other hand, was completely taken aback and, for the first time since he arrived, appeared genuinely surprised.

'King Olise... I did not expect... I mean... that would be... an honour,' he managed to say, unable to wipe the shocked expression off his face.

'Good. Now go and convince your people to set aside any misgivings they may harbour and embrace their king. You must lead by example, Chief Idowu. Let them know that I do not wish to be surrounded by despondent faces, not in my hall, unless they mean to cause offence, in which case I may order my guards to bring me the heads of the men that seek to dampen the mood of this momentous occasion. It would be a shame to ruin such a delightful banquet, do you not think?'

Idowu could not tell if Olise's words were an attempt at humour or whether he truly spoke his mind, but the look on the king's face betrayed no such inclination to lighten the ambience. Idowu then rose from his seat and bowed deeply. 'Thank you, King Olise. You have been most generous. I will speak to my people; they will have no choice but to understand the way of things.' With that, he walked over to join a group of nobles and elders at one of the tables and immediately delved into fervent conversation.

'Do you think it is wise to have such a man on the council, my king? There is little we know about this chief, and how are we sure his intentions are as he speaks? I will grant that he weaves a compelling story, but how much of it is genuine? It could all be an act to gain your confidence and seek an opportunity to betray you, my king,' Odafe stated as he leaned in closer to Olise to avoid his words being overheard.

'It could very well be, though one thing I have learned is that it is always wise to have those that you do not trust under your nose; that way the scent of deceit will not escape you. But your apprehensions are not unfounded. I too am wary of giving this young pup free rein of the council, but he is a man that wields great influence in the region. Do not forget that the islanders are arguably one of the most powerful tribes in the kingdom, and do you really believe them to have been idle for a whole year? No, they have secretly been building their strength, gaining new allies, and increasing their wealth. You are not the only one that possesses *unseen hands*, Odafe,' Olise said with a satisfied smirk.

'If that is so, we will require guarantees to protect you from any potential underhanded deeds that they may be conspiring,' Odafe suggested, rubbing his chin in thought.

'The more reason why I want him with the council in Ife. His being there would curtail his influence in Lagos. His people would not dare act without the express commands of their chief. Stubborn as they might be, they hold their rule of law and traditions dearly. For as long as their chief is our *guest*, they will dance to whatever tune my drums beat.'

Odafe looked thoughtful as he eyed the islanders arrayed about the room. 'That may not be enough, my king. I feel that there is more we could do to assure their loyalty. A contingency of sorts if you will.'

'And what do you have in mind?'

'I believe that there is nothing a few abductions would not solve. That seems to be the most appropriate course of action, my king.'

'Really? That is your grand plan? Need I remind you, we have already been down that path, at the behest of my mother, no less, and look at how that ended.'

'I am aware, but this time we can make subtle… adjustments. Besides their children, who do you believe to be most precious to these people? It is their wives, their sisters and, most especially, their mothers. Rather than locking them away in some far-off settlement, we take them to Ife and hand them over to the care of your personal guards, not a ramble of local militia or untrained peasants with cutlasses. We can provide them with every comfort that the palace offers, and fulfil their every need, but in truth, they would be in a gilded cage. This may yet serve as a further incentive for the young chief to stay in Ife. Who would not want to be closer to their dear mother?'

Olise studied Odafe for a few heartbeats as he processed his word. 'Odafe, you are truly a detestable individual, but I cannot deny that there is merit in your proposal. At the very least, that will serve as a deterrent for any plans the islanders may or may not be plotting. I will think on it.'

'My king, if this thing must be done, which I believe it should, we cannot afford to delay. All their elders, nobles and warriors of note are here under your roof, leaving the city vulnerable. I can rally a group of scouts and warriors uniquely adept in this type of undertaking. They can leave tonight under the cover of moonlight, taking the jungle passes to avoid raising suspicion and in two, maybe three days, the women will be secure in Ife.'

It dawned on Olise that this could not be the first time Odafe had done such a thing from his confidence and the methodology he proposed. However, the idea did not entirely sit well with Olise. More recently, he had made a concerted effort to limit his darker tendencies, and to use innocents in a political game like the pieces on an *ncho* board was the very sort of legacy he was choosing to distance himself from.

'This is not a decision that I can take lightly. There are many sins on my conscience, and every addition to that list needs to be worthy of the damnation that awaits me.'

It was Odafe's turn to be taken aback. He would never have thought Olise would speak of conscience and repercussions. It was true that ever since King Jide's execution and the ritualistic human sacrifices a year ago that paved the way for Olise to ascend the throne, he had not been the same man, as if he had lost a part of himself, a part that had died with those that spilt their blood for him to bear his crown. This deeply concerned Odafe.

'My King, damnation awaits us all, so I see no reason to deprive my darkness in a world full of wickedness and suffering. Let me take the burden of your sins, for I will bear them gladly. You do not have to but speak the words, a sign will suffice, and I will see it done. There is no better option than what I propose.'

Olise thought for a moment longer and then nodded his head almost imperceptibly, which prompted a wolfish grin to spread across Odafe's face. He wasted not a heartbeat and stood from his chair, the wooden legs scraping audibly across the concrete flagstones in his haste.

'Your will, my king.' With that, he was gone, out to gather his band of cutthroats, leaving Olise alone with his thoughts in a hall full of strangers.

TO STAND BEFORE THE STORM

Three thousand warriors on horseback stood unmoving in the shadow of the two colossal statues depicting emirs of old riding into battle, marking the gateway to the greatest city in the north. The sculptures were thought to be hundreds of years old, which was evident from their weathered features and faces that were now barely discernible. Despite their age, the very presence of these historical relics, in a land where countless monuments and architectural feats of man succumbed to the unforgiving turn of time's wheel, was a symbol of the greatness of the Hausa. They represented the people's inimitability – their love for art, their ingenuity, but most of all, their dominance and strength.

The mounted warriors of flesh, standing motionless in their disciplined rows, were the quintessence of the statues behind them, a spectacle that was enough to conjure dread in the hearts of anyone who cast eyes upon this magnificent display of power.

All the warriors had their sights directed towards the rising sun in the east, as they observed the illumination slowly emerge from the horizon to ward off the shades of night and spread across the unbroken sea of golden sand, exposing its subtle iridescence as the rays of light reflected off inanimate objects created by the hands of man scattered amongst the creations of gods.

The morning winds picked up slightly with the arrival of the sun, sending wisps of sand between the legs of the horses and causing them to snort and swirl their tails, but they otherwise remained as unmoving as the riders that sat upon their backs. The horsemen's solemn vigil had lasted a day and a night, which they had all accepted voluntarily and willingly, abstaining from food, bearing the heat of the noon sun and the chill of the long night. Such was their devotion to the man they awaited. The one they had ridden into battle with and bled for, and others had died for. The one that they would follow wherever he commanded, even down to the gates of the underworld. He was known by many names; the prince of two kingdoms, the fearless one, and the spear of the south, but these brave men simply knew him as Prince Toju.

They had wished to follow him over the undulating sand dunes, to range far beyond their kingdom, past the desolate and barren northern borders, but he had forbidden them, insisting that this was a journey meant for him alone. They elected the highest-named warriors within their ranks to intercede on behalf of the collective. They implored those that had the ear of the prince, but none had been able to convince him once his mind was set on a path. Now, all they could do was wait, and wait they did, anxiously, as the day had stretched, the night had fallen, and the sun had risen again.

Despite the bonds of loyalty and the sense of duty that shackled them, these warriors had secretly taken an oath to follow in the prince's hoof trails if another day were to pass without word, regardless of the consequences that awaited them. They had sworn to ride to the ends of the earth if necessary and return with the prince or not at all. But for now, they waited.

As the sun moved across the cloudless azure sky and the shadows of the gathered men shortened over the sands, someone spotted movement in the distance, no more than a speck of black against gold. It was certainly a rider moving with as much speed as the sands allowed, but the men held their positions, not willing to break formation for a lone messenger or merchant. And then the keenest eyes discerned the distinctive armour, the sword, and the bearing of the rider. Elation erupted through the ranks; their prince had returned unharmed. The horsemen shrieked their signature war cry in unison, renting the air and startling the steeds, causing them to stamp nervously in the sands.

Scores of kakakis blared from the city walls announcing the return of the prince, and the city blossomed as a petal showered with water. Soon after, the northern princes spilt from the gates on their magnificent mounts, relief etched on their faces, as they guided their horses towards the front of the line of warriors, eager to be the first to receive Toju.

Danjuma looked every bit the emir-in-waiting on his black stallion, wearing a matching black kaftan with gold patterns and threading. A bejewelled curved dagger hanging from his belt was the only weapon he carried, but his personal guards were never too far behind, as he manoeuvred his horse with his feet wrapped in snakeskin sandals that wound around his shin and disappeared up into the folds of his attire.

'I told you he would return. Did I not, brothers? Yet again, Prince Toju has proved himself invaluable to our people. He is truly a remarkable man,' Usman said, unable to contain his happiness as he shielded his eyes against the sun.

'Indeed, he is. We can only hope that he also bears good tidings with him, although my heart is filled with doubt,' Danjuma replied as he squinted into the distance.

'Come now, brother. We can at least rejoice in the fact that he is back, and seemingly in one piece, eh? Whatever message he bears, we will accept it graciously. For now, a feast must be prepared. I am sure that he craves proper food after being in the company of savages. Who knows what culinary horrors he would have had to endure?' Usman said prompting laughter from the other princes.

'You talk as if he has been held captive for many moons. It was only one night, Usman. Besides, I doubt he would have been treated unkindly, given that he was an emissary of the great emir,' one of the younger princes retorted.

'Well, we shall soon learn of his adventures,' said another.

A moment later, Toju wheeled his horse to a halt a few paces away from the line of horsemen. He was covered in dust but, even in this state, there was no denying the authority and confidence he exuded from the way he sat his horse and the look he wore on his face.

'Well met, princes.' He offered them a brief smile. 'Prince Danjuma.' He inclined his head slightly to the first prince of the north. 'I would have arrived sooner, but I am sure you can appreciate the sensitivity of the task I was given. The duration could not be helped. I trust I did not miss much in my absence,' Toju said as he scanned the familiar faces beaming back at him.

'The only thing that passed in your absence was time, Prince Toju. However, my sister may feel differently. What message do you bring from the Fulani people?' Danjuma asked, clearly keen to learn more and not waste time with pleasantries.

Toju straightened in his saddle, which did not go unnoticed by the princes. 'The news I bear is not one that will fall favourably on the ears of the great emir. The Fulani have amassed a large army, far greater than I could have imagined, and they do not intend to barter with us over lands or titles. They intend to conquer all of the north under the guise of spreading their pious teachings and ideals of what they believe to be the one true religion. War is coming, Prince Danjuma. I fear it is unavoidable.'

Usman's smile slowly faded, as did the blithe expressions on the faces of the other princes as they all looked to their older sibling. However, Danjuma's mien remained as it had been before receiving the message.

After a few heartbeats, he spoke. 'It is as I thought. I knew this day would come eventually; I had only hoped that it would not be so soon. But the further you turn away from your destiny, the more it will seek you.' Just then, the sun shone over him with the same intensity that now burned in his eyes. He looked at the warriors behind him, still in their neat ranks waiting patiently. He turned to the princes, favouring each of them with a look that inspired unwavering confidence. Then, he returned his gaze to Toju.

'I will summon all the north's nobility to attend the great emir in counsel. The time for treating with these Fulani people is at an end, no more words need be exchanged. I will grant them the war they so desperately crave and see to it that our lands are purged of those that would dare to threaten our great nation. We will convene once the lords arrive; right now, you deserve rest and refreshment, Prince Toju. There will be plenty of time to share your knowledge on the Fulani, as I am sure the emir will be eager to understand the mettle of the man that leads these people.'

'The great emir may be slightly disappointed, as the Fulani are not led by a man. A woman sits at the head of these people, a great shahbanu. She commands not only the Fulani but hundreds of conquered nations, all answering to her voice alone,' Toju replied.

This drew gasps and astonished looks from the princes. It was clear that they could not even conceive of a female leading an all-conquering army, one that was so feared for its ruthlessness in its quest to subjugate so many kingdoms and their people.

'How can that be possible? You mean to tell us that this shahbanu can rule such a force? If that is so, this war is as good as won,' said one of the princes triumphantly.

'If that is your first thought, then that, young prince, is your first mistake. Your second mistake and possibly your last would be to ride into battle against her believing that her delicate composition somehow gives you the advantage on the field. How do you think she has come to command some of the most feared and renowned warrior tribes from far across the dunes? It is because she possesses everything that a great leader has, and more, and many rulers possess nothing of what she has. She is a natural strategist, intelligent, cunning, ruthless, and obsessed with her devotion to her God and the spreading of his word. She is an adversary like none that I have seen before, and certainly not one to be treated with anything less than our undivided attention.'

'But a… woman…' whispered one of the other princes, clearly still perplexed after Toju's revelation.

'If Prince Toju says that this is a person we need to take seriously, then we should heed his words. I trust his judgement implicitly,' Usman said, addressing his siblings as he wheeled his horse around to stand closer to Toju.

Toju appreciated the confident words from the second prince in line to the northern empire. Usman had always been a true ally and genuine friend to him, ever since their paths had crossed on the shifting windswept sands of the northern border. Usman had made it known that he would support Toju in all his endeavours, and that support was reciprocated by the southern prince. In their eyes, they were brothers, not bound by the ties of birth but by the bond they had forged on the blood-soaked battlefields of the north.

Danjuma had remained silent throughout the exchange between his siblings and Prince Toju, as he digested the news of the shahbanu. He was known to take his own counsel and was rarely ever influenced by others, rather choosing to evaluate issues from all possible angles before coming to a conclusion. A few moments went by as the princes continued to trade words, and then he nodded to himself as if striking some internal agreement, before raising his hand for quiet before he spoke.

'It matters not that the Fulani are led by a woman, what is important is the intent of this shahbanu and how we respond. As preposterous as it may sound to some of you that a woman can lead such an all-consuming tribe, nothing can be taken for granted. She deserves as much of our attention as we would afford any invading warlord, perhaps more. Prince Toju has the right of it; if she commands such a force, I hasten to believe that the benefit of her rule is of immense value to her people and, in return, she demands absolute loyalty from them. Her sex may also be of more profound significance to her people than we can even begin to comprehend, that, in and of itself could be the greater danger. So, what was initially perceived as another raiding tribe could suddenly develop into an unrivalled threat, the likes of which we have never seen.'

All the horsed princes looked on in silence as Danjuma's words sank in, and a sense of foreboding took root in their minds. However, Toju was undeterred by what he had learned and by the insight that the emir-in-waiting had shared. His thoughts had already drifted to Habibah, who awaited him behind the city walls. She would be anxious to learn that he had returned safely, and he suddenly yearned to breathe her scent and hold her soft body close to his.

'Lord prince, if there is nothing else, I am for a hot bath to wash away the stench of my travels.'

'Hot bath?' Usman asked incredulously. 'You have been among these people for one turn of the sun, and they have already managed to turn you into a savage.'

'You will not believe the wonders it does to ease the tension in your muscles. Do not dismiss the idea before you have tried it, prince, you may come to favour it. Besides, there is much we can learn from other cultures, whether they are considered debased or not. That is how we evolve,' Toju replied with a sly wink. He then turned to Danjuma, bowed to him, then guided his horse through the ranks of his waiting warriors and towards the imposing figures that guarded the gates.

The scent of jasmine with a hint of citrus wafted through the long arched stone hallway that led to Habibah's chambers. The familiar smell conjured a pleasant memory of the princess that stirred some emotion deep within Toju and he could not help the smile it brought to his face, so he hastened his steps.

As the sound of his leather sandals scraping across the rough flagstone floor reverberated off the walls, he saw maids bearing bundles of cloth and furs hurrying towards him, busily chatting to themselves in hushed tones, oblivious to his presence. When they noticed him, they stopped in their tracks, surprised, but managed to offer him a respectful curtsy before hastily disappearing through a doorway that led to another section of the palace, presumably to undertake some tasks instructed by the princess.

Habibah had always been particular regarding the management of her household, and Toju imagined that she had ordered their rooms to be cleaned meticulously in preparation to receive him once the horns blared across the city announcing his arrival. Her attention to detail was impeccable in matters concerning their palace dwellings, just as Toju's was on the battlefield. They could not have been better suited to each other if they had been handpicked by the gods themselves.

The fragrances that assaulted his senses were stronger as he reached the threshold to her room, which made him hesitate for a split heartbeat before he pushed the wooden door open slowly. Habibah's quarters were spacious, with a large window fitted with exquisitely carved wooden grills that dominated the room. The glow of the morning sun permeated through, bathing the room in a hue of orange that appeared to set the room ablaze, which only aided to enhance the ambience in the space, and there, standing directly before the window, was Habibah. Wisps of smoke from burning incense danced in the sunlight and played about her silhouette like moths around a flame. In that light, and the way she stood there with her back turned to him, he thought she was a goddess made flesh come to greet his triumphant return.

He gently closed the door behind him without a word, and only when the soft click of it shutting sounded did she turn to him. Her deep brown eyes found his and held him fast. Her smooth and unblemished facial features slowly began to crack, and a relieved smile spread across her lips. She reached out to him and, without knowing when, they had both crossed the length of the room to embrace for several heartbeats before finally releasing each other.

'It took you long enough to return to me. I thought you had been taken when you did not return with the setting of yesterday's sun. No one slept for fear of what message the morning would bring.'

'You had nothing to be concerned about. The journey was hard going, and it would have been foolish to travel at night. So, I had the pleasure of experiencing the Fulani people's hospitality. I must confess that the thought of holding you in my arms again put the wind at my back to get me here as soon as dawn broke,' Toju replied as he held Habibah at arm's length and drank in her features.

She looked at him, amused, with a raised eyebrow. 'It seems that you found some charm on your travels. Are you certain you were not tortured?'

'Far from it.' He laughed. 'It was quite… enlightening, in more ways than I expected.'

'So, these Fulani people mean to seek peaceful coexistence on our borders?'

His expression hardened ever so subtly. 'On the contrary. They mean to conquer all the lands from here to the far shores of the south, and I do not think they intend to stop there either. I fear that we will not see peace for some time to come, which only makes my position more difficult. By all accounts, I should ride back to my homelands to offer my brother the much-needed support I promised him. Even though he is more than capable, my oath to him remains. But I know that once the Fulani descend on the north, no hands can be spared. I only saw a fraction of the force that the Fulani purport to have at their disposal, and if their words prove true, the north will require every able-bodied fighting man to help in its defence, or risk getting swept away by the tide that is now gathering momentum.'

Habibah's expression mirrored the dread she felt in her heart and the pit of her stomach. She had suspected that war might be inevitable, but she had harboured a glimmer of hope that wisdom and compromise would prevail. She suddenly felt foolish for being so naïve.

'That is unfortunate. I prayed that the gods would deliver us from the clutches of war, but it seems that, in their divine knowledge, they deem that it must be so.'

'This has nothing to do with the gods but more with the desires of man, or woman in this case, and the greed that undoubtedly manifests with the acquisition of great power. There is no denying that we will stare into the face of oblivion, but the north is strong and will certainly match whatever is thrown at it. Of that, I have no doubt.'

'Are you telling me that the biggest threat, by your estimation, that we may ever face is led by a woman?'

'Yes, and a formidable one, spurred by the wind that flows under the wings of her fate and countless nations. Her sole purpose is to indoctrinate every tribe across the lands, whether it be against their wishes or otherwise. The constancy of her ideology is far more dangerous than any typical invading lord simply seeking to acquire lands and power. Hers is more about absolute domination and servitude to her faith or total annihilation. There is no middle ground. One such as her cannot be allowed to succeed, for the whole realm as we know it, north and south alike, will be eternally imperilled. So, war cannot be avoided.'

Habibah was quiet for a moment as she peered off through the window into the distance. 'I see. And what of your brother? What shall we do about your oath and the obligations you have in the south?'

Toju smiled sadly at the mention of the word "we", a reminder that Habibah would stand behind any decision he made, and follow him wherever he chose to place his feet. This only made his love for her swell further, and he thanked the god *Ogun* for preserving his life long enough to stand before her on this day.

'I am deeply torn. I never planned to stay in the north longer than necessary, but I cannot deny that my time here has been nothing short of a blessing. In truth, I feel I am bound to these lands as much as I am to the south. I have built the foundations of a legacy from the strength of my own hands, not from the name of my father or the bloodline that preceded me. My brother needs me now but, more than ever, so does the north. Can I really turn my back on a threat that will have far-reaching consequences and affect all the tribes of our people just in the pursuit of vengeance? I do not know.' Toju said with his head lowered to the floor.

Habibah softly stroked his cheek down to the base of his chin, then tilted his head upwards from the floor to look directly into her eyes. She felt the weight of the decision he battled with, saw the wariness in his eyes and wished she could take it all away.

'My love, I cannot relieve your burden, but know that I am here to support you and hold you up when the load you bear is too heavy. You are not alone in this, just as I swore to you on the day of our union. This is my only duty, until my last breath.'

'That gives me great comfort, Habibah. You are my strength, and I will always be there to protect you.'

She hesitated. 'It is not only I that needs to be protected. It is not only the north that you must fight for…'

She took his hand and placed it on her stomach before covering it with both of her hands.

He looked at her, searching her eyes, shocked, surprised, anticipation registering on his face. He looked down at their hands and back at her face framed by the rays of the sun that still shone through the room.

'Are you…' He dared not finish the words, overwhelming joy, trepidation, excitement, and fear all vying for supremacy at the forefront of his emotions.

She nodded vigorously, eyes welling up, biting down on her bottom lip in a bid to maintain her composure. It did not last, and she began to cry and laugh softly at the same time, tears streaming down her soft cheeks and sparkling in the sun.

Toju felt a sensation he had never known in his twenty years of existence and tears came unbidden to his eyes, as he looked on in silence at the sight of his beautiful wife. He knew then what must be done. At that moment, everything came into perspective and his eyes opened with a clarity that he had not before possessed. This was much bigger than him or any personal desires or dreams. This was everything, and he suddenly knew what it truly meant to have something to fight for, and if so fated, to die for.

UNDER THE WINGS OF DESTINY

A multitude of voices rose in dispute as the atmosphere in the hall quickly descended into chaos. Fingers were pointed, accusations and insults, as well as spittle, were spewed, and hands were hovering dangerously close to sword hilts and dagger handles. It was impossible to decipher the words being spoken when so many contested to be heard at once. Every comment was indistinguishable, and just below the surface of the building tension, violence threatened to erupt.

Amid the cacophony, Essien sat on his highchair facing the gathered men. His index and middle fingers were pressed to his temple, as he attempted and failed to massage the constant throbbing behind his eyes. The noise only made his migraine worse, and he was tempted to rise from his seat and walk out of the hall without a word, though that would only exacerbate matters. He had lost the room before he had even set foot in it, as he was the focal point of the vituperation and rage being hurled in his direction by all the elders, lords and warriors of repute.

They blamed him for the disastrous loss of not one, but two of their most important and strategic strongholds, which effectively rendered their forces defenceless and cut off from reaching the mainland by road or by river, extinguishing any hope of reinforcements from neighbouring allies.

Against the will of the elders, Essien had convinced them that the war in the east was as good as won if they focused their offensive on the boundary of the river near the town of Aviara, where the Calabar held several supply points and was home to one of their most heavily defended garrisons. This proposal had initially been dismissed outright and labelled as reckless, until Essien had revealed the visit from the queen dowager, Ekaete, who had come to him with priceless information on an imminent attack by the westerners.

This admission was met with further derision, especially as the old guard of the Calabar held nothing but hatred in their hearts towards the monarchy that occupied the ancestral seat of power in the west, the very people they held responsible for the divide between the two tribes. This was until Essien spoke of the dark magic he had witnessed with his own eyes, along with all the details of the westerners' plans that could not be disputed. His claims were corroborated by Essien's personal guards, one of whom was still in a state of paralysis from his foolish attempt to lay a hand on the queen regent. The man was then brought before the assembly and examined. He was shaken, prodded, and even cut with a knife but nothing seemed to rouse him from his stupor. And then one of the famed Calabar warriors stepped forward. He was a huge and ruthless man known to have at least one hundred souls on his blade. He hit the guard with an almighty, earth-shattering slap, so loud that it could have risen the dead, sending the poor man somersaulting into the arms of a crowd of waiting men, but still nothing. Essien had then explained that the boy prince himself would be leading the assault, and a chance to sever the head of the snake was too good an opportunity to pass. That was all it took to convince the assembly, although some of them accepted only grudgingly, and before long the entire Calabar army, save for a handful of reserves, was racing towards the borders near Aviara. Only to be met with defeat.

The battle had begun just as Essien had envisioned it, every detail of the westerners' strategy had been exactly as Ekaete had predicted it to be, and the Calabar warriors quickly capitalised on the knowledge they had been granted. As a result, they found early success in thwarting the westerners' progress by intercepting them at a pinch point in the rivers, where they could funnel their enemy into an area where they could be picked off by spearmen on land and pinned down by the Calabar fleet blocking their advance. They also sent warriors into the narrow strips of land where they knew western reinforcements would be lying in wait, and engaged them before they could join the battle and support their tribesmen.

The odds had been firmly in their favour as the unsuspecting westerners were set upon and reaped from the earth in great numbers. The boy prince had even been identified; not only that, but several witnesses saw him struck down by a spear and plunge into the murky river to a certain death. And then the tide of battle had changed.

It was later relayed by warriors who had fled the battle that the boy prince had emerged from the river like a wrathful god come to release *Esu's* fury upon them. Some said he appeared to be propelled by some unseen hand, which confirmed that death was his companion, and no living man could oppose him. This also supported the narrative of the boy's meteoric rise and unparalleled success in conquering most of the eastern provinces in such a short time, something that many renowned and accomplished men before him had attempted and failed.

In any case, the very sight of the prince wrought the fear of *Esu* in the hearts of the Calabar warriors and simultaneously invigorated the hearts of the westerners, who then fought with such savagery that every man they faced was butchered like a ram on the eve of a festival. Those that witnessed the slaughter of their Calabar tribesmen all but threw down their weapons, turned their boats around and fled. Many were abandoned, left to the fate of the westerners. Some attempted to swim for their lives and men drowned, were killed, or taken hostage.

The Calabar warriors that returned were a fraction of the force that sailed out to meet the prince on a wave of euphoria from the scent of victory heavy in the air. Now, they were utterly defeated, disgraced, and petrified of the so-called devil they had awoken, and the repercussions they knew to expect for their actions. Rumours and fear swept through the Calabar camp like a disease that had no cure. Even the elders and hardened veterans that remained behind had little to say other than to project their outrage, which was in truth their poorly veiled terror, onto Essien, who they accused of being the architect of their demise.

'You have condemned us to certain ruin!'

'What would your father think to see how you have squandered your birth right and dammed this great tribe to hell? He would be turning in his grave!'

'It was a mistake to seat you at the head of this tribe. You are not fit to call yourself a chief!'

'You are a disgrace to our ancestors, an abomination to your lineage!'

And so it went, a barrage of insults, denunciations, and threats. Essien just sat through it all in silence, whilst trying to nurse the growing pounding in his head. Then he suddenly thought to himself how easy it was for these men to stand before him and voice their contempt when he had done all he could for the greater good of his people. He had tried to bring an end to the war that had affected so many and brought nothing but misery to thousands. His blood began to boil at the thought of the injustice of it all and he finally snapped.

'SILENCE!' he roared so suddenly that it immediately cut through all the noise. Heads spun in his direction and mouths hung open astonished.

'How dare you all raise your voices to me so, when all I have done is to seek victory against a foe that none of you have been able to defeat? While I sat back and allowed you so-called men of wisdom and military knowledge to attempt strategy after failed strategy, none of which has gained us a single foot of land, and now you dare to condemn me for trying to win?'

'But win we did not and, on top of that, we have lost the bulk of our strength! At least our strategy sought to preserve our men and take on minimal losses; now you have thrown all that to the wind!' countered one of the elders.

'Be quiet, baba! Your *strategies* are only suitable for cowards – to attack and retreat, never gaining ground, never inflicting enough damage on the enemy to be spoken of. Is this the sum of our people? Is this the way of our great warriors? And you dare talk to me about my lineage?' Essien was incandescent. The throbbing in his head had been replaced with a white-hot flame that blazed and coursed through his body. He was usually calm and composed, mainly due to his drinking habits, but he was no weakling and everyone in that room knew the fighting skill he possessed, despite his amicable disposition. All he needed was an excuse, just one more foul remark to remind these men that he was chief, and his word was law, even in the face of defeat.

'I took a risk. A gamble with the fates to secure our place in this realm, something none of you had the liver to attempt. We have failed, but I can go to my grave knowing that I lived without fear, and I followed my instincts. Besides, the battle would have been won if not for our men turning on their heels like dogs with their tails between their legs! We had the westerners; everything was laid out on a platter for us, every single detail of their plans, and yet our so-called warriors allowed superstition to influence their hearts and their legs, and somehow, I am the one to blame? I should have every man that returned from battle executed and damn this tribe to *Esu's* dark halls! What good are warriors if they do not stand and fight against their enemies and face their fears like men?' Essien stood from his chair and cast a scornful eye over the silent congregation before him, most avoiding his stare, seemingly deflated by the truths they had been forced to swallow.

As if on cue, one of the guards burst through the doors of the hall, tripped, and fell in his haste before scrambling to his feet and frantically seeking out Essien, who he bounded towards with a look of pure terror plastered on his face.

'My chief, the westerners are here!' he exclaimed. His manner was panicked almost to the point of insanity.

'Calm yourself down, you fool! Are you a child? What do you mean, the westerners are here? Speak!' Essien bellowed. His blood was still boiling from his earlier confrontation, and he was in no mood for nuisances. Everyone around him seemed to induce an irritation that he had suppressed for so long, and now he simply did not care for the thoughts of anyone.

'They… they came out of nowhere, bearing spears and fire… our… our men fled from them claiming that they were evil spirits seeking retribution! The town is surrounded, chief! The gods are punishing us!' The man shrieked in a voice so shrill he could compete with any maiden singing traditional songs. His words immediately evoked a bout of nervous conversations and hysterical reactions, some more animated than others. Meanwhile, Essien remained composed as he processed the information relayed to him, and subconsciously regretted his earlier remark about his tribe being damned. Mayhap the gods have abandoned them after all, he thought.

He looked across the room at all the worried faces about him and came to a decision. This was perhaps the single most important decision he would ever make during his relatively short reign as chief of the Calabar. He inhaled deeply and breathed out through his half-open mouth slowly.

'I see only two options before us,' he said as the noise started to die down and people strained to hear him. 'We can either fight, and most certainly face extinction, though we would at least retain our dignity, or we could attempt to negotiate a truce. I have no problem standing against the prince if this is your desire. What have I got to lose? I no longer possess your respect, nor do I have your confidence, but I could regain it with the spilling of my blood, not that it would matter if we were all to die here today, but the satisfaction of hearing the words spoken would make it worthwhile. Also, what better opportunity would there be for those that have been screaming for blood? Now is as good a chance as any to prove yourselves, do you not think?' He purposefully looked at several warriors who had earlier claimed that he was too weak to lead. They bowed their heads in defeat, once more avoiding his gaze. 'No? No bold words? No speeches on how you would rid our lands of the enemy? It amazes me to see how quickly some lose their tongue once the cold reality of death comes seeking an audience.'

'We do not have time for your mockery! We could be set upon at any moment!' pleaded one of the elders.

'On the contrary, baba. Now is *precisely* the time for mockery. You cannot choose only to endure the things that best suit you.'

'What if we were to surrender? How can we be sure that the prince will be willing to negotiate adequate terms?' another elder asked.

'How do you expect me to answer that? I may be many things but a predictor of fortune I am not. By all accounts, the prince is a reasonable man, but we did try to kill him, so there is that issue,' Essien replied as he calmly picked up a horn of palm wine that had conveniently been placed on the stool next to him.

The sounds of a town in chaos could now be discerned from within the hall; there seemed to be some fighting, or rather dying, and the screams of both men and women could be heard clearly above the din.

'Now would be the time to decide the fate of our tribe. I recall someone said I was unfit to rule so, do let me know how you intend to address this matter collectively.' With that, Essien sat back in his chair and made himself comfortable. Whether it was the drink that soothed his nerves, the warm sensation trickling down his throat and spreading out to his extremities, or whether he had truly reached a point of not caring enough about the outcome, no one in the room could tell. More anxious chattering followed as men discussed their options, some armed themselves and some attempted to barricade the doors, which Essien found highly amusing, knowing that the intruders could simply torch the building and be done with all the occupants.

Suddenly, the doors were forced open, and an errant piece flew from the frame and struck a man square in the face, sending him sprawling on the floor. The opening created by the absent doors instantly ushered in the odour of battle – burning wood, the coppery smell of blood and the unmistakable scent of terror. Men began to file into the space now created before the entrance, first a pair of grizzled warriors and then many more behind them. From their twisted, almost deranged expressions, it was obvious that they only had one purpose that could not be misconstrued. Their eyes, hardened eyes that had seen countless battles and unspeakable horrors, emanated pugnacity, and their weapons, some stained with blood, foretold certain death. However, none of them uttered a word as they scanned the room for potential threats.

Essien drained the last of his drink, wiped his mouth with the back of his hand, then rose from his chair a little too quickly, and he was rewarded with a momentary feeling of light-headedness, which he shook off easily, being the seasoned drunkard. His personal guards, who had remained by his side throughout the earlier heated debate flanked him, hands on spears and swords ready to defend their chief at his command.

When Essien realised that none of his companions was prepared to address the westerners, he stepped forward. 'Where is your prince?' Essien shouted from across the room to the newcomers in his Calabar dialect, which was only met with violent stares and unintelligible grunts. He had no grasp of the western tongue of Yoruba, so he tried again using hand gestures to convey the message.

'Your prince?' he asked again, this time pointing at the men and cupping his hands around his brow as if to represent a crown. No response, and then the men lining the doorway parted and slowly began to spread out along the walls of the hall to make room for the arrival of the prince.

When Niran stepped into the room, it was as if a god had decided to grace them with his presence, a divinity made flesh. The prince was every bit the conquering lord. His look of absolute authority belied his youthful appearance. Half of his chest was bare, the other half hidden under an improvised cloth wrapped around his torso and looped over his left shoulder, evidence that he had indeed taken a wound from a Calabar spear in battle. An animal pelt, presumably a leopard, hung from his other shoulder and was fastened to his belt with leather strings. Even in this un-regal state, there could be no mistaking him for a mere warrior. He stood erect with his head held high; his footsteps were sure and his manner resolute. A beautifully crafted scabbard inlaid with what appeared to be gold and bronze hung from his waist attached to a fine leather belt, which also held a dagger. Essien's admiration for the prince was instant. Despite the boy being wounded, he chose to endure his discomfort and stand beside the men who had waged war in his name, the very epitome of a leader of men. *How could this attitude not be applauded and respected?* he thought.

The prince purposely took the time to assess every man in the room, scrutinising each individual and committing their features to memory. They all withered under the gaze of his hazel eyes, none of them able to hold his penetrating stare, besides Essien.

Behind the prince stood a knot of warriors, veterans from their appearance, men who were immediately distinguishable in rank and status from the first set of warriors that had breached the doors of the hall. There was a tall and chiselled warrior who casually held a spear, with sad eyes that did little to conceal the violence and deadliness that lay behind them. He had small markings on his cheeks, which were rumoured to be the motifs of the modakeke, further confirming that the boy was one of the princes of Ife. Beside him stood a slightly shorter warrior, young and lean of muscle, but also bearing the tell-tale signs of a man skilled at arms from his stance and the multitude of scar tissues snaking around his forearms. And then there was a stout, muscular and imposing figure flanked by two huge brutes wielding vicious two-handed axes. This could only be the high chief of the Igbo; Zogo the black. The Igbo warrior had a face like thunder, dark hooded eyes over a scowl that could disperse a storm. He was a solid man, thick like an old tree stump with powerful hands that could probably crush a skull. He looked as if he was ready to murder everyone in the room with little to no provocation, and Essien's hopes of having a reasoned discussion slowly began to fade.

But he was a chief in his own right, even if his people held him in no such esteem, and he would act the part, especially since not one of the Calabar men seemed prepared to stand out and potentially be the first to receive the prince's judgement.

'You must be the prince, Niran, if I'm not mistaken,' Essien ventured, and belatedly realised that the boy may not have an ear for the Calabar tongue. He was about to revert to hand gestures when the prince spoke.

'I am Prince Niran, and you must be Chief Essien,' Niran replied in flawless Calabar. For a heartbeat, Essien was taken aback by the prince's grasp of his native tongue, then he remembered that it had always been said that the prince was a knowledgeable boy, blessed with the faculties to speak many of the languages of the tribes, including some of the ancient dialects, which the late King Jide was also famed for. He was a true reflection of his father.

'It is unfortunate that we must first meet in such... unfavourable conditions. Nonetheless, it is an honour to be in the presence of a son of the fabled King Jide,' Essien intoned, which drew some bitter looks from some of his tribesmen, evidently not keen on his heaping praise on their would-be executioner.

'Unfortunate is indeed the word. It should never have come to this, but such is the way of the world and the path we have willingly chosen to tread. I will not waste any time with pleasantries but address you directly – your town is surrounded and most of your warriors have surrendered, the brave amongst them slain. There is no need to progress with any further hostilities, as you now lack the capacity to do so. Every town, village and stronghold held by your tribe for as far as the crow flies has been captured and is now under my hand. The only option available to you is to lay down your arms and swear to me in the presence of every man here, and I will gladly spare your lives and discuss the terms of a favourable agreement with your people. However, should you choose to refuse my offer, there can only be one outcome.' Niran spread his arms open, indicating the men around him. No more needed to be said. He had delivered his message calmly but firmly and it had carried through the room, which was now devoid of sound.

Essien looked around at his fellow tribesmen; some wore a mask of defiance, some one of fear, but most bore the solemn expression of resignation and acceptance of their fate as a tribe that would soon be lost to the world. Essien, however, still felt a twinge of optimism, and cleared his throat before he replied.

'That is very generous of you, Prince Niran. As it so happens, before you arrived, we were debating whether to make our last stand and die with our spears in hand or submit to you.' He paused for effect, and some of his people clearly held their breath. 'A decision was not concluded but I feel obliged to speak on behalf of my people. There is no need for further bloodshed. Long have our tribes fought, but the fighting has done nothing but perpetuate misery and suffering. I for one have seen enough of this meaningless tribal division and resentment driven by feuds long past. I am willing to lay down my spear before you, but I would only do so with the guarantee of some concessions,' Essien finished as he looked on in anticipation of the prince's response.

Niran observed the chief for a few heartbeats and then swept his gaze across the room. The disapproval written on the faces of some of the Calabar tribesmen was not lost on him.

'It pleases me that you can see beyond the differences wrought by our elders. Know that I am not without sympathy for your plight and that which will be forsaken in the acceptance of my proposal – your commitment to your tribe, your pride, and possibly the vows you pledged to your forebears. However, if we are truly to see an end to the fighting and the eradication of the preconceived lines of division that run between our tribes, then this is the path that must be taken.'

'And what makes you believe that you are that ruler, eh? What gives you the right over our people? Our ancestors have presided over these lands for as long as there was soil to walk upon!' spat an older Calabar warrior named Atai, whose face contorted with hatred.

Niran unhurriedly turned to face the man that spoke and fixed him with a silent glare. 'Baba, my father taught me to respect the words of my elders, so I will disregard the tone in which you have chosen to address me, but only this once. A man of your age should know that *my* ancestors have ruled over these lands for as long as these lands have been established in our civilisation. Admittedly, the kings of old always chose not to impose their rule on your province, leaving your people to govern as they saw fit, but there has never been a denial of the hierarchy that existed between our people. I only wish to follow the traditions that have been in place since long before even your time, with the intention to re-establish laws that will protect the self-governance of your people. That is the only concession I am willing to grant you. But you will recognise my bloodline and its place on the tree of kingship.'

'Essien does not speak for me!' another warrior shouted. 'We are born warriors and would rather die standing than grovel at the feet of another pompous Yoruba monarch!' It seemed more had found their tongue as they voiced their disapproval. Essien was appalled at the sudden outburst and visibly struggled to reign in his tribesmen, but it was clear that all respect for the chief had been lost.

The warriors who occupied the entrance to the hall were all tense as they tried to comprehend the words being spoken. Foreign as the language was, there was no mistaking the intent behind the words from the aggressive body language and malice directed towards them, and all were expecting the room to descend into violence at any moment. Some moved closer to the prince, ready to protect him if it came to it, but even with the sudden shift in the atmosphere, Niran's expression had altered not a fraction. He raised his good arm, appealing for silence, and slowly the voices died down to hear the words of the prince.

'It seems that we are at an impasse, and it is also clear to me that even within your tribe the seeds of division have sprouted and borne fruit. If you are unable to master your own courts, how do you propose to serve your people? Have they not suffered enough? Do you not wish to see your tribe prosper?'

'We rule our people on our own terms!' shouted another Calabar warrior.

'Remember to whom you speak, warrior. The prince has been gracious in his restraint and has swallowed the insults and denigration that have been spewed before him. A snake can only be stoned for so long before it strikes,' Seun replied in equally flawless Calabar, his spear now in both hands with the broad head now angled in the direction of the crowd. Niran raised his hand again, but this time towards his blood-guard before he spoke.

'You have listened to me, but it appears that you have not heard my words; I do not intend to manage the way in which you oversee your people. You have your own culture and traditions which I cannot claim to truly understand, nor would I want to influence, but therein lies our strength as a people. As a nation. Our shared differences should bind us rather than drive division – and our unique perspectives, our differing skill sets – these are but a few attributes which we possess, that will form the cornerstones in the creation of a diverse kingdom with a depth of knowledge and capabilities. I believe that every tribe should have their own ruler, someone that is true to the bloodline of those people, but every ruler should be held accountable to someone other than the people they are sworn to serve. A person who ensures that the threads that hold the seams of the kingdom's fabric remain intact.'

'Your uncle is doing such a fine job of promoting unity,' someone said, prompting mocking laughter. 'How are we to know that the rule of law under your hand is not an extension of his? After all, you are of the same bloodline.'

'I assure you that blood is the only thing that I share with my uncle. He will answer for his undoing of our great kingdom and for all the blood that soaks his hands, that I swear before you in the eyes of all our gods.'

Adebola moved closer to Niran. 'I do not understand their guttural tongue, but it is obvious to me that you will not win their trust so easily. I say we should be done with them while we have the opportunity, rather than grant them the privilege of your mercy only to allow them the time to rebuild their strength and later sting us in the back like the tail of a scorpion, at a time when you least expect it.'

Zogo had been listening intently throughout the entire discussion, but had remained silent with his arms crossed, observing the men that stood before them. He had some comprehension of the Calabar tongue but could by no means speak it fluently.

'No. That would be a mistake. Look about you, these are not the faces of men without honour. They have been humiliated and their pride crushed, but I see fallible men driven by their desire for justice, regardless of how misplaced their judgement appears to be. The prince's words have done enough for them to consider the possibility of an alternative solution to continued hostilities, certainly for those amongst them that hold any voice of authority. With a little more persuasion, they might all come to see the benefit of the prince's proposal,' Zogo said to both Niran and Adebola, but the latter was not entirely convinced from the sour expression on his face.

Niran then turned to the Calabar people once more. 'My fellow countrymen, I do not want to prolong this discussion unnecessarily. You must choose the path which you intend to walk. I would like to see a peaceful resolution to this conflict but if my words have not sufficiently satisfied you of my intentions for our collective future, speak now.' There was a touch of iron in Niran's tone, one that was unyielding as the many swords held in the hands of the gathered men.

Once again, Essien stepped forward. 'Prince Niran, I have given voice to my opinion, but I am bound by birth and honour to stand beside the decision of my people, whatever that decision may be.' He turned to face some of the elders waiting for them to deliver the message that would spell the fate of their tribe. It was clear that he had masterfully proven his commitment and solidarity for his people, winning them over in one fell swoop. Niran admired him for that.

Some of the Calabar elders huddled together and briefly conferred amongst themselves in hushed tones, occasionally casting an eye at the westerners before one of them addressed the prince.

'We would like to counter your offer, but I would plead that you do not dismiss our proposal out of hand before you fully understand our words. There can be no forgiveness for the breaking of the ancient laws of guest rights and the spilling of the blood of our tribesman, Abassi, during the reign of your father. Not to mention the slight on the honour of our people being denied the justice that was deserved and demanded by the law of our traditions, irrespective of the status of the perpetrator.'

'The events of which you speak happened long before my time, and I would further say that this would also be true for most of the men who stand here today, and those that have given their lives in the pursuit of upholding a principle,' Niran countered.

The elder who spoke raised his hands in a gesture of patience so he could further elaborate his words. 'Yes, Prince Niran, but if we set aside our principles and dignity, what then truly defines us as a people? Feuds are passed on through the generations like the names we all bear so proudly. Turning a blind eye to the plights of our forebears is akin to spitting in the face of their memory. That said, I agree that our people, Calabar, Yoruba and Igbo alike, have endured much suffering, and if a peaceful resolution can be found, I would rather we all work towards it.' He then paused for emphasis and stole a quick glance at Essien, who had not been party to whatever the old timers had concluded.

'If it pleases you, I recommend that our tribes are unified by the bonding of blood. That is the only true guarantee that none here today would seek further retribution.'

Niran narrowed his eyes, knowing all too well what was being proposed, but wanted the words spoken plainly. 'What exactly are you proposing, baba?

'I propose that our tribes be bound through a union of marriage. We do not seek land, which we have in abundance, though some of the territories you have recently captured can be discussed, nor do we seek empty titles. We believe that marriage is the only true means by which we can even attempt to salvage any remnants of the trust between our tribes. Either a bride of worthy blood is sought from our people and wedded to you, prince, or a similar arrangement is made for our chief. Either option would be satisfactory to us.' Essien's head snapped round at neck-breaking speed at the mention of his title, clearly not expecting the terms he might be forced to abide by. He opened his mouth to protest, but then thought about his precarious position and the sacrifices he would undoubtedly need to make to gain the full trust and respect of his people. He decided to clamp his mouth shut and remain silent.

By contrast, Niran had already anticipated the possibility of such a proposal, and had previously discussed the prospect with the most senior members of his alliance as an extreme but feasible option, one that had now come to bear. They were prepared for the sacrifice that would come with this eventuality.

'You are aware that I have no female siblings, and I have pledged that I will not take a bride until peace has been restored to our kingdom. After all, how can I be deserving of the happiness of marital bliss when so many of our people are suffering? These are my principles – devotion to those that lack the voice to speak. However, I do see the reasoning

behind your proposal, and I am prepared to explore another possibility.' It was Niran's turn to glance at the men at his side. He surreptitiously exchanged a look with Zogo, who responded with an almost imperceptible nod of his head, and then Niran addressed the Calabar contingents.

'As the grace of the gods would have it, Chief Zogo here has agreed to grant the hand of his eldest daughter in marriage to Chief Essien. Their offspring will possess the blood and nobility of both great tribes, and they will be bound to my house through the ancient ties that have always been held between our Yoruba and Igbo ancestors. Also, considering it from a more practical perspective, there is a provincial benefit, since both Calabar and Igbo share a border. This alliance will serve to fortify your respective lands and deter any foreign threats, not to mention the benefit of unlocking the trading routes that have long been hampered by the regional conflict. This will usher in more opportunities for our collective people, and ultimately the entire kingdom. I trust that this proposal is satisfactory.'

The Calabar were hard-pressed to find fault with Niran's proposal, despite their efforts, and this was evident from the subtle nods of approval and excited mutterings from most of the gathered tribesmen. All, in fact, besides a small knot of men and Essien, who wore the look of a reprimanded child; however, he knew that this was the only realistic choice that would ensure an end to the intertribal conflict and see him fully regain the favour of his people. He silently sent up a prayer to the gods, beseeching them to take pity on him and at least make his bride-to-be easy on the eye, but looking across the room at the solid, scowling Igbo chief who was to be his father-in-law, he highly doubted it.

'Now I can see why so many sing your praises as a man worthy of his father's name, Prince Niran. One can only admire your shrewd approach to such a… politically sensitive matter. We accept your offer and hope that this will prove to you that no further enmity will be directed towards you or your allies. Now that our ambitions are aligned, we hope that this will serve as a new beginning for all our tribes,' A Calabar elder remarked as he bowed his head, the first display of genuine reverence that Niran had received from this stubborn tribe of warriors since he set foot in their lands.

He applauded them for their otherwise graceful acknowledgement of defeat and acceptance of the terms he had offered. However, it was essential that he made his position clear and that there was no mistaking that he would preside over all the eastern provinces. He would have no choice but to establish a hierarchy to ensure that everyone knew their place in society, to avoid any future disputes.

'This is a good start but, as you have stated, it is only the beginning, and the path to unequivocal trust between us will be a long one. Once the wedding rites have been observed, I am prepared to grant your tribe three moons to adapt to our newfound alliance and an opportunity to rebuild your community. There is much to do in regaining not only the trust of our leaders and warriors, but also that of our people. They must be put before all else, and this union will go a long way in salving the wounds we have all been inflicted with. However, on the rising of the third moon, I will require your spears and your oaths before all the gods. This I cannot compromise. There can be no mercy for those that would seek to oppose me, and justice will not be denied me for those responsible for the demise of my late father and the brave men that gave their lives in support of his vision.' Niran searched the eyes of the leading Calabar tribesmen in turn, fixing them with his unyielding hazel stare, seeking any glimmer of doubt or defiance. He saw none.

The elder who had recommended the union conferred with his tribesmen briefly before turning back to the prince and bowing again. 'You are most magnanimous, my prince. We can but accept your decree and look towards a better future for all our people.' That was the first time any of the Calabar had referred to Niran as their prince, a sentiment which was not lost on him. Perhaps there was hope for their co-dependent future after all, he mused.

'That looks like a good sign. At least they now appear to give you the respect that you demand, my prince. But what has been agreed?' Adebola asked expectantly. Seun began to summarise the key points of the conversation to Adebola, and he listened intently.

'On the face of it, all the talk seems to be favourable, but is it genuine? Can we really risk opening our arms to our foes that only a short while ago would have liked nothing more than to see our blood cover the soil?' Adebola asked, looking towards Niran, Seun and Zogo in turn.

'It is Chief Zogo who bears the brunt of the risk. For the greater good of our kingdom, he is prepared to gamble with no less than his own bloodline. I sense no ill in Essien and even though he does not wield much power amongst his people, his influence will be essential in time, and with our support, it will grow beyond anything we have seen here today. He for one will not dishonour the terms of our agreement and he will be instrumental in pacifying any flames of dissent before they have a chance to sprout wings. Of that I am certain,' Niran responded.

'For my daughter's sake, I sincerely hope so,' Zogo remarked as he scrutinised his son-in-law-to-be.

'They will not soon forget that we could have simply eradicated their tribe to a man, but instead, we chose to show mercy. That alone is bound to count for something in the days to come,' Seun pointed out.

'Indeed, it will. Now that all is settled, let us welcome our new allies and congratulate Chief Essien.' With that, Niran walked towards the gathered Calabar tribesmen and extended his hand in friendship, which the people were all too eager to clasp.

Towards the back of the knot of Calabar an elderly warrior stood silently, surrounded by his men, his face barely concealing the venom that he held in his heart, fists balled up and veins in his forearm protruding. Atai refused to be seduced by the honey-coated words of the young prince. As far as he was concerned, no words or talk of unification of houses could atone for the years of bloodshed his family had endured. As a cousin to the late chief – Essien's father – he had vowed that only death would prevent him from fulfilling the old chief's wishes of visiting the same grief and shame his people had endured at the hands of the Yoruba on the descendants of those responsible, and he was determined to see it through, even if it went against everything his tribe now stood for. Blood was the only answer.

Shortly after Niran's confrontation with the people of Calabar, he withdrew the main body of his army to the border city of Aviara to recover from his injuries, but left behind a contingent of a few hundred warriors to lend a hand to the Calabar in rebuilding their town. In truth, this was an intentional action on Niran's part to keep abreast of any potential deviations from the protocols agreed with the Calabar. In the event of splinters appearing in the relatively fragile structure of power, he would have no choice but to intervene. He was on the cusp of realising lasting stability in the eastern province, something his late father had failed to achieve, and nothing would prevent him from fulfilling that part of King Jide's legacy. However, his newly acquired vassals could not be thankful enough for the additional manpower loaned to them. The town had been devastated during the invasion and much support was needed to bring it back to more than a shadow of its past glory.

Despite the noble courts of the Calabar suing for peace, Niran's intention to pacify the entire region and facilitate some semblance of past democracy did not occur instantly. He sent out envoys to the furthest provinces in the east to spread word of the events in the River-lands and appeal to the chiefs and leaders to lay down their spears and accept the peace that had now been sealed by the union of the Calabar and the Igbo.

With the blessings of both Zogo and Essien, invitations to the impending nuptials had been extended to a selection of leaders with influence, to bear witness and to partake in the breaking of kola nuts and sharing of palm wine. This would also serve as an opportunity to hold court with the men of note in the region, allowing them to give voice to any residual grievances and disputes with a view of burying all ill intent in the gravel once and for all, never to be spoken of again.

The prince's messages and summons were well received by the populace, and before long, the war had all but dwindled to a handful of domestic skirmishes that did little to affect the agreements brokered in the east. Most of the fighting men of the west and east alike returned to their homes to tearful and joyous reunions with loved ones after so long in the field. As the gods demanded their share of blood, many had not returned, slain over the years of continuous conflict. Lost souls left on the fields of blood, hatred, and despair, reclaimed by the earth where all men were destined to return. These brave men were not forgotten; their brothers-in-arms told the stories of how they had lived and died, but above all, how their sacrifices had influenced the outcome of the peace now firmly within grasp, a far cry from the history of violence that had moulded the lives of so many. Now, this Prince Niran, son of the once beloved King Jide, had laid the foundation to pave the way for a better future for those fortunate enough to have survived the conflict, and those yet to come.

It did not escape the prince's notice that the air of solemnity that accompanied the returning warriors clouded the region like a plague of locusts primed to descend on the masses. He understood how the harsh realities of war could consume the hearts of the bereaved, rendering them numb to the world. The heavy toll of life lost weighed uncomfortably on his shoulders, despite it being a burden that he alone should never have had to bear. This was a flaw in his character that he could never quite dispel – his tendency to take on the responsibility for the suffering of others. He was determined to do anything he could to soothe their aching hearts, knowing full well that there was nothing he could offer them that could truly take their pain away. Still, he hoped that his empathy would be the first stone in the foundation of the bridge he intended to build in his attempt to gain the trust of the people.

He decided that the least he could do was to find some way of honouring the fallen, as he knew that most would never get the acknowledgement they deserved. He resolved to personally visit the villages, towns and cities in the region that had answered the drums of war to pay his respects. This way he could engage with the people directly, hear their stories, show them the scars he had earned in the conflict and offer whatever assistance he could realistically provide, be it resources providing them with the means by which they could begin to rebuild, manpower donated by each of his vassals to labour their abandoned farmlands, or just an ear for them to vent their anger.

This gesture was highly unfavourable with some of the lesser Calabar chiefs, who feared that Niran would win their people over with his open compassion. Niran's actions were something that they, as lords of those lands, had never been compelled to consider, which might expose their ineptitude as rulers, but the prince would not be deterred.

Once he had recovered sufficiently from his wounds, he spent the next moon travelling across the region, visiting every settlement from the Igbo-held borders of the west to the furthest provinces in the east, meeting with his would-be subjects. They soon came to the realisation that, despite the prince's status and the lore that followed his family's name, he saw himself as no better than those he led into battle, and was a monarch that truly valued his people and the contributions they made to the betterment of the kingdom. This gesture alone and the tale of it swept through the east, propelled by the winds that spelt the coming of change. Soon, his name was

on every lip and was sung in awe and reverence, but mostly in songs of love.

Another moon passed before the wedding took place. Chiefs and tribal leaders, great and small, from all across the River-lands, joined the Igbo in celebration. Essien had paid the price of a queen's dowry to Zogo and his family, confirming that the war had done nothing to diminish the wealth of the Calabar.

Copious amounts of food stock, including tubers of yam and cassava, sugar canes, exotic fruits and kola nuts, heaped onto carts and drawn by horses, were brought and laid at the feet of the Igbo chief, filling the compound of his townhouse. Along with baskets of precious metals, ingots of gold, bronze and iron ore, and bundles of traditional materials for the women, which were all accompanied by herds of cattle. There was also enough fish to feed a small village, smoked and skewered on sticks and stacked in baskets.

As custom dictated, the groom travelled to the house of his future father-in-law, to initiate the introduction of the two households. Since the two chiefs had already been acquainted, this display was a mere formality. The dowry was then presented to Zogo, and if he deemed it to be unbefitting of his daughter's hand, he would turn the groom away but, in this case, the dowry was more than sufficient, so the Igbo chief officially accepted the gifts and the marriage would proceed as arranged.

Zogo's daughter, Ngozi, was then brought out, followed by the women of the Igbo tribe, and her hand was placed into Essien's, symbolising the bride leaving one household and entering another to be one with the groom. To Essien's pleasant surprise, Zogo's only daughter was nothing like the menacing and taciturn warrior chief; where Zogo was as dark as the night skies, Ngozi's skin bore the beige complexion of the northern sands; he was stout and bulging with muscle, she was tall and voluptuous. She did, however, possess her father's dark eyes, broad nose, and square jawline, but her other womanly features more than compensated for the resemblance with her father. So, Essien was relieved by the appearance of his wife and was further overjoyed to find out they both possessed similar commonalities – shared passion for their traditions and other personality traits, even their love for palm wine, which may not be a good combination being that Essien was often considered to be on the cusp of being a full-time drunk – once they began to converse.

The pair made a fitting couple as they talked enthusiastically, and their clothing choices effortlessly complimented each other. Ropes of orange coral beads of varying lengths wound about Ngozi's neck, hanging down to her navel, with more on her wrists and ankles. A matching set of beads was made into a crown of sorts that covered her head, with pieces that extended down on either side that framed her face. She was dressed in a tight-fitting wrapper of burgundy accessorised with patterns and embroideries of intricate detail. Essien also wore a thick rope of orange coral beads hung around his neck and down to his stomach, over a pure white wrapper that was tied in a knot above his left shoulder, exposing his arm and part of his bulky chest. He wore a cap matching the burgundy of Ngozi's attire – the colours of Zogo's house – in respect for the family.

The prince, the honoured guest of the occasion, escorted by his retinue of trusted warriors, gave the couple his blessing, which was then repeated by several of the leading chiefs and lords of the Igbo and River-lands. Rams were sacrificed and rites were observed, paving the way to the celebrations that progressed well into a night illuminated by a full moon and fires that burned with a similar fervency to that of those in attendance.

Later that evening, when stomachs had been filled and the unceasing flow of palm wine and other alcoholic beverages had loosened tongues and dissolved inhibitions, men and women who had once been enemies now shared in each other's happiness, embracing, dancing, clinking horns of wine and exchanging tales that aroused raucous laughter that rose into the night skies. The fires that burned around the compound served to enhance the ambience and animate the features of the people, the orange glow illuminating smiling faces and reflecting in eyes that shone bright with the sparkle of renewed hope.

In a corner slightly removed from the excitement, Niran sat with Zogo, Seun and Adebola around a small fire as they observed the scene before them.

'I fail to recall the last time I witnessed a celebration such as this, nor do I think the region has seen one either. It is a welcome change to all the bloodshed and misery from the last few years, I must say,' Adebola remarked as he sipped on a horn of watered-down palm wine in his attempt to remain reasonably sober. Niran and Seun seldom drank, satisfied with their skins of water, while Zogo indulged in a large ram's horn full of the finest palm wine to be had and did not appear to be affected in the least by the strong drink.

'Indeed. The joy shared by the people is something wondrous to behold. Who would have thought that a day like this would ever come to pass, eh? Your late father would be beaming with pride if he ever witnessed such a day,' Zogo replied, with a sad smile as he looked down at the horn in his hand.

He raised it up high to the heavens. 'I prayed his dream of unity in the kingdom would be realised in his lifetime. Even though the gods had deemed it not so, they granted us you, my dear prince, and King Jide's legacy and likeness will never be extinguished. This is to Prince Niran!' Zogo downed the remaining contents of his horn and smacked his lips satisfactorily.

'I'll drink to that,' Adebola said as he followed suit and raised his horn to his lips, drinking deeply.

'You have my thanks, but I cannot entirely share in your jubilation. There is no denying that we have achieved much over the last few moons, but the road ahead of us is still a long one to travel. We still have my uncle to contend with; the west remains firmly ensnared in his clutches with no sign of him relinquishing his hold,' Niran replied as he looked on at the well-wishers parading and cavorting about the compound, oblivious to the world that surrounded them.

'That is true, but the unification of the east has gone some way in tipping the scales of fate in our favour. Now, we have somewhat more allies to oppose your uncle outright. And if the gods see fit to allow it, we could have the support of Prince Toju in the north. With our combined forces, Olise would not stand a chance, even with the help of Ekaete,' Seun said.

This drew an astonished look from Adebola. 'Have you had word from the prince in the north?' he asked.

'Yes, I have. There may be many lengths of land and a great river between us, but we have found ways by which we communicate.'

Adebola shook his head in awe. 'You never cease to amaze me, my prince. Just when I think I understand you, I discover more layers to be peeled away like the leaves that cover the maize plant. Is there anything you have not prepared for?'

Niran laughed softly. 'I am not nearly as precocious as you may believe me to be. I recognise my failings and seek to better them in my pursuit of peace and unity across the region. Besides, if not for the support and counsel of men such as yourself, there is no way we would have achieved anything. So, I am blessed to be surrounded by great people,' he responded, returning the compliment.

'As for my brother, he faces difficulties of his own. I understand that there is a tribe that is quickly increasing in strength and numbers, the Fulani as they are referred to, that threatens the northern borders. This is a matter that if not addressed swiftly and with force could potentially spill into the southern realms and jeopardise all we have accomplished. Right now, he is committed to securing his newly acquired territory, and rightly so. But know that an offensive against Olise at this moment in time would be a little premature. We cannot consider such action until the northern threat is neutralised and, as Seun mentioned, we can combine our strength with that of my brother.'

'So, all we will do is wait? Do you not fear that precious time could be lost if we do not take advantage of our improved position, especially if word has not yet reached Olise of our new alliances?' Adebola asked.

Zogo shook his head and responded, 'Nothing is certain until the Calabar have pledged their fealty to Prince Niran under the eyes of all the gods. Until that happens, I have little faith in these people. Not even with this wedding. For all we know, there could be spies hiding in plain sight at this very moment, drinking our palm wine, breaking bread with us and engaging in good-humoured conversation, but once the right opportunity presents itself, they would not hesitate to betray us to the false king and his allies.'

'I share these concerns. There will undoubtedly be some men amongst the elite ranks that still harbour ill intents towards our people. The Calabar are a proud tribe and I fail to see how decades of enmity can be washed away in such a short period, despite the union of houses. That was my reasoning behind the granting of three moons for them to come to terms with our agreement. This should be sufficient time to allow for the pestilent weeds amongst the good crops to sprout, and for us to sever them from the soil needed to grow our alliance,' Niran concluded.

'Now I understand,' Adebola said thoughtfully to himself. 'Forgive me, my prince. I admit that I do not possess the eyes to view the ever-shifting landscape in which we must navigate, nor do I have the clarity of mind to anticipate the pitfalls that may await us as you do. Yet another reason why I am grateful that it is you who leads us.' He bowed his head slightly in reverence.

'I merely act in accordance with the will of the people and the greater good of our kingdom. My only hope is that all the hard choices we have been forced to make over the last year will continue to align, just as they have today, to allow the kingdom to start to reap the benefits of a unified nation. There has been too much hardship and unnecessary loss of innocent life. It must all count for something greater than we mere mortal beings can conceive or understand. We have little choice but to follow the path the gods have laid out before us, even if we know not where that path will lead,' Niran said as his thoughts went back to his encounter with the goddess of the river, when he had stared upon the face of darkness, at the very threshold between the land of the living and that of the dead. He stifled an unexpected shiver that ran halfway down his spine, still unsure as to whether it had all been a manifestation of the delirium brought about by the fear of realising one's imminent demise.

'Who knows what the gods have planned for us, eh? All we can do is embrace whatever piece of happiness we are fortunate enough to find despite the ugliness that we are cursed to endure in this world of man. This is the only true way to live,' Seun remarked.

'Yes O, this is true. My only hope is that my actions and the life I have lived is worthy of the pride of my people, but there are times when I fail to dispel the feeling of inadequacy… If only my chief, Olusegun, were here. He was always the voice of reason that I could turn to. How unfair it is to be robbed of such guidance… I pray that I have brought honour to his memory,' Adebola said sadly.

'Do not be so hard on yourself, young man. Olusegun had nothing but praise for you, and he died a happy man fulfilling his duty and sworn oath, not only to King Jide but to the late King Adeosi, grandfather to the prince. I did not see the old man fall amidst the fighting, but I know that he would not have changed his fate for all the gold in the land. And you have fulfilled your duty to him. Were you not tasked with seeking out allies in the east? You did not only accomplish that, but you also found the prince, of all people. Not to mention your instrumental role in getting us to where we are today. If I know old Segun, he will be beaming with pride at the man you have become. I am certain there is little more he could have expected from you. Hold your head high, young man,' Zogo said as he pushed an unopened calabash of palm wine into the warrior's free hand, which instantly cheered him up.

'Thank you, Chief Zogo. Your words bring me some comfort. I do not wish to dampen the mood any further, it is a wedding after all.' Adebola unexpectedly cracked a smile, his earlier melancholy already a distant memory. 'With your permission, my prince, I will take leave and seek a companion to share my palm wine.'

'You have it, Adebola. However, I trust you will not indulge excessively. And please keep your blade close, for you never know where the hyenas prowl.' Niran's words carried a depth that needed no further elaboration.

Adebola's face registered a slight hint of seriousness, then he inclined his head to the prince and did the same to the other men before standing and heading off towards the crowd of people, closely followed by one of his men, who had stood as a sentry at a respectable distance, along with more warriors that made up the guards for the men that sat around the fire.

'He is a good man; a little headstrong, but dependable nonetheless,' Zogo said as they watched Adebola disappear into the crowd before he pulled the stopper out of another calabash and refilled his horn.

'Indeed, he is. We are lucky to have men like him amongst us,' Seun replied.

'I have much use for him.' Niran remarked 'Especially in light of the information that I have recently come to possess.' Zogo paused with his horn halfway to his lips, intrigued, and noticed Seun's knowing expression.

'Word has reached my ears confirming that the garrison at Benin has diminished significantly over the last moon, with Olise moving the bulk of his warriors further west in an effort to crush the threat of rebellion in the region. By all accounts, several western cities that supported my father have yet to pledge their fealty to my uncle. Some even went as far as to openly condemn his rule. I believe that there are more allies to be won in that region.'

Niran had Zogo's full attention, and he saw that the old warrior had a sparkle in his eye, perhaps in anticipation of another opportunity to face Olise in battle and pay him back in kind for the losses the Igbo people had suffered, including the murder of his beloved cousin, Nnamdi. Or at least the chance to inflict a mortal blow on Olise's seemingly untouchable empire.

'I intend to take Benin. With our growing numbers, we could easily overpower what little force remains behind the walls of the city, and with a foothold in Benin, we would control the heart of the trading routes between the east and the west, effectively severing any means of supplies intended to replenish Olise's allies getting through. Besides, what better way would we have to test the loyalties of our new friends?' Niran extended an open palm towards the men of Calabar arrayed around the compound.

'The gods have granted us a rare opportunity, my prince. I will get my best warriors too–'

'No, Chief Zogo.' Niran cut him short. 'You and your men are needed here, in the east. This alliance is fragile, and I can think of no one better to oversee it with a firm hand. You have fought too long in service to your people and my family, and I would not see you risk another battle when we are so close to fulfilling the vision that you and my father so desperately strived to achieve.'

Niran moved closer to the old chief before he could object and placed his hand on his muscular shoulder. 'There is a shortage of men of your calibre; warriors with names that inspire fear and awe in equal measures. Men who still walk the path of the old ways and possess the knowledge needed to guide the younger generation such as myself. You have given more than could ever be asked of you and I cannot afford to lose you, nor can I command you to sheathe your blade, but I would hope that in memory of the love you had for my father and all the brave men that fought alongside you that now walk the halls of the underworld, you would honour my request.'

Zogo sat quietly for a time processing the prince's words. He looked to Seun, who had a sympathetic expression, then back to the young prince.

'Very well. I will stay and see to it that this region remains true to their word and obeys your will, but I would ask that you take my son, Obinna. If I am not able to fight at your side, I would have my own kin stand in my place. That is the only thing I will request of you, my prince.'

'And I will gladly have your son at my side. Thank you for understanding. I know it is not an easy thing I have asked of you, but please know that you are the only person I can trust to govern this region. You have presided over the Igbo tribe for more moons than I have witnessed, and no one commands as much respect as you do in this region. As selfish as it may sound, knowing that you command the east gives me the confidence and the reassurance I require to proceed unwaveringly towards my destiny, whatever that may be.'

They sat in silence for a moment, the only sound between them being the crackle of the fire and the ambient noise created by the revellers. Then Zogo turned to Niran and made to ask him a question, before stopping himself.

'Zogo, you need not hesitate to ask any question of me. Please speak freely,' Niran said, noticing Zogo's hesitance.

'My prince, where do you foresee your destiny, once the false king has been removed…'

Niran knew exactly where this conversation was going but chose to remain quiet and let the words that teased the tongues of many mouths be spoken out loud.

'Have you considered… taking the seat in Ile-Ife? Will you decide to take the throne as you rightfully deserve?'

Niran looked at Zogo for a few heartbeats before he spoke and, as expected, Seun's expression showed a deeper understanding of the question and much more of the answer before it was even given voice.

'I am not the rightful heir to the throne; do not forget that I am but the second child of my father and not the first. That seat belongs to Toju. Only he can claim the crown of our ancestors.'

'I do not mean to cause offence, but your brother the prince is not here. You chose to remain on the soil of your ancestors. You are the one that has fought bitterly for every inch of land gained. You shed your blood, rallied the people, conquered the region, and near enough accomplished the unthinkable. You are worthy of every song that is sung in your name. There is no one better loved, truly loved by the people, and above all, you have the strength of the entire eastern province at your back with men willing to lay down their lives without a moment's thought if only you gave the word. There is no one more deserving of the crown.'

'I appreciate your devotion to me, but please know that my brother does not sit idly just waiting to ride down from the north to stake his claim over the ashes of my uncle's empire. He has done the same as, if not more than, I have . Albeit his efforts are in the north and away from the lands of our ancestors, nonetheless, this is where my father had commanded him to go. You see, he is simply fulfilling his duty to the kingdom as any true son of Ile-Ife should, and I would never presume to consider myself worthy of a seat that was never mine to take. Toju will be king of these lands, as our parents wished it, as our traditions demand it and as the gods have ordained it.'

'As I said, I do not want you to think that I do not respect the wishes of your father. I only give voice to the words of a thousand people that hold you close to their hearts and are unable to reveal their true feelings. You are a better man than most, I have seen siblings kill their own kin just to move further along the line of inheritance. We all stand behind whatever choice you make, my prince.' Zogo offered a bow of his own.

'I appreciate your candour, but this is a topic that I do not wish to explore further. You now know my position on this matter and so it will remain.'

'Understood, my prince.' Zogo bowed once more. 'I think this drink is starting to get the better of me after all! Well, it is time for me to find that daughter of mine before she leaves my household for good. With any luck, I can still convince her to take pity on an old fool and favour me with her fine cooking every so often… I will miss her…'

'The night is still young, Chief Zogo. There is plenty of time to smother her with your affection if she will still have it,' Seun suggested with a sly smile.

'Bah, it is times like this that remind me just how old I am, but I do not doubt that I have been blessed to still feel the warmth of the morning sun and inhale the scent of palm trees on the breeze when many of my peers do not. My prince, I will take my leave. Please do not let this fine calabash of palm wine go to waste. I assure you that you will taste no better in all the east.' Zogo pushed the drink towards Seun with a smile.

'Thank you, Chief Zogo. I may yet take you up on that offer. Enjoy your evening.' Niran paused for a heartbeat then added, 'Zogo, know that without you, none of this would have been possible. You have my eternal gratitude.' Niran inclined his head at the old chief.

'Do not mention it, prince.' With that, Zogo stood from his stool with a slight groan and turned away from the warmth of the fire, his axe-wielding guards seamlessly falling in behind him.

As soon as the chief was out of earshot, Seun turned to the prince. 'I am surprised it took this long for someone to broach the topic regarding the future of our kingdom. Although, if I was a gambling man, I would have wagered my gold on Adebola being the first to speak on it.'

'As would I. In some way, it is better that it came from Zogo. He understands the traditions that define us better than most and he is better equipped at ensuring that my stance is clear amongst our people.'

'I do not doubt that. Hopefully there will be no more talk on the matter. Speaking of Benin, when do you intend to march?'

Niran rotated his wounded shoulder, which was still tender with every movement. 'As soon as reasonably possible, but first, I must receive the oaths of the Calabar. They will spearhead our offensive, so it is vital that the men at our front are bound to us before we commit ourselves to this endeavour. However, we will take precautions as usual.'

'I expect no less from you, my prince,' Seun said with a confident smile as he pulled the stopper from the calabash and placed the drink to his lips.

Three moons passed in relative harmony, and now Niran, surrounded by a selection of his trusted warriors, a mix of men from both the Yoruba ad Igbo tribes, stood on the banks of the river that served as the border between the lands of the Igbo and the Calabar, as the cockerel hailed the arrival of dawn. Forty men were arrayed about the prince's back, all resplendent in their armour and the colours of their tribes. Leathers and bronze were polished to a high sheen, spears and swords were sharpened and gleamed in the morning sun, and expressions were solemn in recognition of the sheer magnitude of the age-old rite that was about to take place.

Once the sun crested the jungle-strewn hills of the far east, chiefs and lords from all across the River-lands came to forsake past animus and pledge their oaths to the prince in the east. Niran had specifically chosen this location, the very site of the last decisive assault and one of the bloodiest marine battles in recent times. It had also been the same place he witnessed the deity of the rivers rise from the murk to pull him away from the brink of darkness. Niran felt that this was the most appropriate place to honour the prophecy she foretold, which had now come to pass. What better tribute could he offer than to have the nobles of the land kneel in her presence, or at least near the waters in which he assumed she resided? After all, this was what she had preserved his life to witness, and in his eyes, it was more her making than it was his.

One after the other, each River lord stepped forward and prostrated before the prince, not caring for the moist soil that clung to and fouled their garments, swearing their loyalty, their spears and their devoted support of their new overlord. Each supplicant bore a gift of great value as a symbol of respect, which Niran accepted gracefully, and he showed them the respect they deserved in kind, issuing gifts of his own as a token of the bond of friendship that had now been forged for hopefully a generation.

By the time each lord had performed the necessary rites, the sun had reached its highest point in the sky, and Niran's heart swelled with pride as he gazed upon the multitude of renowned warriors that blanketed the river's shores, all united in his name. He thanked the goddess *Yemoja* in silent prayer for the blessing of this day, something he had fought for, bled for, and willed to come to pass for more than a year, bringing him closer to fulfilling his pledge to his family and all the fallen souls of Ile-Ife.

A great feast was to be prepared to mark the occasion right there by the river, and herds of cattle were brought along to feed the hundreds of mouths and to serve as sacrifices to the gods. But first, Niran wanted to address his new allies and inform them of his plans to retake Benin.

'Men of the River-lands. Men of the great Calabar and Igbo tribes. I do not stand before you a king, nor do I stand as any liege lord demanding servitude. I stand here as an ally, one that will spend my last breath correcting the wrongs that have kept our great tribes apart. This is what my father, the late King Jide, envisioned. This is what he strived for his entire life and sadly, it was this that which killed him. He wanted nothing more than for our people to come together as one, for us to embrace our differences and find that which unifies us. And this, my friends, is what we have achieved today. Though we are but a fraction of the kingdom, what has occurred here is a testament to what can be achieved if we are compelled to work towards it. The root cause of all this great kingdom's misfortunes sits on a throne that he had no right to claim, and I will see to it that the false king receives the retribution that he deserves. We lack the strength to confront him now, but in time we will have all the strength we need to bring him to justice. However, I do not intend to remain idle while our nation erodes from the tide of ruin that Olise has cursed us with. I intend to take our kingdom back piece by piece, like the termites that chip away at the mighty mahogany tree until they manage to burrow deep into the core and irrevocably undermine its integrity. Benin is where I intend to strike. I will take back the resources that my uncle so desperately relies upon. I will take the trading routes, cutting away his supplies.

This is where I will hurt him. If you yearn to see Olise fail as I do, this is where we can inflict the cracks that will eventually spread until the empire he has built fractures and crumbles away into oblivion. Join me, let us take this land and place it back in the hands of the people.'

A shout of support sounded, followed by a crescendo of voices united in support of the prince's words. Nothing more needed to be said. He had done what his father had failed to do. He, second prince of Ile-Ife, had the hearts but, more importantly, the spears, of the east, propelled by the taste of vengeance that was coated on the tongues of the masses.

NO CURE FOR
A HEART FULL OF
MALICE

True to his words, with his sights firmly set on Benin, Niran wasted barely a moon in assembling an army, an assortment of warriors under his colours, to march towards one of the most ancient cities of the western tribes. The surrounding lands of Benin had still not healed from the last battle that had taken place here; the land remained barren and unfertile with large patches stubbornly refusing to yield even weeds, soil that had long lost its granularity and was dry and brittle underfoot, and burnt-out, twisted trees that would never bear the luscious green they once boasted. Remnants of a battle long fought were still discernible, left untouched even by thieves and scavengers, not willing to incur the curse of the fallen souls that were rumoured to roam the lands in the dead of night. No life form dwelled here, not even rats. All that remained was a city in the distance surrounded by walls and shut away from the world around it.

As they marched in grave silence, Niran drew images from his youth in his mind's eye of a countryside filled with greenery and bustling with travellers, traders and all manner of townspeople, a stark contrast to the image that welcomed him.

One of his first thoughts was to personally oversee the restoration of the lands by sparing no expense in applying new methods of farming and irrigation and, most importantly, promoting the trading routes, which would undoubtedly serve as the lifeline for the region and the kingdom. And then his thoughts went to his father's final battle and the realisation that he now walked the same path that his father had trod but a year ago. The thought instantly darkened his mood.

A handful of the warriors in Niran's company had fought on that fated day, veterans who had managed to flee from the carnage, and the sadness of relived horrors was awash on their faces. Niran refused to have his men fall to the same fate as those of their predecessors – men who had marched to Benin but had never returned to their homes, so he shed his melancholy and held his head high for all to see so that there could be no doubt in their hearts.

Unlike his father, Niran had planned every step of this invasion, as he knew all too well that it was near impossible to storm the city head-on and not expect to endure significant casualties.

Two moons earlier, he had employed the services of nomad masquerades, who travelled across the region to entertain the masses, for a fee. They were known throughout the land for their performances and highly regarded for their energetic and acrobatic displays, along with their elaborate masks and colourful outfits. Many believed that the history behind their performances stemmed from a time when men entertained the gods that ruled the earth, and it was considered that the tradition also served to ward off malevolent spirits, which, coincidentally, was appropriate for a place like Benin, which had seen so much death and destruction.

Under the prince's instructions, they had travelled to the city along with a full complement of musicians, jugglers, contortionists, fire-eaters, and others of varying vocations including healers, seamstresses, tanners, and the like. However, years of living hand-to-mouth and surviving harsh landscapes had taught this group of unusual characters more skills than those they used simply to entertain. Rough living had also taught them the arts of subterfuge, thievery, and espionage along with the customary skillsets to complement them.

They were tasked with spying on the city to record and communicate any and every detail of note that could tilt the balance of the scale in Niran's favour. It was intended that this would simply be a reconnaissance action; however, it turned out to be something entirely different, and Niran got much more than he had ever imagined possible.

After days of living amongst the citizens and seamlessly integrating themselves within the society, the masquerades had managed to identify and abduct several high-ranking warriors, including the very man tasked by Olise to govern the city. They were all incapacitated with herbal concoctions and spirited out of the city gates without arousing suspicion, and then delivered to a scouting warrior party sent by Niran, outside the limits of the city.

When the news of their success reached Niran, he immediately sent out envoys to the city ahead of his main army to proclaim that he had assumed control from within the walls, claiming to have men working at his behest and capable of carrying out his bidding at will. The proof of his claim was the missing warriors and city officials, who were later displayed kneeling before the gates of the city, outside spear-throwing range, bound with swords to their throats. This last detail had been an ingenuity formulated by one of the warriors in Niran's advance party, but the image had more than effectively served its purpose.

Now, as Niran and his army approached the city, they were greeted by the two immense iron-reinforced timber gates, swung outwards and open wide like arms extended ready to embrace them. And all of this had been accomplished without a single drop of blood, which made Niran's legend soar to near-stratospheric levels.

The prince marched through the city with a little over a thousand spears at his back, a small number compared to the army his father had amassed a year ago for this very purpose. The occupying warriors had already thrown down their weapons and stood with their heads bowed, awaiting whatever fate the prince deemed suitable for defeated men, and the citizens rejoiced the arrival of a true son of Ife or, as they referred to him, a son of the soil.

Niran wasted no time in establishing a new hierarchy, placing Adebola in charge of the city and Obinna as his second-in-command. He then took the oaths of Olise's warriors, including those who had been captured, promising to establish a new council with the previous governor at the helm. The prince's display of mercy more than won the trust, admiration, and respect of Olise's former warriors and officials, which led them to disclose everything they knew that could serve the prince in the coming moons, for when he would eventually decide to move on the capital city of Ile-Ife and overthrow Olise for good.

Niran also set about employing labourers, which he paid for with plundered gold, to clear the surrounding lands beyond the walls. This had been an undertaking plagued with contention amongst the populace, which had been solved by sourcing labourers from across the lands, men and women who shared none of the superstition possessed by the people of Benin, who believed that the souls of the perished still roamed the lands where they had fallen Before long, the surrounding area, albeit a shadow of what it had been, began to take shape and give life to new potential.

Niran then called for reinforcements to establish settlements along the eastern passes and similarly to the south, down to the town of Warri, and the northern settlement of Owo. Within two moons, the prince had secured his foothold on the entire eastern region, establishing lines of communication between each of the provinces with garrisons, which served as checkpoints, secure trading routes and a self-sustaining network of resources.

He retreated southeast to a small town west of Irri, the border city to the lands of the Calabar, which he claimed as his court and base of operations. It was strategically located in the heart of the east with easy access to all the major cities and garrisons, no more than a day or two's horse ride from his most trusted chiefs and allies.

With every rise of the sun, more people flocked to his cause, drawn in by the lore that surrounded his name and the tales of his accomplishments, like mosquitos to the scent of blood, clinging to him and feeding off his legend, willing to spend their lives in service to the bearer of the bloodline of kings.

'Who would have thought, amidst the burning rubble of Ife, with you and your brother fleeing like endangered animals, that you would be standing here today? A conqueror of an entire province with thousands of spears behind you. No one can deny that the gods watch over you, my prince,' Seun remarked as he stood with the prince in a large townhouse that overlooked a tranquil stream of clear turquoise at the edge of a forest teeming with wildlife.

'No, I would never have imagined my fate leading me here. I certainly could not have seen it through all the smoke that consumed Ife and blinded the path ahead,' Niran replied with a sad smile, recalling that harrowing day. 'As far as we have come, the tale of our struggle is yet to be concluded; not until a son of Ile-Ife takes his rightful place on the throne can we truly reflect on our journey.'

'Well, given how many warriors have added to our strength over the last moon, I dare say that we will soon be able to launch a meaningful challenge against your uncle, even without the assistance of Prince Toju.' Seun replied.

Niran flexed his aching shoulder, wincing slightly as he rotated it slowly. It was still tender to the touch and had not healed fully, despite all the herbal remedies and concoctions prescribed by the skilled healers who had seen to the wound. It was his fault, in truth, as he had often disregarded their advice to refrain from strenuous activities, but a man in his position found it almost impossible to do so. 'That may be so, but I will favour his council nonetheless, just as we planned before we were separated. He should be the first one to set foot on the reclaimed soil of our ancestors, and I will gladly follow behind him.'

'I understand, my prince, but I am certain that by now word must have reached Olise's ears of the mounting threat he faces with your presence. He will most likely be weaving a plot, or several for that matter, to see that that day never comes to pass. But it pleases me to think that he would be profoundly disturbed by the thought of an army marching to face him in battle, led by the nephew he had failed to murder, no less.' Seun mused.

'Truth be told, Ekaete is the one I most fear. Although Olise has the strength of the tribes and men who would gladly carry out his bidding, I have no doubt that she is the shadow that precedes him when the sun is at his back. It is no secret that she pulls the threads that hold his allies together. One cannot underestimate someone that possesses that much power over the people and has the deadly determination to see her line succeed.'

Seun scratched at the tribal mark on his cheek thoughtfully. 'This is true. Even though I am not one given to superstition, the very thought of her troubles me… deeply.'

'One battle at a time, my friend. Ekaete will receive that which is due to her, and if the gods so decree it, we will face her as we would any other mortal – with a heart devoid of fear and our spears in our hands.'

Just then, there was a rap at the heavy timber door to Niran's chambers.

'You may enter,' Niran called, turning towards the entrance just before Lanre pushed the doors open to stand between the wood and stone arch that held it in place.

'My prince, some Calabar nobles have just arrived and are requesting an audience with you. They say they wish to discuss a matter of grave concern that requires your urgent attention.'

Niran looked to Seun, who shook his head unknowingly, confirming that neither of them had any knowledge of any matters of note concerning the kingdom.

'It is probably some domestic squabble between some of the lesser lords. I can see to them and send them on their way,' Seun suggested expectantly; but, after a moment's thought, Niran dismissed it.

'No, I will not be seen to turn my back on my people. Lanre, send them in, but ensure that their swords and spears are relinquished at the gates.'

'Your will, my prince,' Lanre said with a bow as he disappeared behind the door.

Turning to Seun, Niran said, 'Ready a messenger to travel to Chief Zogo and the Igbo chiefs. I would have them attend me when they are able. I am of a mind to send envoys to the west. Judging from reports that have filtered back, the chief of the region is one that could become a great ally to us. Some are even claiming that this chief is of royal lineage. Any man with such a claim deserves to be taken seriously, but I cannot deny that I am more than a little intrigued to see if any of these claims hold water.'

Seun bowed low. 'I will see to it at once, my prince.' He then turned towards the door and headed out to ready the fastest rider he could find, leaving Niran behind a roughly hewn wooden table with a littering of rolled-up maps of cowhide.

As he turned the corner to Niran's chambers, some Calabar nobles were making their way in the opposite direction. There were four of them, big men with hardened faces, wearing unkempt beards, scars and the look of men who had seen their fair share of violence.

As Seun came up beside the men, he recognised the one that led the others; he was a lower Calabar lord they called Atai. Seun distinctly recalled that this lord had been one of the few that had openly voiced his contempt for the prince's proposal when a bargain was struck with the Calabar. He had also shown no sign of genuine acceptance or submission during the swearing of all the Calabar chiefs and elders to Prince Niran.

His blood instantly chilled in his veins, and he felt the unsettling feeling of foreboding wash over him, which stopped him dead in his tracks as the men continued past. They had hardly acknowledged him and avoided making eye contact, which made their appearance all the more suspicious.

'You there, wait!' Seun demanded, but they simply ignored him and now hastened their steps to the prince's dwelling. 'I said HALT!' he shouted, reaching for the sword at his waist. Then one of the men spun on his heel and now raced towards Seun, with murderous intent clear in his eyes. The others hurried forward to the prince's door and shouldered their way in forcefully before slamming the doors shut behind them.

'GUARDS! THE PRINCE IS IN DANGER!' Seun roared as he drew his sword and charged to meet the man now brandishing a dagger. These men would have all been disarmed; however, they must have managed to conceal smaller weapons that eluded the detection of the men posted at the gate. Seun would deal with them later, now, all that mattered was that he got to the prince in time.

The man coming for him snarled something unintelligible and tried to use his speed to overwhelm Seun, jabbing with his blade at neck height, but he was no match for the blood-guard who moved with desperation to fulfil the very duty he was put on earth to carry out – protect the blood of the royal line of Ife.

The dagger shot forward with remarkable speed and was barely a hand's length away from Seun's throat before he tipped his head to the side, the blade just nipping his exposed neck ever so slightly, tracing a thin red line, too shallow a cut to be noticed. Both men now shot past each other while Seun's sword followed his body's trajectory and swept horizontally and upwards, slashing his attacker's midriff just under his boiled leather breastplate, splitting him open to reveal the contents of his stomach. The attacker, still moving forward, instantly lost all control of his legs, which buckled under his weight, fell to his knees, and then planted his face in the wooden flooring, dead.

Seun had not even bothered to stop; he just raced to the door and slammed his shoulder into it with all his body weight and momentum. He backed up and ran into the door again, but it held fast, and he frantically kicked at the centre of the door repeatedly, all the while shouting to the guards. He could now hear fighting, the unmistakable clash of iron emanating from other parts of the dwelling. This was no random attack; it was well-planned and executed almost perfectly. *How could we not have seen this coming?* Seun thought as he continued to kick, shoulder, and throw himself at the doors with urgency and mounting despair just to stand at his prince's side.

Niran looked up from behind the table in his chambers as his door was slammed shut and its wooden beam dropped onto the twin iron holders on either side of the wall, barricading the room, the noise reverberating in the confines of his chambers. Before the door stood three men, chests heaving from the exertion of running and the adrenaline coursing through their veins. Niran immediately distinguished Atai, who stood foremost; a look of pure hatred plastered on his grizzled face.

The prince searched the eyes of each man and saw no compromise in them. They had come here with one purpose in mind, but he would be dammed if he gave them the satisfaction of showing any fear, especially to this group of ungrateful miscreants. He calmly and surreptitiously scanned the room to locate his sword, which was a step away from him leaning against a stool to his rear right-hand side.

'Atai. What is the meaning of this intrusion? Have you no respect for your liege lord? What makes you think you can just barge in here at will?'

'Spare your words, boy. You know why I am here. Did you really think that I would accept the rulings of a child when greater men than you have tried and have failed miserably?'

'Of all the Calabar chiefs, I always knew that the hatred in *your* heart would not soon be sated. It was written in your eyes every time our paths crossed, and I knew that you were one that I needed to watch very closely.'

'Well, you failed in that regard! I have outsmarted the supposed most intelligent man in the whole realm. To catch you here unawares, exposed, weak, this brings joy to my blackened heart. I could not have asked for a better outcome. Know this, prince, I care not for whatever those grovelling

Calabar fools agreed to, traitors all, and Essien, he is the greatest disappointment of them all. His father would have had him killed for his spineless deeds. Capitulating so easily and handing over the entire province without so much as a decent fight. I will see to him just as soon as I wipe my blade clean of your blood,' Atai said with an evil smile, and all three men now produced blades of varying lengths.

Niran shook his head sadly as he regarded Atai. 'So, you are both an oath breaker and traitor. There is much you could have learned, Atai, but I fear that this will be your final lesson. You see, I knew that you and your supporters would eventually try your hands at treachery, despite the words of fealty you swore before the gods. So, I was forced to take appropriate... precautions. I am sure that it did not escape your attention that your hometown has seen an influx of Igbo warriors, nor that a garrison was established but a short march away from your gates. And just how many of your people did you manage to convince to accompany you here? Eight? Maybe ten? Why do you think your supporters suddenly turned their backs on you? It is because I intervened, and your conspiring was revealed to me. I will give you credit for seeing your plans through, even without the full support of your people. That shows your determination. And I must admit that I never suspected that you would act so quickly, so I suppose your hand holds the spear. But know this, your family and those of the men foolish enough to have followed you will be taken, and they will, unfortunately, share in your punishment. None of you will leave here alive.'

The evil smile that had graced the lips of Atai evaporated like a puddle of rain in the blistering sunlight, as the weight of Niran's words sank in. The two men with him also exchanged uncertain and troubled looks, realising that they had just committed the lives of their loved ones to the same fate that awaited them if they failed, or indeed, as was now evident, if they succeeded. This was a fool's endeavour.

'I do not care what happens to me now. This is the destiny that has been designed for me right from the start, and this very moment will define my life and those of the real Calabar people, who still hold true to our values. Once you die, my life, the lives of my family, will have stood for something!' Atai shot back; fear mixed with conviction blazing in his wild eyes.

'No, Atai. You are mistaken. There are no songs for traitors. No stones carved with your deeds. Your family name would be too bitter a taste in the mouths of those who once knew it. People would rather spit that word out and see it mixed with the dirt on the ground to be trampled upon underfoot, and the memory of it lost, worn away like the rocks that edge the waterfalls. Do what you must, but know that nothing is ever given or taken so easily.' Niran had genuine sorrow in his eyes as he spoke, but he was entirely at peace with every decision he had made to lead him to this moment in time, and he was ready for whatever outcome lay before him.

Without warning, one of the men beside Atai roared a war cry and lunged forward. Niran instinctively had two reactions, the first being to upend the table between him and the men, sending scrolls flying and fouling the man's advance, and the second being to reach for his sword and clear it from its sheath quickly enough to face his adversaries. However, he instantly regretted his first action, as the movement caused his still-healing wound to open anew, sending a jolt of pain down his arm, followed by some blood that now soiled the thin beige kaftan he wore. He still managed to reach for his sword, ignoring the pain, allowing his years of training and experience to take over.

Despite his injury, the prince moved with deadly speed as he grabbed the hilt of his sword with one hand, ripping it from the scabbard with the other, and then launched the scabbard towards Atai, just as the first man that had lunged came colliding into the overturned table. The man had been too eager in his attack and now he fell over the table and dropped his blade in the process, which skidded across the floor harmlessly out of reach. Before he could regain his feet, Niran took one quick step forward and drove his sword deep into the exposed back of the man, who never saw it coming and now lay sprawled over the table, still.

Atai and the other warrior immediately tried to circle the prince from either end of the room, cutting off his retreat, gripping their blades tightly, perspiration clear on their foreheads, as they readied themselves to attack.

Niran watched them calmly as he withdrew his sword from the dead man. His arm was afire with pain, but he forced his expression to remain impassive.

'You are bleeding, young prince. Why delay the inevitable? Throw down your sword. I promise to make it quick,' Atai said, sneering.

'You will have to take my sword if you so desire it. What are you waiting for?'

With that, both attackers came charging in from opposite directions, seeking blood.

Atai reached Niran first, attempting a jab, which the prince deflected, and immediately had to twist his line of defence to the other assailant, who aimed for his ribs. The prince managed to parry the attack with the centre of his sword and quickly tried to swing it at Atai, who leaped back out of the way before coming in again for another attack.

Niran decided to change tactics and press his own attack towards Atai, hoping to get around him and have his attackers on one side, but the Calabar warrior anticipated his strategy and held his ground, not willing to be moved aside.

Heedless of the danger and assessing the precarious nature of his position, Niran pushed forward and released a succession of strikes, thrusting at chest height, forcing Atai to cede ground. He turned just in time to avoid a slash from the other man, which he stooped under, the blade just missing the crown of his head by a few finger lengths. He came up quickly, feigned to the left, then slashed downwards, catching his opponent in the leg and provoking a satisfying howl of pain.

Niran spun around quickly, sensing Atai's proximity to him from his heavy panting, and narrowly parried a thrust aimed at his arm. He turned again to the second man and planted a vicious kick on the man's chest, sending him flailing backwards and hitting the ground hard. Niran then leaped over the fallen table with the first downed man, landed awkwardly and slipped, but managed to stop his fall with his free arm, causing a lance of pain, before springing to his feet again. He was now close to the door and attempted to lift the heavy timber beam out of place with his injured arm, but his shoulder failed him, sending more pain to his extremities. He bit down on his agony, released his grip on the beam and spun to face his opponents, the second man now coming to his feet and limping slightly, trying not to put too much pressure on his wounded leg.

All three men, breathing hard, sucking in as much air as their lungs would accommodate, eyed each other.

'I have to say that you are a much better fighter than I would have ever given you credit for, young prince. I expected this to be over swiftly, but I see that you have some fight in you.' Atai spat in grudging admiration.

'Save your flattery, Atai, and talk with your iron!' Niran was moving again, determined to dictate the pace of the fight. He swung his sword, both hands gripping the pommel, downwards from a high guard, which struck Atai's raised long dagger with an audible clash. As he pressed down on Atai's blade, Niran shifted his weight to his right, releasing the pressure on Atai's sword hand, then reversed the pommel upwards, under the raised blade and into the Calabar warrior's face. The impact split his top lip and smashed into his nose, breaking it instantly. Without waiting for a reaction, Niran swept his sword horizontally at the other man, catching him off guard and slicing him across the chest. The leather breastplate saved the man, but the blade still managed to cut through the tough material to leave a bloody line where it had touched exposed flesh.

The warrior, regaining his composure quickly, moved into Niran's guard, and lashed out with his blade at Niran's arm, scoring a cut of his own. The laceration would have been much deeper if the prince had not moved slightly at the last moment, but blood gushed from the wound, leaving a pattern of bloody droplets on the wooden floor.

'You broke my nose! I'll have your head for that!' Atai roared, cupping his ruined nose in his hands, now streaming with blood that pooled at his feet. The other warrior had his hand to his chest, which came away bloody, his eyes betraying the fear that he felt, knowing that the prince would have killed him by now if it had been a fair fight.

Just then, a heavy pounding on the door drew the attention of all the men. The noise was desperate; banging and chopping, the men on the other side obviously trying to break the doors down with whatever objects or weapons they could lay their hands on. Niran could faintly make out the voice of Seun encouraging the men to make haste. Salvation was but two inches of timber away; all he had to do was to survive a while longer for his own men to knock down the door and deliver him from those that thirsted for his blood, but the wariness he felt could not be denied. His left arm and shoulder were practically useless, the old spear wound split wide open; his right arm was in agony, blood seeping down his forearm and making the grip on his sword slippery and awkward. All his muscles ached, and he winced with every movement.

The two Calabar warriors, sensing the urgency, decided to press forward. Both men jumped at the prince simultaneously. Atai was shouting incoherently as he attempted a slash at the prince's throat. In his rage he missed his mark, Niran stepping harmlessly out of reach; however, the other man was on him. He went in low, and Niran just about managed to turn the blade away with his sword but tool a punch to the face, sending his vision into brilliant whiteness. The blow was not thrown with any real power behind it, or with much skill, but it had connected well enough and forced the prince down to his knee.

While Niran desperately tried to clear the haze from his head, he swung his sword wildly from left to right from his crouched position to fend off his attackers, and luckily caught one of his assailants on the shin, cutting right through it. The warrior screamed out and dropped to the ground clutching at his severed limb. The man was delirious from the pain, howling like a tormented animal and drowning out every other sound in the room.

Atai looked down at his companion in horror, momentarily frozen on the spot. This gave Niran the respite he needed to gain his feet and launch himself at the warrior, seeking to take advantage of the situation.

As he barrelled forward, his balance was off, still dazed from the earlier blow, and his sword point missed its mark by a few inches. He was aiming to run Atai through the chest but ended up impaling him in the shoulder.

Atai cried out as Niran's momentum carried him forward, causing him to collide with the warrior and they both fell backwards in a heap of tangled limbs. When Atai hit the floor, the sword was wrenched from Niran's grasp, cutting through more ligaments in the man's shoulder as it fell away, prompting an increased pitch in the man's bellows. Niran had landed on top of Atai and tried to grab for his throat, but the Calabar warrior still held his blade and rammed it into Niran's side, once, twice, before Niran could relinquish his hold of Atai's neck and grab for the arm that held the blade to wrestle it free.

Both men struggled against each other, eventually rolling over and smearing the floor with their blood. Atai was now on top, using his body weight to force his hand down and the blade into Niran's exposed neck.

Atai had a mad sneer on his face, teeth stained red with blood, and elongated strands of blood mixed with saliva drooling from his mouth down onto Niran's face.

'You will die here, prince. I will avenge my people with my last breath!'

A loud bang sounded at the door. The timber beam buckled at the centre and a shower of stone dust fell from the iron holders, which were being slowly pulled from the wall.

Atai looked up for a fraction of a heartbeat and Niran drove his knee into the warrior's ribs, winding him. The pressure was released, and Niran rolled clear and came up on one knee, clutching at the wounds in his side. There was blood everywhere and he felt light-headed, his vision beginning to fade.

Atai struggled to his feet and leaned against a wall, breathing heavily out of his open mouth, unable to draw in air through his disfigured nose. He pointed his dagger at Niran threateningly, 'Say your prayers, boy. You will be seeing the gods presently!'

Niran looked around for his sword, but it was out of reach. He then saw the glint of metal and noticed the dagger his first attacker had dropped amidst a pile of scrolls and other discarded items. Atai came in, blade poised to deliver a fatal blow, Niran rolled away towards the dagger, snatched it up from the floor, and then spun to meet Atai's attack.

The Calabar warrior slowed a fraction when he saw the dagger in the prince's hand, but still lashed out with two ferocious slashes, back and forth. Niran, now on his feet, parried the first and tried to sidestep the second, but he was too slow and was struck in the biceps. He almost lost his weapon, but managed to cling to it as he pivoted on the ball of his foot, coming around Atai's outstretched arm, and rammed the dagger down through his collarbone. Atai's eyes went wide, but he grabbed Niran and pulled him close before burying his blade deep in the prince's stomach.

They both stood there for a moment, each man still gripping the hilt of his blade, silently acknowledging each other as true warriors that lived and died by their word, before disengaging; Atai falling flat on his back with the dagger still lodged in him, and the prince dropping to both knees. Niran watched as Atai attempted to pull the dagger free, but his hands grasped weakly at the air before falling to his side as life left his eyes.

Niran looked down at his bloodstained hands and knew that there was no recovery from his wounds. He looked up at nothing and mouthed a silent prayer to *Yemoja*, thanking her for sparing his life long enough to fulfil his father's life-long ambitions of bringing the Calabar people back into the fold of the kingdom, for granting him the strength to take back Benin when so many had failed, and for the overwhelming love and support of the people. He knew they would rally around his brother when the time came for Ife to be liberated, but he shed tears knowing that he would not witness the day, nor would he see the face of his brother again.

Suddenly, an unusual calm befell his surroundings; the faint sounds of the moaning warrior still clutching at his leg fell away, the noise from the door being forced softened to a gentle knocking, and all he could hear were the sounds of home, the sounds of Ife; trees swaying in the breeze, birdsong sweet and melodic, the feel of rustling leaves and bushes brushing against his palm, water from the stream gently lapping against the bank, wildlife amongst the foliage where he and his brothers had played and hunted as children. He heard laughter, the sound of children, Enitan and Toju chasing after him, the voice of his father calling to them happily and his mother humming an old folk song, watching all of them with love in her eyes. His nose was filled with the scent of the rain before a storm, the many species of plants indigenous to

Ile-Ife. The smell of life. A ray of sunlight shone through the window, warming his brow. He reached out, splitting the lines of light with his fingers, watching it dance around his hand. Then he slumped to the floor, just as the holders of the timber beam came flying off the wall and men poured into the room brandishing weapons.

The scene before them was one telling a tale of violence and the remarkable bravery of a prince that had devoted his life to his people and refused to succumb to the tyranny of man, even in the face of certain death.

Seun rushed to Niran's side and cradled him in his arms, delicately feeling about his body, looking for the sources of all the blood that painted the floor in crimson. He then let out a cry of pure anguish, pain, sorrow, and heartbreak; so deep and resonating was his cry that it chilled the blood of every man present.

SUBSCRIBE
TO MY NEWSLETTER AT

www.de-bajo.com/books

for updates, character artwork and sneak previews on the upcoming books in the Fractured Kingdom Series.